Song For A Nurse

Sonja Collavoce

This novel's story, character and many of its buildings are fictitious. Certain long-standing institutions, agencies and public offices are mentioned but the characters involved are wholly imaginary. Any similarities the reader may discern must be attributed to the reader's vivid imagination!

Song For A Nurse

Cardiff at the end of the 1970s is an exciting place to be, and the City Central Infirmary sees its share of medical drama. However, Julia and Mandy, two newly-qualified young nurses, are unprepared for the events which develop.

Schemes and lies are being woven within the huge, imposing old hospital, but what can these young women do?

DRAMATIS PERSONAE

Julia Harry – a newly qualified staff nurse.

Mandy Jacob – her best friend, another newly qualified staff nurse

Mitch Walker – a music graduate and aspiring rock star

Dr Marcus Battencourt - senior house officer

Dr Neil Hancock – a crony of Marcus Battencourt.

Mr Anscombe – a maverick but hugely talented senior registrar

Phil Ellis – overworked and kind Casualty registrar

Aneira Thomas – a first-year student nurse, on her second placement

Richie – an affable, well-liked porter

Sister Winter – a capable, no-nonsense ward sister of the highest calibre

Sister Daksha Patel - Junior sister, efficient but appreciates a laugh

Sister Ann Peters - Casualty sister

Maggie Hubert – an acid-tongued auxiliary nurse with a long-term grudge against staff nurses and students.

Charlie – Mitch's flatmate, an art graduate.

Miss Marshall – the aptly named warden of the nurses' home

Steph Saunders – head of Artist and Repertoire department at Cosmo Records, a cougar if there ever was one.

Monster – lead singer of the Bartok Boys

Eddie – bassist in the Bartok Boys

Jeff – enigmatic lead guitarist in the Bartok Boys

Dai the Drummer – drummer in the Bartok Boys

Maria Esposito – an Italian S.E.N.

Sister Hunter – a formidable Night Sister of forty years experience.

Alison – a sweet young thing, can manage a few backing vocals

Andy – a police constable

Gillian Evans – a cheeky second year student nurse

Susan Bowen – another cheeky second year

Cali – a indomitable Jamaican domestic.

Sexy Sam – aka Detective Inspector Samuel Enoch, devastatingly good looking officer in C.I.D.

GLOSSARY OF ABBREVIATIONS AND MEDICAL TERMS

C.C.I – City Central Infirmary

T.A – Terence Adams ward, male surgical

Willie Meckett – William Meckett ward, male medical

B/P – blood pressure

TPR – temperature, pulse, respirations

PUO – pyrexia (high temperature) of unknown origin.

IV – intravenous.

Perf – perforated duodenal ulcer (stomach ulcer)

Obs – observations of B/P and TPR

MSU – mid-stream specimen of urine.

FOB – faeces for occult blood, a sample obtained in a pot and sent for analysis to find hidden blood

SHO – Senior House Officer (A doctor of lowly status but sometimes with a huge ego)

Reg – Registrar (senior to SHO)

Hemineverin – used to treat patients with alcohol withdrawal.

Narcan (Naloxone) – antidote to opiates.

C and S – culture and sensitivity (i.e. what bug is causing the problem)

SEN – State Enrolled Nurse, a qualified nurse who has completed two years of training as opposed to three years as completed by...

...an SRN – State Registered Nurse.

Kardex - nursing notes

Paeds – Children's ward

Gasman – anaesthetist

Diff – Cardiff

Aseptic Technique (Phase One) – A method of carrying out a sterile procedure so that there is minimum risk of introducing infection. Achieved by the sterility of the equipment and a non-touch method.

Backs round – the relieving of pressure areas and repositioning of non-ambulent patients

Sluice – the room where all the bedpans and urinals are stored, where any "dirty" tasks are carried out, eg urine testing, and where contaminated materials are disposed of. Habitat of student nurses.

Myocardial Infarction (M.I.) - heart attack.

Universal Container – a small, cylindrical pot, as used for urine samples.

Contents

Chapter One **Overflow**

Julia kicked off her black, leather shoes and flung herself onto the bed, not bothering to remove her stiff, white cap or her cloak. She felt unbelievably exhausted, physically and mentally, the yearned-for status of being qualified was most definitely tempered by the burden of responsibility.

What a shift, she thought wearily, what a bloody shift. Haemorrhaging wounds, perforated appendices and worst of all, the alcoholic on intravenous Hemineverin who, believing he was being held captive by the Nazis, had tried to climb out of the window, still attached to his drip. At least Sister Winter had been working a late with her, so she hadn't had to take charge as well. Ten o'clock on a bitterly cold January night. In just over nine hours she would be back on duty again, she'd better get some sleep, or maybe eat something? Outside, the wind was picking up, and it was starting to rain. Through the big, bay window of her room in the rambling old Victorian nurses' home she watched an ambulance hurtling along the road, blue lights flashing, its siren sounding intermittently. Maybe another patient for her ward? Just as she was drawing the curtains to shut out the night, she caught sight of her friend Mandy, rushing home along the pavement like a caped crusader, battling against the weather. Time to put the kettle on.

"Dear God, what possessed me to become a nurse?" Mandy groaned, accepting the mug of coffee.

Julia chuckled wryly. "Yep. Must have been one hell of a demon who possessed us when we were even considering it! "

Mandy closed her eyes, lying back on the flower printed duvet which adorned Julia's bed, abandoning the coffee. "Yes, the four headed demon of Pee, Poo, Puke and Pus. And Willie Meckett was full. Full to capacity. And we're supposed to be on intake tomorrow. Don't let me fall asleep here, will you? I am in grave danger of doing just that. You doubling back on an early as well tomorrow?"

Julia removed all the pins from her dark red hair and shook it loose. "Yes indeed I am. And we're on intake as well. Plus a theatre list of eleven! You know what? You can bugger off to your own room now, Fanny-Ann. I'm going to make myself a Marmite sandwich and hope to fall asleep before midnight. Nite-nite!" She pushed her friend gently off the bed and steered her towards the door.

"Goodnight, oh Mistress Meanie !" Mandy grumbled as she tottered wearily to her own room across the corridor, pausing to admire the new nameplate on her door: Staff Nurse Amanda Jacob. She smiled in satisfaction."See you in the morning. I'll give you a knock at quarter to seven. Or maybe ten to?"

Julia rolled her eyes in mock exasperation, locked her door and made for the food cupboard.

At least it had stopped raining, thought Julia gratefully, as she and Mandy hurried down the main road which led to City Central Infirmary. Their black cloaks weren't really warm enough for the chilly morning, but the walk only took five minutes or so. The impressive building loomed austerely against the still dark sky, massive and imposing, like a medieval castle in the middle of modern Cardiff.

The old hospital was already bustling with activity, the smell of bacon and eggs wafting down the main corridor as the heavy, silvery meal wagons were pushed into each ward by the early shift porters. Domestics in maroon overalls busily mopped floors and gossiped about the Royal Family, as well as that other 'royal' family on the TV show, Dallas, while nurses of every grade headed for their various wards.

"Catch ya later!" Mandy stopped at the top of the stairs, turning to the left for William Meckett ward, leaving her friend to carry on straight ahead to Terence Adams ward and whatever awaited her.

2

Hanging up her cloak in the staff room, Julia caught a glimpse of herself in the mirror. She had yet to get used to seeing herself in the blue uniform of a staff nurse, she still got a kick out of it.

"Well, Staff Nurse Harry," she whispered to her reflection, "let's face the fray!"

By ten o'clock, the theatre list was well under way, the majority of the patients had been washed and Julia was just finishing the medicine round with a nervous first year student, on her second placement.

"Staff Harry!" The ward clerk leaned out of the office, telephone in her hand. "Willie Meckett on the phone. Can we take a medical admission?"

"Where's Sister?" Julia looked up from the antibiotics she was checking.

"Still at break. What shall I say?" The clerk's voice sounded urgent.

"Hang on." She turned to the student. "Stay by this medicine trolley, and do not leave it. Understand?" The student nodded, petrified, as Julia hurried over to the office, taking the phone from the clerk.

"Staff Harry speaking."

"Hya chick! 'Tis your dear friend Mandy here! Sorry about this, love, but we are full – as you know – and we have a young man down in Cas who needs a cubicle. Now rumour has it that Terence Adams has a cube. Chap has pyrexia of unknown origin. Needs barrier nursing. Miss Graham has okayed it."

Julia groaned inwardly. There was nothing for it, she'd have to accept the case. Sister Winter would not be pleased, but if the Nursing Officer had authorised it there was nothing else to be done.

"Tell Cas to send him up, but ask them to give us twenty minutes or so to get the cube ready."

Returning to the medicine round, she was amused to see that the student had taken her literally, and her yellow-clad form was clinging to the trolley as if her life depended on it. She remembered her own second placement, and how nervous she had been, how strange surgery had seemed after three months on a medical ward. Bringing herself back to the current crisis with a snap, she got through the rest of the round as efficiently as possible, before instructing the student how to prepare the cubicle for the new patient.

"Now, Nurse Thomas, you get the bed ready and I'll show you how to set up the barrier nursing equipment." The student looked blank. Julia sighed – what on earth did they teach them in the training institute these days..?

Mandy kept her promise and the porters duly arrived with the new patient exactly half an hour later, accompanied by a surly looking S.E.N.

"Name's Mitchell Walker, twenty three years old." She handed Julia a set of notes and x-rays, plus a white plastic bag of belongings. "He's had a lumbar puncture, results not through yet. The S.H.O has clerked him but we haven't completed all the demographics. Guess you lot'll have to do that, won't you?" She smiled sweetly at Julia, then left as quickly as she decently could. Cow, thought Julia.

The young man appeared distressed, restlessly throwing back the sheet.

"They keep asking if I'm going to make it! Am I going to die? My head hurts so much!" He was clearly agitated, sweat glistening on his pale face, his dark hair sticking wetly to his forehead.

Julia looked sharply at the porters. "What's he talking about?"

"Oh, he heard us asking the Casualty registrar if we were to take him to Willie Meckett. Coz we knew they were full." The older porter had the grace to look sheepish. "All I said was "Willie Meckett?" The reg said no. And he must have thought..."

Flashing a withering look at two men, Julia turned her attention to the young patient.

4

"Don't be daft! Of course you're not going to die! You're in good hands here. Now these two strong lads are going to transfer you to this comfortable bed, and Nurse Thomas and I will look after you. In fact, I will allocate Nurse Thomas as your very own special nurse." The student looked at her in horror. What on earth would that entail? And barrier nursing?

"All will be well." Julia's voice was firm. She threw a warning glance at the quaking student and started the admission procedure.

The afternoon staff looked so fresh in their clean uniforms, they made Julia feel quite grubby; a third year student was perched on the desk,but the more junior student had to stand, while the senior staff nurse and Julia sat in distinguished comfort for the lunchtime handover in the office.

"And last of all we have a medical patient. Mitchell Walker. Overflow from Willie Meckett. P.U.O. Results from the lumbar puncture indicate viral meningitis. We've been barrier nursing him, but his blood cultures aren't back yet, so we'll continue to isolate him until they are. He's had a good sleep and seems pretty lucid now." Julia glanced around, apologetically. "It's been mayhem here this morning so I'm afraid I haven't had a chance to complete the Kardex, and the student was called to Theatre to collect Mr Edwards after his hemicolectomy because Theatre is short staffed, so..."

The senior staff nurse, known for her exacting approach to life, frowned. "Can you do it before you go to break, Staff?"

Julia sighed. She was starving. "Sure. No problem. Well, that's the happy family, folks, have a great shift." She handed the ward keys over to the other staff nurse, gathered up the necessary documentation and headed for the cubicle, putting on a mask, gown and gloves before entering.

Mitchell Walker was only pretending to be asleep. His headache had subsided, thank God, but he wanted a chance to look at Julia without her realising. Pity about that mask, it hid her mouth, he couldn't tell if she was smiling or not. But those eyes, those huge grey eyes, he could drown in them. She tapped him gently on the shoulder, before sitting down next to the bed.

"Mr Walker? Sorry to disturb you but I really need to ask you a few more questions."

He opened his eyes properly. "No problem. I was only dozing. And call me Mitch, everyone else does."

"Okay, Mitch. We've got your basic information, but I just need your occupation, any telephone contact numbers and your medical history."

"Can't you take your mask off, Nurse? And what's your name? Your name badge is under your gown."

"I'm Staff Nurse Harry. And I'm sorry, the mask stays on until your blood results come back."

He grinned. "Harry's a strange name for a girl."

"Ha-ha. Very funny. At least you're well enough to joke. If you insist, my name's Julia."

"Julia. Good name, I like it."

"Great, now let me get on with my work."

Twenty minutes later, Julia had established that Mitch was a musician, a graduate from Cardiff's Royal College of Music and Drama, where he now worked as a clerical officer while waiting for his Big Break. He came from mid-Wales, where his parents ran a farm.

He started to look anxious again. "Julia, I'm desperate, and I mean *desperate* for a pee. Where's the bog?" He started to sit up in bed.

"Pee in this." She handed him a urinal. "We need a sample anyway."

"I can't pee in that! In front of you!" He looked at her, horrified. "I'm getting up." Mitch's long legs swung over the bed and he tried to stand up.

6

"Get back in bed! You only had a lumbar puncture this morning!" Julia tried to push him back, but he was too strong for her and staggered to his feet. The blood drained from his face and his lanky frame swayed.

"Help!" Julia tried valiantly to support him.

The door burst open. "Let him go, Staff!" Julia was mortified yet grateful. Her cry for assistance had been heard by Mr Robinson, the surgical consultant himself, back on the ward for a brief round. Taller even than Mitch, he grabbed the young man's shoulders and eased him gently onto the floor.

"Only a faint, I think, Staff. We'll leave him there a while until his blood pressure settles. Stay with him and I'll get Sister."

Kneeling beside Mitch, Julia took his pulse. Quite fast and thready at ninety beats a minute. As she held his wrist, Mitch grabbed her hand tightly, murmuring confusedly.

"Don't leave me, Nurse. I love you."

A chuckle from the doorway heralded the capable figure of Sister Winter, hastily donning a gown and mask.

"Charming our wayward patient into submission, Staff?"

Julia blushed. "He's talking rubbish! I couldn't stop him from getting out of bed, I'm sorry."

"No need to apologise. He's the one owing you an apology! You could have hurt yourself, trying to hold him up! Check his B/P and if it's okay we'll get him back to bed."

Ten minutes later Mitch was once more tucked up in bed, having meekly used the urinal as instructed.

"I'm off to break now." Julia recorded his blood pressure on the chart at the foot of the bed. "Someone will be along soon to check your temperature and give you a quick wash and freshen up."

"Aw, can't you do it?" He grinned at her wickedly.

"Enough of your sauce! And don't be giving Student Nurse Thomas a hard time either!" Her tummy gave a loud rumble and her only thought as she rushed to the canteen at half past one was whether there'd be any chips left...

Mitch Walker stood in the foyer of the Infirmary, clutching his belongings in the same plastic bag that had accompanied him to Terence Adams when he was admitted, four days ago. His legs still felt a bit like jelly but at least his headache had gone for good. He hoped his mate Charlie wouldn't be much longer, it was draughty where he was waiting, people coming and going all the time through the big doors at the front entrance. After days of restricted activity and hospital food he was relieved to be going home. Well, going back to the poky ground floor flat in Allensbank Road. His parents had begged him to return to Llanidloes, but Mitch was keen to get back to work and his music. Once his mother got him back in her clutches, he'd be stuck there for weeks, being force fed cawl and home made bread. No doubt she'd put in an appearance quickly enough, as soon as she could get away from the farm, but lambing season was almost upon them, so that would divert her maternal instinct for a while.

Where on earth was Charlie? He'd promised to pick him up at mid-day and now it was almost twenty past twelve. Maybe he was having a problem with the Mini. But if he didn't show up by half past he'd catch a bus, sod it.

He hadn't seen much more of that nice Staff Harry. She must have been on her days off. The other staff were okay, but Julia Harry had captured his imagination. Tall and slim, that incredible russet hair pinned up under that hat – he tried to imagine it all tumbling down. He could feel a song coming on....

He was jolted out of his reverie by a loud honking as an ancient grey Mini pulled up outside. At last! My own bog, my own bed and lamb kebabs, here I come, he thought gleefully

8

Chapter Two **Funky's**

The rapping on the door got more insistent. "Get a move on, Jules! The taxi's due in a minute!"

"Hang on! Almost ready!" Julia hastily applied yet another coat of mascara to her already heavily made up eyes, then gabbed her velvet jacket and bag, just finding enough time to check her appearance in the mirror. Yes. She'd do. Black drainpipe jeans, tight black T-shirt, plenty of black eyeshadow and her deep auburn hair a huge, tousled mess.

Mandy was waiting impatiently on the landing, dressed almost identically to Julia, apart from the drainpipes. No matter how skinny she got, her thighs remained rather curvy, which did not suit the androgynous punk look one bit. No, she'd stick to her Wranglers.

The taxi beeped its horn outside.

"C'mon!" Mandy propelled her friend down the stairs, and out of the front door, shutting it with a slam, before they flung themselves down on the back seat of the cab.

"Funky's, please." Mandy could hardly contain her excitement.

Julia looked at her in surprise. "I thought we were going to Chi-Chi's tonight?"

"For goodness' sake, Julia! It's Thursday night! Nurses and Students night! Free entry! You got your union card? And there's a band on as well. I think it's Dr Feelgood! Whoo hoo!" Mandy was quivering with anticipation.

"I don't mind. But if I had known we were off to Funky's I'd have worn my old boots instead of these little beauties!" She looked down in resignation at her brand new brothel creepers. "I hope they're waterproof..."

The taxi purred its way along the frosty, moonlit Porthnewydd Avenue, passing the Infirmary, with all its brightly lit windows gleaming in the darkness. Julia looked at her watch. Eight o'clock. They'd be doing the backs round now, and checking all the post-op meds. But she was off duty, and the night was hers for the taking. The taxi turned left by the railway bridge near Queen Street, before arriving at their destination in Carlo Street.

The heavy thud of a bass guitar resonated through the darkness as they showed their cards at the door.

"Dr Feelgood?" Mandy looked hopefully at the bald headed bouncer, who shiftily avoided eye contact.

"Sorry, love. They, er, got the dates wrong on the poster. We've got Bartok Boys tonight."

Mandy frowned in annoyance, and, turning to Julia, sighed. "Chi-Chi's it is, then?"

Julia shook her head. "It's cold out here, it's warm in there, it's free, we're here, let's go in." Muttering crossly in disappointment, the pair made their way resignedly down the dimly lit corridor which led to the crowded main hall.

The bar was packed with students and off duty nurses, three deep in places. Julia groaned. How on earth would they ever get served? As if she could read her mind, Mandy volunteered, "Well, since I've brought us here under false pretences, I'll get them in. You go and check out the band, and I'll be back as soon as I can. Half a lager?" Julia nodded, then made her way towards the stage.

10

"Sound check, one-two, one-two!" The skinny, blond singer was leaping about, while the bassist twiddled some dials on an amplifier, the drummer looking bored as he twirled his sticks. The singer grabbed the microphone again and continued his repartee.

"Well, hello all you drunken students and gorgeous, sexy nurses!" Julia groaned with embarrassment as he continued, pushing his flowing blond locks back from his deathly pale face. "The Bartok Boys are ready to go! We'll kick off with a couple of songs you already know, then we'll treat you to a few of our own compositions."

From the obscurity of the other side of the stage, a keyboard played the intro to L.A. Woman. Julia moved around to the right to get a better look. And there he was. Tall, dark and totally absorbed in the music. It was Mitch Walker.

Julia hadn't realised just how tall he was, she had only really seen him either sitting in bed or in a chair. She also hadn't realised just how attractive he was. Only goes to show how ghastly those hospital gowns made you look, she thought. This was proving to be a very interesting evening out.

Mitch's eyes were narrowed in concentration as he played, his dark hair flopping over his forehead. Then Julia was nudged sharply."They're quite good, aren't they?" Mandy was back with the drinks.

"They certainly are." Julia took a sip of lager,not taking her eyes off Mitch. "Christ, this lager's disgusting!"

"Should slow you down a bit, then!" Mandy giggled, glancing around for any possible prey.

But Julia's attention was solely on the band. The floor in front of the stage was thronged with girls, goggle eyed and lusting after the lead singer, who was a professional show-off, prancing about like a demented rabbit, but he could sing well enough, she supposed. Every so often, he'd run his hands through his rippling fair hair, as if trying to eradicate the slightly receding hair-line, which would probably end up in a monks' tonsure within a couple of years. By complete contrast, the lead guitarist stood there, perfectly motionless, an enigmatic half-smile on his lips as he concentrated on his solo. Mitch continued to play, oblivious to the crowd, remaining in his own musical world. Julia had known he was a musician, but in a rock band? He'd never mentioned it.

"D'you wanna dance?" An arm snaked around her waist, and a drunken face leered at her, breathing beer fumes into her face.

Julia recoiled in disgust. "Push off, you tosser, I'm here to watch the band." Her rejected suitor staggered away, trying his luck with Mandy instead, only to be given the same treatment.

By now the floor was an inch deep in beer and cider, such a delightful alcoholic blend, which by the end of the evening would also be enhanced by a fair few dollops of vomit. Julia, worried about the state of her new shoes, battled her way through the heaving, sweaty bodies to the edge of the dance floor, which was marginally drier, leaving Mandy to the more welcome attentions of a red-haired dental student she'd had her eye on for ages, having attended the dental hospital with toothache a few weeks ago and been treated by the six foot ginger nut Kevin.

At half time, the band left their instruments on the stage, and jumped down onto the floor, where the lead singer was immediately surrounded by adoring fans. Julia tried to spot Mitch. Then oh, my God, he was walking towards her, purposefully.

"It's you." His delighted grin spoke volumes.

"You look a lot better." Julia found she was gripping her glass so hard it was in danger of shattering.

"You're not kidding!" He laughed. "That was one hell of a headache I had. What are you doing here?"

"Um...I guess I came to see the band. Only you lot don't look or sound much like Dr Feelgood!"

Mitch feigned offence. "But we're miles better than them! Don't you reckon..?" His voice trailed away, suddenly uncertain.

"Actually, you are pretty good. I suppose if you'd been rubbish, this lot would have buggered off by now. No. I tell a lie." Mitch's face fell. "You were amazing!"

"Honestly? Bloody hell, that's great. You staying until the end? Will you hang around for a quick chat?"

"I'll consider it,"she replied, smiling, "in fact, I've now considered it. Yeah, I'll stick around!"

Thus encouraged, Mitch hurried over to his band mates, and the singer, who was busy chatting up a bunch of second year physiotherapy students. He looked over his shoulder to check if she was still there. And she was, giving him a discreet wink as she turned away to look for Mandy.

The hall was almost empty. The overhead lights had been switched back on, and any glamour that had been there earlier had faded, showing the band for the youthful boys they really were, with pale, tired faces, yawning their heads off, busily packing away. Mandy had long since departed, saying she was going home, with a besotted Kevin in tow.

"Can I help at all?" Julia felt useless as she stood there, nursing an empty glass while the band busied themselves with leads, cables and amplifiers.

"Not really." Mitch carefully zipped up his keyboard case. "But I'm done now, just got to wait for the others. Can I get you a drink?"

"No, I'm good, thanks. Working tomorrow."
"You won't get much sleep then!" Mitch looked concerned. "It's half past eleven now! You'll be on duty again at half past seven!"

"Nah, I'm on a late. A nice lie-in for me, thank you very much! I really enjoyed your band, though. It's been a great evening."

13

He took her hand and led her to sit down at one of the few tables that were near the bar.

"Look, I'd offer you a lift home, but we came here in the van, and it's stuffed full of our gear. But, what I wanted to say–what I wanted to ask was-" Julia smiled as he struggled for the words.

"Can I meet you again? I know you're working late tomorrow, but the day after? Saturday? I haven't got a gig or anything, we could go for a drink?"

"That would be really nice." Yes, yes yes!she thought, happily. "What about the Five Oaks? In Oak Street?"

"Yes! And I would suggest we go for a meal, but I'm skint. I can cook for us though! How does spag bol chez moi grab you?"

"Sounds good to me." She got up to go. "Say, seven o'clock at the Five Oaks?"

"It's a date!" He out his hand on her shoulder. "You know, I'm so glad we bumped into each other again!"

"Me too." Lucky, lucky me, she thought.

"Will you be okay getting home?" He frowned in concern. "Have you booked a taxi?"

"I'll be fine." She felt on top of the world. "I haven't lived in Cardiff for three and a half years without knowing how to get myself home safely! I'll see you Saturday." Gathering up her bag and jacket, she threw him a big smile and headed for the door.

Chapter Three **Nipple to knee**

Friday morning dawned bright and breezy, as though winter was finally letting up and allowing spring to offer a preview of better weather to come. Julia opened one eye and squinted at her alarm clock; ten past nine. She would have just enough time to pop into town and look for something new to wear for Saturday night before reporting for duty at one o'clock. She wondered how Mandy had got on with the delightful Kevin. There was no sound coming from her room. Maybe she was having a lie-in as well, she was a day off today, after all.

Yawning and stretching, Julia pulled on her dressing gown and made her way down the corridor to the communal bathroom. Just as she was about to start running a bath, a tall figure suddenly leapt out from one of the toilet cubicles.

"Bloody hell!" Julia jumped in alarm. This was no nurse, but the dental student, clad most inadequately in Mandy's pink satin dressing gown.

"Sorry! Didn't mean to startle you!" He blushed deeply to match the fetching rose tint of the dressing gown.

"No problem. You'd better keep out of sight in case the home warden spots you. I hardly think you'd pass for a staff nurse!" His face went even redder, blending in with his hair perfectly, and, pulling the gown even more tightly around his narrow hips, scuttled off to Mandy's room. Miss Marshall would have a fit if she caught an illicit male visitor at this time of the day, especially one as bizarrely dressed as Kevin...

So, what had Mandy been up to, she wondered, pouring a few drops of Fenjal into the bath water. It was a devil to clean, but so what? She decided she'd just ignore it and let Mandy deal with it when she had a bath later. Julia had a pretty good idea as to Mandy's bedroom activities, but felt a bit surprised. On the first night? Ah well, she thought, slipping down under the scented water, no doubt Mandy would tell her everything in the fullness of time. Or would she..?

Having rummaged through the rails at Miss Selfridge, and dithered over the dresses at Dorothy Perkins, Julia finally found what she was looking for in Wallis. Ordinarily she wouldn't even venture into this store, it was beyond her means. But she still had some Christmas money left over, so in she went, to emerge triumphantly fifteen minutes later with a beautiful pair of brown velvet jeans.

Glancing at her watch as she walked briskly down Queen Street, dodging the other shoppers, pigeons and buskers, she thought she had just enough time to call in to Marks and Spencers to buy something for her lunch. Why not, she thought to herself, let's treat myself.

Reaching out to select a tub of prawn cocktail, someone tapped her lightly on the shoulder.

"Hello." The voice brought an instant smile to her lips, and she turned round to see Mitch standing there, a shopping basket in his hand. Her face lit up as her heart did somersaults.

"Hi! How are you? Busy shopping?" She looked down at his empty basket.

"I'm looking for a birthday present for my mother. She's fifty at the end of the month, I might pop home for that. But I don't know what to get her."

"Do you need help?"

"Bloody hell, yes! Lead the way, Staff Harry!"

"Ssh..don't call me that! Julia is fine! C'mon!" Smiling, she escorted him down to the underwear department, taking just five minutes to pull out a pretty, pale blue dressing gown.

"What size is your mother?" Julia held the delicate garment up in front of her.

"Ooh, I have no idea. A bit bigger than you, but not as tall, I think. Try it on for me?"

"Okay, if I must." She removed her jacket and on it went, over her thick jumper. "It's fine. Plenty of room even over my clothes. You gonna buy it?"

"I am, indeed. And I'm going to buy you a coffee too. Would that be acceptable to Madam?"

Julia grinned at him. "That would be fab. Where shall we go? I only have about half an hour before I need to go home to change for work."

The pair were soon tucked up in a cafe around the corner, with two cappuccinos and a toasted sandwich for Mitch.

"This is an illicit date," he smiled, "I'm not supposed to be seeing you until tomorrow night."

"Don't worry," she whispered, chuckling,"I won't tell anybody."

He laughed. "So how long is your shift this afternoon?"

"One o'clock until nine o'clock. But that's if it's calm and quiet, which I doubt it will be."

He reached for her hand over the sugar bowl. "This is such a bonus, seeing you now. You know, you look so different out of uniform, younger I guess, especially with your hair loose."

"Ah, it's the air of authority the uniform gives us. Mind you, we need it, with difficult patients like you!"

"Me?! I was like a little lamb when I was in, I gave you no trouble at all."

"Hmm." She smiled wryly. "Is this your lunch break? It's very early. Only quarter to twelve."

"Yep. But it was so quiet in the office I asked the manager if I could go early to avoid all the lunchtime shoppers. I hate shopping."

The minutes ticked by all too speedily, and reluctantly, Julia decided it was time to go. "It's getting late now, I have to get back."

They both stood up.

"Until tomorrow, then. And we'll have a proper talk then." Shyly, he leaned over and kissed her on the cheek.

"Yes, until tomorrow." Blushing deeply, yet deliriously happy, she waved goodbye and started to hurry home.

The afternoon shift had started out fairly quietly, until half past three, that is, when Sylvia Cross, the part-time S.E.N. who was due in at four, rang in sick. That left Julia to work the shift with Maggie Hubert, an auxiliary nurse who must have graduated from the Josef Stalin School of Charm. Maggie hated qualified nurses and students with a vengeance, doing as little as possible, preferring to beetle off to the sluice for a sly cigarette when Julia was busy and unable to catch her in the act.

"Terence Adams, Staff speaking." Julia wearily answered the phone for the fifth time in as many minutes. Surely Maggie could have answered it?

"Hi, Staff." A smooth, English accent poured like warm honey into her ear. "It's Marcus here. We've got a perf coming up soon. Forty-two year old rugby player, can you prep him for theatre stat?"

Honestly, Julia thought, the airs that Marcus Battencourt gave himself, anyone would think he was a consultant rather than a lowly S.H.O.

"Yes, of course, Dr Battencourt. I'll get a bed ready right away."

"Muchas gracias," came the slick reply, "and please call me Marcus, er, Staff..?"

"Harry. Staff Harry. Okay, send him up." Her heart sank. I'll have to ring for help with the post op meds, she thought, anxiously, there's simply not enough time to do everything. She decided to ring Llanfair ward to ask them to send their student over for half an hour or so. Where the hell was that bloody Maggie? She looked down the Nightingale ward, despondently, twenty four men all her responsibility, intravenous infusions in progress at every other bed, catheters hopefully patent and draining, wound drains likewise, obs waiting to be recorded. Maggie was perfectly able to check pulses and temperatures, however Julia very much doubted they'd been done. But there was no more time left to be worrying, as her new admission was being wheeled through the double doors at the entrance of the ward.

A feeling of utter frustration overwhelmed Julia, and her usual calm tolerance went flying out of the office window.

"Maggie! Nurse Hubert! Please get on with the post-op obs as quick as you can, and then do the fluid charts after emptying the catheters." Her sharp tone startled the lazy auxiliary into a surprised response.

"But what about my break?" Maggie's petulant mouth turned down in indignation.

"It'll have to wait. Now please get on with it, sharp-ish." Julia turned her attentions to her new patient, leaving a fuming Maggie scowling as she started to carry out her instructions.

Rob Thomas was a big chap, proudly telling Julia, in between painful spasms, that he was a prop forward for St Peter's R.F.C

"Do I really have to have this tube up my nose, Nurse?" He fingered the naso-gastric tube unhappily, then winced as another wave of pain shot through him.

19

"You'd be vomiting blood if it wasn't there." Julia saw no point in beating about the bush. "It's keeping your stomach empty. Now I'll get you ready for theatre and call a porter."

"A porter? Am I going somewhere else?"

"No." Julia fastened a name band around his wrist, struggling to make it secure, as her patient was big-boned to say the least. "You can't have any hair where the surgeon needs to operate. So we get a porter up to do that."

"Do what?" Rob Thomas was sweating profusely now.

"Shave you. Now enough questions, I'm just going to ring for a porter and get your pre-med. Don't be tempted to drink anything, please, it will complicate things, okay?" She put a Nil By Mouth sign above his bed.

"Yes, Matron." He attempted a weak grin at her, but Julia could see he was in a great deal of pain and extremely nervous.

She picked up the phone in the office and rang the Porters' Lodge.

"Staff Harry here, T.A. Can one of you come up and do a pre-op shave please?"

There was a heavy sigh at the other end of the line. "Ooh, I don't know about that. We're two chaps short this evening, family bereavement and stuff, and there's a stiff on Llanfair ward needs collecting."

Julia sighed impatiently. She really didn't want to know the reasons for their staff shortages.

"So can you send someone up or not? My patient's scheduled for theatre at seven thirty."

Another heavy sigh. "Well, I'll see what I can do."

"Well be as quick as you can." Julia was fast losing patience. She slammed the phone down angrily, when it rang again.

20

"Hi, Staff Harry, Marcus here again. The perf's going to theatre at seven now, not half past, because our darling senior reg wants to finish at a decent time as he's going out to dinner with our darling consultant. Bloody drugs rep do or something equally lucrative. I'll be up in a mo to do the consent form. The gasman has already seen him in Cas."

Julia wanted to burst into tears. "Fine, she replied, evenly, "I'll get him ready." I'll have to prep him myself, she thought.

Despite three years of nurse training, and three months as a qualified staff nurse on a busy surgical ward, Julia had never had to carry out a nipple to knee shave on a man before, there'd always been a porter available, or a male nurse. And this was a youngish man...

Shit, she thought, shit, shit, shit.

Rob Thomas didn't know what on earth to make of it all as she wheeled a trolley to his bedside, gowned, masked and gloved. What the hell was she going to do to him? Pulling the curtains around the bed, she smiled bravely beneath her mask.

"Won't take long, can you just lift your gown for me, please, Mr Thomas?"

Struggling to remain calm, her patient did as he was asked, then examined the ceiling for any non-existent cobwebs, praying for divine intervention, his face becoming redder by the second.

Julia swiftly removed the hair from his chest and abdomen, then, as she reached his nether regions, she tentatively reached forward her gloved hand, to lift his appendage in order to shave around it. Just as she was gingerly holding it between her finger and thumb, the curtain was yanked back briskly, and an irate voice exclaimed,

"It's not an unexploded bloody bomb, Staff! It won't go off any second! Give that razor to me! I'm off to dinner at eight thirty, I haven't got all day!" The senior registrar, not known for his tact or bedside manner,

21

grabbed the razor from her, and took over, with a smirking Marcus Battencourt standing behind him.

Julia fled to the sluice, seeking comfort amidst the gleaming bedpans and urine bottles. She leaned back against the closed door. Her cheeks were on fire as she played back the scene. How humiliating. Tears filled her eyes and she battled against the need to weep loudly and unrestrainedly. Control yourself, she muttered, pretending to clean the sink, keep calm.

The door opened. "Can I go to break, now?" Maggie Hubert stood there, hand on hip, a smug look on her face.

"Yes, off you go." At least the presence of the irritating auxiliary had the beneficial effect of making her pull herself together. What a dreadful evening, and another two hours to go...

By twenty past nine, Julia was finally making her way down the main corridor, strangely quiet after the bustle of the ward. Somehow she had managed to get through the shift. Making a mental note to ensure she did not share a shift with Maggie in the near future, she passed the Theatre suite.

"Hi there." A voice called from the darkened depths of the anaesthetic department. It was Marcus Battencourt."You okay?"

"Of course I am, why wouldn't I be?" Julia was not in the mood for his suave chatter.

"Alright, don't be so shirty. Can I walk with you as far as Path Lab? I'm taking this choice specimen down there." He grinned, brandishing a gruesome-looking lump of red tissue in a specimen jar.

Julia looked him up and down. He was such a dandy, good looking, but rather affected. Foppish blond hair artfully slicked back, an immaculate white shirt and a cravat. A bloody cravat!

"Sure." She was too tired to argue.

22

"Anscombe is such a bastard, isn't he?"

"If you are referring to Mr Anscombe our wonderful senior reg, then I'm afraid I'd be inclined to agree with you." Julia looked stonily ahead.

"Oh, don't take it to heart, sweetie. His bark is worse than his bite!"

"Really?" Julia was disinclined to continue the conversation. Thankfully, they'd reached the Path Lab, and the parting of their ways.

"Look, Staff Harry, or may I call you..?" He put his hand on her shoulder.

"Staff Harry is fine,"she replied coldly. "And I really must be getting home, I'm on duty again at seven thirty."

"As you wish, fair lady." And giving her the benefit of his super trouper smile, he turned around and walked in the opposite direction.

Thank God for that, she thought, jadedly, pushing though the black rubber doors and out into the dark January night.

The temperature had plummeted, and the icy air took her breath away as she made her way along the path that led from the main body of the hospital, past the nurses' home, to the Gap in the Wall on the main road where the student nurses would catch the hospital bus every morning, if they were working in the other Cardiff hospitals. The full moon shone brightly down on Porthnewydd Avenue and the pavements sparkled with frost. Orange double decker buses rolled by, destined for Llanrumney and St Mellons, taking bingo players and late shift workers back to their warm homes. Friday night revellers shouted and laughed as they departed from the watering holes of Roath and Splott, heading for the bright lights of the city centre. Well, that'll be me tomorrow night, she thought happily.

Chapter Four Julie the goat

Saturdays on Terence Adams could be relaxed and calm, unless, of course it was on emergency intake. Thankfully, this particular weekend it wasn't, so the sunlit ward had an almost holiday-like atmosphere, so different from the fraught, manic shift the previous night. Rob Thomas was making a good recovery from his operation, and Mr Anscombe with his smooth talking sidekick, Marcus Battencourt, did not put in an appearance.

How lovely it was, thought Julia, to be able to take time to do things properly, and even find the opportunity to do a teaching session with the student nurses.

"See you tomorrow afternoon!" She waved goodbye to the late shift staff, pulling her cloak on as she left the ward.

Porthnewydd Avenue was quieter than usual. Normally, at four o'clock on a Saturday, it would be busy with traffic, but then she remembered, there was a rugby international today, England against Wales. Flanders, the trauma ward directly below T.A, would be busy tonight, she thought wryly. Alcohol-induced head injuries and fractures would find their way there, and probably the odd facial fracture would end up on her ward too. But not my problem tonight, she concluded joyfully, as she opened the big front door to the nurses' home.

Julia stood on the bed in order to examine her full length appearance in the dressing table mirror. Her new brown velvet jeans were so tight she could hardly sit down in them, but they were seriously gorgeous, especially teamed with the cream silk shirt she'd borrowed from Mandy.

Mandy was being very coy about her new boyfriend, and just giggled when Julia had asked her about her bedroom antics with Kevin. That confirmed her suspicions, the First Night Floozie...

Looking at her watch, she gasped. Almost ten to seven. Grabbing her bag and her sheepskin coat from the wardrobe, she rushed along the corridor and down the stairs. As she walked quickly down Porthnewydd Avenue, her breath hung on the freezing air. It was a clear, starry night, but no moon as yet. Julia wondered how the evening would work out. Mitch seemed quite special. She'd had a few casual boyfriends since she'd lived in Cardiff, but none of them had amounted to much. Even after three and a half years, she was still feeling hurt about Paul and the way he had treated her. She had tried hard to forget him, him and his lager-swilling rugby friends and the whole social set up back home. Julia had thrown herself into nursing with total commitment, resulting in her coming top in her hospital finals. But she was still sad inside...he'd called her frigid, he'd called her wooden and cold...she wasn't like the other girls, he'd said. Maybe it was her Roman Catholic upbringing, but she had always been told by her mother, her sisters, her grandmother, not to give herself to a man too easily. And to be truthful, she hadn't really wanted to anyway, not with Paul...

The Five Oaks pub stood on the corner of Oak Street, an old fashioned black and white building next to some terraced houses. As she opened the door, Julia scanned the smoke filled bar. Where was he?

Somebody tapped her shoulder. "You looking for someone?" Mitch was grinning at her. "I was loitering with intent outside, I wasn't sure where you'd be." He looked great, tight black jeans, white T-shirt and a leather jacket, every inch the rock musician.

"Hi." She suddenly felt shy, unsure of herself.

"Shall we sit somewhere? I'll get us a drink. What do you fancy?"

"Um, half a cider, please. I'll get the next round in, though!"

They managed to squeeze themselves into a corner seat. "Well this is cosy!" He moved closer to her in order to make room for the old man who had decided to join their table.

"So, you're obviously not from the Diff! Not with that accent. Where's home?" He took a sip of his Guiness.

"I'm from Llangennech, near Llanelli."

"Llangennech? Wow! All those massive waves and miles of sand! Are you a surfie?!"

Julia laughed. "Oh, everyone mixes them up. Llangennech, where I'm from, is a small village in Carmarthenshire, about two miles up from Llanelli, Llangenn*ith* is the coastal village on the Gower. And no, I'm not a surfie! Anyway, tell me more about your music. You didn't say you played in a rock band! I was so gobsmacked to see you playing in Funky's."

"It was gobsmackingly great to see you there, too." He reached over and shyly stroked her hand. Julia felt a prickle of warmth steal up her arm.."As for my musical career, well I was obviously not going to be a natural at farming or rugby, so I started piano lessons when I was about seven. My poor mother had to drive me all the way to Newtown for the lessons. I passed every one of my exams and started playing the organ in church just after my fourteenth birthday. God, that used to make me so nervous, even though there were only half a dozen people in the congregation at each service! But then I discovered rock music! Bye bye church organ, hello Pink Floyd. Jesus, I'll never forget the day when I met my nemesis! I thought I was alone in the church after morning service, so I was thumping out some punk rock and the vicar caught me!" He laughed at the memory. "Then I auditioned for the College here in Cardiff, and here I am now! I've even sent some of the band's original stuff off to Cosmo records, they're the new pretender to the record companies' crowns! Polydor, look to your laurels! What about you?"

"Me? Oh, I'm not musical!"

"No, not music! Tell me more about yourself. Why you became a nurse, for example."

"Okay."She took a sip of cider. "I did all languages in school, for A-level as well."

"And you got them?"

"Yes, got an A in English, a B in Spanish and French."

"So why didn't you go to Uni? You're obviously shit hot at those subjects. Why nursing for God's sake?"

She frowned at him, but not unkindly. "Nursing is more than bedpans and thermometers, you know."

"I'm sorry,"he mumbled, suitably chastised. "Go on. Tell me why. I really want to know."

"Boy trouble."She looked down at her hands. "I was going out with a local boy, Paul, we were together for about two years. He wanted more from me than I was prepared to give, so he dumped me."

"He wanted to get engaged or something?" Mitch's dark eyes scrutinised her closely.

"No, don't be daft. He, you know, he wanted other things..." She blushed. "Do you mind if we don't discuss that here? Anyway, I suddenly didn't want to go to Uni any longer. I didn't want to be part of that free and easy lifestyle. I think I wanted a more secure environment. So I applied to Cardiff to do my general nursing, and here I am."

Their attention was suddenly drawn to a scuffling and a small commotion in the far corner. A plump old man was slowly getting to his feet, brandishing a trombone, which he started to play, to the crowd's delight. It was a tune Julia had never heard before, but one she would certainly remember afterwards. The crowd started cheering and clapping along to the music, and when the old musician stopped playing in order to sing the chorus, they all joined in,

Julie the Goat, Julie the Goat

She's a right sweet darling

In her black and white coat!

Julie the Goat, Julie the Goat

She's pretty and charming,

She's Julie the Goat

Mitch looked at Julia in astonishment, then they both burst out laughing. "Do you reckon he should audition for your band?" Julia giggled, tears running down her face.

"Hmm, maybe if we're desperate! I think it's time to have some spag bol back at my place, what d'you reckon?"

Julia grabbed her coat."I'm in favour of that. I can't wait to sample your cooking. Let's go!"

It was only about a twenty minute walk from the Five Oaks to Mitch's flat in Allensbank Road. As they walked along the dark streets of Cardiff, Mitch's hand gradually found its way into hers. It felt so right, Julia squeezed it gently by way of response. Mitch cast a sideways glance at her when she wasn't looking – such a sweet face, with the sprinkling of freckles over her upturned nose and the wide, generous mouth. And those amazing eyes...

"Excuse the mess, won't you?" Mitch opened the gaudily painted front door. "And ignore the purple paint. Everything is purple in our flat. My flat mate Charlie is an art graduate and has weird taste!"

"Is he joining us for dinner?" Julia grinned impishly, as she followed him into the hallway, the tiled floor being carpeted with scores of unopened envelopes, old newspapers and takeaway menus. A slight smell of damp hung in the air.

"No way! I've bunged him a fiver to go out and leave us alone. I think he's buggered off to Newport to see his ex-girlfriend. He still holds a candle for her, but she's not interested. The stupid bastard, he keeps on trying!"

Entering the main room, Julia could see that Mitch had made a huge effort. It was reasonably clean, and any clutter had been artfully hidden behind the ancient red sofa, but not hidden well enough to escape a nurse's sharp scrutiny. A small table had been draped with a white piece of material and shining glasses, spoons and forks were placed in readiness. Tall red candles had been placed in Mateus Rose bottles, which Mitch was struggling to light with a lighter he'd found on the mantelpiece.

"A glass of Piat D'Or for Madam?"

"If it's red, it'll do." Julia plonked herself down on the sofa, pulling out a heavy music manuscript from behind a cushion, which was digging into her, painfully. "What's this?"

He uncorked the wine. "It's my latest work. I've been composing an album. The band played a couple of songs from it on Thursday. I'm kinda hoping we'll get signed up by a record company." He sighed. "It's stupidly difficult, though. It's so competitive. Basically, it's just a matter of luck, being in the right place at the right time."

"Well, I wish you all the luck in the world. Then when you're famous I can tell everyone I had my supper made from me by the celebrated star, Mitch Walker!" She raised her glass to him in a toast.

Joining her on the sofa, he put his arm around her shoulder. "I'd like it very much if you and I have lots more suppers together, not just tonight."

"Do you go home very often?" She snuggled up to him, loving every minute of this. "I can't imagine the train service to Llanidloes is terribly regular!"

"You remembered where I'm from! From the ward! Ha ha! Well done, Staff Harry!"

"I told you there's more to nursing than people think. We have to have computer brains and the investigative skills of a detective too! So! Do you go home often? For any particular reason?"

"Ah, I see what you mean. No, I don't go home for any special reason." He grinned down at her. "Apart from my parents, and my Nan, there's no-one else in Llanidloes who draws me back. And no-one special in Cardiff either. That answer your question?"

"Perfectly."

They continued to talk until Mitch leaped to his feet. "I forgot to turn the oven on! Bugger! Our dinner won't be ready for another half hour at this rate!" He rushed off to the kitchen, returning a couple of minutes later, settling down once more on the sofa.

"And as I already know that the delightful Paul no longer pulls you back home, I was wondering - what about here, in the Diff? Any dashing young doctors wooing you? There must be scores of them!"

Julia smiled wryly. "You must be kidding. Most of them are nothing but a pain the backside—oh, don't get me wrong, there are some decent enough S.H.O's out there -"

"S.H.O's?"

"Senior House Officer. Junior doctor. Yeah, there are some decent ones, but they're usually already engaged or they're women! Yeah, the women are generally pretty nice. Much nicer, in fact." A wicked grin challenged him to contradict her, but he merely smiled and waited for her to continue.

31

She tapped his hand, reassuringly."No, I'm completely unattached, thank you very much."

"That's good." He pulled her closer, stroking her hair gently. She lay her head on his shoulder.

"You know I've been dreaming of this moment for bloody ages!" His voice was hardly more than a whisper. "Ever since I saw you that first time in hospital, I couldn't get you out of my mind. You kept popping up into my thoughts all the time, with your lovely red hair and beautiful eyes."

"Sounds like the start of a famous song!" She laughed. "But Dolly Parton has already done that one!"

"I could write a song about you, though. Maybe one day..." His eyes had a faraway look about them.

"You're a born romantic, you are."Julia teased. "I bet you say that to all the groupies!"

He shook his head, seriously. "No, I'm not like that, please believe me. Now Monster, on the other hand..."

"Monster?" Julia giggled.

"Our lead singer. We call him Monster on account of him boasting about the size of his, er, you know!"

"Jesus!" Julia chortled. "I've heard it all now. What about him?"

"He grabs his opportunities whenever he can, and I can tell you there are lots of opportunities for him. The girls throw themselves at him. I can't see why. He's a good singer, and okay looking I guess, but the I.Q and personality of a gnat."

"He's not as good looking as you. Or as talented." Julia put her hand on his.

Blushing, he smiled at her. "That's very kind of you. I'm glad you don't find me repulsive. Because I find you wildly attractive, and despite my intentions – which were entirely honourable - I think I'm going to have to kiss you."

Julia turned her face towards him, her eyes huge and shining in the candlelight. He brushed her parted lips with his, then drew her into his arms, kissing her slowly and softly. She offered no resistance.

"What about dinner?" She murmured, stroking his face with her fingertips.

"It can wait." His whisper was barely audible, but the urgency of his kisses conveyed the depth of his desire. Her lips were soft and inviting, he liked the way she melted into his arms and returned his kisses with an ardour matching his own. There was no doubting the chemistry between them.

Pulling away from him to catch her breath, Julia suddenly felt timid. "It's been ages since I've been kissed. And I've never been kissed like that before in my life."

"Me too." He kissed her again, his hand reaching around, searching for her breast, softly cupping it in his hand. She tried to push it away, but that insistent hand kept returning to its goal. She really shouldn't let him...

His hand strayed to the waistband of her velvet jeans, then ventured further south, moving down to her inner thighs, and yet again she tried to remove his wandering hand.

"I'm sorry, "he murmured, "I want you so badly. Forgive me."

Julia had never experienced feelings like this before. With Paul, it had been so different, he used to grope her with all the tenderness of a scrum half desperate to win the ball. This was breathtaking. Wild thoughts were racing through her feverishly excited mind.

"Nothing to forgive," she whispered back. Thus encouraged, he increased his endeavours, and succeeded in reaching her breast once more, this time his hand was given free rein. How sensual it felt, how she wanted him to continue, but he'd think her easy, surely? Yet she wanted him badly, too.

He pulled her to her feet. "I think we'd be more comfortable in my room, what d'you think?" She nodded mutely, following him compliantly. An image of her mother's serious face flashed into her head, then flashed out again quickly. Julia was filled with a longing she'd never felt with any other boyfriend, she felt directed by her own desire.

Closing the door and locking it behind them, he kissed her again, all the while undoing the pearly buttons of her silk shirt.

"Do you want this?" His voice was loaded with meaning. "Am I moving too fast? Please tell me, is this what you want?"

"Yes. No. I think I do...I don't really think I should...you'll think I'm..." Like Mandy, she thought.

"Ssh..."He silenced her protests with his kisses. "Take your shirt off."

Her face was on fire, but that was nothing compared to the heat within her prim, Catholic little soul, which was becoming more incandescent by the minute. Mitch did not wait for her to reply, but eased the silky garment over her shoulders, letting it drop to the floor. Julia looked down, embarrassed, covering herself with her arms.

"Don't be shy, let me see you." Nervously, she dropped her arms, raising her eyes to him, anxiously.

He stood back, taking her in. Her beautiful white breasts were only just contained by the lacy, white bra; she was breathing deeply, rapidly. God, he had never wanted a girl as much as he wanted her right now.

"You are so lovely, so perfect." He caressed her bare arms, then unhooked her bra, which she struggled to keep from falling off. "I just want to stare at you for hours, but I also want to do other things to you... Let me see you..." Reluctantly, she relaxed, allowing her bra to fall away. Mitch felt his desire surge within him, and he reached forward to caress her breasts with both hands. She shivered with pleasure at his touch. Surely this wasn't wrong?

He ran his fingers through her long red hair, then picked her up and put her on the bed.

"I've been longing to do that from the moment I saw you on the ward." He continued to stroke her breasts, kissing her all the while, until Julia felt she would go mad with longing. She let his hands roam wherever he wanted, finally allowing him to unzip her jeans.

"You'll have to help me take these off,"he laughed quietly. Julia complied, then lay back on the pillow. This could not possibly be wrong, she thought, this felt so right.

He stood up to undress himself, all the while watching her, not taking his eyes off her. God, she was stunning, those long white legs, that glorious auburn hair spilling over the pillow, those delightful breasts.

Lying down next to her, he could sense her trembling. Taking her in his arms, brushing her hair out of her eyes, he asked, "You okay? Hey, this isn't this your first time, is it?"

"Yes, "she whispered, "I'm afraid it is." Oh, Jesus, she thought, this is it. Do I stop him now?

He hugged her close. "Then I'll be very slow and gentle, please don't worry, my angel." He slowly eased her knickers down, before removing them in one swift action. His hand wandered down to her mons veneris, and he fondled her lightly for a few minutes, until she felt she could stand it no longer. His caresses grew more rhythmical, and suddenly Julia felt an incredible wave of pleasure wash over her.

"Oh my God!" She gasped. "Wow!"

Mitch smiled. "I think you're ready now, gorgeous girl. Prepare for your deflowering, Mitch Walker is claiming it for his own." She was aware of his legs moving hers apart, she sensed his hardness against her thigh, pressing on her, wanting access.

"You don't have to, Julia, you can change your mind - but I do want you so much."

She gazed up at those dark eyes of his, eyes brilliant with desire and longing. "I'm ready."

He slowly parted her hesitant thighs, then positioned himself in readiness, before gradually pushing his manhood into her tight, virginal cave.

All Julia felt was a brief, sharp pain as Mitch entered her, then gave herself up to his pelvic rotations and deep, but tender thrusts. It was sheer bliss.

They lay entwined amidst a tangle of sheets, not speaking, just enjoying the closeness. Julia felt incredibly happy and relaxed. She knew now she'd been right to refuse Paul's demands. She'd never felt this way about him, there was no comparison. Mitch stirred beside her.

"If I smoked I'd be having a fag right now." He grinned at her. "But I don't, so I won't. Was that really your first time? Was it okay? Are you okay? Were you really still a virgin at the ripe old age of twenty-one?" There was genuine concern in his voice.

Julia wriggled, aware of a stickiness underneath her thighs. "Yes, I really was. I think when we get up you'll, er, see the evidence of my chastity! And yes, I am okay. And it was more than okay, Mitch! It was amazing! You're amazing!"She smiled up at him.

He leaned over to kiss her, saying quietly, "I think I love you, Staff Nurse Harry. I think I love you a lot."

"I think I love you too, Mitch Walker, a lot."

The spaghetti bolognese was just about edible, but Julia and Mitch didn't care. They were too busy talking, laughing, telling each other about their

36

pasts, their hopes, their dreams. Julia skilfully avoided the subject of Paul. Why should that no-good bugger intrude on this wonderful evening?

"So do you want to become a ward sister, like that Sister Winter? I can just see you in a navy dress, bossing everyone about." He grinned cheekily, reaching for his wine glass.

"I don't know about that. I'm not sure what I want to do next. Maybe midwifery? That's what lots of my friends will be doing. But I want to staff on T.A. a while longer, I'm enjoying it—on the whole." And she proceeded to tell him about Anscombe and his antics the other night.

Mitch grimaced."He sounds a load of trouble!"

"Indeed he does, but having said that, he's a good surgeon. So if you ever have appendicitis, and he's on call, you'd be bloody grateful!"

"I can assure you I have no intention whatsoever of returning to hospital for a very long time!" They both laughed.

"When can I see you again?" He was suddenly serious. Julia breathed a silent sigh of relief. At least it hadn't been a one night stand. She couldn't have borne it if it had been, she knew she had taken a risk by sleeping with him, but she hadn't been able to help herself.

"I've got two days off at the end of next week – Thursday and Friday. I know you work office hours, but..?"

"I know! I'll work all of my lunch breaks this week, and go in an hour early each day so I can have Friday off! We can catch a train to Penarth or something! Get something to eat while we're there! What do you say?"

"Sounds great! Shall I meet you at Queen Street station? Say about two o'clock? The trains go every half an hour, I think."

"It's a date. Let's hope it's sunny. Nothing worse than strolling along the sea front in a howling gale."

Julia looked at her watch. "It's nearly ten o'clock. Was that a phone box I saw just down the road? I need to ring a taxi."

"I'll walk you home." Mitch leapt to his feet, reaching for his coat.

"Indeed you will not! It's late. All the drunks will be roaming the streets after the match. There was a mugging in Roath only last week. You can see me to the phone box and wait with me until the taxi arrives if you want."

"Are you sure?" He didn't seem happy about this.

"Absolutely sure. The man who got mugged ended up on my ward with a fractured zygoma!"

"A what?"

"His face got bashed in! Now where's my coat?"

"One last kiss before you go, Julia, just one." He held out his hands in supplication.

Laughing, she fell into his arms, and kissed him a very long goodnight.

As the taxi pulled away, Julia turned to wave. Mitch was standing by the lamp post, his dark hair illuminated and made golden by the street light, his face serious. He was waving back, and didn't return to his flat until the taxi had turned the corner.

Julia smiled to herself, as she snuggled in to the back seat of the cab.

"130 Porthnewydd Avenue, please." She fumbled in her purse to get the money ready.

"You a nurse?" The taxi driver paused at some traffic lights."I'm taking you to the nurses' home, innit?"

Julia hesitated. "Er, yes. Why?"

"Coz there's discount for nurses, that's why. Twenny percent off."

"Great!" What a satisfying end, she thought, grinning, what a gratifying end to a perfect evening.

Chapter Five The bitter winds of January

The bright, sunny weather which had lulled everyone into a false hope of spring suddenly transformed itself into iron-grey, bitingly cold conditions. As she shivered her way down Porthnewydd Avenue to start her late shift on Tuesday afternoon, Julia felt her eyes watering as the arctic blast relentlessly sent the mercury plummeting, the wind whipping her face like a heartless bully, cutting into her very soul, making her long for her sheepskin coat.

On days like this she missed home, Cardiff seemed too big, too impersonal, nothing green to relieve the stark concrete edifices of the city centre. Uncompromising and bleak, the buildings seemed to remind her how small and insignificant she was. She missed the warmth of her family, the perfectly cooked meals, the comfort of her kind grandmother who lived next door, even the bickering between her older sisters. She wondered what they were all doing, back home in Llangennech. She'd been the only one to spread her wings and leave home. Rachel and Sarah were content to remain in the modest, semi-detached house on the outskirts of the village, Rachel teaching in a local primary school and Sarah working in the main post office down in Llanelli.

A lorry hooted at her as it drove past, the passenger leaning out of the window shouting suggestive remarks about sexy nurses. Thankfully, she'd already reached the Gap in the Wall, and, slipping through it quickly, was able to ignore her lewd admirers.

The hospital was its usual busy self, people hurrying in all directions, nurses rushing to their wards to start the afternoon shift, junior doctors strutting importantly down the corridor, their stethoscopes dangling around their necks like over-used fashion accessories, office staff walking more sedately from the Admin department with bundles of medical records in their arms, and porters transferring patients in wheelchairs and

41

on theatre trolleys. It was like a complete, self-sufficient little world, a microcosm, with its own rules, social etiquette, terminology and values. A world she loved and was proud to be part of.

"Afternoon, Staff Harry!" A loud and cheerful voice broke through her daydreams. A tall, bulky, rosy-cheeked porter was approaching, pushing a trolley full of clean linen.

"Richie! How are you! How's your wife and the new baby?" Julia was delighted to see him. Richie was the friendliest, most helpful senior porter in the Infirmary and universally popular.

"Can't you see the bags under my eyes?" He pulled a comical face. "The little blighter, she stays awake all night and sleeps all day!"

"Bless her! Bet you love her to bits, though. See you later!" Waving goodbye to Richie, she ran up the stairs to Terence Adams.

The treatment room door quietly opened and someone silently slipped inside. Julia looked up from her surgical dressing preparation. Student Nurse Aneira Thomas stood there, sniffing loudly, her face blotchy and her eyes red, her fair curly hair doing its best to escape from under her cap. She looked like a little girl dressed up in a nurse's uniform, her yellow dress slightly too long and baggy for her tiny frame.

"What on earth's the matter?" Julia abandoned her work, feeling concern for the young girl.

"Sister told me to find you. She said I'm to observe you doing the dressing on Mr Jackson."

"Yes, of course. That's fine. But why are you crying?"

Aneira sat down suddenly on a footstool, and burst into more noisy tears.

"I- I can't tell you. I feel such a fool. I'll never make a nurse. I don't know why I ever thought I could be." Julia crouched down beside her, putting her arm around the student.

"What's happened?"

Aneira sobbed even louder, unable to form the words necessary to speak. Sighing in exasperation, Julia handed her some Clini-roll to blow her nose. "Right, I'll go and have a word with Sister, and you can scrub down this trolley – including the wheels, mind you – and then we'll go and do the dressing." Aneira nodded, thankfully, as Julia marched from the room.

Daksha Patel, the junior sister, was in the office, completing the reports. Julia sat down opposite her."What's up with the first-year? She's in a right state!"

Sister Patel glanced up from her writing, a serious expression on her face. Then she burst out laughing. "Oh, I must seem so cruel, but it was hysterically funny, Julia. You would have laughed too. Our poor little student has just been totally humiliated, and the second years have done nothing but keep on about it all morning, spiteful little devils."

"Go on, I'm all ears!"

"Well, you know old Mrs Hustwick in the cubicle? She's the medical patient we took from Weston ward? Stroke patient, and not for resuscitation? Well, we called her family in this morning, she seemed close to death's door, she was dyspnoeic and drifting in and out of consciousness. I allocated the student to be there, to pop in every few minutes and monitor the situation. Well, Nurse Thomas was just carrying out oral care when she noticed Mrs Hustwick wasn't breathing any more. She took her pulse, quite rightly, and couldn't find it. There were about four family members around the bed. So our little student took it upon herself to pronounce Mrs Hustwick dead. One of the second years was outside the door, and she heard Nurse Thomas saying quietly to the daughter, "I'm afraid she's gone." The second year went into the cubicle as well, to see Nurse Thomas closing the patient's eyes. Suddenly, Mrs Hustwick gave a yell and sat bolt upright in bed. You can imagine how

43

startled everyone was! And the student, in all her embarrassment, said, "Oh, she's not dead, after all."

Julia chuckled. "Poor, poor girl. No wonder she's upset. And how is Mrs Hustwick now?"

"Eating her rice pudding and swearing at her children. I reckon she's good for another week or so yet!"

"I'll go and reassure poor Aneira, then. I'll tell her a couple of horror stories from my own training!" Julia laughed and returned to the treatment room, where a calmer Nurse Thomas was awaiting her trolley inspection.

"Right, then."Julia reached for a dressing pack. "That looks just fine and dandy. Well done, Nurse Thomas. Just fetch me a disposal bag and a sachet of sterile saline, and we're ready to rock!" She smiled at Aneira in encouragement, who beamed back, happy to be a student nurse once again.

"Do you fancy joining us for a drink on Friday night?" A wave of Paco Rabanne almost asphyxiated Julia as the silky voice of Marcus Battencourt interrupted her report writing. Looking up, she shook her head. "I'm sorry, I'll be out most of the day, not sure when I'll get back. What's the occasion?"

"Oh, nothing special. A couple of the chaps from medical are starting their trauma placement in a few weeks. It's a sort of farewell drink, I suppose. I think your friend Mandy is going."

Julia raised an eyebrow. "Really?" What about Kevin, she wondered.

"Well, if you change your mind we'll be in the Marshlands around seven o'clock."

"Ok, thanks for asking me. Now if you don't mind, I'd better be getting on." And with a dismissive smile, she returned to her paperwork, totally oblivious to the fact that her aloof attitude towards Marcus only served to fire up his interest in her. Unused to being rejected, smarting slightly from her indifference, he swept up the ward, running his fingers through his blond hair, winking at the student nurses, who all blushed and giggled as he swanned past them. What a plonker, thought Julia.

Up in the canteen at supper time, Julia was just sitting down to her cauliflower cheese and grilled tomatoes when a group of junior doctors sat down adjacent to her, laughing loudly and talking in plummy, resonant accents. Marcus Battencourt was holding court. He hadn't spotted her, he was too busy regaling his colleagues with gross tales from theatre that afternoon, striving to impress them and, unfortunately, largely succeeding. Julia kept her head down and concentrated on her dinner.

But a burly figure bearing a tray was heading for her table."Hya, chick! Can I join you? I want to ask you about the baby!" Richie the porter squeezed into the seat opposite her, placing an overflowing plate of pie and chips in front of him.

"Sure! Mind you, I'm not paeds trained, other than the usual three months!" Julia forked up some cauliflower. "How can I be of help?"

"Well, she's got this rash on her backside. Vaseline don't work. Nappy cream don't work. My missus is going nuts. She won't ring the health visitor, coz she's an old battle axe." He shook the ketchup bottle vigorously before emptying it all over his food.

"Well, if she was a patient on the ward, I'd say leave off all the fancy stuff, keep the area clean and dry – and that means changing her nappy more often - and you could try letting her have a kick on the floor without a nappy, let the air get at her little bottom. But it could be thrush, your wife may have to bite the bullet and ring the health visitor and get it checked."

"Ooh, that's a thought! I'll tell the missus! Thank you! Is it ok to stay here? I'm not bothering you, am I?"

45

"Not at all." Julia laughed. "Better than having to listen to those numbskulls over there!"

"Bloody idiots, they are." Richie concentrated on shovelling as much food into his mouth as he could.

Julia couldn't help overhearing the talk at the doctors' table.

"That brunette from William Meckett, now she's seriously smart." A tubby little SHO was noisily slurping his tea. "Bit of a goer, by all accounts." He grinned, lasciviously.

"You mean that Mandy? She's coming on Friday. Wouldn't mind having a crack at her. Yes, I've heard she has a rather Scandinavian approach to fornication." His deeply tanned friend chuckled. "Likes to put it about, does our Mandy!"

Julia stared at them, aghast. Richie also put down his knife and fork.

"Thought she was going out with one of the Woodentops?" Dr Tubby started peeling a banana.

Marcus sniggered. "I doubt she'll be with him much longer, not once she keeps better company on Friday, and we can show her a good time, if you get my drift."

"Right." Richie got to his feet. Oh, no, thought Julia in horror, what's he going to say?

Richie walked slowly over to the doctors' table, putting his big hands down on it, glaring at the astonished men.

"Don't you ever let me hear you prats talk about one of our nurses like that again. D'you hear me? Staff Nurse Jacob is a lovely gal, too good for the likes of you lot. And as for her boyfriend, I think you'd better reconsider what you call him and the other dental students. I mean, it would be dreadful if word got around that you doctors called them Woodentops, innit? I don't think you'd be getting any anaesthetic in your fat gobs if you turned up for a filling!" Richie's normally placid face had

46

turned puce with fury. "And if you've finished your dinners, why don't you just push off and get on with your jobs, eh?"

He returned to sit next to Julia, while the doctors beat a hasty exit, leaving their half-eaten food behind, Marcus Battencourt attempting to salvage his wounded ego by saying loudly, "Better go and save some more lives, chaps."

"They're a bloody disgrace, that lot." Richie moodily put his knife and fork together. "Nobs, the lot of them."

"You tell 'em, Richie!" Julia pushed her plate away, her appetite suddenly gone. "I guess they'll get their comeuppance sooner or later." Thank God all men weren't like them, she thought, thank God for decent men like Mitch.

On Thursday evening Julia knocked loudly on Mandy's door, trying to be heard above the blast of E.L.O 's "Don't Get Me Down." Eventually the door opened, Mandy stood there, dressed in just her bra and French knickers, brushing her teeth, her dark hair in rollers.

"C'm in," she spluttered, flecks of Colgate flying everywhere. Several pairs of jeans and a mountain of shirts littered the floor, with discarded shoes adding to the general chaos. "Can't decide what to wear." She spat the toothpaste out into her sink.

"Where are you off to, then?" Julia sat down on the only available area of the bed which wasn't covered with underwear.

"Seeing Kev. We're going to the Clarence for a drink, then back to Med club, coz it's Thursday night."

"So you and he...I mean, you're still seeing him?" Julia wasn't quite sure how to word this.

Mandy looked up in surprise, all the while applying deodorant to her armpits.

47

"Of course I am. Why wouldn't I be? Chap deserves another chance!" She hastily selected a pair of navy corduroy dungarees, and squeezed her curvy legs into them.

Julia hesitated."I was in the canteen the night before last and Marcus Battencourt and his cronies were there, talking about this shindig tomorrow night, to which you, my sweet girl, were reported to be going – without Kev."

"Oh that!" Mandy struggled with the braces. " Give us a hand with these, Jules. Well, Neil Hancock from our ward is leaving to start his trauma placement in a few weeks, and he asked me to go for a drink with the gang. What's wrong with that?"

Julia paused. How could she possibly tell Mandy what the doctors had said, and that as far as they were concerned, she already had a bit of a reputation, was theirs for the taking.

"Well, be careful, won't you?"

"What on earth are you on about?" Mandy was getting cross now.

"Well, what if this Neil wants more than just a drink?" Julia blushed.

"Well, that's up to me, isn't it? I mean, it's my body, I can do what I please, can't I? I'm not ashamed of that fact! I'm not engaged or anything. Why can't I simply enjoy myself?"

Julia had no answer for her, no reply that Mandy would have been happy to hear, at any rate. Sighing, she got up to go. "Well, enjoy tonight, and tomorrow night, but look after yourself, yeah?"

"I fully intend to!" Happy once more, Mandy took the rollers out of her hair, shaking the lustrous brown curls about her shoulders. "And you enjoy your little outing tomorrow, too."

"I will."And with a strange sense of foreboding, Julia returned to her own room, drawing the curtains against the howling wind, and for the rest of the evening played solitaire with her troublesome concerns.

Mitch could hardly stop his hands from shaking as he tore open the white envelope. His name and address had been handwritten, it had a Cardiff postmark, and had a second class stamp on it.

Dear Mr Walker,

Thank you for sending Cosmo Records examples of your band's work. The recordings were forwarded to me at the Cae Taff studio centre, as I am the Artist and Repertoire manager. We have listened to your tapes and would be extremely interested in meeting you and your band to discuss the possibility of a live studio test/recording.

Please could you (together with your colleagues)attend our studios in Cathedral Road at twelve o'clock on Friday the 21st January. We may be contacted on the phone number at the top of the page.

Yours sincerely,

Steph Saunders

Caer Taff Studio Centre

Mitch closed his eyes in sheer joy, then kissed the letter."Yes!" He breathed. Then shouted as loudly as he could, "We've done it! We've bloody done it! Whoo hoo!" Prancing around the kitchen in his boxer shorts, he grabbed his half drunk tea, and looked at his reflection in the dusty mirror, raising the chipped mug in self-congratulation. "Success, here we come!"

"Where are you going?" Charlie sleepily staggered into the room, scratching his hairless chest, his ancient dressing gown flapping open to reveal bright green longjohns.

"Nowhere with you, Charlie boy, and certainly not wearing those monstrosities. Band's got an audition of sorts! With Cosmo Records! Bloody hell! I can't believe it!"

"Brilliant, you lucky bastard! When is it?" Charlie snatched the letter from him, scanning it rapidly. "Hey! It's today! Shit, man! You've got to be there in an hour! It's eleven o'clock now!"

"Fucking hell! I'm meeting Julia at two. And I won't be able to get hold of the others that quickly, they're in work. I'll have to go it alone. But I won't be there two bloody hours, will I?"

Charlie looked doubtful, but said nothing, not wanting to burst the bubble of excitement which was enveloping his flatmate. Mitch dashed into his bedroom, for the first time in his life wondering what on earth he should wear...

No bus or taxi would have propelled Mitch to his destination faster than he did on foot. As he breathlessly raced along Queen Street, then past the Castle, a thousand wild and wonderful thoughts were also racing through his head. What would Monster think of all this? And Dai the drummer? He was engaged to be married, he was a bit older than the rest of them. Jeff, the lead guitarist, was doing his P.H.D. in physics, would he have the time to commit if anything came of it? As for Eddie the bassist, he'd been talking about moving to Stevenage, to commute to London in search of a new job. And what if they made it? Where would it lead? A record deal? Christ, this could go anywhere!

He glanced at his watch as he slowed down to cross the road by St David's Hospital. Ten to twelve. He'd just make it. As he swapped the bag holding his heavy manuscript to his other hand, a couple of midwives were hurrying through the main entrance of the hospital. He'd have another mad dash back across town to get back to Queen Street station to meet Julia by two o'clock. He be stinking of sweat by then, despite the wintry day.

Pushing open the glass door of the building, a he felt a tropical blast of the central heating. Unaccustomed to such opulent heat, and wearing a thick duffel coat, he began to perspire profusely. The cool blonde behind the reception desk looked up.

"Can I help you?"

"Er, yes. I've got a twelve o'clock appointment. Mitch Walker." He was panting with nerves and exhaustion.

"Ah yes. Miss Saunders will be with you shortly. She's running a little behind schedule. Take a seat over there." She pointed to a row of easy chairs half obscured from general view by a forest of artificial plants.

Mitch shifted uneasily from foot to foot, "Um, will it be a lot later? I have to be back in town by two o'clock."

The secretary removed her glasses and regarded him with incredulity. "You do realise Miss Saunders is a very busy woman? And you are aware that Cosmo Records is second only to Virgin? Not many young hopefuls such as yourself are given such an opportunity. If you want to see her, then I suggest you sit down over there and she'll be with you quite soon."

There was nothing more to be said. Mitch obediently took his place behind a massive, fake rubber plant, and thumbed absent-mindedly through an ancient copy of Music Scene, not reading a single word. His stomach churned uncomfortably, and an unaccustomed feeling of anxiety was creeping through him.

The secretary's phone rang.

"Good afternoon, Caer Taff Studio Centre, how may I help you? Ah yes, Mr Leonard. How are you? Yes, I'll put you straight through." She pressed a button on her switchboard. "Deke Leonard on the phone, Miss Saunders, he's calling from the States, says he's come across another possibility you may be interested in." Mitch's mouth hung open in disbelief. Here he was, in the same building as the people who dealt with the likes of Deke Leonard! He simply had to make this work, this was his golden opportunity.

"Coffee?" The arctic blonde smiled glacially at him.

"Er, no thanks." He really hoped Deke Leonard wouldn't be on the phone for ages. The huge art deco clock on the wall now said half past twelve. Gazing out of the window, he could see people hurrying down the road, hunched up against the bitterly cold wind which was blowing from the north. He and Julia would be freezing cold in Penarth. Maybe they should abandon that plan and go to the cinema instead. The new Star Trek film was showing. Then perhaps they could go for a drink afterwards, and then...possibly back to her place? Charlie was busy working on a painting in their flat. There'd be no way he could be bribed to get lost today.

Finally, at quarter past one, the phone buzzed. "Mr Walker? Yes, I'll bring him in now. Follow me." Another chilly smile, and the secretary stood up to usher Mitch through a padded door at the far end of the room.

Steph Saunders was about forty, with artfully streaked blond hair and bright red lipstick. Her rather macho pinstriped suit hid a lean,fit body.

"Steph Saunders." She held out her hand, which Mitch shook rather cautiously.

"Hi, Miss Saunders, I'm Mitch."

"Call me Steph. I'm the A and R manager for Cosmo Records and it'll be me you'll be working with if all goes ahead as hoped. Please, make yourself comfortable." Mitch sat down gingerly on a leather armchair. "I'm seriously impressed with your tapes. Are you the singer?"

"Er, no, I'm the keyboard player and I wrote the music and the lyrics."

"Better and better!" Steph rubbed her hands in delight. "So. I'm speaking with the main man! I take it your other band members couldn't make it?"

"The letter only arrived this morning." Mitch wished he didn't sound so apologetic. It wasn't his fault the studio only got in touch last minute.

"No problem. We'll arrange another date with them once we've sorted a few things out. What I have in mind is to arrange a recording session with you guys, see how that works out, possibly change the band's name – I mean, Bartok Boys? I don't think so." She laughed mockingly. "And if we like each other – and I'm pretty sure we will - we can organise some contracts and take it from there."

"Wow!" Mitch felt taken aback at the speed with which things were happening. "This is amazing!"

"Do you have a portfolio? Of your work?"

Mitch pulled out his manuscripts from the carrier bag, handing them to Steph as though they were the Crown Jewels.

"Right. I'm just going to get one or two of these photocopied – don't worry, you have the copyright - and then we can arrange a date. I'll be right back." She swept out of the room, leaving a stunned Mitch sitting in his chair, unable to believe his luck. But then he checked the time again. Shit, it was almost twenty to two. He prayed she wouldn't be ages. However, she was true to her word and came right back, but with a fat, middle aged man in her wake.

"This is Stan. He's our sound engineer. I was just telling him about you. He listened to your tapes with me the other day."

"Hi, Stan." Mitch wondered where this was leading.

"I'll leave you in Stan's capable hands, Mitch, then I'll be in touch. This is your address, right?" She checked her paperwork. "In Allensbank Road? Seeing as you've no phone I'll call by next week some time and bring you over to meet the team. Then we can firm up a date for the recording."

Stan put his chubby hand on Mitch's shoulder."D'you wanna come see the studio? I thought I'd give you the heads-up on the set up, so you know what to expect when you and the guys come in for a studio test."

53

"Sure." Mitch's heart was sinking. There was no way he'd make it back to Queen Street in time now. He had to think quickly. "I've only got a few minutes spare, though, I have to catch a train at two o'clock."

"Ah! Trains come and go, there'll be another one to catch! I won't keep you long, follow me."

So Mitch reluctantly followed Stan into the Holy of Holies, the Caer Taff studio itself.

The sky had turned an even darker grey as Julia stood shivering at the entrance to Queen Street station. She hadn't bothered buying a ticket, the weather looked so grim, maybe they should go for a coffee or something instead? She huddled into her sheepskin coat, and dug her freezing hands deeper into her pockets. She'd forgotten her gloves, dammit, but had remembered her long woolly scarf which doubled up as a hood.

Five past two. Where was he? At least there were trains every half an hour to Penarth, so they could just catch the next one. The seagulls shrieked harshly as they swooped low over the street to find rich pickings in the discarded, half-eaten sandwiches and chip trays. Julia hoped Mitch would arrive soon. She started shivering. Stamping her feet on the ground to try and keep them warm, she checked the time again. Almost quarter past. People weren't strolling or ambling anywhere today, they were all in a mad rush to get to wherever they were going. Anywhere was warmer then here. She walked over to the kiosk which sold sweets and magazines, and idly picked up a copy of Company magazine. Before she started to skim through it, the eagle eyes of the old woman behind the counter glared at her, so she hastily replaced it.

How much longer should she wait? The station clock was now saying twenty-five past. She felt it was mocking her with the speed with which the second hand was ticking by. Despite the freezing temperature she wanted time to stop, to wait, wait until Mitch showed up...

Julia felt sick with disappointment. He obviously wasn't coming. She'd give him until half past, then she'd have to go home. All her old concerns came flooding back. She'd clearly been a one-night stand for him. How could she have been so naïve? He'd used her, then like a toy which had lost its appeal, he'd tossed her aside. How could she have been so taken in by him? He had seemed so genuine. That made it all the worse.

Half past two. Sadly, Julia turned around, and started walking wretchedly down the road, looking back occasionally just in case he turned up. But he didn't. As she turned onto Porthnewydd Avenue she felt something cold lightly touch her face. It had started to snow.

Chapter Six The Marshlands

Mitch ran so fast his sides were hurting. People must have thought he was a nutcase, belting along clutching a carrier bag. Christ, it was cold. It was also extremely late, twenty past two in fact. Would Julia still be there? It looked as though it was going to snow. She would be freezing. So many conflicting emotions were surging through him now. Elation at the thought the band were probably going to get signed up, concern about the reaction of the others and high anxiety about being late. She would think he'd stood her up. He groaned inwardly. What a bloody situation.

At two minutes after half past two he arrived at the station, looking frantically for the redhead he'd fallen hopelessly in love with. He scanned the entrance, then ran onto the platform, hoping to catch a glimpse of her russet hair, her pale, pretty face. But she wasn't there. She wasn't there at all.

"Come on, Julia! Open the door!" Mandy tried the handle again, to no avail. "Right. I'm giving you another ten minutes and if you don't unlock this bloody door by then I'm calling Miss Marshall." Julia heard Mandy's steps retreating back to her own room across the corridor. Pulling the duvet over her head, she curled up into a ball, great sobs racking her body, weeping without stopping. Men were such bastards, her mother and sisters were right. Only her father, her gorgeous father, was genuine, kind and true. She would never trust a man ever again, she thought. She reached out to her bedside cabinet for more Kleenex to blow her nose. The floor was littered with scrunched up lumps of damp tissue. Snotfetti, she thought to herself. But there was no way she would allow Mandy to call the warden. Easing herself slowly out of bed, she caught her reflection in the dressing table mirror. God, what a mess. Her hair was all over the shop, her eyes were just two slits of red with twin rivers of mascara running down her cheeks, and her nose was an luminous crimson. Pulling on her towelling dressing gown over her striped pyjamas, she unlocked the door and walked over to Mandy's room, opening the door quietly.

"Come here, you daft bugger!" Mandy held out her arms and Julia fell into them, crying once again. "He's really not worth it, he's not worth wasting all this energy on. So he stood you up? It happens to all of us eventually. Why is this getting to you so much?" She stroked Julia's tangled hair.

"It's just that, you know, I er..." Julia sniffed into her sodden handful of Kleenex. "I thought it meant something to him." She looked down in complete embarrassment.

"What are you talking about? Meant what?" Mandy looked puzzled.

"Well, he and I, er, you know…" Julia's voice trailed away miserably.

The penny dropped. "You slept with him, didn't you?"

Julia nodded, sorrowfully. "Yes. And now I regret it."

"Why? Oh my God, you don't think you could be pregnant?"

"No, I'm on the pill anyway, to stop me having to take time off every month because of dysmen. No, it's not that. You see, I was a virgin. I was a bloody *virgin,* Mandy!"Her voice rose, getting angry. "He took my virginity, and now he's dumped me!"

Mandy hugged her again. "I wish I could make things better for you. He's a sod to do that. But your trouble is you wear you heart on your sleeve. Maybe you should be more like me, love 'em and leave 'em. I mean, look at Kev! He was okay and stuff, but he had as much clue about foreplay as a starfish in a game of poker. I kicked him into touch yesterday!"

Julia shook her head. "I can't be like that. It's not in my nature. But it was amazing, Mandy, I never realised how lovely it was going to be. But now I won't ever see him again." And she started weeping afresh.

58

Mandy sighed in despair. Nothing she said right now would make her friend feel any better. She looked out of the bedroom window, which opened out onto the flat roof of the common room underneath. In summer, she and Julia would sunbathe on it, slathering themselves with coconut oil, listening to the radio, gossiping and waving at the disapproving old woman who worked in the solicitor's office across the way, who would scowl at them when they emerged through the window in their bikinis. But today it was covered in a blanket of white. The snow was still coming down, softly, gently, relentlessly, making the garden below look like a scene from The Lion, The Witch and The Wardrobe. Any moment now, she could expect Mr Tumnus to come trotting along holding his umbrella. But all Julia would want right now was for Mitch to come trotting along...

There was a discreet knock at the door. "May I come in?"

"Sure, Miss Marshall!" Mandy nudged Julia, who hastily dried her eyes.

The door opened and who could be mistaken for Mrs Thatcher's twin sister elegantly stepped inside.

"There's a message for you, Staff Harry." Julia smiled, despite her distress. Always formal, always so ladylike! Miss Marshall handed her a note. "Terence Adams has just rung me on the internal phone. They want to know if you can change your late shift tomorrow to nights? They want you to go on nights for a week, as there's a lot of sickness among the night staff. Can you do it?"

"Yes, that's fine. Will you ring them for me?" Julia blew her nose, noisily.

"Yes, of course, my dear." Miss Marshall twisted her pearls thoughtfully. "Are you feeling well, though, Staff? You seem a bit under the weather."

"I've a bit of a cold, that's all." Julia smiled bravely. "I'll be right as rain by tomorrow night."

"Good. Well, I'll be getting on, then. And Staff Jacob?"

Mandy looked up, the picture of guilt.

"You and I are going to fall out if you leave all your dirty saucepans in the kitchen sink again. Judy the cleaner had to wash them, and it's really not her job. Good afternoon."

"Yes, Miss Marshall." Mandy stuck out her tongue behind the retreating back of the warden, who shut the door as gracefully as she had opened it.

"She always makes me feel like a naughty schoolgirl." Mandy lobbed some orange peel into an overflowing waste paper bin and missed.

"Well, stop behaving like one then, innit? You're always leaving your dishes in the sink."
"You're obviously feeling better. I know! Come with me to the Marshlands tonight. Come on! It'll take your mind off things. It's only down the road, and you can always come home early if you want to."

"I'll think about it." Julia stared out of the window. The common room roof was now about three inches thick with snow, immaculate and unblemished, a virginal carpet of white, waiting for some little bird or mouse to come pattering along and defile its purity. Julia sighed heavily. Why did everything always come back to her lost virginity..?

Mitch unhappily threw his manuscripts onto the table, and wondered what he should do next. How on earth could he get in touch with her? He didn't even know where she lived. But surely the ward would know where? Fumbling in his pocket for some change, he emerged onto the snowy street, making for the phone box.

"Can you put me through to Terence Adams ward, please?" He put an extra five pence piece in just to make sure. After what seemed like ages, the phone was answered.

"Terence Adams, Sister speaking." Hell, he hadn't expected that. He thought the clerk would have answered.

"Er, I wonder if you can tell me where I can find Julia Harry, your staff nurse. Do you have her address? I need to contact her."

60

"Oh, I'm terribly sorry." This wasn't Sister Winter, this woman's voice sounded Indian, or Pakistani. "We don't give staff details out to the public. Security reasons, you understand."

"Ah, of course. I'm sorry to have troubled you. I wonder if you could - ." But she had put the phone down. Feeling forlorn and helpless, he replaced the receiver and walked slowly back to his flat, his hands in his pockets, his head hanging down dejectedly.

The flat had never seemed so empty, so cold and unwelcoming. Charlie must have gone out, he'd left the place in a mess, paintbrushes and half-completed canvases everywhere. He'd also turned down the heating when he'd buggered off, it was freezing. Mitch sighed. He should have been with Julia now, cuddling with her in the cinema, or even throwing snowballs at her before hugging her and kissing her. If he had only been on time.

He had a band practice at seven. The snow wasn't too bad as yet. And what news he had to tell the others. Suddenly feeling drained and exhausted, Mitch threw himself down on the sofa, still wearing his coat, putting his feet up and closing his eyes. I know, he thought, determinedly, she's had Thursday and today off, that means she'll be in work tomorrow. I'll go there. I'll bloody go there. Satisfied for the time being with his decision, he drifted off to sleep.

There was something about snow that brought about a sense of childlike glee amongst the residents at the nurses' home. The whiteness outside seemed to illuminate the rooms of the building, everything seemed bright and unreal. The students launched a snowball fight against the qualifieds in the front garden, shrieking in delight as they hurled their icy missiles at each other, all protocol forgotten in the fun of the moment. The students and qualified staff who worked at the C.C.I. thanked their lucky stars they didn't work in the other hospitals, because those poor nurses were stranded there, the buses which ferried them being unable to make their way through the thick snow; only the ambulances were operational, and these were used judiciously. Having to spend the night on the floor of the ward's day room with few home comforts was no-one's idea of a fun night out.

At half past seven, Julia and Mandy made their way carefully down a snowy Porthnewydd Avenue. Hardly any cars drove past them, it was strangely silent. Thick flakes of snow continued to fall, there seemed no end to it. Tripping over a snow-covered kerb, Julia fell headlong into a three foot high drift.

"That's a good start. My jeans are drenched now!" Hastily, she scrambled to her feet, looking around to see if anyone had seen her.

"My socks are soaking wet! We've only walked a hundred yards!" Mandy complained bitterly.

"Should have worn our wellies, I suppose." Julia pulled her hood further over her head. "At least this duffel coat is warm, I've had it since the lower sixth in grammar school." They turned the corner at the Infirmary and hurried as quickly as they dared to the old Marshlands

A welcome contrast awaited them as they entered the pub. Brightly lit, warm, jam-packed with off duty nurses, doctors, porters and ancillary staff, the noisy bar was bouncing with high spirits. Shaking off the snow from their boots, the girls pushed their way to the crowded bar. The energetic barmaid, Myrna, was vigorously pulling pints, her pale breasts jiggling about above the low neckline of her scarlet top. All male eyes were riveted on those quivering cuties, but Myrna was oblivious, her attention fixed on her job. Julia often wondered privately if Myrna was thyrotoxic, her eyes were always so huge and staring, her movements furiously frenetic. Did she ever take a rest? But then her reverie was interrupted.

"Didn't expect to see you here." A familiar voice whispered in her ear, and a hand was placed lightly on her shoulder. Julia turned around.

"Oh, hi Dr Battencourt." She forced a smile.

"Oh, come on. We're both off duty. Call me Marcus for God's sake!"

Julia smiled. "Okay. Hello, *Marcus*."

"That's better. I thought you weren't coming, you were out today?"

"Change of plans."

"It's Julia, isn't it? Your name, I mean." His voice softened, his probing eyes looking straight into her grey ones.

"Yes." She accepted a half of lager from Mandy, who had forged ahead successfully and been served within minutes.

"Is Neil here?" Mandy scanned the room. "He promised me a drink, the bugger."

"He's over in the corner, with Jason from Gynae." Marcus jerked his head in the direction of a small group of junior doctors. "But you'd better get your skates on if you fancy your chances with him, Veronica from Goldilocks Ward has had her beady eye on him for weeks." Marcus smirked into his gin and tonic. His well-aimed comment hit its mark, and Mandy bridled. Veronica was the junior sister on Goldilocks, the children's ward, a Farah Fawcett lookalike, with flicked back blond hair and a Duo-tan, which Julia and Mandy always considered absolutely daft, in the middle of winter.

"I'll see you in a minute, Jules." Mandy started elbowing her way through the crowd. "I'm owed a drink."

Marcus chuckled as Mandy disappeared into the throng of drinkers, searching for Neil and her anticipated half a cider. "She certainly enjoys life!"

"What's that supposed to mean?" Julia challenged. "Are you implying something? Mandy is my best mate, remember."

Marcus had the grace to look abashed. "No offence meant. Look, shall we try and get a seat?"

By half past nine. Julia was still chewing on her half a lager, but reluctantly accepted a glass of white wine from Marcus. Her heart wasn't in this, it didn't feel right, somehow. Marcus was quite funny, managing to make her giggle occasionally, and his acerbic wit was admittedly pretty entertaining, but he wasn't managing to lift her spirits. Why wasn't she finding him attractive? All the other girls seemed to be swooning at his bloody feet. Tall, blond, confident...he should be ticking all the boxes. But somehow, he wasn't...or maybe he was? She smiled hesitantly up at him.

Seizing the moment, he put his hand on her shoulder.

"Can I see you tomorrow? Are you working? I'm stopping over at the on-call doctors' quarters tonight, I'd never get back to the Heath in this snow."

"Sorry, I'm on nights tomorrow, I'll need to get some kip. But thanks, anyway." She smiled wearily at him. "Maybe some other time."

Marcus stared at her in incredulity. "You're playing incredibly hard to get, you know that?"

Julia shook her head. "Oh, I don't play games, Marcus, I can assure you. I'm sure there's lots of people around who enjoy that sort of manipulative mind-game stuff, but I'm not one of them."

He lowered his voice, stroking her cheek. "You're also extremely pretty, Julia. How about if I take you out to dinner next week? Let's go to the Dubrovnik, shall we? My treat!" He looked immensely pleased with himself.

"I'll let you know in a couple of days, okay?" Julia got up. "I'm off home now. Mandy's having a good time, but I'm tired. I'll catch up with you soon." She pulled on her duffel coat.

He leapt to his feet. "I'll walk you home!"

"No, I'll be fine. You stay here with your friends and enjoy the rest of the evening."

"Very well, oh heartless woman!" He leaned forward and pecked her on the cheek. "Goodnight, and don't slip on the ice."

"I won't." Turning round, she headed for the door, leaving an exasperated Marcus watching her, wondering what on earth he was doing wrong, was he losing his touch..?

As she walked back up a silent Porthnewydd Avenue, the moon shone down on what should have been considered a beautiful scene. But Julia was unable to appreciate the sparkling white roads, the snow-moussed cars and hedges, the big, old houses which had been temporarily transformed into alpine lodges. Her heart was heavy, her thoughts turned to Mitch. Was he with some other girl? Was he kissing her? Would she ever see him again? Julia wondered what he was doing now...

"For Christ's sake, Monster! Do you have to show up pissed all the time?" Mitch crunched up his empty Coke can and flung it down in anger. "We've just been given a crack at making it big, we've only got a couple of practices left before we go to the studio, and you come here fucking arseholes! For fuck's *sake!*" Dai, Jeff and Eddie sat silently, guessing what was coming next.

"Jesus, man, lighten up, will ya!" Monster staggered slightly as he tried and failed to secure his microphone to the stand. "Can't a chap have a few jars without his mates getting all whiney on him? You're nothing but a nag, Mitch, let's face it."

"Er, he does have a point, Monster," Dai volunteered quietly. "You're always drunk. Or high."

"Oh, so you're in on it too, are you?" Monster swung round in fury, his pale face suffused with rage. "Well, guys, I'm out of this crappy set up. I'm always getting picked on. You know what? I can make it without you bastards. I'm off." He kicked at the mic stand, which fell over with a crash. Then silence. A collective holding of breath awaited the next line.

"Consider yourself sacked. Fired. Now piss off before I throw you out." Mitch's words were spoken quietly enough but his menacing tone was enough to make Monster beat a hasty exit, swearing loudly. "You can't fire me, you wanker! I just fucking fired myself!" He slammed the practice room door shut after him.

"Oh, bloody hell." Eddie put his head in his hands. "We're stuffed." The excited mood of only half an hour ago had evaporated.

"How the hell are we going to find another singer by next week?" Mitch sighed heavily. "I'm sorry guys, I should have tried to calm him down, it was my fault."

"Not at all." Dai juggled his drumsticks. "He had it coming, it was long overdue, we couldn't have carried on much longer. Every bloody rehearsal full of shouting and swearing. It's not your fault, Mitch."

"Let's carry on with the rehearsal anyway." Eddie decided to take charge. "Mitch, you'll have to sing lead for a bit, or maybe Jeff?"

The tall, serious Jeff shook his head. "No way, guys. I can't sing a sodding note. Go for it, Mitch. Let's warm up with something easy, let's try it out. You've been doing backing for ages, anyway."

"C'mon, Mitch, we'll do 'Feel Like Makin' Love.' Ready?" Eddie was poised to start.

"Oh, alright then." Mitch switched on his keyboard.

"Okay!" Dai shouted. "A-one-two-three-FOUR!"

Mitch's voice was shaky and uncertain to start with, but as the song progressed, it grew stronger and more confident. His voice was quite different to Monster's, more melodic, less harsh. As the last note faded away, Mitch looked up apprehensively.

66

"Well?"

The others looked at him in amazement, big smiles on their faces.

"Fucking hell, Mitch!" Jeff laughed in disbelief. "Where've you been all my life? That was cracking!"

"Really?" Mitch was reluctant to believe them.

"Absolutely." Dai put down his sticks. "That was shit hot, mate. I don't think we need to look elsewhere. I reckon Monster has done us a favour here! Yabadabadoo!"

"But can you learn all the songs by next week?" Ever serious, Jeff started thinking of the practicalities. "It'll be hard work."

"I know half of them anyway." Mitch started to feel relieved. "Well, if you guys are sure..."

"A hundred percent." Eddie slapped him on the back. "Welcome to your new role of songwriter, lyricist, keyboard player and lead singer!"

Mitch laughed. "You forgot my role as musical director as well! Now, let's get to work, you lazy sods!"

Back at his flat later, Mitch settled down to write some lyrics. But a pretty, pale face with luminous grey eyes and shining red hair kept stealing into his mind, distracting him, inviting a melancholic mood to creep over him. Almost unconsciously, he began to write...

Julia, my lover, won't you come back to me

I miss you so,

You know I need you now

Like the desert needs the rain

Julia, you're my life, you're the star in my sky, and you know why -

Give me one more try...

Chapter Seven The nights of Terence Adams

The snow had hardened to a lethal royal icing on the frozen streets of Cardiff. Mitch tentatively inched his way along the glassy pavements, not taking his eyes off his feet. One slip and he could take a dive – and where could that lead? A fractured wrist? How ironic, he thought, if he should end up back in the Infirmary...

And that was where he was going. Mitch had reckoned that if he showed up on Terence Adams around two o'clock, Julia would be there. If she'd been an early shift, she would have had her lunch break, and if she was a late shift she'd definitely be there. Pleased with his plan, he continued at a snail's pace along City Road, thinking of what he would say to her. He hoped she wasn't going to be really angry with him. She must think him such a bastard, taking her virginity, then apparently dumping her. God, what must she think of him? He couldn't wait to see her, but dare not hurry in case he slipped and fell.

Terence Adams was busy, he could tell. As he entered the ward, there were nurses bustling to and fro, the phone was ringing constantly. Anxiously, he looked around for a familiar face, but he couldn't see anyone he recognised. Nervously, he knocked on the door of the office, and took a step inside.

"Er, excuse me..."

The ward sister looked up from writing her notes. "Hello? Can I help you?" It must be the sister he'd spoken to the other day. Sister Patel smiled encouragingly, her big brown eyes friendly and warm. Thus heartened, Mitch cleared his throat.

"I'm looking for Julia Harry? Your staff nurse? I was a patient here only recently." Maybe she'll think I've come to thank her, he thought, hopefully.

"Oh, I'm afraid Staff Harry is on night duty now. Can I take a message?" But before he could reply, the phone rang again. "Emergency admission? Yes, of course, send him right up, I'll get the bed ready." Turning to Mitch, she said, "I'm sorry, this isn't a very good time. Would you excuse me?" And she hurried from the office, leaving Mitch standing in the doorway, wondering what on earth he should do now. However, luck was on his side, for who should be returning from her break was that little student nurse who'd looked after him. The blond one.

"Hey! It's Nurse Thomas, isn't it?"
Aneira smiled, then blushed. "Hi, yes! Are you feeling better?"

"Well, I'd feel a lot better if you could pass a message on for me? To Julia Harry? She's on nights, I've been told, and I've been trying to get in touch with her."

"Yes, of course! Do you need some paper?"

"Can you get me some? I'll write it now!" Mitch was feeling desperate.

Aneira fished in her pocket, and pulled out a tiny note-book and pen. Handing it to him, she said, "I'll put it in the message book, she'll get it when she comes on duty, then. So don't write anything personal!" The student giggled.

Hastily, Mitch scribbled a brief message.

Dear Julia, Sorry I missed you the other day, events overtook me and I was terribly late. Can you get in touch with me at the College? I'm in the main office. Mitch x

He ripped it out, quickly folded it up and handed it to Aneira.

"What's that?" The sulky voice of Maggie Hubert interrupted the transaction.

"Oh, this man wants a message left for Staff Harry. I was going to put it in the message book." Aneira started to look worried, Maggie was bound to report her to Sister for chatting when she was supposed to be back from lunch and at work.

"I'll take that." Maggie snatched the note from Aneira's little hand and stuffed it in her pocket. "I'll put it in the message book for you, Nurse Thomas. Now you get back to your work, Mr James is asking for a bedpan." Maggie smiled nastily at Mitch, her bright, painted lips revealing nicotine-stained teeth. "You'd better go now, we don't allow members of the public to go roaming around the wards." She swung around and stalked down the ward, head in the air.

Bitch, thought Mitch, returning to the main corridor. Ah well, he would just have to hope that Julia would get the note. He could hardly come back here in the night-time, they'd probably call the porters to throw him out. He would just have to hope...

Maggie unfolded the note and read it. With a smirk, she opened the bottom drawer of the office desk, where they kept all the extra stationary, and shoved Mitch's message underneath all the papers, closing the drawer with a satisfying slam.

It was dark when Julia threw back the duvet. Fortunately she'd been able to nod off and grab a couple of hours sleep in readiness for her shift that night. She glanced at the alarm clock. Half past seven. Enough time for a quick bath and get ready to leave by half past eight. Pulling her still-damp uniform off the radiator, she spread a towel on the floor and started to iron it. This was her favourite uniform dress, she'd taken it in at the waist so it actually fitted her quite nicely. She'd be in charge this shift, more than likely. It was a Saturday night, so unless they were on intake it should be reasonably quiet. Maybe there'd be one of the third-years on with her, someone competent whom she could rely on.

Still in an optimistic frame of mind, she had a quick snack of Ryvitas with peanut butter, and by twenty-five past eight was closing the big front door of the nurses' home. No cape for her this evening, it was still bitingly cold. She pulled the belt of her old, green duffel coat more tightly around her, and set off down the slippery pavement, hoping her starched hat wouldn't get creased in the carrier bag she was holding. At least her sensible, black nurse's shoes seemed to grip the ice quite well.

"Could you possibly lend me some money for me to buy some food, my dear?" A refined, English voice called to her from the house across the street. Julia groaned. Caitlyn McDuff was waving at her hopefully, wrapped in several shawls and wearing a massive woolly hat.

"Sorry, Miss McDuff! I've got to go to work!" Julia smiled weakly at the woman, who was brandishing a half-empty brandy bottle, from which she was taking hefty swigs. Caitlyn McDuff had been a patient when Julia had done her three month stint in Psychiatry as a student nurse, but upon her discharge, had been placed in a bed and breakfast hostel across the road from the nurses' home.

"Oh, you poor dahling! Going to work! Never mind, I think I'll go in for a bit, it's quite cold out here, and I may be having a visit from His Worship the mayor this evening. I've been asked to speak at City Hall! On my book about Tennyson, you know!"

"Oh, that's nice!" said Julia, politely, going along with the fantasy. Caitlyn suffered from manic-depression, and was prone to delusions of grandeur when she was manic, which she clearly was this evening. Poor Caitlyn, thought Julia, what a way to end up, obviously an educated woman at some point, but now a lonely, crazy alcoholic. Thankfully, Caitlyn found the bitter weather too much to bear, and soon retreated indoors, leaving Julia to carry on walking down the treacherous road to the Infirmary.

"And the only new admission is in the first bed. He's a twenty year old appendicitis, going to theatre as soon as they ring to say they're sending the porters up for him. Name is Peter Webster, he's had his pre-med, so shouldn't be too long before theatre rings, the student is just finishing admitting him now." Sister Patel closed the Kardex and handed the ward keys over to Julia. "Oh, some chap called by this afternoon, looking for you."

Julia's heart leapt. "Who was he? What was his name?"

"Oh, I don't know, we were really busy." Daksha Patel pulled on her black cardigan. "I expect he'll call back at some point – if he really fancies you!" She chuckled and waved goodbye as she hurried to the staff room, the rest of the day staff following in her wake. Julia's heart beat quickly. Could it have been Mitch? Pinning the keys to the inside of her pocket, she quickly read through the notes she'd made during handover, not really absorbing the information. What if it was him?

"Shall I aska da student to do ten o'clock obs, Staff? Or you wanna she help you with da meds?" The little Italian S.E.N, Maria Esposito, was busy organising the fluid charts.

"Um, it's Nurse Edwards, isn't it? The third year?Yes, she's pretty quick, let her do the obs and we'll do the medicines together. Shouldn't take us too long."

The night stretched ahead of her, eleven hours of observations, checking wounds, relieving pressure on vulnerable skin, giving post-op analgesia, answering the phone and responding to patients' buzzers. At least they were no longer on intake, and unless they had a problem, there'd be no need to summon the on-call doctor, although Marcus Battencourt was off this evening, anyway.

The hospital was transformed at night. The hustle and bustle of the daytime activities vanished, to be replaced by an almost sacrosanct atmosphere, where night nurses spoke in hushed tones and walked silently along the wards and corridors. The only lights were the overhead bedlamps of the patients, and the main office light was replaced by a single angle-poise lamp. Julia loved the nocturnal character of the Infirmary, there was nothing quite like it.

73

At ten past ten, just after she'd finished the medicine round with Maria, the ward doors opened and the porters arrived, pushing a theatre trolley. "Patient for theatre? Peter Webster?"

"Theatre was supposed to ring first." Julia took the paperwork from them in annoyance.

"Guess they forgot." The younger of the porters looked shamefaced. "Sorry, Staff."

"Never mind." Julia sighed, showing them to Pete Webster's bed, and starting to check his wristband. "Nurse Edwards? Can you escort Mr Webster to theatre please?"

The ward clock showed half-past three. Julia yawned, desperately trying to stop herself from falling asleep. It was a quiet shift, no drama, no emergencies. The young lad who'd had his appendix removed was recovering nicely and all the patients were asleep. The silence remained unbroken, apart from the occasional snore, or the uninhibited passing of wind which differentiated the male ward from the female. The student had been sent over to Llanfair ward to help out, as one of their S.E.N.s had gone home with diarrhoea and vomiting. Maria had gone to break.

Julia looked down at the report she was writing for handover. The words seemed to dance a jig before her tired eyes and her pen slipped from her fingers. She shook her head in an effort to stay awake. Maybe she should make some coffee. Getting up from the office desk, she put on her cardigan, it always got so cold around three o'clock in the morning, even in the middle of summer. Glancing down the Nightingale ward to check all was well before going into the kitchen, she saw Maria walking from the patients' bathroom across to the sluice. That was strange, she hadn't seen her return from break. What if she'd been asleep and hadn't noticed her? How awful! She hurried towards the sluice to apologise. No patient stirred. Bumping into one of the beds in her haste, she silently cursed and rubbed her sore knee.

The light was on in the sluice, it was never turned off, the staff were always in and out of it, there was no point. Opening the door wide, Julia peeped inside, ready to make her excuses.

It was empty. No-one was there. But she was sure she'd seen Maria. Where could she have gone? A cold rush of air blew into her face. Seeing that the window was slightly open, she shut it tight. Noiselessly closing the door, she looked up and down the ward. The S.E.N. was nowhere to be seen. An icy trickle of fear crept down her spine, and her heart beat faster. What was Maria playing at? Julia checked the treatment room, the kitchen – nobody was there. Returning to the office, she attempted her report-writing once more, trembling with fear.

"Hya, Julia! You gonna go up for break now?" Julia jumped in fright as Maria appeared at the door.

"Where've you been, Maria?" Julia was almost in tears.

"Whassa matter, tesora? You looka like you seen a ghost!" Maria put her handbag away under the desk.

"I – I thought I just saw you going into the sluice. But when I checked, there was no-one in there."

"I know. I was up in da canteen, I just come back. You ok?" Maria put her hand on Julia's quivering shoulder.

"I don't know. I saw someone, Maria. Someone definitely went into the sluice. And then disappeared." Even in the dim light, Julia's pallor was evident.

"Well, maybe da Grey Lady is doing da rounds tonight. But no problem, eh?" Maria picked up the empty coffee mugs from the desk. "Go on, you go for break now."

"Grey Lady? Who is she?" Julia wasn't sure if she wanted to know.

Maria sniffed. "Oh, some stupid story. Everyone see her sometime. She do no harm. But when da patient see her – then there's trouble."

75

"Tell me, please, tell me about her."

Maria sighed. "Oh, okay. But don't blame me if you have-a bad dream! The Grey Lady, she been around a long time. Some say they know who she was, but nobody really knows. She flit about on da wards from time to time, lotsa night staff 'ave seen her. There was a death over on Weston ward earlier on, about half an hour ago. The dear old lady who has now passed away, well she told da auxiliary she'd been comforted by a strange nurse and then ten minutes later – she was dead! Da Grey Lady like to comfort those about to meet their maker. And such strange things on da children's ward as well, I no work there, ever again!" Maria crossed herself. "Now you go to break, cara mia."

As she walked nervously down the deserted corridor and up the stairs to the next floor, Julia couldn't help looking over her shoulder. The desire for sleep had vanished, she was on full alert and her heart was still racing. Had she actually seen a ghost?

"Cheer up, sunshine! You look like you've seen a ghost!" The cheeky young porter sauntered past her lugging a bag of soiled linen.

"Get lost, Steve." Julia was in no mood for his wisecracks tonight, especially when they were uncannily close to the truth. She left the main corridor and turned right to go up the narrow staircase which led to the staff canteen. How many nurses had crept up these steps over the years, she wondered. The place was like a rabbit warren, nooks and crannies everywhere, hidden flights of stairs leading to nurses' accommodation, unexpected twists and turns, plenty of places for ghosts to linger...

The canteen was empty except for Night Sister, who was primly sipping a cup of tea in the far corner, out of her very own, special china cup.

"What can I get for you, Nurse?" Dot the canteen supervisor smiled pleasantly at her. "Beans on toast? Bacon sandwich?"

"Oh dear, not right now. I'll have a milky coffee, that's all."

"You sure, love?" Dot poured the steaming milk into the cup. "You're as pale as a little ghost! You need feeding up, you do."

Touched by Dot's kindness, but fed up with all the ghostly references, Julia took her coffee and considered where she should sit. It would be awkward to sit anywhere else but at the same table as Sister Hunter. Sighing inwardly in resignation, she took a seat opposite the Night Sister.

"May I join you, Sister?"

"Yes of course, Staff Harry. How is Terence Adams? I'll be down to do a round with you after break. I've been rather tied up over in Llanfair this evening, as you can imagine."

Julia smiled privately at the thought of the prim Sister Hunter being tied up. "I'll look forward to it, Sister. Everything is fine on T.A., all under control."

"You have got quite a pallor about you, Staff. Are you unwell? There's a lot of sickness about, you know."

"Er...I'm fine." Julia prayed that the Night Sister wouldn't press the issue, however her prayer went unanswered.

"Hmm. Somehow I think not, Staff. Now I don't want my staff feeling ill or worried in any way. What's the matter?" Sister Hunter smiled gently over her half-moon spectacles.

"Er, forgive me for sounding stupid, Sister, but I think I may have seen a ghost or something..." Julia's voice trailed away, embarrassed.

"Ah. Our Grey Lady." The older woman nodded understandingly.

"You mean you've seen her too?"

Sister Hunter put down her teacup. "I've worked here for forty years, my dear. I've never seen anything."

Julia shivered. " But I did see something..?"

"Staff Harry, this is a very old building which has seen more than its fair share of death, tragedy, trauma and human sorrow. All that energy is stored up in the very fabric of the structure, and I'd be quite surprised if that energy didn't manifest itself in some way. But it's far more likely that you were overtired, and your mind was playing tricks on you. As my dear yoga teacher keeps reminding me, the mind is a powerful thing!" She smiled reassuringly.

Julia looked at Sister Hunter gratefully. The strict, old-school senior nurse certainly didn't seem the type to entertain fantastic ideas about the spirit world. Or do yoga either, for that matter.

"Anyway, Staff Harry, I'll be getting back to work. I will be down on the ward in ten minutes. It's been pleasant talking with you, but let's not dwell on it, shall we?"

"No, Sister, and thank you." Julia smiled, slightly reassured. "Maybe the Grey Lady will retire for the night." She laughed." Now you've put things in perspective for me."

Sister Hunter nodded, sagely and turned to go, Julia watching her make her way through the deserted canteen.

These young girls, thought the Night Sister, such imaginations, they have too much time on their hands, not like it was in my day when we worked non-stop all night, cleaning, ordering, sorting...

Mitch rolled over in bed, the sheets a crumpled mess and the duvet slipping off his cold shoulders. Checking the time on his watch, he sighed wearily. Only ten to four. Where was Lady Sleep when he needed her most? He swung his feet onto the thinly-carpeted floor and pulled on his dressing gown. Rubbing his eyes he sat down on the low window sill and looked out through the grubby net curtains at the magical scene in the street before his eyes. The moon shone brightly down onto the frozen road, as yet unblemished by car tracks, and the stars glittered frostily in the navy sky. But he was in no mood to appreciate the charm of the wintry picture. His mind was restless, he felt anxious. But why? He should be ecstatic, he should be excited beyond belief about the band's good fortune. And he was, he supposed. But his thoughts always kept returning to Julia. When would she contact him? Maybe Monday, he hoped. Rummaging in his bedside cabinet, he pulled out his notepad and continued the lyrics he'd started.

Julia has left me yet I try in vain

To ease the misery and wipe out all the pain;

And I wonder where Julia is tonight

Lord, I want you, Julia,

Like the darkness craves the light.

Chapter Eight After the snow

At ten o'clock on Sunday morning, the flat was colder than the average household fridge. Even in his bedroom, Mitch's breath hung mistily with each exhalation. Reluctantly putting one foot on the floor, he grabbed his jumper from the previous night and shoved it on quickly, over his pyjamas. Looking through the window he was relieved to see there'd been no further snow. The street was criss-crossed with footsteps, several snowmen had arrived on the scene and the Saudi Arabian students next door were running about shrieking, excited at the novelty of it all, pelting each other with snowballs. At least he'd be able to get to band practice that evening, he thought. He rapidly pulled on his jeans, then another jumper and was soon heading out of the front door, looking like Paddington Bear, he was so muffled up against the cold. Time to buy some more milk, he thought, he was fed up of Marvel, and he was overcome by a sudden yearning for some Redy Brek. Central heating for kids and musicians, he grinned at his reflection in the dusty hall mirror, imagining a golden halo surrounding his body. As he shuffled down the street, he felt something wet on his face. It was starting to rain.

The thaw set in rapidly, resulting in dirty-looking clumps of grey snow on the pavements and oily black slush on the roads; the sort of weather that is depressing and untidy, lacking the inspiring beauty of the snow and reminding Mitch of the chaos of his bedroom, with all the manuscripts scattered about on the floor. By Monday morning the white stuff had disappeared completely, and winter resumed its path of uninspiring normality in Cardiff – rain, wind and yet more rain. Mitch spent his day in work answering the phone, issuing tickets, sending out prospectuses and arranging audition dates for the various departments. Every time the phone rang, his heart beat faster. Could it be Julia? Had she been given his note? But as he trudged home at five o'clock, disappointed at the lack of contact from her, he decided on another plan of action. He'd go to the ward tonight, sod it. He'd go there about half past nine. The day staff would have buggered off and Julia – if she was indeed on duty - would be on the ward.

As he cautiously approached the big double doors to Terence Adams for the second time in a few days, he wondered what he should say to her. He couldn't exactly say, "Sorry, I didn't mean to shag you and then stand you up." He had a lot of explaining to do. His mouth was dry and a wave of anxiety swept over him as he tentatively pushed the door open. And there she was, he could see her half way down the ward, marching briskly towards a bed, pushing a trolley. How lovely she looked, he thought, her tiny waist pulled in tightly by her belt, her shapely hips swaying slightly as she walked and her glorious red hair piled up, half hidden by her white cap. However, his reverie was rudely interrupted.

"ARREST!" Julia's loud cry broke through the relative silence of the ward. He could see her pulling the curtains around the bed. "Four two's, Nurse Edwards, quickly!" A student nurse in yellow rushed into the office, picking up the phone. Julia was hidden behind the curtain. What could be happening?

Then all hell broke loose. A bunch of doctors, some in scrubs, shoved past him as though he was invisible, and were sprinting down the corridor to the ward, one of them grabbing a big trolley full of equipment from outside the office on the way. Hot on their heels came a couple of ECG technicians pushing a machine, and some other staff. What was going on? It seemed to be some kind of emergency, the staff were shouting at each other, the urgency in their voices unmistakeable. Unsure what to do next, he retreated a little way back, his eyes glued to the events which were unfolding. It was like a scene from General Hospital.

"Stand clear!" One of the doctors barked out an instruction. Midge couldn't see what was happening. He hoped Julia was okay.

"What are you doing here, son?" Mitch swung round to be faced by a truculent, six foot four Richie, on his way to the ward with a box full of intravenous fluid bags. "You got business on the ward? Can't you see there's a cardiac arrest going on?"

"I er- I'm trying to see..." Mitch's voice faltered. "I was hoping to see Julia..."

"That's not possible. There's an emergency going on. You'd better leave." Richie was getting exasperated with this boy now, and the box was heavy.

Mitch felt desperate. "But, could you pass a message on...or can I hang around a bit..?"

"Get out, go on! Hop it! Before I throw you out myself!" Richie could feel his temper rising. Why couldn't this kid just bugger off?

"But – but – I only want to..." Mitch tried hard to see round Richie's huge bulk.

"OUT! Now! There's people's lives at stake and you're hanging around making a nuisance of yourself like some bloody stage-door johnny! Piss off!"

"Okay, okay, I'm going, there's no need to get shirty." Somehow, his need to see Julia seemed pretty trivial now. She was up to her eyes in a real life or death drama, and here he was, acting like a love struck kid.

Embarrassed and disappointed, Mitch slunk miserably away, feeling like a fool. What had he been thinking..?

"I think we could both do with a cup of tea." Julia smiled wearily at the student. "Off you go and make some, Nurse Edwards, the medicine round can wait ten minutes." The drama of the cardiac arrest had left her totally drained. The area around the patient's bed was a mess, discarded clinical waste and tubing, all of which awaited clearing away. As she returned to the office, the poor man was being transferred in his bed to I.T.U, wired up to monitors and with an oxygen mask covering his mouth, accompanied by a couple of doctors and a nurse. He'd been lucky, it had only been by chance she'd decided to check his wound drain at that point in time. Well, she thought, if you're going to have a cardiac arrest, it's best to have one in hospital, in front of a nurse...

Entering the door of the office, she found Marcus Battencourt locking the door of the controlled drugs cupboard. He smiled reproachfully at her.

"Looking for these, Julia?" He threw her the bunch of keys. "They were on the desk and this door hadn't been locked."

Puzzled, she accepted the keys and sat down. "How did they get there? I thought I'd pinned them inside my pocket as usual. I must have put them down on the desk and forgotten. And how was the door unlocked?"

Marcus shook his head. "No idea. I expect the day staff must have left it like that. Anyway, you did rather well there, I must say. Didn't think you were so strong! Never seen cardiac compressions done with so much energy before!" He crinkled his eyes at her, engagingly.

"If you don't do it properly, it's not worth doing, is it?" Julia's tone was cool "Don't patronise me, Dr Battencourt."

"Oh, c'mon, Julia, I'm only teasing, and you know you can call me Marcus."

Julia sighed. "Oh, okay, *Marcus*."

"And I haven't forgotten about our date, you know." His bleep went off. "Sorry, better dash. Llanfair wants me to write up some post-op meds for a cholecystectomy. Catcha later, flower." And he was gone, with a flourish of his white coat, throwing his stethoscope over his shoulder, almost knocking Nurse Edwards over in his haste.

"Sorry, I've spilled a bit." The student apologised as she placed the tray on the desk.

"No probs, Nurse Edwards. You did really well there. Good girl."

The gangly third year beamed. "Thank you. I didn't do much, just rang for the team and stuff."

"But the "stuff" is very important. You stayed calm, you didn't panic and you reassured the other patients. Well done."

"Who has done well, Staff Harry?" The two nurses looked up from their tea to see the tall, austere figure of Sister Hunter standing in the doorway, immaculate in her perfectly ironed navy uniform, her grey hair severely pulled back in the tightest bun the student had ever seen. They both stood up.

"The student, Sister. Kept a really cool head in the arrest just now, she did, very professional indeed." Julia looked approvingly at Nurse Edwards, who was now blushing deeply.

"Well that's good to hear, Staff, make sure you let Sister Winter know at handover in the morning. All settled now? Everything alright?"

"Er, yes, we were just having a quick cuppa and a debrief before doing the medicine round." Julia hoped she wouldn't be reprimanded for this slight transgression.

"Quite right. Important to look after yourselves as well as the patients, that's what I say. Just remember to check the arrest trolley – and wash your cups, won't you?" And with a twinkle in her eye, she swept regally from the office.

At eight o'clock the next morning, Julia wrapped up her handover, closed the Kardex and reached for her belongings under the desk. "Hope you have a good shift, chaps, I'm off to my bed now! Back on days on Thursday, thank goodness!"

"Sleep well, Julia!" Sister Winter smiled as she took the keys. Julia was just leaving the ward when a breathless little voice behind her whispered, "Staff! Did you get the message?"

Julia turned around to see an anxious Aneira Thomas standing there, a hopeful smile on her little face.

"Message? What message?"

"A young man asked me to give you a message, you know, that boy who was in with meningitis? It was supposed to be in the message book, that's where Nurse Hubert said she was going to put it."

"I haven't seen it, there was nothing there for me last night. But thanks, Nurse Thomas." Julia turned away, trying to conceal her mounting excitement. She wouldn't put it past Maggie Hubert to accidentally 'mislay' a message. So Mitch *had* been to the ward! She felt unbelievably happy as she ran lightly down the staircase, pulling on her duffel coat as she went. He'd tried to contact her! Everything was going to be okay! The early morning sun shone cheerfully in through the stairway window as though saluting her good fortune. Any tiredness from the night shift dissolved and faded away, overpowered by her elation. She would pop by his flat tomorrow, she couldn't wait to see him. Oh, Mitch, she thought, I knew I was right to trust you! As she hurried down the main corridor, she couldn't help grinning like a Cheshire cat at everyone she saw, even at Marcus Battencourt as he followed in the hallowed footsteps of Mr Robinson the surgeon. Marcus smiled back, triumphantly. At last, he thought, my luck is in.

"I'm just popping out, Mandy!" Julia knocked on her door at half past four, as she shrugged on her coat. "Not sure how long I'll be. You in later?"

"Come in, Jules! I'm trying clothes on."

As usual the room was like the fitting room of C and A in the sales. Dresses, skirts and blouses lay draped all over the bed, shoes and handbags littered the floor.

"What are you doing?" Julia burst out laughing, for there was Mandy struggling to fasten a suspender to a stocking top. She was also sporting a pair of black French knickers, a low-cut black, lacy bra, and some shiny black stilletos were lying on the bed in readiness.

"Oh, bugger! Snagged my stockings!" Mandy gave up on her struggle and eased the sheer black stocking down before removing it. "How the hell did our mothers manage wearing all this get up every bloody day?"

"I wouldn't know, Mandy! Why are you all togged up in that stuff? You auditioning for a local strip club?"

"Nah! I'm seeing Neil Hancock later. He wants me to pose for some photographs or something, he's an amateur photographer in his spare time and he needs a model. Said he'd buy me dinner first, in lieu of paying me. How's that for a date, eh?" She grinned, impishly, her dark curls in wanton disarray.

"And he wants you to dress like that?" Mandy raised a well-plucked eyebrow.

"It's called glamour photography, Jules!" Mandy sighed in exasperation. "I have to dress like this!"

"Well, have a lovely time, and don't forget to say cheese!" Julia laughed, teasingly, dodging the towel Mandy threw at her retreating figure as she left the room.

At quarter to five, the sun was beginning its rapid descent onto the western skyline, making her long for home, for west Wales, where there was maternal comfort, an easy way of life and the beautiful Carmarthenshire countryside all around. But here she was, a young nurse in the middle of cosmopolitan Cardiff, having to bear the responsibilities no other twenty-one year old could ever begin to understand. She was just about getting accustomed to the fast pace of living, but sometimes it left her breathless. Setting off with hope in her heart, longing with all her might to see Mitch once more, she started her journey down Porthnewydd Avenue, wondering if she would time her visit to coincide with Mitch's return from work. He finished around five, he'd mentioned, and it would take her about forty-five minutes to get there. She'd knock on the door, she decided - even if he was still out, maybe his flat-mate Charlie would be in. The weather was kind, for once, not a breath of wind ruffled her long chestnut hair, and the temperature, although hardly balmy, was almost in double figures, despite it being still the end of January. Caitlyn McDuff waved vigorously from her window across the road, sporting a bright pink satin dress, so Julia waved back, then hastened her step, not wishing to linger.

The sunset gave the urban scene a softness that was absent in the bright light of day. A peachy glow warmed the grey buildings and the Infirmary looked more like a gothic fairytale castle than ever in the mellow glow. I think I'm beginning to feel at home here, she thought, contentedly.

The smart, white sports car pulled up outside the address she'd been given in Allensbank Road. Jesus, Steph thought, student land once again. Would it never change? She eased her rapacious body out of the driver's seat, and looked around at the insalubrious surroundings.

After a few minutes of rapping on the door, she got fed up and tried the handle. It wasn't locked.

"Hello! Can I come in? The door was open!" Her assertive voice rang through the hallway.

"Shit!" Mitch hastily pulled a grubby towel around his sopping wet torso and looked around desperately for his dressing gown.

"It's only me!" Steph Saunders marched into the main room, where Mitch had, rather absent-mindedly, been reading the South Wales Echo while drying off after his bath. She smiled broadly. "Oh, don't mind me, sunshine! This is the nicest thing I've seen all day!"

Mitch coloured. "Hi Steph, didn't realise you were there!"

"Evidently. I've been knocking for ages, You should get a bell, or even better, a phone!" She plonked herself down on an ancient armchair, crossing her long, black stockinged legs provocatively. He could see a flash of red knickers, he was sure.

"I'll er, be right back!" Mitch backed away into his bedroom, holding the towel protectively around his waist. "Won't be a minute!" He shut the door firmly.

"Take your time, honey, I wasn't sure if you'd be in, but I thought I'd take a chance." She pulled out a nail file and started to work away at her bright red talons.

"Um, I finished early. Not much going on this afternoon." He dressed quickly in the security of the bedroom, before opening the door again. "There, all yours."

Steph smirked, giving a low laugh. "Hmm, if only! But joking aside, I've come to take you over to main office to go through some T's and C's with you, there won't be time to do that when we do the recording. You free now? I can drop you back home after, or we could go for a drink,if you like?"

Christ, he thought, she must be twice his age! She'd eat him for breakfast! He thought fast. "Oh, just drop me back here if that's okay, I've got some mates coming round later."

"A girlfriend?" She teased, playfully.

"Um, not really, just a couple of friends and a few tinnies. I'll get my coat." Bloody hell, he was starting to sweat now, she was a right hoochie mama. Please God, don't let her make a pass at me, he thought.

"My car's just parked on the street." She led the way, with an obedient Mitch following meekly in her wake.

It was almost dark outside, but he could see her car, and whistled. Maybe one day he too would be the proud owner of such a flashy set of wheels. The white TR7 stood shining and ready outside the house. As she opened the passenger door for him, Mitch hoped fervently that the students from next door were watching, however, the road was annoyingly deserted. That is, apart from a slight figure in a green duffel coat, who was watching the scene, unnoticed, from the corner of the street, her huge grey eyes brimming with tears and her face a mask of unutterable sadness.

Julia never remembered much about the walk home. She wept a bit, but the worst feeling was that of numb disappointment. The beautiful sunset had gone, the warmth of the sky had disappeared, the emerging stars seemed cruelly heartless, and the city seemed hostile, unfriendly. He had obviously turned up at the ward to apologise, that was clear, but more than likely to tell her it was all over. All over before it had even begun. At least he'd had the decency to do that, she supposed. And now he was off gadding about with that blond woman. Who the hell was she? How could she afford a car like that? Patently not a nurse, she thought wryly.

Walking helped calm her, it focussed her thoughts. Be brave, Julia, she told herself, pull yourself together. But her heart was heavy. Couples hurried past her, hand in hand, laughing and joking with each other. Students, probably. She could see warm, yellow light spilling out of the terraced windows, and young families settling down for the evening, snug and cosy in their togetherness. How she longed to be part of that. But she remained an outsider, a stranger and an onlooker, mocked by the loving domesticity she was seeing.

Finally arriving back at the nurses' home, she unlocked the massive wooden door and slipped inside, closing it quietly behind her, trying to obliterate the heartache and the painful memory of the boy she'd fallen in love with setting off into the night with another woman. Slowly, she climbed the stairs to the qualified nurses' quarters, hoping fervently that Mandy had already gone out. She couldn't face an interrogation right now.

Flinging herself down on the bed without turning on the light, she closed her eyes. Maybe sleep would help? She could hear the other nurses (students probably) downstairs in the kitchen, laughing and shouting, accusing each other of pinching each others' milk and bread. They don't have a care in the world, she thought sadly.

Just as she was drifting off, there was a knock on the door.

"Staff Harry?" It was the home warden. "Telephone call on the internal phone for you. Can you take it? You know it's not really allowed, but I think it's someone ringing from the Infirmary."

Julia opened the door. "Yes, of course, Miss Marshall. I'll take it right away." Not more bloody nights, she thought despondently. She picked up the receiver from the hall stand.

"Staff Harry speaking?"

"Hi, it's Marcus. Listen, are you free tomorrow night? I can pick you up and we can go into town if you like?" His smooth, caressing tone slipped into her ear like golden syrup.

Julia took a deep breath. "You know what, Marcus? That would be absolutely great! Pick me up at seven."

Replacing the handset, she looked at her face in the hall mirror. "Sod you, Mitch Walker," she muttered, before returning to her room and slamming the door.

Chapter Nine The use of women

"Go on, another one won't hurt you!" Neil Hancock took Mandy's empty glass, grinning broadly. "I must say, you look sensational tonight. I've got some smashing shots of you!" He turned his back to her, and replenished her drink from the well-stocked drinks trolley

Mandy smiled, lying back on the fake sheepskin rug as she accepted the wine. She was feeling quite relaxed. It had been strange at first, parading around Neil's living room in her underwear, striking some rather provocative positions when he requested them, in front of this huge white screen. But she'd soon got into the swing of it. It's only like calender stuff, she thought, a bit saucy perhaps, but where's the harm? Nothing she'd be afraid to show her mother, and that's what mattered at the end of the day. And she could hardly refuse after he'd bought her that amazing dinner at Fontana di Trevi, no expense spared, the best of everything, even vintage Champagne. Not that she knew the difference between a vintage Champagne and a bottle of Asti Spumante – come to think of it, she preferred Asti, she reckoned.

"What will you be doing with all these photos. Neil? Is it for a competition?" Mandy sipped her wine, and made a face. "This still tastes a bit sweet, is it still the Liebfraumilch?"

"Yes, but maybe I haven't chilled it enough. I'll stick it in the fridge later. Maybe we can do some topless shots!" He chuckled lecherously, reaching for his camera and messing around with it.

"No bloody way!" Mandy giggled, drowsily. "I'm game for a laugh, but I draw the line at any Page Three stuff!" She took a big gulp of wine, then lay back once more, closing her eyes. "I just feel so sleepy. So lovely and mellow." She sighed contentedly.

"Sleep for a while, then. Don't mind me. But finish your drink first, it'll get even warmer otherwise." Obediently complying, Mandy drained the wine glass, before settling back down on the rug. Neil watched her closely, observing her limp, languorous body, clad only in the provocative black underwear. He waited patiently for ten minutes, checking his reflection in the mirror – not that it mattered right now. He smoothed down his dark, brown hair and grinned at his handsome, après-ski tanned face. You gorgeous bastard, he thought, smugly. He checked his watch. Should be okay now, he thought. He reached for her foot, removing the shoe. He drew his fingernail under her sole, monitoring her reaction. There was none. Good.

Opening the lounge door, he beckoned to his friend, "You can come in now, she's out of it."

"Leave the stockings and suspenders on her, and put that shoe back on, Tom. Let's lose the bra and knickers, though." The two men soon removed these items from Mandy's unresponsive body.

"Oh, boy, we're in for a treat here, Neil! Oh look! She's even shaved herself! Especially for the camera! What a little beaut! Saves us having to do it!" Tom rubbed his fat hands in glee, his piggy eyes gleaming behind his thick-lensed glasses, which were on the point of steaming up, so intense was his lust. "What shall we do first?"

"Tits, I reckon." Neil positioned his camera, getting the best angle for the shot. "Stand behind her, I won't get you in, obviously, but I want you to rub her tits. Use plenty of baby oil, it's in the cabinet."

"My pleasure, boss!" Tom wasted no further time in applying himself to the task, enthusiastically oiling Mandy's voluptuous breasts with unbridled lust and enjoyment, while Neil snapped away with his camera.

"Right. Now I want some really candid stuff. But I need to get her ripe and ready first!" Neil opened a plastic box, pulling out a a tube of lubricating jelly. "Open her legs, Tom, open those gorgeous chubby little thighs for me!"

With Tom holding Mandy's legs wide apart, Neil started to paint her with the jelly, rubbing it in with his finger, then he squirted some onto his fingers, inserting them deeply into her, thrusting in and out, then smearing the excess all over her genitalia, rendering it red and shining. "That's a good girl," he grunted, "be a good girl for Dr Hancock." He sat up to admire his handiwork. "Stunning, even if I say so myself. What a cracking little honeypot." Back behind his camera, he took photo after photo of the unconscious Mandy, her thighs still being held apart by a gloating Tom.

"Pull her lips apart, Tom, I wanna see her smile!"

Tom giggled, and obliged. "That a wide enough smile, for you, Doctor Hancock? I bet that Woodentop boyfriend of hers doesn't get to see all this, does he?"

"I very much doubt he does, Doctor Mason, in fact I can almost see this patient's tonsils."

"You going to go for the rectal exam next?" Tom's voice was thickening, he was getting seriously turned on.

"Not yet." Neil started to unbuckle his belt. "I'm gonna have a little fun first. Oh, boy, I'm going to enjoy myself, and if you're a good lad, you can too." And he plunged into her, his face a contorted picture of licentiousness and spite. It was over in seconds.

Tom Mason zipped up his jeans, only just managing to do up the button on the straining waistband which supported his beer gut. "I'm quite out of puff after that," he panted, "didn't realise I was so unfit!" Mandy still lay on the sofa, breathing gently, unaware of anything at all.

"Well she hardly put up a struggle, did she? You didn't have to work very hard!" Neil sniggered, putting his camera away carefully. "You know, this Hasselblad 2000 is a smashing little number, pity I'll only get black and white out of it, though."

"Medium format, yes?" Tom took a swig from a bottle of lager. "Can I come round to, er, help you develop these titillating pics?"

"I think you've done enough coming for a while." Neil zipped up the camera case. "Now, I'm going to clean her up and then you can help me dress her. We'll drop her off at the nurses' home, put her on the doorstep and ring the bell. That old fossil warden-person will just think she's pissed. She'll be waking up shortly so let's get a move on." He looked down at Mandy in disgust. "Slag."

"It's seven o'clock!" Julia hammered on Mandy's door. There was no sound. "Come on! You'll be late for work!" Sighing in exasperation, Julia hurried back to her own room to finish getting dressed, sipping a cup of rapidly cooling coffee as she did. After tying her hair up in its usual bun, she returned to Mandy's room.

"Get up, Mandy! I'll have to go without you!"

After what seemed like ages, the door slowly opened. Mandy looked awful. Her hair was all over the place, her face was ghastly pale and her sunken eyes had big, dark circles around them.

"Good God! What's the matter?" Julia brushed past her into the room. "Are you ill?"

Mandy lay back down on her bed. "I can't go in, I feel terrible," she whispered. "I've been vomiting all night, I've hardly slept."
"Hangover, eh?" Julia suggested, wryly.

"Not like any hangover I've ever had before. I can't remember much, either. Jesus, I feel dreadful."

"I'll tell Miss Marshall to keep an eye on you. I'll ring the ward on the internal phone and tell them you're off sick. Look, I'll have to go, it's almost quarter past. I'll see you later, okay?"

Mandy nodded mutely, then rolled over into a foetal position. She wished she could remember...

"And there she was, I found her collapsed on the front step! I don't know how she managed to ring the bell! Couldn't remember getting home, even." Miss Marshall looked sternly at Julia. "What on earth has she been up to? I mean, she's qualified now, she should know she shouldn't go out getting drunk before an early shift."

"I know, Miss Marshall. I've rung the ward, can you keep an eye on her? I have to dash, now, or I'll be late!"

"Yes, of course, Staff. And I'll give her a piece of my mind when she finally surfaces." Miss Marshall sniffed in disapproval, and with a swish of white nylon dressing gown, returned to her apartment.

Jesus, Mary and sweet Joseph, thought Julia as she flew down Porthnewydd Avenue, what a bloody start to the day!

Julia was half way through the ward round with Daksha Patel when the ward clerk summoned the junior sister to the office, leaving Julia to continue accompanying the revered Mr Robinson and his retinue of doctors, which included Marcus Battencourt and the maverick registrar, Anscombe.

"Do we have the chest x-ray results for this patient, Staff?" Mr Robinson asked politely. "I think we need to exclude a chest infection before we discharge him." The elderly patient looked up in delight.

"I can go home?" His weather-beaten face creased into a happy smile.

Mr Robinson nodded, kindly. "Yes, indeed, Mr Shepherd, as long as your x-ray is clear. Staff?" He turned to Julia in expectation.

She smiled at the benevolent consultant. "I chased up the results an hour ago, sir. The radiologist was still reporting on it when I rang. Shall I go and check?"

"Excellent, yes, that would be helpful, Staff." The consultant nodded, pleased at her initiative. "Good work, young lady. I hope these young whipper-snappers take a leaf out of your book!" He chuckled, looking at the junior members of his team, his eyes twinkling. Even Anscombe laughed. Leaving the doctors to their own devices, she went to the office to ring Radiology, only to be met by a harassed Daksha hurrying back to the ward round.

"Julia! I'm so sorry. Can you go over to Willie Meckett to help out? Mandy Jacob is off sick, and they're desperate!" She looked flustered.

"Yes, of course. I was just going to chase up Mr Shepherd's x-ray results, though..."

"Leave that, I'll get the clerk to do it. You'd better hurry, there's only Sister Blake, an auxiliary and a brand new first-year there right now, and they've got six patients on dialysis." Daksha looked apologetic.

"On my way!" Julia gathered up her bag and hurried through the ward doors, oblivious to Marcus Battencourt's proprietorial gaze as she left

Mayhem held sway on Willie Meckett. The normally calm senior sister was dashing around, trying to multi-task, answering buzzers, checking dialysis bags and monitoring blood pressures, in between trying to complete the medicine round. An equally stressed auxiliary was tearing about, striving to wash the bed bound patients and supervise a very green first-year student.

Great, thought Julia, where the hell do I start? Taking a deep breath, she dumped her bag under the office desk and bravely walked up to Sister Blake.

"Hi, Sister, where d'you want me?"

"Oh, thank God!" Sister Blake wiped her hand across her forehead. "I've never been so glad to see anyone! Can you take over the observations, and come and check meds with me when I call you. Oh, and keep a very close eye on the student - Nurse Rees, her name is. It's her first bloody day and she's terrified! And give Sheila the auxiliary a hand with the bed baths? We've got three on bed rest, that's the cubicle and the first two beds. Chap in the cube is in with an acute episode of Crohn's disease, as well as a urine infection plus chest pain and unfortunately is needing a bed pan all the time! The rest of the gang are up to toilet."

"Yes, Sister." Julia put on a plastic apron and set about locating the student, eventually finding the quivering eighteen year old hiding fearfully behind the sluice door.

"Right, Nurse. You can help me do the obs and if anyone buzzes you can answer them – but come back and let me know what they want. Understand?" The student nodded mutely. Almost immediately, the buzzer rang in the cubicle, and the student trotted off to answer. Within seconds she was back.

"Mr Griffiths wants to go to the toilet, Staff."

"Well, take him a bed pan, you do know how to do that, yes?"

"Yes, yes, I can do that." And off she scampered, to the sluice, where Julia could hear her banging and clashing the steel bedpans about.

Julia continued checking blood pressures and recording her findings, but was interrupted by the student.

"Sorry, Staff," she started breathlessly, "he's saying he can't go on a bedpan any more, he says he finds it, er, inhibiting."

Julia rolled her eyes. "Mr Griffiths is on bed rest. That means he's not allowed to get up to the toilet. Oh, I suppose he could use a commode. Okay, Nurse, take him a commode instead." The student dashed off to carry out her latest instruction, leaving Julia to help the auxiliary change the sheets of another bed-bound patient. The student eventually returned, looking quite proud of herself. Things weren't so bad after all, Nurse Rees thought. It was almost half past ten and she hadn't killed anyone, she hadn't got into trouble...

Right, Julia thought, the obs are nearly done, I'll show the student how to do a bed bath, next. However, her good intentions were disturbed by Mr Griffiths' buzzer going yet again. Where's that student, she thought, crossly.

"Nurse! Nurse! Help! I can't get down!" Mr Griffiths' plaintive voice carried down the ward. Puzzled, Julia walked briskly to the cubicle and opened the door. She couldn't believe her eyes. The curtains had been drawn around the bed, and all she could see was Mr Griffiths' bald little head bobbing up and down above the top of them. Bloody hell, she thought, yanking back the curtains quickly. She wanted to burst out laughing, she wanted to call Sister Blake to witness this event, but most of all she wanted help, for there was poor Mr Griffiths perched on a commode, which had been placed on top of the bed. How the hell the student had managed to get him up there in the first place, she never found out.

"Sheila! I need help!"

Between the two of them, the two nurses managed to assist a quaking Mr Griffiths and put him safely back into bed, not looking each other in the eye for fear of laughing openly in front of him.

Returning to the ward, Julia glanced down the ward. There she was, chatting happily to a patient, obviously pleased as punch at her progress. Dear God, thought Julia in despair. "Nurse Rees? Can you come here a minute?"

Chapter Ten Opportunities

Marcus Battencourt's car was just like him. Smart, sleek and showy. Julia could just imagine what Mitch would have to say about it... She brushed away the thought, impatiently. Why did her mind always return to Mitch..?

"Hi!" She greeted Marcus smilingly as she eased her velvet-jeaned bottom into the low-slung seat of his red Mgb Gt. "You're early!"

"Early bird catches the worm!" He grinned at her, showing a row of perfectly straight, white teeth. Daddy must have paid a fortune for that orthodontic work, thought Julia cynically.

He revved up the engine."Right then, I've reserved a table in the Dubrovnik for half past seven, so we'll have time for a quick drink first."

"Great." Julia settled down in the passenger seat . I hope I've got enough money, she thought, anxiously. The Dubrovnik is quite expensive...

The softly-lit restaurant was inviting, attentive waiters showed them to their table and the smell of garlic floated enticingly from the kitchens.

"What do you fancy?" Marcus looked up from the menu.

"Um, I think I'll just have the chicken." It seemed the cheapest option, Julia thought.

"Oh, go on! Have something nice! Have whatever you want! My treat!" He reached over and touched her wrist.

"Oh, very well." She looked up at the expectant waiter. "I'll have the steak Diane, well done, please."

The waiter looked horrified. "Madame is sure? Well done?"

Julia nodded, vigorously. She hated undercooked meat. "What do you want, Marcus?"

"You," he whispered, leaning over the table and gazing into her eyes. Aloud he said, "I'll have the same, but I'll have mine rare. The bloodier the better." Again that wolfish grin. She was aware of other people staring at them. Marcus was certainly good-looking, tall, blond, well-dressed in his expensive leather jacket and tight Levi's What Julia didn't realise is that they were also staring at her, thinking what a stunning couple they made, how they complimented each other. She remained totally unaware how captivating she was, with her waist-length coppery hair, her mesmerising grey eyes and her incredible figure.

"You know, I can't let you pay for all this." Julia buttered a roll, as the waiter opened a bottle of Châteauneuf-du-Pape.

"Stop worrying! Relax! I'm not expecting anything by way of return." He gave her an old-fashioned look. "I got paid some overtime last week, so I'm feeling pretty flush! You can make me dinner some time, okay?" I'll have to play this one carefully, he thought, one false move and she'll bolt, I'll go softly, softly...

Julia laughed, relieved. Taking a sip of her wine, she thought that maybe this evening wasn't going to be too bad, after all.

Everyone was wiping the sweat off their foreheads, the recording studio was so stiflingly hot. The boys were just getting ready to play their last song and Stan was confident they would be able to call it a day as everything was successfully laid down. His colleague, Dan, the second engineer, was grinning from ear to ear. These guys sounded incredible.

Suddenly, the studio door opened and a young, fair haired girl was ushered in by one of Steph Saunders' minions.

"Hi!" She seemed shy and breathless. "I'm Alison. Mitch said you needed a backing singer for tonight? Hi Mitch! Hope I'm not too late!"

"Great!" Mitch greeted her with a hug. "Glad you could make it, Al! We're just doing the last song, you know, the one I got you to listen to in work? You ready to do those backing vocals? You been practising?" He was kind and reassuring. "This song really needs a female voice."

Alison swallowed. Another graduate from the College, she was used to singing and playing piano, but this was a whole new ball game. "I'm ready when you are! I know this song pretty well by now, Mitch, it's amazing!"

"Cheers!" Mitch smiled encouragingly at her. "D'you wanna warm up a bit?" He handed her some earphones. "Guys, play something easy – play 'Feel Like Makin' Love.'Al – put those cans on and sing the first couple of verses just to warm up, yes?" She nodded.

Her voice, uncertain at first, grew in strength as she sang. Half way through, she stopped, her eyes shining.

"Hey! That's a great sound! You're making my voice sound amazing! Can I have some more of that, please?" She dug her little hands into the pockets of her drainpipe jeans, unsure whether she was being too forward.

Stan and Dan looked puzzled from behind the screen.

"What d'you mean, kid?" Stan spoke through the intercom.

"That trill! It's lovely! Can I have some more trill?"

The band looked at each other, dying to laugh.

"D'you mean reverb, chick?" Dan chuckled.

"Yes! Yes! It's brilliant! Give me lots of that trilly reverb!" Alison beamed at the boys, thrilled to be part of this recording, thrilled to hear her somewhat average voice sound so sweet.

"As requested, little gal, you're getting some more trill!" The two sound engineers creased up with laughter as they turned up the dial on the controls. Alison shook back her frizzy blond hair and got ready for the first music recording of her career.

As Steph sidled unnoticed into the room, Mitch started up the chords of his latest song, the song which he'd only finished a few days ago, the song he'd written from his heart, in the depths of despair. Julia.

The others didn't have much to do, the keyboard was the main instrument, and Mitch's voice cut through beautifully. Steph smiled in appreciation, she'd been right to recruit this band. Talent in bucketfuls, she thought in satisfaction, plus they'd appeal to the general public. Youthful, yet experienced and absolutely focussed on their music. But that name would *have* to go...

She stepped forward, clapping slowly. "Well done, you chaps. That was awesome. I'll have a good listen to the recordings and get back to you about releasing one song as your debut single. But – you really need to change your name! Bartok Boys is quite, er, naff? How about 'Playing For Time?' That's quite catchy, yes?" Mitch looked at the others in horror, relieved to see that they were looking equally dismayed.

Unexpectedly, assistance came from the normally quiet Jeff.

"Ahem." He cleared his throat, anxiously. "I think this band should be called The Mitch Walker Band. He's the main man, now, and he composes most of our stuff. He deserves it." He looked at Dai and Eddie for approval.

"I'll second that." Dai nodded in agreement.

"Obvious choice, really," laughed Eddie. "He's the hardest worker as well." And it'll really piss off bloody Monster, he thought happily.

"Hmm...yes, that's got a nice ring to it." Steph chewed thoughtfully on her pen. "Yes, I think we'll run with that. The Mitch Walker Band it shall be. Well, that's about it for now, you guys. We need to have a meeting with you next week, so if you can all come to my office at five o'clock next Friday? Will that suit? You'll be free from work then? We need you to sign some contracts and boring stuff like that!"

They all nodded their assent, and Alison turned to leave, but not before Mitch called her back.

"Hey, you were spot on with those backing vocals. Fantastic! Thank you for helping out. I didn't want a stranger singing for us, not yet anyway."

Alison blushed prettily. "Aw, it was nothing! Just remember me when you're famous! Anyway, who is Julia? It's such a beautiful song."

Mitch pretended to mess about with his keyboard, so she wouldn't see the pain in his eyes. "Oh, she was someone I met once." He turned back to her and grinned. "And we'll put your name on the credits, Al, if this record comes about, don't you worry!"

"Aw, thank you, Mitch. I'll get going now, Derek is picking me up in a few minutes and we're going to the flicks. See you in the office next week?"

"Unfortunately yes! We haven't made our millions yet!" He waved goodbye and watched her hurry out to meet her boyfriend. How he wished Julia was waiting for him outside...

The newly-named Mitch Walker Band then packed away their instruments before heading out into the damp January night, to load up the old van and drive home to dream their dreams of fame and success.

"Thanks for a lovely evening." Julia opened the car door. "I've had a great time."

"No kiss goodnight?" Marcus put a restraining hand on her shoulder. "Just a little one?"

Julia smiled, apologetically. "Yes, of course." She leaned over and pecked him on the cheek. Marcus sighed in exasperation.

"Not like that, like this." And he drew her into his arms, kissing her languorously and probing her reluctant mouth with his tongue. "There. That's better. Now off you go, there's a good girl! Get plenty of sleep, and Dr Battencourt will give you a ring soon." He beamed at her, confident and in control.

Christ, thought Julia, he'll be patting me on the bottom, next. Aloud, she said, "Sure. Anytime. Goodnight, then." She got out of the car, and without looking back, ran lightly up the steps to the nurses' home.

Christ, thought Marcus, why is she so bloody cool with me? And, revving the engine unnecessarily, he sped off into the night.

The lights were off in the hallway, and Julia didn't want to disturb anyone, especially Miss Marshall, who despite her fondness for Julia had a tendency to behave like a mother hen at times, so she crept up the stairs in darkness. She could do without a probing conversation from the home warden this evening. She could see the light shining under Mandy's door, so knocked softly.

"It's Julia. You awake?"

"Yeah, come in."

Mandy looked better, her colour had returned and she was tucked up in bed, drinking Ovaltine and watching something on her tiny black and white portable T.V.

"You okay?" Julia plonked herself on the end of the bed. "What you watching?"

Mandy nodded, draining the last of her hot drink. "Loads better, thanks, back to work tomorrow. What am I watching? I am pretending to be interested in a bloody awful documentary about copulating turtles." She looked up at her friend. "Honestly, Jules, it was not a hangover. I felt so ill, I was vomiting, I can't remember anything much at all."

"I thought you were seeing Neil Hancock. Didn't he bring you home?"

"He must have. I can't remember."

"Hasn't he been in touch? To ask if you're okay?"

Mandy sighed heavily. "Nope. Not a sausage. I even bleeped him this afternoon, from the internal phone, the Sergeant Major was out shopping so I was able to use it on the QT. He never got back to me, though. But maybe he was busy..." Her voice trailed away, miserably. She picked at a loose thread on her quilt cover.

"How did the photo shoot thingy go?" Julia kicked off her shoes and unbuckled her tight jeans.

"Alright, I think. Like I said, I can't remember much." Her face looked so forlorn, so sad, unlike the happy-go-lucky girl she would normally be. Julia felt incredibly sorry for her and hugged her tightly.

"Get some sleep, Mandy, forget about bloody Neil Hancock, yeah? He's a waste of space. And I'll catch up with you tomorrow. You on a late?"

"Yes." Mandy smiled wearily. "See you in the morning, then."

Julia left her snuggling down under the blankets, and after switching off the light for her, crossed the darkened landing to her own room.

Men, she thought to herself, they're more trouble than they're worth...

Chapter Eleven Gut Feelings

Daksha Patel rolled her eyes at Julia as she completed the handover at lunchtime. "There's two new second years started today. Keep an eye on them. Gillian Evans and Susan Bowen. They're right little horrors, full of cheek. This morning I caught them trying to do the obs without a trolley, putting the sphygmomanometer on the beds, would you believe? It makes you wonder what they teach about infection control in the institute these days! And accepting chocolates and grapes from that young lad in the bottom bed."

"I'll keep my eagle eye on them, don't worry," replied Julia grimly. Little buggers, she thought.

"To make matters worse, Miss Graham the nursing officer caught them eating chips from the lunch trolley She went bloody nuts! Anyway, I'm off now." Daksha pulled on her cardigan. "I've got time owing. Sister Winter is on at four, so you're in charge until then. Have a good one!"And with a brilliant smile, she hurried with almost indecent haste from the ward.

The ward was calm, everything was in order. Sister Patel may have been young and newly-promoted, but ran the busy surgical ward with enthusiastic efficiency.

"Nurse Thomas?" Julia called the little first-year over. "We'll start the two o'clock medicine round now, then there's a few dressings to do. You can help me do the first one, then maybe you can do the next one. Yes?"

Aneira blushed in delight. "Oh, yes please!" Honestly, thought Julia in amusement, you'd think I'd given her a hundred quid and a free trip to Spain!

The medicine round passed uneventfully with for once, no interruptions. The office phone was mercifully quiet and everything was up to date. Just as Julia was securing the medicine trolley to the wall, and thinking of asking Aneira to prepare the dressing trolley, her attention was caught by vigorous burst of yellow-clad activity down the bottom end of the ward. Gillian Evans, the new second year, was precariously holding a bedpan and at the same time executing what appeared to be some intricate choreography, all the while waving at someone at the top of the ward. Following the direction of the student's waving, Julia was horrified to spot the other student, Susan Bowen, with an armful of clean linen, also performing the same dance routine, waving madly and grinning from ear to ear. Right, thought Julia, that's it.

"Nurse Evans? Nurse Bowen? In the office. Now!" She hardly raised her voice, she didn't need to, for the outrage in her tone stopped the two errant students in their tracks, and they trotted meekly up to the office, bedpan and linen in their respective arms.

"Is that a used bedpan, Nurse Evans?" Julia glared at the shamefaced student, her hands on her hips.

"Er, no, Staff."Nurse Evans looked down at her feet.

"What the hell do you think you were doing, acting the goat like that while on duty?"

There was silence. Neither nurse responded.

"Come on, I haven't got all day. Or would you prefer I reported you both to the Nursing Officer?" Both young girls paled visibly.

"Um..." Nurse Bowen shuffled uncomfortably. "Well, you see, it's like this -"

"Ssh!" Nurse Evans nudged her with her bedpan-free hand, but Nurse Bowen shrugged her off and continued.

" We were in Tito's last week. I tried to teach Gill- Nurse Evans – a dance routine, you know, like they do in Saturday Night Fever." The student

110

warmed to her theme. "Well, Nurse Evans couldn't quite manage it, so I told her to practise it. And she's got it now, she's quite good." Susan Bowen smiled hopefully at Julia, while Gillian Evans remained silent in total mortification.

"I see. The ward is not the place for such stupidity." Julia's tone was icy. "And seeing as you've so much energy, you can get rid of it by cleaning the sluice, top to bottom, and I will be inspecting it in an hour. I may even take swabs and send them off for culture. If I am not satisfied, I can guarantee that I will be reporting you both to Sister Winter at four o'clock. Understand?"

"Yes, Staff."Both students spoke in unison.

"And let me tell you both that neither of you are much good as dancers anyway," she added acidly, "stick to looking after your patients, that's my advice to you."

"Yes, Staff." Suitably chastened, the pair retreated sheepishly to the sluice, while Aneira looked on goggle-eyed.

"Come on Nurse Thomas, let's start the dressings." Julia marched importantly into the treatment room, Aneira trotting along behind her like an obedient little lamb.

"Excellent, Nurse Thomas. Well done. You did that dressing beautifully." Julia wheeled the trolley out from behind the curtains. "I'll dispose of these soiled dressings and clean everything up, if you can wash your hands and go and prepare Mr Khan for his dressing. He had his laparotomy yesterday."

"What's that, Staff?"

"The surgeon made an incision down his abdomen to find out the cause of his abdominal pain. They couldn't find anything amiss, though. We need to remove his dressing and clean the wound, then re-dress it."

Aneira nodded dutifully.

"Yes, Staff. I'll make sure he's emptied his bladder and has had any necessary analgesics. Then I'll close any windows that may be open nearby. And of course I will make Mr Khan comfortable before explaining the procedure to him." She smiled, hopefully

"Perfect. You're doing really well, Nurse Thomas. Now I won't be very long, so off you go and get him ready."

The late winter sun shone weakly through the treatment room window as Julia disinfected the trolley and prepared it for the next patient. Aneira Thomas was coming along just fine, she thought. Such a sweet little thing, but anyone would think she was about ten years younger than Julia, instead of just three. Better than those two little blighters Gillian Evans and Susan Bowen, who were much too bold and brazen for their own good. Ah well, she considered, Sister Winter and the rest of the qualifieds would soon knock them into shape. As she wiped down the top of the trolley with disinfectant from back to front, she drifted back in time to her own student training. She'd probably been more like Aneira, she pondered, but certainly not as timid.

Julia fastened the disposal bag to the side of the trolley, making sure that any adhesive did not come into contact with the metal – that would be difficult to remove and would provide a breeding ground for pathogens. She loved the serenity of the treatment room, everything orderly and quiet, clean and shining...

A shriek of panic then pierced the air and Aneira appeared at the door, a look of absolute terror on her little face.

"Staff! Come quickly! Please!"

Julia abandoned her work and rushed over. "What's happened?"

"Oh quick! It's Mr Khan! Something terrible has happened!" Julia couldn't get any more sense out of Aneira so hurried over to Mr Khan's bed, slipping between the drawn curtains.

No wonder Aneira had been panicking. Mr Khan lay back in bed, the covers pulled back, a glazed expression on his face. His pyjama top had been unbuttoned in readiness...and his intestines glistened as they lay on his substantial abdomen, obscenely twitching in their snake-like coils.

"Burst abdomen!" Julia's shout alerted the two second years, emerging from the sluice after completing their prescribed cleaning.

"Bleep the reg!" Julia barked out the command, the urgency in her voice ensuring an instant response from Susan Bowen who darted away to the phone. "Tell him we have a burst abdomen. Nurse Evans, get swabs, a bag of saline, and a receiver. Hurry!"

She turned her attention to Mr Khan, who was rapidly becoming clinically shocked.

"My stomach is out, Nurse," he whispered., "my insides are out!"

Thank God he's still got a drip up, thought Julia, making sure it was still running properly. Aloud, she said, "Don't worry Mr Khan, we'll get the doctor here in a second. Hold Nurse Thomas' hand and keep looking at her." She turned to Aneira. "We need to protect the area with saline drapes. Ah, here's Nurse Evans. Well done."

"You're going to be okay, Mr Khan,"Aneira squeezed his hand, "the doctor is on his way." The patient gazed up into her eyes, clinging to her small hand, sweat breaking out on his face.

Just as Julia was placing the saline drapes over the quivering intestines, the curtain was pushed aside, and Mr Anscombe the registrar charged in upon the scene, with Marcus Battencourt following in his wake.

"This the laparotomy from yesterday?" He snatched the notes from Marcus's hand.

"Yes, sir." Even Marcus's habitual composure was shaken by the sight of Mr Khan's spectacular burst abdomen."I'll ring theatre, yes?"

"Yes." Anscombe's curt reply hid his concern. "And get that kid out of here." He nodded towards Aneira, who had gone ghastly pale. "This is no place for a first year. Quick, before she passes out."

Julia hurriedly escorted a shaking Aneira back to the office.

"Sit down for a bit, don't worry, you've been amazing. But it's a difficult situation. Once we've got Mr Khan off to theatre, we'll have a chat about it, yes?" Aneira nodded, grateful to sit down, but couldn't help comparing it to the book she'd been reading last night about Tudor methods of dispatching traitors, who'd been hanged, drawn and quartered...

Within ten minutes, Mr Khan was being rushed back to the operating suite, accompanied by Marcus Battencourt and a nurse from theatre.

Julia called the other two students back into the office. "Well done, you lot." She smiled at the three young girls. "That was pretty scary, yes? But you all did well, nobody panicked and Mr Khan will be fine. It's not something we see every day, in fact it's my first burst abdo as well! You all did so well, I'm proud of you all."

"Thanks, Staff." Susan Bowen's voice was deferential.

"We're sorry about earlier." Gillian Evans was equally humble, in awe of the severity of the recent emergency. "We won't do that again."

"Good." Julia. "Let's forget about it. Carry on the way you mean to go on, behave exactly like you all did just now. Okay, Nurse Thomas, Sister Winter is just coming down the corridor, then you and I can go to break."

Julia and Mandy met at the top of the stairs, cardigans and capes on, ready for the walk home along the damp Porthnewydd Avenue.

"Can't wait for bed, my feet are killing me." Mandy winced as she stooped to run a finger along the inside of her left shoe. "Bloody new shoes. I should have broken them in first. I've got a massive blister."

"It's bleeding a fair bit,"Julia remarked, glancing down at her friend's ankle, "a nice soak in the bath for you, I reckon."

Then all thoughts of painful feet were banished from Mandy's head, for who should be strolling down the corridor but Neil Hancock and Marcus Battencourt, head-to-head in deep conversation. The blood rushed to her face and her heart beat faster.

"Julia!" Her voice was just a whisper. "It's Neil!" She grabbed Julia's arm and squeezed it hard.

"Act cool!" Julia knew quite well that Mandy had as much reserve as a puppy with a toy bone.

"Hi, girls!" Marcus was charm itself. "Off home?"

"Well, we're not exactly about to hit the town, are we, Mandy?" Julia smiled at him, brightly Please, please be chilled, Mands, she prayed.

"Hello, Neil." Mandy smiled hopefully up at him, only to be rewarded with the briefest of grins.

"Sorry, chaps, I've got to get going. People to see, things to do, you know what I mean?" Neil turned abruptly around and ran down the stairs without so much as a backward glance. Julia glanced at Mandy, knowing full well how she was probably feeling.

Mandy's face was like stone. She betrayed no emotion at all. I can't believe this is happening, she thought, it's as though I've become invisible. Dear Lord, what on earth have I done to make him behave this way? She felt sick, lonely and disregarded. "I'll head on home, you guys," she managed to get a few words out, "I'll see you in the morning, Jules." Mechanically, she smiled goodbye and managed to walk down the stairs, her head in a whirl. Tears blinded her eyes as she pushed open the big, rubber doors. Then she spotted him, deep in conversation with Tom

115

Mason, the pair of them chuckling together under the lamplight of the gate outside Chalet Six, the nurses' home.

"Neil?" Her voice faded away miserably as she saw him scuttling away like a thief in the night, casting a sly look at Tom as he went.

"And can I see you again? This weekend?" Marcus grinned confidently at Julia's concerned face. "My place? I can pick you up?"

Julia nodded, absent-mindedly, her thoughts entirely on Mandy and her obvious rejection by Neil.

"Battencourt! Casualty NOW!" The pair sprung apart as the white coated Anscombe pounded past. "Stop your little flirting games and get your upper-class arse into gear! Hear me?" The senior registrar glared through his thick-lensed spectacles as he continued his whirlwind progress towards Casualty.

"Yes, sir." Marcus had the grace to look abashed. Julia smiled to herself. It was good to see him put in his place.

"Hey! Did you hear me?" Marcus tilted her chin upwards. "Sunday? I'll pick you up at seven?"

"What? Sorry, yes, that would be great. I'm off on Sunday." She tried to smile. "Where shall we go?"

"I said we'd go to my place!" Marcus was getting a bit frustrated now. "I'll get us a take-away and we can get a video out, if you like."

"Yeah, sure. Great." Julia's apathy was evident.

"What's the matter? I'm bowled over by your enthusiasm."

"Oh, it's just that I'm wondering why Neil is giving Mandy the cold shoulder. He took her home after their date, and that's the last she's heard from him. Well, she thinks he took her home, she can't remember much."

"Oh, Neil's a bit of a Lothario. Not much Mandy can do about that. I'd just forget about him if I was her."

"Yes, but he's actively avoiding her. He's not even being very friendly, is he?"

Marcus shrugged non-committally "None of my business. Anyway, I'd better crack on. There's a haematemesis in Cas and I've got to go and clerk him. I'll see you on Sunday, then." He leaned over and pecked her on the cheek, before turning around and sauntering off down the corridor. What is it with that girl, he thought, irritably, she's playing incredibly hard to get. He winked at an attractive third year nurse hurrying along past him, eager to get back to the nurses' home. She blushed prettily. Well, he said to himself, I'm obviously not losing my touch, but I'll just have to warm up the Ice Maiden good and proper on Sunday, she'll be like putty in my hands by the time I've finished with her. He watched Julia as she made her way towards the stairs, her pretty face anxious, her slim body almost dancing down the steps with haste...he wanted her badly.

Julia walked home, disconsolately. She let the fine rain bathe her upturned face as she passed through the Gap in the Wall. It wasn't cold at all, just misty and murky. She took her time, wondering what to make of Neil Hancock and his libertine attitude towards poor Mandy. It was highly likely that Mandy had slept with him. Fair enough, she thought, maybe it was a one-night stand, but his avoidance of her was spectacularly cruel. As she crossed the road at Carlton Street, she felt a sudden longing to go home, to escape all these complicated men and their schemes. The mist thickened, and she suddenly became aware of a tall, dark figure appearing menacingly out of the fog. Her heart almost stopped, as the figure loomed closer.

"Evening, Nurse." A night-shift policeman nodded at her from a doorway.

"Evening, Officer." Julia smiled, relieved. "Hope the rain keeps off for you."

"Oh, I'll be okay. Now you get along quickly to your nurses' home. There's some unsavoury characters about this evening."

"Thanks." There certainly are, she thought. And with a quickened step, she hurried along the pavement until she reached the door of the nurses' home.

Chapter Twelve Going home

The four boys sat uncomfortably in the tropically heated office. Steph Saunders was at her most relaxed and urbane in her own warm environment; lush fake plants lined the bright orange walls, and several paintings of the Amalfi coastline added to the general exotic atmosphere. She sat on a swivel chair behind her huge white desk and gave them all a dazzling smile, her bright red lipstick immaculate.

"Thanks for getting here on time. Everything is sorted. You are now a signed band! Congratulations! Coffee, anyone?" They all shook their heads. Let's get on with it, thought Mitch.

Aloud he said, "You mentioned we need a manager now. There's a guy in work who's managed a blues band before, and he's looking to do this type of thing again. He's ready when we are." Steph nodded approvingly

"Great!" She got up and prowled around the room, showing off her long, slender legs in her leather mini skirt. "Now, boys! We're going to release your first single in two weeks. Hopefully this will coincide with Valentine's Day and we'll be able to capitalise on all those little teenyboppers out there!" Mitch cringed, looking at Eddie for support. But Eddie was looking straight ahead, seeing only pound signs, and fast cars...

She continued."We're going to release 'Damned if I Do' as your first single. It's got a great beat and it's danceable too."

Mitch stood up. "No." Steph looked at him in astonishment, her heavily mascara'd eyes fluttering away like demented spiders. "No way. It's got to be 'Julia.' It's a much better song, put 'Damned' on the B side if you want, but it's got be 'Julia' on the A side."

"Oh, dear me, Mitch. No. It's not as marketable. I do know what I'm talking about here, you know." She smiled patronisingly at him.

"I guess you do. But I still want 'Julia' as our first single. If it was good enough for Kate Bush, then it's good enough for us." He stuck his hands in his pockets stubbornly and looked squarely at Steph.

"What on earth are you talking about?" she asked, puzzled.

"Her record company wanted 'James and the Cold Gun' as her first single, but she stuck to her guns – pardon the pun - and look where 'Wuthering Heights' got her! Number one for four weeks!"

Steph sighed, frowning. "Okay. I tell you what. Let's make it a double A single, both songs will be played on the radio. Happy with that?"

"Ecstatic!" Mitch sat down again, beaming, delighted with the outcome. He'd thought it would have been impossible to override any decision made by Steph, a woman used to getting her own way.

"One more thing," she added, returning to her chair, "we need a decent photo of you all, for the single. Gone are the days of plain white record sleeves with a round hole in them. No, the fans will want to see you guys smiling up at them as they rifle through the selection in the shops. So!" Her laser beam eyes scrutinised their reactions. "Happy with that?"

"Sure, fine by me." Eddie smiled in agreement.

Jeff folded his arms, nodding. "Okay. What d'you have in mind?"

She sighed deeply. "I had wanted you guys to be representative of Cardiff. I had visions of you posing outside City Hall, you know, goofing about a bit. But our artistic director has other plans. He wants you out in the middle of bloody nowhere, on a mountain top or somewhere equally dramatic. Wearing dark, dark clothes." She made a face. "So bloody gloomy. But he says it's the current trend. So he's thinking of flying you all up to Scotland next week."

Mitch was thoughtful. "I think it's a cool idea, I like it." Steph raised an eyebrow. He continued. "I think it should be black and white as well. But with our socks visible, and coloured red or something, as a contrast."

120

"Yes!" Steph's eyes lit up. "I like it! I didn't know you were all arty, Mitch."

He had the grace to look embarrassed. "I'm not!" He laughed. "But I share a flat with an artist, and we chat about this sort of thing. I suppose I've just plagiarised one of his ideas!"

"Hey, Mitch!" Dai piped up from a delightful reverie about getting rich and being able to buy a detached house in Cyncoed. "We don't need to go to Scotland! Steph – do you realise where he lives? In the middle of nowhere, loads of mountains, plenty of sheep if he's desperate -" he dodged a feigned slap from Mitch - "and at this time of year there's a pretty good chance of shit weather!"

"Hey, good thinking, Mr Drummer!" Steph looked immensely pleased with him. "We'll save money and time. Well, that wraps up our little meeting. I'll be in touch about the photo shoot, but it could be as early as this Sunday. Can you all make it?"

They all nodded their assent. They were on their way. They were almost there.

The grim winter clouds scudded across an already leaden sky, throwing spiteful showers of hail and sleet upon the band and the rest of the team as they clambered up the steep slopes of the mountainside.

"Whose fucking idea was this?" Dai grumbled as he tripped over a boulder, his boxer's nose bright red with cold.

"Er, yours, actually!" Mitch grinned, edging to the front, clearly used to the terrain. Steph was unrecognisable, her face almost totally hidden by the hood of her parka. She was struggling with the climb, and was longing for the sub-tropical comfort zone of her office, but instead found herself battling the elements on the harsh hillsides of Powys.

"How much further? I don't know if I can go on much longer." She grimaced in discomfort, panting heavily. "The last time I breathed like this was on a one-night stand with a DJ from Radio 1." Jeff looked at Eddie and sniggered.

"We're here, boys!" Mitch stood atop a small hillock, hands on his hips, oblivious to the weather, surveying the countryside below. It always reminded him of a picture in one of his favourite childhood books, it always reminded him of Narnia. "This is where we should do the photo!" He flung his arms wide, as if he owned the place and was the king of all the land. As the others followed his gaze, they could see for miles, hill after hill, fields and meadows one after the other, until they melted away into the horizon. Somewhere down there, far away, was South Wales and the sea. The clouds occasionally parted, allowing a watery sun to light the landscape with amazing colours; dramatic steep slopes were studded with tough little Welsh sheep and the occasional lonely farm lay in sequestered solitude between the rugged, austere mountains. Tiny lights started to twinkle in a few of these isolated dwellings, making Mitch think of his family, of a roaring log fire and a warm, comfortable bed. Red kites swooped and dived in the sky above them and only the occasional car wound its way along the narrow road far below.

"Perfect!" The photographer yelled above the roar of the wind. "We'll do it here! If you guys are ready?"

By four o'clock it was getting quite dark, but Jack the photographer was happy with his shots and the little group started making its way carefully back down to the road.

"Steph? Can I ask a favour?" Mitch caught her arm as she stumbled over an uneven part of the path, unused to her designer hiking boots.

"Sure! Ask away! She grinned at from from the depths of her hood.

"I've got a few days off from work, and if you don't need me for recording or anything, I'll be staying on at my parents' farm, so I was wondering of you could drop me off there? It's only a couple of miles off the main road?"

"Sure, no problem. I'll take you in my car, the others can go with Jack and Stan in the mini van."

"See you guys next week, then!" Mitch grinned as he eased himself into the sports car, rubbing his frozen hands together to get them warm. He'd have been stuffed if she'd said no...

Menna Walker could hardly believe her eyes when a smart, white car rolled up in the farmyard. She peered through the kitchen window, trying to make out who the visitor could be.

"Llew! We've got company!" She hurried to the tiny mirror in the porch, anxiously re-arranging her short, brown hair.

"Who is it?" Mitch's father hurried down the narrow staircase, lowering his head at the arch at the bottom, which could barely accommodate his six foot frame.

"It's MITCH!" Not waiting a moment longer, Menna flung open the kitchen door and threw herself at her son who was emerging from the passenger side. "MITCH! Why didn't you say you were coming home? I haven't aired your bed, and there's only cheese pie for supper -"

"Hush, Mam!" Mitch laughed and hugged her. "It's all been very last minute." He turned to Steph, who was regarding this homecoming scene with predictable cynicism, a wry smile on her face. "Thanks for the lift, Steph, do you want to come in for a cup of tea?"

"No thanks, Mitch. I'd better be off. It's a good two hours from here back to Cardiff. You enjoy your break. I'll see you next week." And, reversing the car skilfully between some milk churns but driving heedlessly over a vegetable patch, she executed a neat three-point turn and roared away down the narrow lane and into the rapidly falling darkness of Powys.

"Well, i Duw, Duw!" Menna hugged her son for the twentieth time. "Are you feeling better? Have you got holidays from work? How long are you home for? And who was that woman? Is she -"

"Hang on, Mam!" Mitch laughed affectionately. "One question at a time! I'll stay a couple of days, then I'll get the train back to Cardiff, if that's okay?"

"Okay? *Tân uffern ar ni!* Of course it's okay!" Menna's round, sweet face beamed with happiness.

"And Steph is a record producer," Mitch continued, " well, she works for a recording company, and she's signed the band!"

"Signed the band?" Mitch's father looked confused. "What does that mean?"

"We've got a recording contract. That means our music will be played on the radio and we'll be paid for it! I'll explain everything properly after tea."

"Oh I see, well done, bach!" Menna's cup was overflowing with maternal joy. Here was her boy, home safe and sound, and on the brink of stardom. But only one stone remained unturned. "So that woman, is she your girlfriend?"

"No," laughed Mitch, "she's old enough to be my mother, mun! No, no girlfriend at the moment." More's the pity, he thought, sadly. "And here's your birthday present. Sorry I missed the party, but it's been so busy in Cardiff!" He handed her the untidily wrapped present, watching anxiously as she started pulling out the pretty dressing gown.

"Oh, cariad bach, that's so kind of you!" She ripped it open. "Oh, so beautiful, and it's my size as well! Clever, you are!" She hugged him yet again.

"That's all the luggage you've brought?" Mr Walker looked down in surprise at Mitch's small duffel bag.

"'Fraid so, Dad. But no worries, I've got plenty of stuff to wear upstairs, and I'm sure Mam's washing machine is in good working order." He grinned wickedly at his mother.

"Cheeky as ever, eh, Llew?" Menna rolled her twinkling eyes at her husband. "Anyway, I'll go and put some sausages in the oven for supper, to go with the cheese pie. Mitch, get along with you upstairs and have a nice hot bath. Supper'll be ready in half an hour."

"Yes, boss!" Mitch pinched an apple from the fruit bowl, then sprinted up the stairs to his room and homespun comfort.

"Your house is really nice, Marcus." Julia wandered around the sitting room, looking at all the photographs on the sideboard and the paintings on the wall. "How on earth can you afford it? I couldn't even consider a mortgage yet. I know your basic pay is a lot more than mine, but still..?"

"Oh, it isn't mine." He uncorked a bottle of bottle of wine. "Dad bought it a few years ago, so I could have somewhere half decent to stay during my time in Cardiff."

"During your time in Cardiff?" Julia accepted the full glass from him. "Sounds like you don't plan on sticking around for much longer?"

"Come on, sit down." He patted the sofa. "Well, I'll stay here for a year or two, I suppose, then I'll head back home to London."

"I see." Julia took a sip of her drink, letting the slightly fizzy wine slip down her throat. "And what will you do back in London?"

"Obs and gynae. And of course, there's all those grim parental expectations to comply with!" He laughed, wryly, putting his hand on her knee.

"Sorry? What do you mean?"

"Well, mama and papa expect me to settle down in a rural GP practice, marry the Right Sort of girl, if you know what I mean, and buy a pile in the country."

"And is that what you want?" Julia was feeling more bewildered by the minute. "Have you already got that Right Girl tucked away back in London?"

Marcus had the grace to appear embarrassed. "It's not what you think, Julia. I've known Annabel for yonks, her brother was at boarding school with me... Look, it's practically an arranged marriage, for Christ's sake! But what she doesn't know won't harm her, will it?" He winked conspiratorially at her.

Julia removed his hand from her knee. "Well, maybe not, but what about how I feel about it? You're confusing me now."

"Oh, don't be like that, sweetheart!" He replaced his hand, and tilted her chin up. "We can have a good time, can't we? Hey, our takeaway will be getting cold unless we scoff it right away! Be a duck and set the table, will you?"

Patronising sod, thought Julia, getting up and going into the kitchen.

Marcus may have been a patronising sod, but over the chicken chow mein and crispy noodles, he had Julia in stitches, telling her stories about the other junior doctors and the scrapes they'd got themselves into. It seemed Marcus loved talking about himself, and he was admittedly pretty good at it. Never mind, thought Julia, it was easier for her like that. She didn't feel like opening up to him, she was content to be entertained by his rather risqué tales and jokes. And surely she would start to develop more of an attachment for him, once she had got over Mitch. She was just in a state of recovery, that was all. And Marcus, in theory, ticked all the boxes; good-looking, witty, charming... Maybe that Annabel wasn't really featuring in his life anyway. Maybe he was teasing her?

"I'll put some music on." Leading her by the hand, back into the sitting room, he went over to the stereo and soon they were sitting side by side again, on the sofa, listening to Hotel California, the lights having been artfully dimmed to a more romantic level.

"You're frightfully attractive, Julia, d'you know that?" He gazed deeply into her eyes, as though trying to mesmerize her. "I don't think you have a clue just how lovely you are. Come here." And he pulled her to him, kissing her slowly and sensually, as his hand caressed her shoulders, her waist then her thighs. He ran his long fingers through her mane of hair, easing her head back as he did so, kissing her throat.

A whirl of muddled thoughts raced through Julia's mind as Marcus's wandering hand continued its determined journey over her body. He was certainly an expert in his field, his movements were smooth and seductive, yet insistent. He lightly stroked her breast, then started lifting her sweater to access his goal more freely. Julia tried to push his hand away.

"No need to be shy, Julia," he whispered, softly, "come on, let me feel these wonderful globes of yours, let me see them. With amazing speed, his hand slipped around to her back and with one smooth move he unhooked her bra, releasing her voluptuous breasts.

"Oh my God, these are wonderful." He jiggled them in both hands, then swiftly raised her sweater up over her head, taking in the erotic sight of Julia lying topless on the sofa, her hands covering her breasts as best they could.

"Let's go to bed." He held out his hand to her.

This isn't right, thought Julia. starting to feel ashamed, looking for her sweater to cover herself up.

"Er, no, I can't, Marcus, it's too soon."

His handsome features settled into a frown. "Chill, relax. Come on, I'll get you another drink." Leaving her standing there in the sitting room, he returned to the kitchen, where Julia could hear him opening cupboards, clanking about with glasses and bottles. Holding her sweater up against her, she tip-toed to the door.

"What are you doing, Marcus?"

He jumped, a curiously guilty expression on his face as he swung round.

"Nothing, just getting you a drink."

"I don't want another glass of wine. I don't want anything to drink." She returned to the sitting room and put her sweater back on, stuffing her bra hurriedly into her bag.

He stormed in after her. "What the hell are you playing at? Isn't this what you wanted? A simple, straightforward fuck?" His face was red with anger, his good looks contorted with fury. She felt as though she'd been slapped.

"I'm going home." Fear started to creep in.

"Yes, you do that. You piss off home, you little prick-teaser," he snarled, "you let me buy you dinner, you let me drive you about in my car, you let me bring you home – and you led me on, yes, you certainly led me on to believe you wanted a shag. Little Nurse Prim and fucking Proper, that's what you want us all to think, isn't it? But you're devious and nothing but a user."

"I am no such thing." Julia struggled into her coat. "And you had better not try contacting me ever again. From now on it's Staff Harry, understand, *Doctor* Battencourt?" Her eyes filled up with tears of shame and indignation, as she grabbed her bag and rushed out of the front door, slamming it hard behind her.

The soft, fine mist swept through Cardiff's night sky, and Julia could just about see the lights of the Gabalfa flyover through the drizzle, like a great, ghostly arc providing a bridge between this world and the next.

Maybe she should flag down a taxi? But no taxis seemed to drive past in this residential area at half past nine on a Sunday night. Thank goodness she was wearing her new brothel creepers. They'd get soaked, but at least she could walk fast in them. She felt strangely detached. Why wasn't she all that upset? She'd felt terrible after being dumped by Mitch. Always Mitch, she thought, sadly, it always came back to Mitch.

What an absolute plonker Marcus was, she considered; actually, she'd had a lucky escape. He was nothing but a nasty, two-timing, self-gratifying bastard. For one terrifying minute she thought he may come after her in the car, to say sorry, perhaps. Then she laughed to herself, dryly. As if he would.

Increasing her speed, she continued her way through the old streets of Roath, only seeing a few passers-by and the occasional car. Not many people would be out at this time on such a filthy night.

Once again, her thoughts strayed to Mitch. I wonder where he is now, she pondered, as she ran up the steps of the nurses' home, I wonder what he's doing...

Mitch was stretched out on his bed, the curtains drawn against the murky winter night. Two days of being spoiled, he thought, two days of good food, warmth, hot baths and no work – although he expected his father would be hoping he'd lend a hand with some early lambing at some point. His bedroom seemed a world away from the cold, sparsely furnished flat he shared with Charlie. Cosy without being chocolate-box pretty, the bedroom was pleasantly old-fashioned, with wooden floorboards, a patchwork quilt and a bookcase rammed with an eclectic variety of books. The only nod to contemporary living was the giant-sized poster of Kate Bush on the wall. He turned off the bedside lamp, closed his eyes and started to drift away into sleep...

She turned to face him and smiled, her beautiful pale face lighting up with pleasure at seeing him. Her auburn hair was floating about her slim body as she reached out to him, he fell into her welcoming arms...

He woke with a start, and looked at the clock. Midnight.

I'll have to find her, he vowed, I can't go on like this, I'll go to the ward again this week. Comforted by his decision, he rolled over and at last found peace in his dreams.

As she applied the Pond's cold cream to remove the make up from her rain-ravaged face, Julia reflected on the evening. I got away relatively unscathed, she considered, that could have gone badly wrong. Who would have thought someone as supposedly refined as Marcus Battencourt would be as abusive and coarse as he'd turned out to be. Wiping the remains of the cream from her cheeks, she remembered that from Tuesday she had three days annual leave. Brilliant, she thought. I'm going home, bugger all the men, I'm going home, home to Llanelli, to Llangennech, to my lovely family.

Thus cheered, she pulled on her dressing gown, found a couple of ten pence pieces in her purse and ran downstairs to the payphone in the hall.

Chapter Thirteen Trains that pass in the night

Julia and Mandy snuggled down in their seats, watching the lights of Cardiff disappear as the train hurtled its way westwards. It was pitch black outside, nothing visible through the dusty windows.

"Best keep our coats on," whispered Julia, "you never know who could be watching!" The pair had escaped from their early shifts as soon as they could, without bothering to change out of their uniforms, in order to catch the five past five Swansea train, and in Julia's case, onwards to Llanelli.

Mandy yawned. "I'm knackered. I daren't go to sleep, though, it's only twenty minutes to Bridgend and if you fall asleep as well, I'm stuffed." Echoing her yawn, Julia replied, "Who's meeting you ?"

"Nobody. My parents have gone on their second bloody honeymoon and my brother is working. So I'll catch the bus."

"Come home with me! Come on! If there's not much going on at your place, why not come back with me?" Julia grinned, pleased with her idea. "You can pay the excess to the ticket collector when he comes round."

Mandy looked doubtful. "Won't your parents mind? And where will I sleep? What about your sisters?"

"We'll sleep at my gran's next-door. I often do that. She's sweet, my Nana, she'll love it if we stay with her. And I can borrow my sister's Mini so I can show you around."

Mandy brightened. "Can you get me back to the station on Friday morning? I'm on a late on Friday."

"No problem! I'm off until next Monday but we can have a good time while you're down! You'd better get your ticket and your purse out fast in case Mr Happy the collector shows up!"

Mandy fumbled in her pocket, pulling out a selection of bits of paper, rummaging through them until she found her ticket.

"What's this?" Julia picked up a crumpled sheet of paper. "Bloody hell, Mands! It's your notes from handover! Good job you haven't written names, just the bed numbers! Hey – what does this mean? You've written T.T by a few of them. What's that mean? Is it some new renal condition I don't know about?"

Mandy giggled. "No, no, no! It stands for awkward, difficult patients – Total Twat."

They burst out laughing, causing the old man sitting across the way to smile at them indulgently.

The train raced along towards Swansea, stopping at Bridgend, then Port Talbot.

"Oh, isn't that lovely?" Mandy peered out of the window. "Look at all those lights! I didn't realise Port Talbot was so pretty! I've only ever driven past it in Dad's car, never been here by train. It's beautiful!"

"You're as bad as my Nana Cook." Julia remarked, dryly. "Those lights are the steel works! If you saw it in daylight, you'd just see miles of factory and heavy industry. Smelly City, we call it! But in the night it is transformed, I have to admit. Nana Cook calls it the Fairyland of South Wales, God bless her!" They continued their journey west, two young nurses who were both intent on leaving behind their busy city lives and their complicated romances, carrying them onwards to Carmarthenshire, to a slower, calmer place, where they could recharge their energies and maybe heal their broken hearts.

The small connecting train from Swansea to Milford Haven slowed to a stop at Gowerton, allowing commuters from offices in Cardiff and Swansea to hurry home to their various houses, before picking up speed again and crossing the Loughor Bridge. A shy half moon shone over the sea, looking at her reflection in the calm, still waters, and a string of lights twinkled over the bay in Penclawdd. Almost home, thought Julia dreamily, how I've missed it. As the train slowed down near Llanelli Station, the pair got up, dragging their bags from the overhead shelf.

Julia scanned the platform for her father, but the view was abruptly blocked by the arriving train from Carmarthen. Oh my God, she thought suddenly, that boy looks a bit like Mitch! The Swansea-bound train was almost empty, and she could see a dark head bent over a magazine, the hair falling forward over the reader's face. Infuriatingly, he did not raise his face...

She was jolted out of her reverie by the train coming to an abrupt stop, throwing the passengers forward into an undignified scramble for the door. Always comes back to Mitch, she thought sadly, picking up her case, would she never be able to forget him..?

"Daddy!" Julia dropped her suitcase on the platform and ran towards her father, who was patiently waiting for her, a big smile on his face. She threw herself into his outstretched arms and hugged him as hard as she could. "Oh, it's so good to see you!"

"Flippin' heck, Julia!" He extricated himself laughingly from Julia's embrace. "You're crushing me to death! And who is this you've brought with you? Why, if it isn't little Nurse Jacob from Bridgend!"

"She's Staff Jacob now, Daddy!" Julia reminded him. "We're terribly important and qualified now!"

"Hello, Mr Harry, lovely to see you again." Mandy grinned at him.

John Harry picked up both the suitcases and they trooped out from the station to the green Morris Marina which was waiting for them on the road.

The shiny new car, with its bright orange cushions in the back window, crawled out of the station and made its way through the town centre. Julia hadn't been home since Christmas. The fairy lights and the tree had disappeared from the Town Hall Square but the old Town Hall clock was still illuminated, and the stately old building looked as beautiful as ever. No matter how wonderfully exciting it was to live in Cardiff, Julia always loved coming home. Cardiff may be cosmopolitan, progressive and multi-cultural, but her home town was so relaxed; everyone was welcomed; Italians rubbed shoulders with Sikhs; Jewish, Polish and German families lived next-door to Welsh households of ancient lineage, and everybody got on. Racial prejudice seemed to have bypassed Llanelli.

The lights were on in the Harry house when they pulled up, Julia's mother waiting impatiently for her daughter's arrival on the doorstep of the 1930's semi, the prim little front garden as immaculate as ever, with pots of winter pansies and primroses in regimented order on the tiny lawn.

Home, thought Julia in relief, home at last.

"Pass the gravy, Rachel," Julia stretched across the table, "this is seriously tasty, Mammy! I haven't had a cooked dinner like this for yonks!"

"I'll second that," Mandy agreed, forking up a roast potato, "and thank you so much for letting me stay, Mrs Harry, especially without any warning."

Jean Harry beamed at the compliments. "Well, you can pay me back by doing the washing up!"
Julia feigned horror. "No! It's Sarah's turn! We're the guests tonight!"
And so the good natured bickering carried on between the three sisters, Mandy enjoying the banter as she wolfed the first decent meal she'd had in days.

Julia's grandmother smiled serenely at the top end of the table, content in the knowledge that all the little chicks were together once more, even if only for a short time.

"So have you met any nice young doctors yet?" Mrs Harry senior twinkled at Julia over her spectacles. "I'm sure they must be queueing up to ask you both for a date." Julia looked at Mandy swiftly, before replying.

"Doctors? You must be kidding! No indeed, Nana, we've no time for doctors, with us it's just work, work ,work. Isn't it Mandy?"

"Oh, yes, that's right," Mandy nodded in agreement, not particularly liking the way the conversation was going, "I'm waiting for Mr Right to come along, some rich managing director or someone like that, and definitely not anyone remotely connected with hospitals!"

If only they knew, thought Julia, looking down at her empty plate, how shocked they would be. A slow flush coloured her pale face, her mother would be horrified. The remaining trails of gravy on her plate resembled brown tears, reminding her of the sadness she'd left behind in Cardiff, she felt quite sick at the memory. Directing the conversation away from this dangerous territory, Julia looked hopefully at her older sister."Can I borrow the Mini tomorrow, Rachel? If I take you and Sarah to work first? And I'll fetch you as well?"

"Sure," Rachel agreed, "but I have to be in by half-past eight, mind, so we'll need to set off by a quarter past. St Mary's is at least fifteen minutes from here. You'll have to be up early." She gave Julia an old-fashioned look, finely honed after years of being the older, wiser, sister.

Julia and Mandy looked at each other in wry amusement. Up and about by a quarter past eight? That was practically a lie-in...

As the two young nurses had been transported westwards through the night, to Llanelli, Mitch had been travelling east. His train stopped at

135

Llanelli Station, but Mitch was too busy reading a music magazine to notice Julia and Mandy alighting on the platform opposite. His father had had to go to Carmarthen for a farmers' meeting, so had given Mitch a lift to catch the train. His other option would have been to travel to Newtown to catch a train from there and it would have taken ages. His compartment was almost empty, so he managed to stretch his long legs under the table and relax. Should he open the tin of Welshcakes now, he considered, or wait until he was back in the flat? His mother had loaded him up with food, he could hardly carry it all. As well as the Welshcakes there was a loaf of home-made bread, a Tupperware bowl full of cawl and a jar of home-made beetroot chutney. Then he imagined Charlie's eyes lighting up with delight at these goodies. Sod it, he thought, I'm starting the Welshcakes now!

He munched away in satisfaction, reading the magazine he'd bought in Smiths' as he ate. As he turned the page, his heart almost stopped. Christ, he thought, almost choking in excitement, this is about us! There was a small article about up and coming bands – and The Mitch Walker Band was listed! Coughing hard on the cake crumbs, he read it again.

"Keep your eyes and ears peeled for this new Welsh band, debut single due out shortly. One not to be missed!"

Yes, he grinned joyfully, we're on our way.

"Anything from the trolley, sir?" The plump little woman smiled down at him.

"Yes, I think I will! I'll have a can of cider, please." As he reached into his pocket for the money, he considered that this was one undisputed reason to celebrate.

Marcus Battencourt strode down the ward of Terence Adams, trying hard not to appear as though he was looking for her. Stupid bitch, he thought. Who the hell did she think she was, rejecting him like that. He caught sight of himself in the office window, and ran his fingers through his blond hair.

"Good morning, Dr Battencourt." Sister Winter handed him a set of notes. "New patient in bed three needs clerking, elective circumcision for tomorrow's list."

"Thanks, Sister." He accepted the notes, an assured smile on his face. "Haven't seen Staff Harry recently. Is she days off?"

Sister Winter chuckled knowingly. "Oh, you leave my young staff nurses alone, you wicked boy! Especially Julia Harry, she's as innocent as a baby, is that one, even though she's a great nurse." Marcus laughed in return, feeling no remorse whatsoever. She's still a fucking tease, he thought. Catching sight of the diminutive Aneira Thomas admitting the new patient in bed number three, all thoughts of Julia were suddenly eradicated from his mind. He watched her, in her too-big uniform, as she laboriously wrote the patient's details in the Kardex, her fluffy blond hair escaping the pins under her cap. Now that's an innocent little virgin if I ever saw one, he thought, lasciviously, and ripe for the plucking and fucking. He cleared his throat. She turned around, startled, her big blue eyes round with apprehension.

"Nurse Thomas," he murmured smoothly, having looked briefly at her name badge, "I wonder if you're free on Saturday night?"

Chapter Fourteen Camelot

The dank undergrowth smelled of dampness and decay, and the going was difficult due to the sodden ground. Despite being stripped of leaves, the trees still managed to block out any of the late afternoon light that struggled to filter through the heavy clouds. Cruel-looking branches reached out to pierce those unfamiliar with the path and even the birds were silent.

"Welcome to Troserch Woods." Julia grinned as her friend stumbled on a particularly muddy part of the path, cursing as her boots squelched in the sludge.

"Why have you brought us here?"

"Oh, Mandy, I thought you liked being spooked! Isn't it creepy!" Julia took Mandy's arm, shivering in the chilly atmosphere of the woodland.

"I couldn't agree more. Don't tell me it's haunted or something."

"Headless horseman, no less. The Headless Horseman of Goitre Wen!" Julia looked at Mandy slyly, then giggled at her friend's horror. "You'll believe anything, you will, you nutter!"

These woods certainly provide the perfect setting for any ghost story, thought Mandy nervously, you could get lost here and not be found for days...

The only sound they could hear was the rushing of the River Morlais as it hurried its swollen way to meet the Loughor river at its tidal reach. There was a sudden rustling in the bushes. Both girls jumped.

"Probably a squirrel or something," said Julia, none too certainly, then jumped again as a crow started screeching its raucous cry from the tree tops. Silence settled around them once more, the light fading every minute, the forestry becoming more sinister all the time.

She looked at her watch. "Time to go back to the car. It's quarter to four and we have to get Rachel at four o'clock."

"Do you believe in ghosts, Mands?" Julia panted slightly as they climbed the steep gradient back to the car.

Mandy looked surprised. "Why? Do you? I thought you were the eternal sceptic!"

"Well, a couple of weeks ago, when I was on nights, I could have sworn I saw something on Terence Adams."

"Saw something?"

"Yes, a nurse who wasn't really there, but I think she was wearing something old fashioned, a cloak possibly. At first I thought it was Maria, but you know the way your eyes play tricks on you on nights?" Julia sighed. "Maria said it was the Grey Lady. Although Sister Hunter - you know, Night Sister - said it was just my imagination." Julia's heart quaked at the memory.

"No way!" Mandy's eyes shone. "You saw the Grey Lady? How amazing is that? I've heard of her. Comforts the dying and stuff."

"Hmm." Talking about ghosts in the dim and chilly twilight no longer seemed such a good idea. "Maybe I was mistaken."

A twig snapped.

"What was that?" Mandy hissed, grabbing Julia's arm.

Julia swallowed. "No idea. But let's get the hell out of here..."

For a Thursday night, the Camelot was noisy and busy. Standing proudly on the corner near the Parish Church, it was full of twenty-somethings who were hell bent on having a good time. Billie-Jo Spears belted out a song from the jukebox and at seven o'clock the bar was packed with shelf-stackers from Tesco's, clerical staff from the Tax Office and exhausted trainee hairdressers from Murray Street. And Julia and Mandy.

"Let's put Bohemian Rhapsody on the jukebox," begged Mandy, "it's such a good value for money song, goes on for ages!"

"Pick another four, then, and pick five for me, you know what I like,"said Julia, getting out her purse, "because if we put fifty pence in, we'll get ten choices."

Mandy got up and wove her way through the crowd to the jukebox at the far end of the room, her curvy figure generating some admiring glances from a group of rugby players propping up the bar.

Good to be home, thought Julia, sipping her glass of Olde English cider, no hassle, no worries. She pulled the last cheese and onion crisp from the packet, hoping that Mandy wouldn't mind. As the disc slipped into action and Sultans of Swing started its familiar guitar intro, Mandy settled down once more next to her friend, tipping the empty crisp packet upside down in disappointment.

"So how did your date go with Casanova Battencourt, then? I forgot to ask you." Mandy drained her half a lager, and picked up the fresh drink which was waiting for her. Julia shook her head.

"A complete disaster. He was just after one thing, and when I didn't give in, he went absolutely nuts. Shouted and swore at me, called me horrible names."

"Oh God, no, I'm so sorry! What happened?" Mandy was suitably shocked. "I mean, he seems so refined."

"We had a takeaway, and some wine – I didn't get pissed, I can promise you – then he set the mood, you know, low lights, nice music, and we started kissing and things, and then when he asked me to go to bed with him, I told him no."

141

"Why not?" Mandy's eyes were like saucers.

"Mandy! I just didn't want to!"

"But he'd bought you a fancy meal in that restaurant, and the takeaway as well-"

Julia exploded."Mandy! How can you say that! Why should I go to bed with a bloke just because he's paying for stuff. I'm not a bloody prostitute! I'm not to be bought! I didn't fancy him. I thought I might have, but I didn't. There was no spark there, not like there was with..." Her voice trailed away miserably.

"Mitch?"

Julia nodded, sorrowfully. "I'm still not over him, Mands. He's in my thoughts all the time. Oh, why did I sleep with him?" She was on the verge of tears and her voice was getting louder.

"Ssh." Mandy patted her hand. "Don't cry, Julia, he's not worth a single tear. But let me ask you: did you sleep with Mitch because you wanted to? You really wanted to?"

Another nod.

"Then there's nothing wrong, nothing wrong at all, with two people who fancy each other like mad, going to bed together, as long as that is what they both want. How can that be wrong?"

"It can't be, I guess, when you put it like that. Oh, Mandy, it was so special with Mitch, so lovely. But I didn't want that with Marcus, and he turned so nasty." Julia sighed heavily.

"Sounds like you had a lucky escape." Mandy furtively lit a cigarette.

"That's what I said to myself. Why are you smoking?"

"Not allowed at home, not allowed in the nurses' home, so I take my chances when I can!" She giggled cheekily. "But I can assure you that Marcus would probably have dumped you pronto if you'd slept with him, and how awful would it have been afterwards, having to work with the bugger as well."

"Bloody terrible, I would have been mortified having to see him day after day."

"So look on the bright side. You were the one that got away, the one he didn't manage to seduce. Game, set and match to you! You know what the other staff nurses call him, don't you?"

"No, tell me."

"G.C.B." Mandy chuckled.

"G.C.B? What on earth does that stand for?"

"Golden Cock Boy. Mind you, I overheard Pat Gravelle from Theatre call him a B.C.S.D the other day!"

"Okay, spill the beans! What does that stand for?"

Mandy chortled. "Big Car Small Dick!"

Julia groaned, but managed to laugh. "So any news from Neil Hancock?"

Mandy scowled. "Neil Hand Cock I call him these days, makes me feel a bit better. Hand always in his pocket, fiddling with himself. I keep trying to imagine him taking the matter in hand in his bathroom, reading a porno mag and sitting on the loo."

Julia shrieked with laughter. "You're hysterical, you are! Your mind is like a sewer – no, it's like the sluice on a geriatric ward after a heavy shift!"

"But I still can't remember much about that evening." Mandy looked worried, a frown furrowing her pretty face.

"D'you think you and he, er..?" Julia didn't know quite how to put it.

"I think we probably did." Mandy lowered her voice to a whisper. "I was quite sore the next day, if you know what I mean, and I had to get some Nystatin as well."

"You got thrush?"

"Yes, as itchy as hell, but it's fine now. Doesn't say much for his technique, does it?" Mandy smiled weakly.

Julia wasn't sure how to respond to this, but felt she should say something."But did you want him to, er, you know? Did he ask or anything?"

Mandy looked close to tears. "I wish I could remember something. Anything. It's all a blank. I know you think I'm a bit free with my favours but I honestly thought I was just going there to have some photos taken, you know? I thought that if Neil thought I looked sexy and stuff, he'd ask me out properly. I didn't just go there just assuming I'd be having a quick shag."

Julia cringed at the crudeness of her words."He's better consigned to the hinterland of your memory bank, Mands."

Mandy sighed then laughed. "Oh, you do make me giggle with the way you put things, sometimes! You should write a book!"

Julia chuckled." Maybe I will, someday. Shall we move on? This may be the Camelot, but we aren't going to find a Sir Kissalot in here anytime soon."

Llanelly House loomed austerely in the dim light of the street lamps, as though disapproving of the girls' restored high spirits. The library was in complete darkness as they strolled past it. W.H. Smith did not merit a second glance from the pair, despite the latest bestsellers being spotlit in the window.

"Where are we going?" Mandy pulled her bomber jacket more tightly around her, ignoring the drunken compliments shouted at them by a couple of young boys sitting on a bench outside Marks and Spencers, drinking a flagon of cider between them.

"The Tavern. It shouldn't be too busy on a Thursday night. There's usually a DJ there as well, a bit of a disco."

"But I'm wearing jeans! And you've got your cords on! Will they let us in?"

"Course they will! This is Llanelli, you know!"

They turned left into a deserted Stepney Street before reaching the junction with Market Street, and arriving at their destination.

The Tavern was busy, music blaring out from the open door.

"All the girls are in pencil skirts, Julia! I knew we'd be underdressed!" Mandy looked in despair at all the local girls wearing tight skirts, black satin. white P.V.C and even faux suede.

"Don't be daft, c'mon, let's go in." And as predicted, there was no objection from the genial bouncer on the door.

The dance floor was packed with the youth of Llanelli, gyrating away to I Will Survive. The David Cassidy lookalike DJ was enjoying his position of power at the turntable, flirting and smiling with the girls, charming them into doting admiration. Randy Bagger hasn't changed much, thought Julia in amusement. The lights flashed pink, yellow and green, the disco ball spun dazzlingly overhead and the the strobe lights pulsed intermittently; all the while the hot, sweaty bodies continued to bounce around the dance floor. You'd never think this was in the middle of Market Street in Llanelli, she considered.

"Shall we have a dance?" Mandy looked hopefully at Julia.

"Maybe in a bit. Let's get a drink, shall we? Although I just want lemonade, I've got to drive you to the station in the morning."

145

Left alone while Mandy went to the bar, Julia looked about her. Nobody here I know any more, she thought sadly, no old school friends. They had all left Llanelli, gone these past three years and not returned, living in places like London, Reading and Manchester. She wondered what they were all doing now...

"Hello, Julia." Someone tapped her on the shoulder.

Swinging round, Julia came face to face with a smirking blast from the past. Paul.

He smiled broadly. "You're looking well." That arrogant swagger was still there. "How's life?"

"I-I'm fine, Paul, thank you. And you?" Julia could feel her face burning. And yet, she thought, what had she ever seen in him? He'd put on weight and had developed a beard, neither of which suited him very much.

"Life's good." He grinned, leering at her tight, black sweater. "You've, er, filled out a bit, haven't you?"

"What on earth are you talking about?"

"Never used to have tits like that when I was with you. Must be on the pill, eh?" He was practically drooling.

"Oh, just get lost, Paul. You obviously haven't changed much."

"Problems, Julia?" Mandy was back with the drinks, glaring at this newcomer, who seemed to be causing her friend some degree of grief.

"This is Paul, Mandy. My ex from long ago."

The tension of the moment intensified when they were joined by one of the pencil-skirt set.

"Who is this, then, Paul?" A small dark haired girl edged her way into the conversation. grabbing his arm proprietorially, looking at the other two girls with hostility written all over her face.

146

"Nobody important." He scornfully turned away. "C'mon Andrea, let's get you a drink."

"Jesus, what a complete arse!" Mandy's jaw was dropping in disbelief. "You were well shot of him!"

Julia smiled serenely. "Yes, I know. But it's taken me until now to realise it. Let's have that dance, Mandy, and then we'll go home and leave the likes of Paul and Andrea to their own devices..."

Brushing her burnished hair before she went to bed, Julia mulled over the past few days. It had been so good to get away, but Monday was looming nearer and nearer, and she'd be back on the ward before she knew it. I need a complete change, she thought, glancing over at an untroubled, sleeping Mandy, who was snoring gently at the wall side of the big double bed. I can't afford a holiday, I can't afford to buy a car, or to take out a loan. But I want to move on, put all this behind me. Suddenly, a masochistic thought stole into her head as she plaited her thick, heavy hair. I know, she thought, rebelliously, I'll go down to Anthony Lee's salon in the morning, after I drop Mandy, I'll show them. I'm going to chop this lot off.

With hope in his heart and determination in his soul, Mitch marched once more along the main corridor of the Infirmary. Five thirty. All the office staff had gone home, and it was relatively quiet. A tall, heavily built porter was lumbering towards him, pushing an elderly woman in a wheelchair. Richie. He glanced suspiciously at Mitch as he went past, as if trying to remember where he's seen him before. At least he won't be hanging about on the ward, thought Mitch in relief. A couple of important looking senior nurses wearing starched, frilly hats passed him, looking disdainfully down their noses at the slightly untidy, yet good-looking youth who was, for some inexplicable reason, wandering around *their* hospital when it wasn't visiting time. What *was* it about hospitals that made him feel so nervous? Maybe it was the smell of disinfectant, or the

147

way everyone else seemed to know exactly where they were going and what they were doing? He could never work in a place like this, he thought, he couldn't stand the hierarchy stuff and the almost militaristic way people behaved. As he reached the top of the staircase, he felt a wave of panic wash over him. What should he say to her? Would she hate him for not turning up at Queen Street? But this time he had come prepared. He felt in his pocket for the carefully folded up letter, which he had sealed in an envelope.

Dear Julia,

I don't know when you'll read this, you may never read it, but if you do it's because you weren't on duty when I called at the ward. I have no means of contacting you – no phone number, no address. I asked the ward sister (the Indian one) but she wouldn't give it to me. I can understand why – I could have been anyone, a serial killer or anything!

I am so so sorry I was late that day at the station. Please can you find it in your heart to forgive me. I haven't been able to stop thinking about you. This is the first love letter I have ever written, by the way.

You know where I live, where I work. Please get in touch.

Mitch. Xxx

Taking a deep breath, he pushed open the heavy doors of Terence Adams, scanning the ward for Julia.

For once the place seemed calm and quiet. The only nurses he could see were some students and a tall, African auxiliary who was emptying the catheter bags. He knocked tentatively on the office door.

"Come in." He recognised the sweet, Indian accent. Pushing the door open, he held his breath. He felt this was his last chance.

148

Daksha Patel wasn't alone. She and Sister Winter were deep in conversation , a pile of notes on the desk. Both nurses smiled at him.

"Hello, young man." The older woman greeted him warmly. "You look a lot better than when I saw you last time. To what do we owe this pleasure? Did you leave something behind on the ward after you were discharged?" Mitch's face was burning.

"Only his heart!" Daksha Patel giggled, her Malteser eyes twinkling. "You were here recently, weren't you? Looking for Julia Harry?"

"Um...yes. That's why I'm here." Mitch shuffled from foot to foot. "Is she here?" There, I've said it, he thought, dreading their reply.

"Well, goodness me, a lot of people seem to be looking for Julia Harry these days!" Sister Winter looked at him in mock annoyance. Let the young buck sweat a bit, she thought.

Mitch looked dismayed. "Someone else has been looking for her as well?"

"Talk of the devil." muttered the senior sister, as the door was flung open wider and Marcus Battencourt swept importantly into the office, brushing Mitch aside. Aloud, she continued, " Our little Staff Harry is on annual leave and won't be back until next week."

"Um...can you give her this?" Mitch handed her the folded envelope, quite crumpled by now. "And say Mitch called by?"

Marcus Battencourt glanced contemptuously at him, shoving past him roughly to reach for the notes trolley. "When you've *time*, Sister, I'd like an ECG ordered for the patient in the cubicle. If you're not too busy." He stomped angrily out of the room, his normally bland features twisted in annoyance.

"Ooh-ooh!" Daksha chortled in delight. "Seems you have a rival, better get your skates on there!" Both women burst out laughing.

"Well, thanks anyway." Mitch backed towards the door.

149

"Don't you worry, Mr Walker." Sister Winter was always good at remembering names. "I'll make sure she gets the letter." Smiling maternally at him, she got up to see him out. Lowering her voice, she added, "I'll make damned sure."

Mandy settled back into her seat as the InterCity 125 sped along from Llanelli to Cardiff. At least there'd been no change of trains at Swansea, at least she was facing forwards and there were only a few people in her carriage. Lucky Julia, she thought wistfully, such a wonderful, close family, such a safe security net into which to fall in troubled times. The train slowed to a halt at Neath. Only a few elderly people got on. Closing her eyes, she pondered on the upsetting events of the previous couple of weeks. She'd always enjoyed herself with boys, had never looked for more than a fun night out, maybe an enjoyable romp between the sheets and a swift, sweet goodbye in the morning. Never feeling guilty or ashamed about her bedtime games, Mandy felt relaxed and confident in her sexuality. But to have been treated the way Neil Hancock had treated her, well, this was a different matter. Perplexed, she tried to put it out of her mind, but it was always there, lurking in the background, like a sly monster mocking her, taunting her with something she couldn't quite understand. What have I done wrong, she wondered, what the hell happened that night..?

"I'm afraid we're fully booked this morning, nothing available until Monday." The salon receptionist smiled in fake regret at Julia, her false nails drumming a beat on the appointments book, in time to "Heart of Glass" which was blaring out of the radio nearby.

"Oh no...I'll be back in Cardiff by then. Is there nothing available at all? I don't mind if Mr Lee can't see me, it's only a straightforward cut." Julia took the elastic band out of her hair and shook it loose, generating an immediate interested response and gasps of admiration from the stylists.

"Julia, my darling!" The man himself rushed over to her and hugged her. "Have you finally decided to let me work wonders with this fabulous mane of yours?" His dark eyes flashed in excitement and he stood back to look at her properly, before running his skilled fingers through her amber locks.

"I only want it cut short, Anthony, nothing special." The other stylists caught their breath in horror. "I am a nurse, after all, so it's either long enough to put up or quite short. And I have decided that at twenty-one it's time to get rid of it." She said it so bravely that Anthony Lee had to hide a smile.

"I can get one of the juniors to do that, then I can re-style it, if you want?"

"That will be fine." Her reply was decisive, although it took every ounce of courage. There was a collective sigh of disappointment from the staff, as a young trainee guided her to a vacant chair, draping a nylon cape over her. Regarding her reflection in the mirror, Julia saw a pale, tired face with masses of long red hair cascading over her shoulders – about to be chopped off for good. The smell of hair lacquer made her eyes water and the drone of the hairdryers almost obliterated the music from the radio. Maybe Mitch wouldn't recognise her any more without her long hair. Maybe it would also deter the likes of Marcus Battencourt for good measure. Great, fantastic.

I wonder what it's like to be a hairdresser, she pondered, idly, watching Anthony Lee as he sashayed in his platform shoes from client to client, his tight, high waisted trousers leaving little to the imagination. The other stylists were all women, every one of them singing along to the next song being played on Radio One. Julia glanced up at the huge posters of models on the walls; would her hair look like any of those styles, she considered. Maybe an elfin look would suit her, or a severe, cropped style? Her daydreaming was disturbed by the appearance of Miss Denise, a stunningly pretty junior stylist with shining blond hair. She brandished the scissors.

"Are you sure about this, honey? Your hair is to die for." She looked sympathetically at Julia.

"I'm sure," replied Julia with a conviction she didn't really feel. "It's time for a change, you know what I mean?"

"Man trouble?" Miss Denise started brushing Julia's hair lovingly and admiringly.

She nodded, miserably. "You could say that."

"They're not worth it, chick. Give us a smile, honey, it'll make me feel a lot better about what I'm being asked to do!" She continued her brushing, trying to build up the courage to carry out this act of what she considered to be utter brutality.

"And that was Donna Summer with MacArthur Park." The DJ's nasal twang rose above the last few bars of the song. *"But before we have the weather forecast, we have a new release. Listen to this, you guys, it's really quite something, all the way from Wales on the Cosmo record label. I give you "Julia," by the Mitch Walker Band!"*

Julia's eyes nearly popped out of her head. She stood up abruptly, the protective cape falling to the floor.

"STOP!"

Miss Denise stepped back in amazement. All the other stylists stopped in their tracks and stared at Julia, who was standing there as though in shock.

"Turn the hairdryers off!" The urgency in her voice elicited an immediate acquiescence. A respectful silence settled over the salon.

Julia listened, unable to believe her ears as the melody played, and Mitch's beautiful voice sang the following lyrics,

Julia, my lover, won't you come back to me
152

You know I need you now,

Like the desert needs the rain,

I miss you so,

Julia, you're my life, you're the star in my sky, and you know why -

Give me one more try...

Miss Denise looked at Julia, astonished. The music continued.

Julia has left me yet I try in vain

To ease the misery and wipe out the pain;

And I wonder where Julia is tonight

Lord, I want you, Julia,

Like the darkness craves the light.

Julia remained motionless, tears pouring down her cheeks, her heart felt as though it would burst.

"Is the song about you?" Miss Denise whispered, reluctant to spoil the moment. Julia slowly nodded, her face ablaze with sheer happiness. Everyone listened intently to the radio, until the very end.

"Well," murmured Miss Denise in awe, "I reckon he is worth it after all."

"Sorry, everyone! I've changed my mind! I have to go now! Please forgive me!" Hugging an astounded Miss Denise and a bemused Anthony, she grabbed her coat and bag and ran to the door.

"I'll be back for a trim soon!" And she was gone.

"It must be love." Anthony Lee shook his head, in wonderment.

Chapter Fifteen A step too far

"But I have to go back to Cardiff today!" Julia regarded her mother's disappointed face in alarm. "Something's come up – oh, please, Mammy, don't be angry!"

Jean Harry looked away, pretending to clean the draining board, trying hard to hide her frustration. "I'm not angry, Julia, it's just that as you were home for a few days, I've asked my mother and your cousins over for a meal tomorrow night – Nana Cook hasn't seen you since Christmas, and goodness knows when you last saw Tracey and Joanne."

"But I was supposed to be getting the seven o'clock train tomorrow night, anyway!" Julia could feel exasperation mounting rapidly. She just wanted to get to Mitch as soon as she possibly could.

"I know, I realise you're on an early shift on Monday, and the Sunday trains leave a lot to be desired, so Daddy said he'd drive you back on Sunday evening."

"Okay." There was nothing more to be said, without appearing terribly ungrateful and mean. "What time will that be?" Maybe she'd still be able to run over to Mitch's flat after she'd been dropped off?

Mrs Harry sighed. "Daddy's working a day shift, he'll be home from the fire station by ten past six or so, then you can go straight away." Providing there's no call-out at half past five, she thought privately, her husband was regularly delayed because of emergencies.

"Right-o. Thank you, Mammy." Julia hugged her mother, resignation damping down her previous excitement. Seeing Mitch would have to wait until Monday, after work. A few days more shouldn't make much difference. "I'm popping over to Nana Harry's, okay? I said I'd help her sort out some old photos and things."

Mrs Harry senior lived alone in the house directly next-door to her son and daughter-in-law. Both properties were identical, except that the old lady's house was about thirty years in the past, with old, dark furniture, turkey red rugs and net curtains at the windows, yet filled with the smell of lavender Pledge, home-made cakes and love.

The morning was bright and sunny, the emerging daffodils danced and swayed in the late winter breeze as Julia opened the front door.

"It's Julia, Nana! I'm just going upstairs then I'll give you a hand with the photos!"

"Lovely, cariad! I'll put the kettle on." Her grandmother's voice echoed through the sunlit passage.

Julia ran up the stairs, also carpeted in turkey red, and threw herself onto the pink, candlewick bedspread, looking out at the sun shining on the River Morlais as it wound its way sleepily to the estuary.

Her world suddenly seemed alright again. She should have known, deep down, that Mitch hadn't used her, she should have trusted her innermost feelings, they were usually right. But her stubborn pride had overcome everything and she'd allowed herself to get sucked into a mire of self-pity and outrage. She couldn't wait to see him. A flock of starlings swooped and dived in perfect unison over the river; Julia smiled. She always thought they should be collectively known as a fuss of starlings, on account of all the racket they made. Rolling onto her back, she closed her eyes, feeling the heat of the sun through the window warm her pale face. How intoxicating and unbelievable was it that Mitch had written a song about her? Unwilling as yet to share this with her sisters, she hugged her secret to herself, enjoying the complete romance of it all. She was his muse, she supposed, and he had written a song for a nurse, a song about her.

"Julia, cariad, I'm pouring the tea!"

Julia swung her legs over the bed. "On my way, Nana, and I'll have a piece of toast as well!"

Chi-Chi's bar was quiet for a Saturday night. The subdued lighting and subtle background music seemed the epitome of sophistication to Aneira, as she self-consciously sipped her shandy.

"So, are you from this neck of the woods?" Marcus Battencourt was effortlessly elegant in white chinos and a pale lemon polo shirt, a white sweater thrown casually around his shoulders. He leaned against a pillar, pouring himself a glass of wine from the half-bottle he had just bought.

"Er, no, I'm from Ystradgynlais." Aneira blushed deeply, as though embarrassed at hailing from a village with such an unpronounceable name.

Marcus laughed. "Where the hell is that?"

"Um, the Swansea Valley."

"Ah, I see." He didn't see really, and wasn't that interested either, but he could put on a good show when necessary. "So why come all the way to Cardiff to train? Why not go to Swansea? Singleton, for example?"

"My sister trained here, and she's a staff nurse, now. I'm sort of following in her footsteps." She laughed, nervously.

Marcus looked down at her with a slight degree of affection. She certainly looked different out of that over-sized uniform, her fair hair loose, cascading in frothy curls over her small shoulders. Little Aneira was actually very pretty indeed, in her pink angora jumper and tight blue jeans. It would be like shagging the fairy off the Christmas tree.

"Well, hello there!" Marcus's callous thoughts were rudely interrupted by a slap on the back, which heralded the arrival of Neil Hancock, popping up like a pantomime demon, deeply tanned, his dark brown eyes sparkling with mischief. "You've descended to the ranks of first years, now, eh, Battencourt?" He laughed patronisingly.

Aneira looked down at her feet, mortified.

"Enough of your mockery, Hancock." Marcus winked at his friend. "Aneira and I were just enjoying a quiet drink. It's refreshing to find an innocent young girl, these days, don't you think?" As he toyed playfully with a strand of her hair. Aneira didn't know where to put herself. She wasn't sure if they were being serious or if she was being teased.

"A very pretty, innocent young girl, I have to say." Neil leered at her appreciatively, his wicked eyes lingering a fraction of a second too long on her angora-covered breasts. "I'm an amateur photographer, you know." He put his hand on her shoulder. "Would you let me take some photos of you one day? I can just see you in white, your hair all wafting about, a sort of spiritual look, you know?"

Marcus struggled to keep a straight face. "Enough of your poaching, old bean." He removed Marcus's hand from Aneira's quivering shoulder. "Now push off, like a good chap. You're cramping my style!"

"If you insist." Neil turned to go, but not before he took Aneira's tiny hand and planted a protracted kiss on it. "Au revoir, ma cherie. And don't forget the offer of the photo shoot!" He flashed a wide smile at her, revealing brilliantly white teeth, then headed for a group of older women in the far corner.

Marcus returned his attentions to Aneira. "Take no notice of Hancock, he's a right womaniser! So, getting back to us. I don't want to rush things, we'll finish our drinks and I'll drop you off at the nurses' home in the Infirmary, that's where you live, yes?"

Aneira nodded. "You seem to know an awful lot about me," she giggled, uncertainly.

"I make it my business." He looked over his shoulder, trying to see what progress Neil Hancock was making with his new prey. Focussing once again on his own target, he stroked Aneira's cheek. "But for now, we'll take tiny baby steps, yes?" She nodded again, relieved, having felt out of her depth in this upmarket environment. "I'll drop you off, and make a date for some time next week? And you can come back to my place, we can get a takeaway and watch a film. How does that suit you?"

"That sounds lovely." Smiling gratefully up at him, she wondered what on earth he saw in her. She was nothing like all the other women in the bar, who seemed so gorgeously sophisticated and worldly wise, with their painted lips, high heels and perfect hair. He seemed so kind as well. She was a very fortunate girl, she thought.

His voice dropped to a whisper, slipping his arm around her waist. "But let's keep this between ourselves, yes? Our own special secret. We don't want the hospital gossips wagging their tongues about us, do we?"

She shook her head, horrified at the thought of being the subject of any rumours or speculation on the ward.

"Let's head for home, then, sweetie pie." He propelled her towards the door, putting her coat over her shoulders. "I'll take care of you, you can trust me, you know."

She thought her heart would burst with happiness.

Five to four. Surely to God the lates should be back from break by now? Julia anxiously re-arranged the Kardex and tidied up the office desk.

"Um, Staff?" A breathless voice piped up from the doorway. Aneira. "Is there any chance I can swap with someone for Friday? I'm down for a late but I've, er, got to go out. If I ask one of the second years to change, would that be okay?" Hope was written all over her sweet little face.

Julia smiled, indulgently. "Aren't you getting ready to go home? It's four o'clock! Yes of course you can swap. Let me know if you're successful and I'll change it on the rota. Anything special? A hot date?" She winked, teasingly.

159

Aneira blushed. "Er, no, nothing special. Thanks, Staff." And she fled, grabbing her cardigan, before Julia could ask any more awkward questions.

The ward door opened, and Sister Winter, a third year student and miserable Maggie Hubert strolled in, chattering away, seemingly in no great hurry.

"Sister, can I go now, it's five past four? Everything's in order, the post-op obs have been done and I've put the medicine charts here on the desk ready for the post-op analgesics." She handed over the keys.

"Off you go, Staff. You got a hot date or something?" Sister Winter grinned. "Oh! I almost forgot! A chap called by last week and left a note for you." She rummaged in the bottom drawer and pulled out the crumpled note Mitch had left. Everyone stared at Julia, as though expecting her to open it in front of them.

"Cheers, Sister!" Julia took the letter, triumphantly, grinning in particular at a furious Maggie Hubert and brushing past Marcus Battencourt in her hurry to escape the ward. She dashed into the staff cloakroom, locked the door and tore it open. She read the words aloud, a lump in her throat. How could she have doubted him? Euphoria surged through her, she wanted to laugh loudly, she wanted to announce to the world "Mitch Walker loves me! And I love Mitch Walker!" Gleefully she kissed the note, then read it again, as if trying to memorise every single precious word. She couldn't wait to see him, to tell him how much she'd missed him, how much she loved him...

As she folded it up and put it in her pocket, she considered that he must have suffered too, maybe as much as she had. But now everything was going to be alright.

Back in the office, Sister Winter was keen to divert attention away from the departing Julia.

"Ah, Dr Battencourt. Can you write up some pre meds, please? And I just need to check our stock levels of Omnopon,." She opened the controlled drugs cabinet, leaving a sulky Marcus Battencourt standing in the doorway, watching a buoyant Julia walking swiftly down the corridor, pulling the pins from her hair and shaking loose her long, russet locks, as she went.

That bloody bitch Julia Harry, he thought in irritation, the one that got away.

It may have been a pleasant evening, still light and sunny, but Julia had no time to spare. She needed to get to the Royal College before five, and it was a quarter past four now. An old man at the bus stop outside St Agnes' Church touched his cap at her. "Lovely day, nurse, innit?"

Bugger, thought Julia as the number 47 came to a halt in front of her, is it that obvious? She supposed the flat black shoes and black tights gave the game away, really.

"Greyfriars Road, please!" She fished in her purse for the right change.

"Well, there's Welshie you are, innit? Where you from, then?" The cheerful driver gave her the ticket.

Julia was tempted to say Wales, but the driver was only being kind. "Llanelli, I'm from down west." She took her ticket and sat down in one of the front seats. Pulling out a tiny hand mirror from her bag, she hastily applied a little more eyeliner and used her finger to smear some apricot gloss on her lips. Shit, she thought, did I wash my hands before I left the ward? Ah, well, she considered, too late now. Then she pulled out the letter again. As she re-read it, a blissful smile spread across her face, putting more of a glow on it than any make up could ever achieve. She watched the hustle and bustle of the city centre, people rushing everywhere, always in a hurry...but she was in a hurry herself, this afternoon, she was going to see Mitch very soon. Her heart was thumping away so hard, she felt sure that the woman behind her could hear it. Her mouth was dry, hastily she searched in her bag for some Polos – just in case, she thought.

161

"Hello. Can you tell me where I can find Mitch Walker?"

The miserable-looking receptionist glared at her from behind large, pink-rimmed glasses. "He's in General Office." She looked as though she was chewing a wasp.

"Where's that?" Julia was quite out of breath now, having run all the way from the bus stop.

"Down there." Miss Scowly-Face nodded her head towards some double doors on the left. "What do you want him for anyway?" But her question remained unanswered, as Julia had already bolted for the doors.

The office was noisy, the phones were going constantly and there was a happy buzz of conversation. Julia looked desperately around for Mitch. Where was he? Then suddenly, she set eyes on a tiny blond girl, her head bent industriously over a computer. Aneira? What on earth could she be doing here?

"Ahem. Hello?"

The blond girl looked up. Ah, thought Julia, not Aneira at all.

"Is Mitch Walker around?" Her hands were sweating and her cheeks were on fire.

The blond girl smiled. "I'll call him for you. He's only in the photocopying room." She walked over to an open door. "Mitch! Someone to see you!"

"Hang on, Alison! Just on the last ten copies!" His voice could be heard just above the noise of the typewriters and general din of the office.

Alison returned to her desk. "He hates photocopying, he'll do anything to get out of it." Her tone was friendly and warm. "I'm Alison, by the way." She extended her hand.

"I'm Julia." She took her hand tentatively, then registered the shock on Alison's face.

"Julia!" Alison's voice was a mere whisper, her eyes like saucers. "Oh my God! You're *Julia? The* Julia?!" People nearby stopped talking and stared.

"All done, I'm not doing another bloody copy again this week, and that's final!" Mitch emerged from the photocopying room, a bundle of forms in his arms. He glanced up from his armful of papers and saw her standing there, her old green duffel coat tightly belted, her long hair untidily pushed back over her ears, her gentle face anxious and uncertain – and she had never looked more beautiful.

"Jesus *Christ!*" The papers were unceremoniously dropped onto the floor, and he stood silently, unable to believe his eyes. "Am I seeing things? Is it really you?"

Julia nodded shyly. Mitch approached her slowly, as if in a dream, his arms outstretched. "Come here, my gorgeous girl, come here." And he pulled her into his arms, buried his head in her shoulder and whispered, "I love you, I love you so much."

"I love you too, Mitch. It's been a horrible few weeks. I'm so glad I heard your record on the radio, so glad I've read your letter." Her grey eyes were shining with tears of joy, and he drew her closer still, and kissed her tenderly, passionately, endlessly. They kissed on and on, oblivious to the cheers of the office staff, and their standing ovation, and the sour face of the receptionist as she popped her head around the door to see what all the fuss was about.

They meandered back through the streets of Cardiff, saturated with their love for each other, having no thought for anything, only their rapturous elation. They seemed a world apart from the office workers and commuters who were rushing for their buses and trains; they were completely wrapped up in their own little world, a symbiotic entity.

As they wandered past the Sherman Theatre, the sun was setting behind them and the light was fading. He pulled her onto a nearby bench, putting his arms around her.

"I've dreamed of this moment so many times over the past few weeks." He stroked her hair, tenderly. "You have bewitched me, you wicked woman. I've hardly thought of anything else."

"I was besides myself," she replied, "I honestly thought you'd dumped me. I don't think I've ever been so sad in my entire life. I tried to put it behind me, move on and stuff, but I just couldn't."

"With that doctor?" Mitch asked, wryly.

Julia reddened. There was no point denying it. "Yes, I went on a date with him, out of sheer bloody-mindedness more than anything else. But it was awful, he was awful. And nothing happened, if you know what I mean."

He hugged her closer. "I understand. Christ, he made me feel so bloody jealous. He was on the ward when I delivered the letter, the look he gave me, Jesus! And your ward sister was stirring things up as well! Her and that Indian sister, they were having a right old laugh about it. But I got the distinct impression that they were on my side. He's a bit of a plonker, isn't he?"

"He most definitely is." Julia snuggled closer to him. "But I don't want to talk about him, now. I'm just glad, relieved, happy, that we're together. But something is bothering me, Mitch."

"What?" His face was all concern.

"Who was that blond woman? The one with the flashy car?" She looked up at him anxiously.

"Oh, you mean Steph!" Mitch laughed. "She's the woman who signed us up, from the record company. She's old enough to be my mother!"

"Ah, I see!" The relief in her voice was evident. "God, I'm so glad we're here together now. I was thinking of you all the time, I kept imagining I

164

was seeing you everywhere. I even thought I saw you on the opposite train when my train was pulling in to Llanelli!"

He squeezed her hand gently. "It probably was me on that train, I was going back to Cardiff. If only I'd have realised you were so close – I'd have jumped right off my train and grabbed you – like this!" And he pulled her towards him again, kissing her passionately, to the amusement of an old lady walking a pug nearby.

"So what do we do now?" Julia came up for air.

"Well, Charlie is going out at seven, he's meeting a girl and going to the flicks or something. So..?"

"That's pretty convenient!" She grinned from ear to ear. "But I must advise you, Mr Walker, that I have come straight from work, and I feel honour bound to inform you that, as a nurse, I have an embarrassing problem."

"What's that?"

"My feet."

"Your feet?" Mitch was nonplussed.

"They smell, they stink! They're atrocious! I've been on my feet since seven o'clock this morning, and I haven't even changed my shoes. So be prepared for a nuclear fallout!" And she burst out laughing.

"C'mon," he chuckled, "let's go home."

Aneira stared in fascination at the lava lamp in the corner of the lounge, changing from green to blue to red. Marcus's house was so different to her small, terraced house back home in Ystradgynlais. Big, cream sofas and a beige carpet rendered the room luxurious and inviting; there was even a drinks table, supporting premium brands of whisky, gin and vodka. How wonderful it must be to live like this...

"Red wine or another glass of white?"

Startled out of her daydream, she called back, "Um, could I have a glass of lemonade, please? I don't really drink much."

Marcus popped his head around the door of the kitchen, a bland smile on his face. "Sure, of course, just give me a sec."

Aneira settled back into the squashy sofa, still unable to believe her luck at getting a second date with someone like Marcus Battencourt. She hadn't been able to eat much of her Indian takeaway, she was too nervous and apprehensive. What if he tried to kiss her? He'd only pecked her on the cheek when he'd dropped her off the other night. She hoped there was no chicken stuck between her teeth. And what if her breath smelled of curry? Surreptitiously she fumbled in her bag for the tiny bottle of Apple Blossom scent, stuck out her tongue and dabbed some of the perfume onto it. She winced – disgusting. But better to suffer than to be humiliated by having halitosis. Feeling pleased with herself at having remembered the medical term from her last essay, she fluffed out her hair and waited for Marcus to return. Briefly closing her eyes – she was feeling quite drowsy - she wondered what her friends back home in the village would say if they could see her now? Being entertained by a doctor, given wine and being driven around in his sports car? They would be surprised, she reckoned, and jealous. She was definitely feeling sleepy now, and failed to prevent an enormous yawn from developing.

"I'm not that boring, surely." Laughing, Marcus plonked himself next to her, handing her a glass of lemonade.

"Oh, no, not at all!" She took the glass from him. "I was just feeling a bit tired, that's all. I've been up since six and I didn't sleep that well last night, I was too..." She stopped, embarrassed.

"Excited?" He finished for her, grinning complacently. She looked away, feeling foolish. To disguise her discomfiture she took a big gulp of the fizzy drink.

"Thirsty?"

166

She nodded. "I think Indian food can be quite salty."

"Drink up then, there's plenty more." He watched approvingly as she drained the glass. "That's my girl."

He moved closer to her, putting his arm around her shoulders. "You're frightfully attractive, Angharad."

"My name's Aneira," she whispered, mesmerised by his intense gaze.

"Yes, that's what I meant. Bloody Welsh names!" He laughed softly. "I don't think you realise just how attractive you are. May I kiss you?"

It's going to happen, she thought in joyful terror, he;s going to kiss me. Her small, pink mouth opened almost involuntarily as his lips met hers, welcoming his probing tongue and responding with enthusiasm.

This is going really well, Marcus thought, she's like a little lamb to the slaughter, should only take me a quarter of an hour to get her really loosened up. His hands stole around to her tiny but perfectly formed breasts. She made a feeble attempt to resist, but quickly surrendered to his insistence. She felt so relaxed, as though she was floating on air. His hand moved south and started to creep up her leg, under her denim skirt, seeking gratification, easing her slim, child-like thighs apart as he started to pull down her ribbed tights.

"Let me get to fantasy land, let me pleasure you," he murmured, pushing his fingers into her lacy knickers, "I want you so badly." He started to ease her knickers down.

"Mustn't do this," she mumbled, groggily, "I don't think we should..." She was seeing two of everything now, Marcus's voice seemed to be coming from miles away.

He put a finger to her lips."Hush, my angel. You know you want this, come on, let's go to bed. Let Doctor Battencourt take you to heaven." He pulled her to her feet, intending to lead her upstairs, but to his horror she collapsed like a rag doll onto the carpet, completely lifeless and as pale as death.

"Hey! Wake up!" He slapped her face lightly, and prised open her eyelids. But there was no reaction and her pupils were like pin points. Alarmingly, her face and lips were ghastly pale and her breathing was shallow.

"Shit, fuck, oh my fucking God!" Panicking, he checked her breathing then lifted her up off the floor. Grabbing his car keys he carried her outside and bundled her limp form in to the car.

As he sped away, he cursed his stupidity. "You fucking idiot, Battencourt. You've gone a step too far this time!"

Chapter Sixteen Dangerous secret

"HELP!" He was running as fast as he could through the ambulance entrance of C.C.I's Casualty. It was as if he was in a nightmare, his legs felt like lead and he could hardly get his words out. Where the hell were the porters when you needed them?

"Help! I need help here!" Thank God Aneira was as light as a feather or he'd never have been able to carry her so quickly and easily from the car.

"Bring her over here!" The senior sister was quick to appear on the scene, already drawing the curtains around one of the trolleys in the emergency assessment area.

"I found her outside the main entrance, Sister." Marcus panted as he placed Aneira's unconscious body onto the trolley. "Pissed or something, I think. Can't get a response, but she's breathing okay."

"Doctor Battencourt?" The sister recognised him in surprise. "Well, good job you found her, you of all people. Nurse Howard!" A tall second year appeared at the bottom of the trolley.

"Yes, Sister Peters?"

"Bleep the reg, quickly, and ask Staff Dixon to admit the facial laceration, oh, and fetch the resus trolley – just in case..."she added under her breath. "Who is she?" She put Aneira into the unconscious position and removed the pillow. The girl looked no more than a twelve year old child lying there.

Marcus had been dreading this question, but there seemed no point in lying, he'd only get found out once someone recognised her. "I think she's one of the students from T. A., er, Thomas I think her surname is."

Sister Peters swiftly checked the comatose girl's pulse and blood pressure. "One of our own students, eh? Well, I'll contact Terence Adams once this little lass is stable and on the ward." She looked up at an ashen Marcus. "We'll take over from here, thanks, Doctor Battencourt." She glanced curiously at him. "Are you okay? You've gone quite pale. But don't worry. We'll let her know about her good Samaritan when she comes round."

"Er – okay. Right then. I'll be off." Sweating profusely under her searching scrutiny he turned and left as quickly as he respectably could. She'll be okay, he kept telling himself, There's no real damage done. How was I to know she'd react like that? But deep down he felt he was losing control, had overstepped the mark and could find himself in serious trouble. Unless, of course, he took matters into his own hands...

"I'm not sure what we're dealing with here, Sister." Phil Ellis the Casualty registrar shook his head in puzzlement. "Clinical signs suggest some sort of overdose but what the hell could she have taken?"

"Shall I call the consultant?" Sister Peters replaced the sheet over Aneira's inert figure.

"You better had, she's well out of it, and can you do gastric lavage too, please. We need to send bloods to Tox-Base as well."

"I'll set it up right away." She opened the curtain to leave, but was intercepted by a worried Sister Winter and an apoplectic Anscombe.

"Why the hell weren't we called immediately?" He pushed his colleague aside to take a closer look at the patient. Flouting all hospital protocol, he rapidly assessed the situation, checking Aneira's vital signs, looking into her eyes with his torch. Oh my dear Lord, he thought in horror, as he took in Aneira's deathly pallor. As he held her wrist to take her pulse it seemed to him that any excess force would break it; she was as fragile as a china doll. A wave of intense concern and outrage engulfed him. What the hell were her parents thinking, letting an innocent kid like this come up to the city to train as a nurse?

"Word certainly travels fast in the Infirmary." Phil Ellis muttered, but was too much in awe of his senior colleague to object.

"You've seen these eyes, Ellis? What the hell have you been doing for the past half hour?" Anscombe barked the questions directly at Phil. "Pin points! Bloody pin points! Get some Narcan going here, then get her warded ASAP! She's one of our own, for Christ's sake!"And he swept angrily away, knocking over the sphygmomanometer in his fury.

"Opiates?" Sister Winter whispered in horror to the Casualty sister. "She's only a baby, and an extremely innocent one at that."

Ann Peters shrugged, unhappily. "Who knows? I expect we'll know more when she surfaces. Her obs are stable now, and after she's had the Narcan we'll do a stomach washout, then up to the ward. There's no respiratory distress, ITU doesn't need to be alerted, she won't need intubating. They're full, anyway."

Sister Winter stroked the young girl's hand. "Poor little thing. Let me know how things go, Ann. We're all very concerned." What on earth are we going to tell her parents, she thought as she made her way out of Casualty, and more importantly, what exactly has happened to her?

"She's mumbling something, Sister!" The student nurse shouted excitedly, as she removed the blood pressure cuff from Aneira's thin arm.

Aneira's eyes were rolling about in her head, and she appeared distressed, but her colour had improved and she was grabbing at the Venflon which was linked to the IVI in her wrist..

"She's saying something about having some lemonade. Sister. Do you think she's thirsty? Shall I get her some water?"

Ann Peters came bustling over, leaving the tramp whose facial laceration she was dressing.

"Goodness me, no, Nurse Howard! She's only semi-conscious, she could choke. Her IVI is providing her with all the fluids she needs right now. If she continues to ask for a drink then you can moisten her tongue with some ice, but nothing more."

"Yes, Sister, of course." And the student scuttled off to the tiny kitchen to fetch some ice cubes.

"Narcan's having an effect?" Phil Ellis joined Sister Peters at Aneira's side, anxiety written all over his face. It had not been a pleasant experience being shown up by Anscombe. He hated these overdoses, always so tricky, he much preferred the straightforward, bread and butter trauma cases.

Sister Peters checked Aneira's pupil reactions again. "Seems it's working. Her pupils are responding more briskly now. Can we get her up to Weston ward shortly?"

"Don't see why not." Phil Ellis referred to his notes. "And get Sister Winter over when she's warded, we have scant details about her."

"I'll ring the ward now." What a shift she thought, as she picked up the phone. Thank God it's nearly nine o'clock.

Marcus walked through the hospital with a feeling of trepidation. Tonight the building seemed to be sinister, unfriendly. It felt as though he was walking through a dark cloud. He thought everyone was looking at him oddly, suspiciously. And through the dark cloud had shone the super-trouper lights of Sister Peter's probing stare. Had she suspected anything? But he was guilty of nothing, nothing at all. He hadn't done anything wrong, he kept reminding himself, feeding himself the lie until he actually started to believe it. The main corridor seemed endless this

172

evening, stretching far away into the gloom of the hospital's night shift persona.

"Evening, Doctor Battencourt." Richie the porter nodded at him, his face surly and uncompromising, as he lumbered down the corridor towards him, thankfully turning a sharp left towards Flanders wards. Marcus stared after him. Am I being paranoid, he thought? He could have sworn Richie had muttered something under his breath as he had passed by. Wise up, he told himself, you're being stupid. Anyway, he had far more important things to consider. Hastily he pulled on the white coat he'd picked up in the doctors' mess, then ran quickly up the stairs to the first floor of the hospital then turned left. The corridor was deserted. Except – was that a nurse or a visitor he could see at the far end? A nurse, he thought, strangely dressed in grey? Surely none of them wore grey..? He shivered, unaccountably. Banishing any illogical thoughts from his determined mind, he turned right into Weston ward. Putting a broad, winning smile on his handsome face, he pushed open the doors of the female medical ward, where the plump and pretty night nurse was filling in some charts at one of the beds.

"Good evening, Staff." He was at his most charming, he might wish to screw her in the near future. "I understand you have a little girl here, the one that I rescued from the steps of the hospital itself this very evening. Can you show me her bed, please?"

Aneira struggled to open her eyes. The cubicle was in semi-darkness. Someone was calling her name, but she just wanted to go back to sleep.

"Aneira!" The voice was whispering in her ear. "It's Marcus. Look at me." She moaned quietly, turning her head to and fro. He tapped her smooth cheek lightly. Her eyelids, still wearing the sparkly blue eyeshadow from the disastrous evening, fluttered slightly, and she seemed to wake up a little.

"Marcus! Oh, Marcus!" She reached out to him, weakly, trying to put her hands around his neck. "What happened to me? Take me back to your house? Please? I'm so sorry I fell asleep, I -"

Abruptly he untangled himself from her embrace. "Be quiet," he hissed, "you were never in my house, you did not spend the evening with me, you will say nothing to anyone, do you understand?"

"But – but – why? We were having such a lovely time, until..." She started to try to sit up.

"Shut up!" Roughly, he pushed her back onto the pillow. "If you know what's good for you, you'll keep your mouth shut. Understand?"

She nodded, scared. Where was the captivating doctor who had swept her off her feet and treated her so romantically? Why had he turned into this cold, harshly spoken man? Tears filled her eyes.

"Will we see each other again?" The desperation in her voice was pitiful.

"No. Never. And if I hear that you have told anyone – anyone at all – about what has happened tonight, then I will inform the whole bloody hospital that you are nothing but a little slut, a cheap little slut who lets any chap have his way with her on the very first date."

Aneira gasped in horror, then burst into noisy tears. "I didn't do that! I wouldn't do that! We never did -"

"Shut the fuck up!" He was getting really angry now. Why wouldn't she just do as he said? "Remember what I just said. Keep. Your. Mouth. Shut." He stormed off, but closed the cubicle door discreetly, just managing to compose himself and give a smiling wave to the staff nurse.

"All done?" She really fancied the pants off Marcus Battencourt, he was such a bloody good-looking bloke. "Did she remember anything?"

"Nah, she was just talking bollocks. Got herself a bit upset about everything. Probably had too much Blue Nun with some bloke or

174

something! She'll calm down though." He edged closer and closer to the ward entrance, anxious to make himself scarce.

"So what exactly happened?" The staff nurse's curiosity was getting the better of her. Marcus was keen to go, but to withhold basic facts would only attract unwanted attention.

"Well, I was just driving up to the hospital, and there she was, on the steps of the main entrance. Collapsed in a heap. I thought she was pissed out of her brain, so I picked her up and carried her into Cas."

The staff nurse took a sharp intake of breath. How bloody romantic was that? "Well, you certainly are a Sir Galahad," she giggled flirtatiously, "I wouldn't mind being rescued like that!"

Well, you'd have to lose about two stone first before I'd be able to pick you up, Marcus thought, spitefully. "Well, thanks again, Staff – er – Lundy, isn't it? Sorry to have interrupted your work. Toodle pip!" And he stalked importantly from the ward, leaving her gazing longingly after him. Maybe he'll ask me out before much longer, she thought wistfully. I'll start my diet next week...

With an air of confidence he didn't entirely feel, he made his way forcefully along the ward corridor which led out to the main first story thoroughfare, running his fingers through his perfect blond hair.

All was quiet. No nurses rushed about, no office staff hurried to and fro at this time of night. The lifts were silent. The lights shone, yet the whole place seemed shadowy, sombre. The hospital seemed like a great, sleeping monster, but all the while keeping one watchful eye open, observing him, monitoring his every move. He was under scrutiny. The building knew everything about him, he felt. Uneasy now, he directed his steps towards the staircase.

"Dr Battencourt!" The words were hardly more than a whisper, a murmur on a breath of wind that wasn't there. He looked around. The corridor stretched for eternity before his frightened gaze.

"Who said that?" Wildly, he searched for the hidden voice, his eyes narrowing with suspicion. "Come on, show yourself!"

A heavy sigh. A swish of clothing. What the hell was going on? Had someone been following him? Was it that bloody porter?

A glimpse of grey, a hazy figure, disappearing swiftly around the corner. Someone had definitely been watching him, but who the hell could it have been?

He raced recklessly down the stairs, almost falling in his haste to escape his stalker, intent on reaching his car, normality and a stiff whisky.

Julia sighed contentedly, feeling Mitch's arm snake around her slim waist. By way of response she entwined her long legs around his, feeling his hips thrust closer to hers.

"Not again, young man?" She giggled, in anticipation, her hands reaching down to stroke him into even more desire, feeling him stiffening.

"I can't get enough of you!" His mumbled reply was cut short by her grabbing him and kissing him ferociously.

"You know what they say about redheads!" She panted, lustfully. "Hot blooded, passionate! Are you sure you can handle me?!"

"And you were a bloody virgin only a few weeks ago!" He laughed in delight as she flung herself on top of him, her long tresses covering his face. "It hasn't taken you long to learn the pleasures of the flesh!"

"Ah, but I've had a good teacher!" She took his face in both hands and gazed at him, her eyes ablaze with love and excitement. She kissed him again, running her tongue along his teeth, then down his throat, to his chest, nibbling playfully on his nipples.

Abruptly, he pulled away. "Well, Staff Harry, your lessons haven't ended yet!" And he lay her down flat on the bed, licking her breasts, her stomach, always heading downwards, sensing her becoming rigid with anticipation, until he reached her most sensitive parts. She arched her body towards his searching mouth, feeling the ecstasy sweep over her as his wicked tongue found her delicate rosebud...

Bliss.

"Are the results back from Tox-Base yet?" Sister Hunter confronted Phil Ellis at the main desk in Casualty.

"You mean that little waif of the night up on Weston?" He was seriously exhausted now, having been on the go for the past twelve hours.

"The very same. Aneira Thomas, I think her name is. And?" She drew herself up to her full height. Phil Ellis may be extremely tired, she realised, but the welfare of her nurses was her uppermost concern.

"Opiate poisoning." He closed a set of notes abruptly. "I've asked the ward staff to speak to her about it in the morning, and maybe get the psych team to have a word with her."

Sister Hunter shook her head. "I'd be very surprised if this was intentional. Maybe she's dabbled in something without realising it, who knows, but as far as I can gather from the day staff on Terence Adams she is a God-fearing Baptist, chapel three times on a Sunday, you know what I mean?"

"Hmm. The quiet ones are sometimes the worst."

"Very cynical of you, Phil." Sister Hunter glanced at her fob watch. "It's almost midnight. I'll pop along to the ward later and if she's awake, I'll have a little word with her. Why don't you get some sleep?"

"Can't. There's a threatened abortion expected in any minute and the gynae reg is still in theatre with an ectopic pregnancy. So..." He shrugged in resignation.

"Who'd work in the NHS, eh?" She smiled, dryly, as she checked the night report before leaving for the wards.

Weston ward was silent, only the occasional overhead bedlamp provided any illumination; the night nurse was head down, busy filling out the fluid charts for the following day, and the auxiliary was measuring the fluid output of a patient on peritoneal dialysis.

"Staff Lundy?"

The staff nurse jumped. "Sister Hunter, good evening." Deferentially, she got to her feet.

"And how is little Nurse Thomas, now?" Sister Hunter walked purposefully to the cubicle.

"Er, quite comfortable, Sister." Kath Lundy trotted behind the senior nurse, dutifully. "She's been able to give us some information, so we've got her home address and date of birth as well. It's her birthday tomorrow, poor dab."

"But no mention as to what happened?" A frown creased the night sister's forehead. "Any information about that?"

"Nothing at all." Staff Nurse Lundy quietly opened the door of the cubicle. "She says she can't remember anything."

"You may leave us now, Staff. I'm sure you've plenty to keep you busy." The dismissive smile on her face was perfectly understood, and the staff nurse discreetly retreated to the office.

Aneira was sleeping, her fair hair spread out on the pillow. She looked so fragile, so delicate, it seemed a shame to wake her. But Sister Hunter was on a mission. Something was very wrong here, she thought, very wrong indeed.

"Nurse Thomas," she whispered gently. "Can you hear me?"

Aneira slowly opened her eyes. "Yes."

Sister Hunter sat down next to the bed. "Tell me, my dear, what happened to you? It's important that we know, for your own safety and well-being."

"I can't remember anything." Aneira pulled the sheet up to her eyes, as if it would protect her, peering over it like a frightened rabbit.

"Have you tried to harm yourself? Are you pregnant?" The older woman put a reassuring hand on Aneira's. "I won't judge you, my dear, I'm only trying to help."

But Aneira simply burst into tears once more. "I can't remember anything, sorry Sister, I'm sorry."

Sister Hunter got up to go. "Never mind, my dear, all will be well. Once you are up and about you should go home to your family for a short stay, build yourself up, then maybe you will be able to remember. The day staff may ask the psychiatrist to see you tomorrow, to make sure you haven't tried to harm yourself."

Aneira nodded silently, watching the night sister open the door, then blurted out, "I haven't tried to harm myself, I would never do that, and I'm not pregnant, I'm not that sort of girl, if you know what I mean. I just can't remember..." Sister Hunter nodded understandingly.

"Go back to sleep, my dear. You'll feel better in the morning."

Aneira retreated beneath the sheets, feeling as though her whole world was collapsing in on her, as if she was being punished for something she knew nothing about, was innocent of. How she suddenly longed for the close community of Welsh village life, the orderly little streets of terraced houses where everything was reliable and predictable. How she wished she was back in the valley, where everyone went to chapel on a Sunday morning, then the club on a Sunday afternoon to listen to music and get drunk, where it was safe to get drunk, and everyone laughed, danced and hugged. Where the children played in the park and mothers chattered on the benches, where cawl was made on a Friday afternoon and eaten with wooden spoons. Where the tall trees on the mountains sternly surveyed the land, observing and protecting them all, where she felt safe...

Turning onto her side, she closed her eyes, despairing of her situation, feeling frightened and so terribly alone...

Chapter Seventeen Elsie's

"Honestly! You and Mitch are behaving like conjoined twins! It's as though you're joined at the hip! And you've only been reunited for two days!" Mandy shared the umbrella more equally over them as the two nurses battled their way down Porthnewydd Anvenue, on their way to start a late shift. "But I am glad for you, Jules. It's so nice to see you happy and smiling again." Then she cursed like a fishwife as a car raced past them, spraying them with dirty water from the many puddles on the oily tarmac.

"Mandy! Such language from a responsible staff nurse!" They both burst out laughing.

"Are you going to pop over to Weston to see that little student?" Mandy tried desperately to protect her white hat from the slanting rain which was doing its best to drench it.

"Yes, indeed I will. I'll go over in my first break. I can't believe she took an overdose, or was taking illegal drugs. She's not that sort." She shook her head in incredulity. "She's one of life's innocents."

Mandy gave her playful dig in the ribs. "You should know! Anyway, here we are, the Gap in the Wall ready and waiting for us as usual. Brace yourself, Jules, let's face the music!"

Weston was a hive of activity, the consultant's round just coming to an end and the visitors starting to queue at the entrance to the ward. Julia managed to slip in to Aneira's cubicle unnoticed by the draconian ward sister who was attending the physician and his entourage with the utmost reverence.

"Staff Harry!" Aneira sat up in bed, a pale little ghost surrounded by acres of white hospital sheets.

"Please call me Julia. You're off duty right now and I'm at break, I'm your visitor and you're the patient." Julia smiled kindly at the young girl and sat down next to the bed.

Aneira continued to look anxious. "Thank you for coming to see me."

"When are they letting you go home?" Julia placed the grapes she'd brought on the locker.

"Tomorrow, I think. I'm going home to Ystradgynlais for a week or so. Sister Hunter has organised my sick leave. But - "

"But what?" With dismay Julia watched huge tears roll down Aneira's cheeks. "Look, Aneira, I know something bad is troubling you. But you don't have to tell me about it. Not until you're ready. But I'm here for you, you can talk to me at anytime. I only live up the road, so if I'm not in work, you know where you can get hold of me, you can even ring on the internal phone if you like, no-one will mind."

Aneira smiled, grateful. "Thanks, Staff – sorry, Julia. Maybe after I come back to work?"

"As I said, anytime. Now you get some rest. I'd better make myself scarce or Sister Honey will be on my case!"

Aneira managed a giggle. "Not very sweet, is she, Sister Honey?"

Julia laughed. "You'd better not let her hear you say that!" But she was relieved to see that at least the kid still had a sense of humour.

"What are you sniggering about?" Richie scowled in annoyance at young Steve, the junior porter. The porters' lodge was empty, apart from them. Steve had his size nines up on the ancient wooden table and he was sipping a mug of builder's tea. "And take those filthy shoes off that table!

They're right next to my sandwiches, you dirty bugger! Where the hell d'you think you are? In a bleedin' pig sty?"

"Sorry, Richie." Steve obediently did as he was told and removed his feet, but carried on chortling away to himself.

"I asked you – what are you laughing about? What's the bloody joke?" Richie found the younger man irritating to say the least, such a clever dick, always had an answer for everything.

"Nothing." Steve furtively put something back in his pocket.

Richie's sharp eyes missed nothing. "Give it here, c'mon, hand it over!"

"I ain't done nothing!" Steve wore a pained expression, as if dismayed Richie was doubting his honesty.

"I don't bloody care. What's that you're hiding? You ain't leaving until I get to see what you're up to, understand?"

Steve sighed dramatically, and reluctantly pulled out what appeared to be a small photograph. Looking at it again, he chuckled, and held it to his chest. "What's it worth, then, guv? How much you gonna pay me to have a squint at this?"

Irritation boiling over, Richie snatched the photo from the junior porter. As he glanced at it, a wave of horror swept through him.

"Where did you get this?" He could hardly get the words out. "This is bloody pornography!" Richie was aghast at what he was seeing.

"Aw, c'mon, Rich, she's bloody gorgeous! Phwoah! Look at those tits, and what that bloke is doing to her!And you can see every thing! Hey, give it back!" He tried to grab the photo back from Richie, but was too slow.

"Where did you get it?" Richie still couldn't believe his eyes. "WHERE?" He grabbed Steve by the collar, shaking him like a terrier with a rat.

"Um – I-er -in the doctors' mess." Steve saw no point in lying, Richie was on a mission and as he was six inches taller and three stone heavier than him, he thought he'd better come clean. "There was a group of them posh buggers having a laugh about something the other day, and when I came in to bleed the radiator, they all pushed off. But one of them, that Doctor Hancock I think it was, you know, the Italian-looking one, well he dropped it, see."

"And so you kept it for yourself? So you could have a bloody wank in the boiler room, is it? You filthy little pervert, get out of my sight! And if I find out you've told anyone about this, you're dead fucking meat! Get it?"

Scared, Steve nodded meekly and beat a hasty exit as fast as he possibly could.

Richie sat down heavily on one of the scruffy armchairs in the small, old-fashioned room. He looked at the photo again, in disbelief. The girl looked as though she was asleep, unaware of what was going on. Unaware that she was the subject of a pornographic photo. Unaware of what was being done to her. But the worst thing was that he knew her. His heart sank as he realised with certainty that he recognised her. Staff Nurse Mandy Jacob.

Julia often wondered where the demarcation line lay between Roath and Splott.

Roath, with its seemingly aristocratic three story, bay-windowed houses, was a world apart from the modest terraces of Splott. Despite Splott's sparkling street names of Gold Street, Sapphire Street and Topaz Street, any shining distinction was undeniably tarnished. The word Splott would cause raised eyebrows, shaking of heads and a cacophony of tut-tuts. Common, dangerous, lower class.

But, when she used to live at the rear of the nurses' home as a student, she would look out at the roof tops of Splott, especially in the evening as the sun was setting, and would think how familiar it looked, how much like

Llanelli. She'd be filled with *hiraeth*, such a longing for home. Splott. Why did it have such a tainted reputation? Then when she'd qualified, she'd moved to the front of the building which overlooked Porthnewydd Avenue itself. Porthnewydd Avenue: an essential artery of the busy Cardiff network, lined with huge Victorian houses, most of which had been converted into solicitors' offices, medical practices and small hotels. As she walked towards the Five Oaks to meet Mitch, it was already dark; buses rushed past with their weary passengers homeward bound, and students hurried along the broad pavements to their various flats and bedsits.

To her left was the much maligned Splott, to her right the more aesthetically pleasing Roath. But all the people Julia had ever met from Splott were decent, welcoming and friendly. Whereas she could think of quite a few unsavoury characters who lived in the more upmarket Roath. She supposed all towns had their districts of notoriety, deserved or not. Passing the library, already brightly lit and ready for late visitors, she considered her own home town. The New Dock area was deemed to be terribly downmarket, frowned upon by many Llanelli residents, yet her mother had been born and brought up there, had been happy there and looked upon the area with love and nostalgia.

"Gotcha!" A pair of arms encircled her waist and swung her around, before a pair of lips crushed her mouth in a passionate kiss. Laughing, she broke away from Mitch's embrace.

"You nutter! But the nicest sort of nutter, I have to say!"

He grinned at her, appreciating her autumnal beauty, breathing in her favourite perfume, Kiku.

"Shall we go in?" He took her arm and opened the door of the pub, but she held back.

"You know what? It sounds crowded in there. I'm not in the mood for crowds tonight. Why don't we go back to my room? I've got a bottle of red in the cupboard..." She smiled mischievously at him.

"Oh, you wicked woman! You're trying to corrupt me, tempting me with wine and other promises."

"What promises?" She feigned indignation.

"Promises you'd better keep!" He cuddled her. "Let's go then, but what about your landlady?"

"Miss Marshall? The warden? I'm her blue-eyed girl! But even I will have to make sure you're gone by midnight."

He glanced at his watch. "Ten past seven now. That gives us almost five hours before one of us turns into a pumpkin. Lead on, oh temptress, lead on!"

They lay sandwiched together in her single bed, the duvet half on the floor, in the aftermath of their lovemaking. The ceiling was periodically illuminated by cars driving along the road, despite the curtains being drawn at the huge bay window. Lindisfarne's "Run for Home" played quietly on Julia's cassette player in the corner, and an empty bottle of Piat D'Or lay on its side next to the bed.

"I used to play this song all the time when I was first up in Cardiff, and I was homesick." She hugged him. "But now I can play it for a different reason, because it'll always remind me of this evening"

"But what about my song?" He pretended shock. "Haven't you bought my record yet?"

"Oh ye of little faith." She slid out of bed and walked naked across the room, Mitch enjoying the sight of her narrow waist, her pert, high bottom and her slim, endless legs as she went. Pulling open the wardrobe door, she pulled out a carrier bag, and carried it back over to him, Mitch appreciating the front view this time.

"Look inside!" She sat down next to him and watched his expression as he opened the bag.

"Jesus, Julia! You've bought ten – no, hang on – twelve copies!" He burst out laughing.

"I know. I went into Smith's yesterday and I bought one for every member of my family. One for Sarah, one for Rachel, one for my parents – I didn't get one for Nana Harry because she hasn't got a record player or anything – one for Nana Cook, one for -"

"Okay, okay!" He stopped her chatter with his kisses and pulled her back into bed.

"I'm bloody starving. You got anything nice to eat?" Mitch could feel his tummy rumbling away like a steam train. Peering into her small food cupboard, Julia shook her head, glumly.

"How d'you fancy baked beans on toast? Or baked beans and Smash? Or to be really exotic, we could have baked beans a la Julia?"

"Ooh, that sounds interesting! What's that?" Mitch could guess what was coming.

"It's baked beans. My speciality, though, is to eat them cold, straight from the tin!"

"I think I'll pass on that." Mitch started to pull on his jeans.

"I know! Let's go to Elsie's!"

"Where's that? Is it far? Is it expensive? And will it be open at -" he checked the time "-half past eleven?"

"Ah, you're an Elsie virgin. Well, it's open until the customers decide to go home, it is not expensive, and it's just around the corner in Carlton Street. I tell you, it's an experience not to be missed. You haven't lived, my boy, until you've tried their spag bol!"

"Better than mine?" He did up her bra for her, kissing her on the neck.

"It's er, unbelievable."

There was a knock at the door.

"Shit!" Julia whispered. "It's Miss Marshall!"

Another knock.

"Julia! It's me, Mandy! You still up? I though I heard you talking!"

Heaving a sigh of relief, Julia pulled on her dressing gown and opened the door.

"Hi, Mandy! We're just off out."

Mandy's face fell. "Oh, bugger. I was just wondering if you wanted to get some fish and chips with me, I'm as hungry as hell."

"Well, come with us to Elsie's then!" Julia looked at Mitch for approval, and he nodded.

"Ooh, now that's an offer I cannot refuse! Hang on, I'll get my coat!"

Julia grinned up at Mitch. "You're gonna love this!"

The steamed up windows of the dingy little cafe hid the identities of the customers as effectively as thick, net curtains. At midnight, it was packed, and the three were hard pressed to find a table. Sitting on the Dock of the Bay was belting out of the juke box and a group of seriously drunk girls was attempting to sing along. One of them fell off her chair, to the great mirth of her friends.

"Should have seen her in Tito's," shrieked one of them, "she was bloody amazing!" More raucous laughter. Nobody paid any attention to them at all.

Mitch looked incredulously at his companions. Where the hell had they brought him? Julia giggled at Mitch's expression.

"You two sit down and I'll go and order. What do you fancy?"

"You recommended the spag bol – I'll have that." Mitch handed her some coins.

"Ooh – I'll have sausage, egg and chips with a splash of curry!" Mandy was almost drooling at the thought of this gastronomic delight. There was more food on the floor than on the menu, and Julia had to pick her way carefully around the tables to avoid slipping.

Just as she was returning to her table, there was a bellow from the far corner of the restaurant.

"What 'ew looking at? 'Ew asking for a fight or what?." Two burly chaps, plastered in tattoos, very much the worse for wear, drunk as skunks, pushed back their chairs and glared at each other over the remains of their burgers and chips.

Automatically, without anyone batting an eyelid or even a false eyelash, everyone in the vicinity picked up their plates and moved out of the line of fire. Mitch looked alarmed. Shouldn't they leave immediately?

"Don't worry," Mandy patted his arm reassuringly, "they'll just bash the shit out of each other, then calm down." She was right. Burly chap number one threw an amazingly accurate right hook, considering he was out of his skull, and chap number two went spinning off into the opposite corner, where he sat down on a hastily vacated chair, momentarily stunned. Encouraged by the success of his attack, the assailant moved in for a second chance to wallop his victim, scrambling over the chairs in his haste. All the diners watched in fascination, plates, knives and forks safely in their hands, as the victim suddenly leapt to his feet, having lulled his attacker into a false sense of security, throwing his bulky body against his attacker, who went sprawling, face down, onto the food-splattered floor.

"Ow! You've knocked me filling out!" The guy on the floor was almost in tears. "I'll have to go to the dentist now!" He opened his mouth wide for all to appreciate.

"Oh, jeez, no!" The other chap leapt over to check. "Ooh, yeah, I can see! Sorry about that, pal." Seconds later they were shaking hands, all good mates again, everything forgiven.

"I take it that it's a regular occurrence, then?" Mitch chuckled, quietly.

"More or less."Mandy searched in her purse for the right change to pay Julia.

There was a squawking from the Tito gang. "How you getting home? I haven't got any money left? Can you lend us some?"

"Oh, calm down, Chrissie," said the blonde who was wearing a black ra-ra skirt. "Just sit here with us for a couple more hours and we'll cadge a lift off Milko when his float floats by. Hahaha! Floats by!" They screamed with laughter again.

Ten minutes later, Mitch was looking down in disbelief at the plate of food, described on the stained, plastic menu as "Spagetty Bollonaise." It resembled a mass of writhing worms, topped with what could only be described as brown slush with the odd diced carrot thrown in. Yet Julia seemed to be enjoying it immensely, tucking in with gusto, and Mandy couldn't shovel her meal in fast enough, either. Must be something about nurses, he thought, they'll eat anything... Tentatively, he started to fork it up. It was certainly memorable...

"God, these chips are to die for!" Mandy forked up a couple of those heavenly items and dipped them in the curry sauce. "Do you want one, Mitch?"

"Er, no thanks, I'll stick with the pasta." He continued in his brave endeavours, picking his way around the overcooked spaghetti, looking thoughtfully at the tomato sauce bottle, wondering if it might improve things a bit. "You nurses can't half eat!"

190

"Oh, we love our nosh!" Mandy happily wiped her plate clean with a slice of bread and butter. "I remember when I was doing nights on paeds, I was always so hungry I ended up eating the Farley's rusks and baby rice."

"You little devil!" Julia laughed, slurping up a strand of pasta in a very unladylike manner. "Those poor babies, going without so that plump little Nurse Mandy could stuff her face!"

Mandy's face was a picture of mock indignation. "I bet you did some wicked things when you were a student, Jules! C'mon, what was the naughtiest thing you did?" She looked slyly at Mitch, then Julia, daring her friend to fess up.

Her tongue loosened by the three glasses of wine earlier in the evening, Julia grinned at her audience. "Well, once again it's when I was on nights. You see, nurses drink buckets of coffee during night shifts to stay awake, but because of the effects of certain hormones, namely anti-diuretic hormone, we don't wee it all out at night, and it builds up. So when we try to sleep during the day, our full bladders keep waking us up. Now my room was at the far end of the corridor – remember Mands? - and the loos were miles away. I was so knackered when I woke up for a wee, I couldn't be bothered to trot down to the bathrooms , so I – er - "

"You bloody peed in your sink! You did, didn't you!" Mandy creased up laughing, with Julia joining in, tears running down her face.

"You're spot on!" Turning to Mitch, she said, "You sure you want to associate with me after that little confession?"

Mitch groaned in mock despair. "I dunno, you girls, you look so innocent, the pair of you, but you're nothing but a couple of scoundrels!" He returned his attention to his rapidly cooling plate of food, but soon pushed it away, Mandy eyeing it beadily.

"And do you remember two little first-years who'd just been allocated their uniforms?" Julia was on a roll now.

191

"Oh, sweet Jesus, don't remind me!" Mandy hid her face in her hands. "I'll never live that one down!"

"I realise you two are on a pleasant trip down memory lane, but I'm not familiar with the territory. C'mon, spill the beans!" Mitch feigned annoyance.

"We-ell," Julia dropped her voice to a whisper, "Mands and I were so bloody chuffed to get our uniforms, we put them on, hats, cloaks and all, and strolled right into the middle of town wearing them! I can't believe we did that! The looks people were giving us! We even went into Marks and Spencers!"

"So what was wrong with that?" Mitch couldn't understand the problem.

"Well, apart from looking like two idiots, it would have been instant dismissal!"

"So we try not to remember that event!" Mandy finished for her. "Happy days, eh?" The two girls giggled again.

The door of the cafe opened, allowing a cool gust of air into the fuggy atmosphere.

"Ooh, watch out, here comes Andy Pandy!" One of the Tito trio, a hefty brunette, sniggered in delight, as the door opened and a tall, uniformed policeman tried to slide in unnoticed. "Hya, Andy, lovely boy! How ya doing? Catch any nasty murderers tonight?" She got up and put her heavily braceleted arms around his neck, which he swiftly removed with the ease of one accustomed to such an event, although his cheeks were burning with embarrassment.

"Thought I heard shouting." He made his way over to Julia's table.

"Nah, all good here, Officer." The owner of the cafe, who resembled a heavyweight wrestler herself, winked at him. "All good, all quiet. Everyone behaving themselves, like, innit?"

Andy removed his helmet. "Any chance of a cuppa, Elsie?" He turned to the three at the table. "Evening, Staff Harry! Or should I say good morning? Okay if I join you?"

"Sure!" Julia pulled out a chair. She could sense Mitch bristling next to her. "Mitch, Andy is our local copper! The cop shop is just across the road. Often accompanies drunks and vagabonds to Casualty and if he's very unlucky, up to the ward! If we're feeling sorry for him, he gets a cup of Horlicks before he leaves!"

"Oh, I see. How's it going?" Mitch extended his hand, which Andy accepted.

"Been a bit of a quiet night. Could have sworn I saw some fisticuffs going on a few minutes ago, but those windows are so bloody filthy it's impossible to be certain."

The female wrestler brought his coffee. "On the 'ouse, love, coz we thinks the world of you, we does!" She plonked a smacker of a kiss on his cheek.

"Cheers, Elsie." Grinning, he turned to Mandy, looking at her properly for the first time. "I haven't seen you around the hospital. Do you work there too?"

"Yes, I staff on male medical, mostly kidney patients."

She was really pretty, he decided. He liked the way her glossy dark hair curled over her shoulders, her merry blue eyes sparkling in mischief as she smiled at him.

"Sorry, I didn't catch your name?" How else was he going to find that out, he thought, why didn't Julia just introduce him, like she'd done with her boyfriend?

"That's because I haven't told you yet!" Mandy giggled, pushing away her empty plate.

"Go on then. Your name, please! Because withholding any information which could be used in evidence later may possibly harm your case!" Christ, he thought to himself, I'm bloody flirting with her!

"Mandy. Mandy Jacob. And you are Constable, Sergeant..?"

"Police Constable Andrew Greenleigh-Peters. But you can call me Andy."

He's seriously attractive, thought Mandy, trying to suppress a hiccup, praying there wasn't any curry sauce on her chin or food between her teeth. Verging on the strawberry blond, his short hair was a whisker's breath short of being ginger, his open, freckled face both boyish and friendly. There was nothing suave or sophisticated about Andy, she considered, he seemed wholesome and ordinary. And extremely good looking.

Aware of the electricity that was starting to crackle between her friend and the police officer, Julia turned to Mitch.

"You going to walk me home, then? Can you manage it after all that food?" She looked down in amusement at Mitch's half-eaten spaghetti bolognese.

"Oh, I reckon I can manage a few steps. Let's go."

"Will you be okay, Mands?" Julia put her coat on. "Shall we wait for you?"

"Er, she'll be fine with me. I'll make sure she gets home safe." Bugger off, you two, thought Andy, impatiently.

"Yes, you go on home. I'm enjoying my little chat with Andy, so see you later!" Waving dismissively at the pair, she turned her attention back to Andy.

"Now, where were we?"

Kissing Julia goodnight outside the nurses' home, Mitch looked up at the stars and thanked them fervently for his good fortune. Life was looking rather good, he thought, bloody brilliant, in fact.

She hugged him close, burying her face in his denim jacket. "Will I see you on Friday? I'm on a late tomorrow so it'll be difficult after work."

He released her from his embrace. "I've got a meeting with Steph Saunders on Friday, at four o'clock, about an album they're considering. But anytime after that?"

"I finish at four, so..?" She gazed up at him, happily. Her eyes were shining as brightly as those benevolent stars, he thought.

"I know! Come straight over to the studio! Steph usually runs late, she has no concept of time-keeping. You can meet her then. She's ancient, you'll soon see she's no bloody threat to you!"

"You dull bugger!" She punched his arm playfully. "After all the agony we both felt when we had that terrible misunderstanding, I don't think there's any room left for doubt in our relationship."

Mitch burst out laughing. "Ooh! We're having a relationship are we?"

"I expect you could call it that."

"I don't know about you, but I think it's a bit more than that, what d'you reckon?" He pulled her close once more, kissing her gently, unaware of the curious, yet smiling face of Miss Marshall as she peered through the net curtains of her ground floor flat.

Young love, she thought, wistfully, and it passed me by so many years ago...

"So he wrote a song about her, and it's gone in at number twenty-five in the charts! He named it after her as well – Julia! How cool is that?"

"That guy? Mitch? He's a rock star?" Andy looked incredulously at Mandy, before draining the rest of his second cup of coffee.

"I wouldn't go that far. Let's just say his band is on the brink. But Mitch is a nice guy, and those two are so well-matched, don't you think?"

I'd like to be well-matched with you, he found himself thinking. "Shall we make tracks? We're the last ones here, and I've got to be back at the station by one o'clock."

Grabbing her coat, Mandy got up. "Well, you haven't got very far to go have you? It's only across the road! Rumour has it around these parts that Elsie even lobs bacon sarnies over to you after closing time!"

Andy laughed. Mandy liked the way he crinkled his eyes when he laughed, she liked his wide, friendly grin, she liked his occasional bashfulness, despite his professional assertiveness. In fact, she thought, I like him a lot.

"By the time I walk you home and get back, it'll be almost one."

Mandy glanced at her watch. Half past twelve. The nurses' home was only a five minute walk from the cafe, so maybe Andy was planning on the scenic route...

They wandered along the dark roads of Splott, taking their time, talking about their jobs and the pressures involved.

"Do you like being a nurse?" In the anonymity of the night-time street, his uniformed arm found its way around her small, plump shoulders. Was he being too forward, he considered, anxiously. But she didn't seem to mind, in fact, he was sure she was walking closer to him, now. Hell, she definitely was, she seemed to be snuggling up under his arm. His heart started to beat faster.

"It's all I've ever wanted to be. I love being a staff nurse, I'm really happy in my job – no, you can't really call it a job, it's my life, I suppose. What about you?"

"Well, on the whole it's great, but I can take or leave the shifts, especially nights. But then, if I hadn't been on nights tonight, I wouldn't have bumped into you, would I?"

They stopped and looked at each other. His face was so serious, yet his expression so young and trusting... Where is this going, Mandy thought, apprehensively, the disastrous evening with Neil Hancock still fresh in her memory. I hope it won't end before it's even started...

"I, er, can I see you again?" He seemed to have trouble getting the words out.

Mandy sighed in happy relief. "That would be lovely." She wanted to throw her arms around him and shout out "Yes, yes, yes!" But, remembering Julia's advice from a few weeks ago, she decided to play it cool. Well, luke warm anyway.

He swallowed, uncertain if he'd been too forward. "How about Saturday night? The pictures?" The eagerness in his voice touched her.

"Perfect." Her heart was doing somersaults. "Do I meet you somewhere?"

"No, I'll call for you at about half past six, if that suits you. I only live up the road in Rumney, still with my parents, believe it or not!"

"That'll be fine."

His hand found hers, and they continued up the road until they reached the nurses' home.

"Well, goodnight, then. I'll watch you go in. Best to be safe, you never know."

Smiling back at him, Mandy climbed the old, stone steps to the front door. As she fitted the key in the lock, she failed to notice the net curtains at the ground floor flat window twitching once more.

Miss Marshall sighed, nostalgia sweeping over her, as she remembered another certain policeman, many years ago, on those very steps. Sadly, she moved away from the window, and returned to her lonely sitting room, her Ovaltine and her bitter-sweet memories. A sad half moon shone down on that big, old house in the wee, small hours of a February night, as a sentimental oldish woman pulled down the covers of her single bed, thinking of her youth, of missed chances and dances forgotten, longing for what might have been...

Half a mile down the road, Sister Hunter pushed open the Casualty office door with her usual aplomb. A couple of second year students jumped to their feet and pushed away rogue strands of hair that were escaping from their hats.

"Is Dr Ellis about?" She scanned the small room as if half expecting the registrar to be hiding amongst the empty coffee cups and filing cabinets.

"Er, he's behind you, Sister." The shorter of the students pointed at the doorway.

"Hmph." Sister Hunter turned to see a world-weary Phil Ellis standing there, holding a bundle of notes. "A word, please, Phil, let's go somewhere quieter." Turning to the students, she continued. "And clear away those cups before I'm back, understand?"

"Yes, Sister." And they grinned at each other behind her retreating back, dutifully grabbing the dirty cups and empty sandwich wrappers.

In the relative peace of treatment room B, Sister Hunter sat down and indicated to her colleague to do likewise.

"I'm not happy with the situation, Phil."

He looked puzzled. "About what? Drinking coffee after midnight? Student nurses lolling about in the office instead of cleaning the sluice?"

"Don't be facetious." She withered him with a look. "I'm referring to little Aneira Thomas, the student who was admitted the other night, you know, the opiate poisoning."

"Ah yes. How is she, anyway?" He pushed back an unruly lock of dark hair from his furrowed brow.

"Still back home in the Valleys. I've been thinking, do you suppose we should involve the police?"

"Seriously?" Phil felt surprised, he hadn't considered this, maybe he should have..?

Sister Hunter looked uncomfortable. "I'm not sure. Of course, it all depends on what Nurse Thomas wants to do, if anything. So far, she's disclosed nothing. It's as though she's afraid. I know she's a timid little thing anyway, according to Sister Winter, but...oh, I don't know." She got up and automatically reorganised a pile of sterile dressings on the work surface, sighing heavily. "I've got a bad feeling about this, Phil, one I can't ignore."

"Well, if anything comes to light, I'll let you know, although I doubt we'll hear much more about the matter now, not here in Cas."

"Of course. Well, I'm off to break now. Have a good shift."

"Thanks, Sister, you too." He watched her walk stiffly away, her posture ramrod straight. What a formidable woman, he thought, I'd bloody hate to get on the wrong side of her.

"Ambulance control on the phone, Dr Ellis!" The nurse's voice echoed through the empty corridor. "R.T.A. on the way !"

Here we go again, he thought tiredly, all hopes of a bacon sandwich fading fast from his exhausted mind.

Chapter Eighteen Keeping Secrets

The ward seemed strangely quiet as Julia hung up her coat in the locker room. Normally, at handover, she'd be able to hear the buzz of chatter, the clatter of the lunchtime crockery being cleared away and the racket of the SluiceMaster as it roared into action at the end of a busy morning.

Where is everyone, she thought, shoving her bag neatly under the desk, before settling down in readiness to take Report.

A few minutes later there was still no sign of anyone, so she got up and walked into the ward itself. Suddenly, there was an almighty chorus of voices, male and female, high and low, all singing together, at full volume,

Julia, my lover, won't you come back to me

I miss you so,

You know I need you now

Like the desert needs the rain

Julia, you're my life, you're the star in my sky, and you know why -

Give me one more try...

Turning crimson in embarrassment, Julia burst out laughing, tears filling her eyes. All the patients who were well enough were singing their hearts out, accompanied by Sister Winter, the pesky second years and Dorcas the Nigerian auxiliary. Even Dr Gupta, the normally shy anaesthetist, had gone down on one knee and was holding his hands out in supplication, trying not to laugh.

Sister Winter rushed to hug her."We heard it on the radio! The Mitch Walker band! The young lad who was here!" She could hardly contain her delight.

"And it's all about you! And it's in the top twenty now!" Student Nurse Bowen was practically hopping with excitement.

"Didn't take us long to put two and two together!" They were joined by a grinning Mr Anscombe. "I must say we've never had a rock star as a patient on the ward before. Now don't let it go to your head, Staff Harry. Sister, let's get on with our work, shall we?" And he turned around importantly, followed by a surly-faced Marcus Battencourt, who'd been lurking on the periphery, resentful of all the attention being bestowed upon Julia, jealous of the fact that he'd never managed to bed her, and that she'd found someone else so quickly, wasn't even pining over him, the stupid cow....

I've never seen Mr Anscombe smile before, thought Julia in amusement, oblivious to Marcus's scowling expression. Beaming from ear to ear and with a spring in her step, she returned to the office in readiness for the one o'clock handover.

"Can you check Mr Powell's pulse, Nurse Evans, before I give him his digoxin?" Julia checked the patient's treatment chart. "If it's over sixty we can give it."

Obediently, the student picked up the patient's wrist, and checked her fob watch. After a few seconds, she reported confidently that it was seventy beats per minute.

Julia frowned. Really, those second years need to be brought in line, she thought. "Now, Nurse Evans, you only took that pulse for a few seconds, so how can you possibly tell me it was seventy?"

Nurse Evans had the grace to blush. "Well, er, sorry, Staff, I counted for fifteen seconds and multiplied by four."

"I see." Julia's tone was glacial. "So, you are assuming that Mr Powell's pulse was steady, regular and strong, after only feeling it for fifteen seconds? What if the remaining forty-five seconds showed you a thin, thready, irregular pulse? That could be highly significant. Take it again, for a full minute this time, please."

Shamefacedly, the student did as she was told.

Feeling she may have been a little harsh on the student, Julia wheeled the trolley back to its station next to the office, Nurse Evans following meekly.

"You'd better go to break, now. I know I told you off just now, but it's so important you don't get into bad habits while you are still a student. You are a good, kind nurse, all you need to do is dot the i's and cross the t's. You'll be fine, Nurse Evans." She smiled kindly at the young girl.

"Yes, Staff, thank you, Staff." The student beamed with pleasure.

"Tell me, do you live in the same nurses' home as Aneira Thomas?" Julia secured the trolley to the wall. "I was wondering when she was coming back?"

"Yes, she lives a few rooms down from me. She rang the home warden yesterday, she's coming back next Monday. Does anyone know anything more, Staff?"

Julia shook her head. "Your guess is as good as mine. But I'll catch up with her once she's settled in. If you see her before I do, tell her I've been asking about her, yes?"

"Yes, Staff, of course." The student picked up her bag and headed out of the ward. "And I've done the fluid charts too!" She grinned cheerfully, before pushing the heavy doors and trotting off to the canteen.

"Well done!" Julia rolled her eyes at the girl's irrepressible exuberance, but smiled indulgently and carried on gathering up the treatment charts for the post-operative analgesics.

Steph Saunders had changed the colour of her hair. The sleek, blond bob had disappeared, and had been replaced by a shock of bright orange spikes. An enormous pair of sunglasses and a leather cat suit completed the look. Mitch hardly recognised her, but he had to admit that for a wrinkly, her body was absolutely stunning.

"Mitch! Darling!" She crossed the beige carpet on her six inch heels and enveloped him in a bear hug, almost suffocating him, her heavy, cloying perfume making his stomach turn over. "Congratulations! Number twelve in the charts! You must be so thrilled! We've so much to discuss, you're in demand, honey!"

Mitch allowed her to propel him into a plush swivel chair.

"I've been in touch with your manager." Removing her sunglasses to reveal heavily made-up eyes, she referred to a sheet of paper she was holding. "Max Morrison?" Mitch nodded. "He'll be explaining the royalties and payments to the band when you meet with him-let's see-on Wednesday next week?" Again, Mitch nodded.

Steph stalked her way across the room to a small, occasional table and poured herself a large Scotch. "Care to join me, Mitch?" He shook his head, wanting her to get on with it.

Taking a large slug of the whisky, she beamed at him. "How does Top of the Pops grab you?" She paused for dramatic effect, eager to see his reaction.

"Television? Us? The band?" He hadn't been expecting this. This was all happening incredibly fast. He felt as though he was on a roller coaster ride without access to the brakes.

"Well, of course! You ready for this? I mean, we'll have to kit you out properly, can't have you guys appearing on the telly in baggy T-shirts and scruffy jeans! I was thinking maybe matching black satin suits, or possibly all denim, no, white denim. What do you reckon?"

"Um...not sure about anything matching, or anything satin, Steph." But he was saved from having to field any further suggestions by a subtle knock on the door. The Ice Maiden receptionist put her head around it.

"Sorry to interrupt, Miss Saunders, but there's someone here to see Mr Walker."

Steph sighed in annoyance. "Are you expecting someone, Mitch? Oh, go on then, send them in!" She was even more disgruntled when a bashful Julia was ushered in. "Who the hell are you?"

"Sorry, am I disturbing you?" Julia was mortified at Steph's rudeness, her pronounced Welsh accent even more obvious than usual.

Mitch got up, walked over to Julia and put his arm around her. "This is Julia, my girlfriend."

Steph's jaw dropped. She regarded Julia with disbelief. Pretty enough, she reckoned, but as dowdy as hell. Flat, black lace ups, an old duffel coat and hair done up in some sort of top knot. Realising what was going through Steph's mind, Mitch added, "Julia's a nurse, she's just finished her shift."

"Ah, I see." Patently, Steph did not. Why is he hanging around with that frump, she thought, when he could have the pick of thousands of groupies? Doesn't he realise that having a girlfriend is serious no-no for wannabe rock stars? She'd be a millstone around his neck. Julia seemed to read her thoughts only too clearly, and looked ready to do a runner.

"I just wanted Julia to meet you, Steph. If that's okay?" He dropped his arm to Julia's waist, tightening his grip, protectively.

"Hmm. Right. Hi there, Julia." Then she did a double take. "Whoa! Now I get it! Julia? *Julia!*" Her sunglasses nearly fell off their perch on top of her orange spikes, and she moved closer to Julia to get a better look, circling and scrutinising her from top to bottom. "So you're the mystery girl. I had absolutely no idea, no idea at all that you were a real person. You're not what I'd have expected, I must say."

Julia didn't know where to put herself. She stared at the carpet, wishing it would open and swallow her up.

"Julia's a staff nurse at the Infirmary. She looked after me when I was in with meningitis." Mitch was starting to feel fed up with Steph and her insulting remarks, his temper started to rise. "And she runs a ward with thirty patients in it, she knows how to resuscitate a patient if they have a cardiac arrest, she has to deal with burst abdomens-and she's only twenty bloody one years old! Nursing isn't just bedpans and thermometers, you know!"

Julia smiled at his last few words. He'd remembered them from their first date.

"Okay, don't get your knickers in a twist, Mitch." Sighing heavily, Steph sat down on one of the squashy sofas. "But there's one thing I have to make very clear. On no account are you to disclose to anyone that you're in a relationship-at all. Do you understand? If any of the teenyboppers find out that you wrote the song about her, they'll dump you, drop you like a hot potato, before you've even started!" Julia uneasily recalled the reception she'd received on the ward from all the staff and patients. Well, she thought, you could hardly call any of them teenyboppers...

"For Christ's sake why? What's the problem with having a girlfriend?" Mitch couldn't keep the frustration out of his voice.

Another major sigh from Steph. "Don't you get it? Do I have to spell it out for you? You're young, good-looking, you're in a successful band. There won't be many young fans that won't have a poster of you and the band on their walls after our publicity staff get to work. Those little girls will be dreaming their passionate teenage dreams about you, longing for you, wanting your autograph, imagining you asking them out, they'll be practising kissing on their arms, then they'll be kissing their mirrors, pretending they're kissing you! In their naïve imaginations, they are Julia. But if they think for one second that you're spoken for-forget it."

Julia's heart was sinking. After all the angst of the previous few weeks, another hurdle, an unwelcome obstacle was now being placed in front of her.

"I suppose I get where you're coming from." Mitch had to choose his words carefully. "Okay, I won't broadcast the fact that Julia and I are an item-a very serious item -" he smiled and kissed Julia's cheek, "-but I've bust a gut to get her, and I have no intention of giving her up-ever."

"Very well." Steph resigned herself that Mitch was no longer her property, not totally, anyway. "So about Top of the Pops..."

Julia breathed in sharply, looking up at Mitch with shining eyes. "Top of the Pops? My God!"

"Can Julia come with me when we go up to London for it?" Mitch could guess what the answer would be, but he thought he'd try his luck anyway. Steph gave him a very old-fashioned look, then shook her head.

"Sorry. Out of the question. No significant others allowed. The audience is selected months in advance."

Mitch sighed, and squeezed Julia's hand. "Will you mind if you can't come?"

She swallowed hard, the lump in her throat making it difficult. "Of course I'll mind. But you should do it! I want you to do it! What an opportunity!" Being brave is tough, she thought, miserably.

Mitch kissed her again, much to Steph's chagrin.

"Of course," Steph grinned evilly, "he'll have to watch out for Legs and Co! They'll be there too, dancing around looking gorgeous, maybe they'll bump into each other backstage!"

That's it, thought Mitch, sensing Julia's increasing despondency, enough is enough. "Well, it's been great talking with you Steph. I'll see Max as scheduled. We have to bugger off now, see you next week, then." And, grabbing Julia's arm, he steered her out of the office, through reception and into the cold February evening.

Steph watched them go, chewing her Biro thoughtfully. I wonder just how hungry he is, she thought, I hope he isn't going to throw it all away over a homely little nurse from the sticks. Her heart hardened, and she shoved her unhappy memories to the back of her mind, trying desperately to forget all her broken relationships, the unfaithful lovers and the shattered romances of her youth.

"That film may have been called "The Fog" but it's worse out here!" Mandy looked in dismay at the thick folds of mist that were hiding the buildings at the other side of the street. "It's going to be tricky navigating our way through this Andy. I've never seen such bad fog in Cardiff!"

Putting his arm around her, he led her to a nearby bus stop. "What shall we do next?" He checked his watch. "It's only nine o'clock. Shall we get some fish and chips? Or go for a drink?"

Mandy shivered, and pulled the collar of her smart, corduroy coat up over her neck. "Oh, let's just go home, shall we? I've got a Vesta curry in the cupboard, I think, and half a bottle of wine."

"Back to the nurses' home?" Andy sounded surprised. "Is that allowed?" The number 47 bus loomed out of the murky night, not registering the couple who were deep in conversation, and carried on towards Porthnewydd Avenue.

"Of course it's allowed," Mandy giggled, "but you're supposed to be gone by midnight. Miss Marshall will turn you into a pumpkin if you stay too long!"

"Well, that's one bus we've missed. Let's walk?"

"Why not? But I'm bloody freezing!" Mandy shivered theatrically, prompting Andy to remove his grammar school scarf and drape it around her exposed neck.

They couldn't even see more than a few yards ahead. Any light from the shops and pubs merely diffused out over the fronds of mist that were swirling eerily before them.

I wonder what's on his agenda, thought Mandy, he seems quite old-fashioned, straight-laced. Maybe he thinks I'm the same... But he really is something special, I don't want to get it wrong...

They continued their journey home at a snail's pace, the visibility so poor they couldn't even make out the Infirmary when they crossed the road which led up to it.

I hope she doesn't think I'm only after one thing, he thought, anxiously, as they passed the Gap in the Wall, she seems such a nice girl, one of the nicest I've ever met.

The fog seemed to deaden any traffic noise, and their walk home was hushed yet companionable, the pair holding hands, making idle conversation, but both apprehensive about the remainder of the evening.

Mandy's room was identical to Julia's, but faced south over the flat roof of the common room. Much more untidy than Julia, Mandy lived in a constant state of disarray, with underwear drying on the radiator, books and magazines strewn over the floor and dirty mugs lying in desperate hope of a wash in the tiny sink. A demi-john full of cloudy red wine bubbled away hopefully in the corner.

"It wasn't very nice, was it?" Mandy pulled a face and relieved Andy of his half-eaten plate of chow mein , putting it down on the ugly brown Flotex carpet beside the bed, where they were both perched.

"Doesn't matter, Mandy." He pulled her closer to him. "As long as it extended the evening, that's all I wanted, anyway."

"I've just realised something!" She giggled, nervously, feeling suddenly awkward. "What a pair we make!"

209

He looked puzzled. "What d'you mean?"

"Mandy and Andy! You couldn't have made it up!" Her laughter was so infectious he started chuckling as well, but not for long.

"Sounds okay to me." His voice sounded serious again. "Do you mind if I kiss you, Mandy?" He scrutinised her face to check her reaction, relieved to see she was grinning broadly.

"I thought you'd never ask!" She held up her open, happy face to his, her eyes sparkling and joyful. He put his arms around her and kissed her gently, brushing away her dark, brown curls from her cheeks, breathing in her warm perfume, sweet and musky.

They kissed on and on for what seemed like hours, enjoying the closeness, totally in tune with each other.

Coming up for air, Andy smiled down at her flushed face. "I don't want to rush things, Mandy, I don't want to spoil things. Let's just take it slowly?"

Feeling a cold hand squeezing her heart, her spirits sank. "You don't fancy me?" The disappointment in her voice took him by surprise.

"Of course I do! I'd be crazy not to! You're perfect, you're pretty, and an amazing figure!"

"I'm not too plump?" She was suddenly aware of her curvy thighs which looked even more chubby when squashed down on the bed.

"Don't be daft! I think you are absolutely gorgeous! Everything about you is fantastic." Lowering his voice he continued. "I fancy you like mad. I've thought about you constantly since that night in Elsie's. I just don't want to overstep the mark, that's all. I don't want to scare you off or anything."

He thinks I'm an innocent virgin, she thought uneasily, do I pretend to be one?

"I've had a few girlfriends in my time," he went on, "but none of them are a patch on you. You just tick all the boxes, you're attractive, you're funny, witty, intelligent."

"Well, I could say the same about you," she smiled, deciding to reveal nothing at the moment. Keep my powder dry, that's what I'll do, she thought.

There was a knock at the door, making them both jump. Mandy hurried to answer it. Julia wouldn't be bothering her now, surely?

"Coming!" She opened the door a couple of inches.

"Good evening, Staff Jacob." Miss Marshall's low voice was as cool as ever. "I hope you don't mind me knocking but it's almost twenty to twelve. I know you have a young man with you, so I thought I'd remind you. Goodnight." And she was gone, leaving a faint trail of Tweed perfume in her wake.

Shit. Bugger. Mandy shut the door and closed her eyes, feeling the blood rush to her face.

"Did she call me a young man?" Andy grinned.

"Oh, she's still living in the fifties! But I guess it'll have to be goodnight, then." She sighed in annoyance.

"Never mind, there's always tomorrow. Are you off?"

Mandy shook her head dejectedly. "'Fraid not. I'm on a late. How are you fixed next week?"

"This is my long weekend, which finishes tomorrow. But I'm off on Tuesday. Any good?"

"Perfect! I'm an early shift so we can meet up in the evening if you like?"

"Okay, then, shall we go for a drink in the Clarence, I can call by for you around seven?"

211

"That's great. I'll look forward to it." She couldn't keep the enthusiasm out of her voice.

" Not as much as me. It's been a lovely evening, Mandy. And thank you for that culinary surprise! I definitely wasn't expecting that! It certainly put Elsie's in the shade!"

They both laughed, then he bent down to kiss her goodnight, his hands remaining chastely around her shoulders. But there was no denying the passion, the desire of their embrace.

"Well, I guess it's goodnight. I'll see you out."

"And I'll see you on Tuesday."

As she closed the huge door behind her, Mandy quietly went back upstairs after turning off the hall light, her thoughts in a turmoil. As she locked her own bedroom door, she re-lived the evening. He was so incredibly considerate, so unbelievably thoughtful and attentive. And he hadn't tried anything on. He hadn't even tried to grope her. He must think her such an innocent. What would happen when he found out she wasn't? Mandy remembered the policeman she'd had a few dates with a year or so back; he hadn't been so restrained, and they'd jumped into bed on the first date. What if he worked with Andy? What if he found out that Andy was seeing her? Would he boast about his conquest? Oh, crap, she thought anxiously. She sat down at her dressing table to remove her make-up. She regarded her reflection critically, her eyes huge with worry in the rather dusty mirror. She didn't see the sweet, happy face that Andy liked so much, or the dancing, mischievous eyes, she could only see a pale face filled with trepidation. As she worked the Anne French cleansing milk into her cheeks, she felt worn out, confused and yet, at the same time, deliriously happy.

Moving over to the window to draw the curtains, she looked out at the misty scene. The garden was invisible, it was as though the whole house was floating on a sea of grey. Only one or two lights were on in the students' wing across the roof of the common room. Suddenly, her room seemed enormous and unfriendly.

Unwilling to allow her melancholic mood get the better of her, she hastily changed into her striped pyjamas and leapt into bed, pulling the duvet over her head to keep the phantoms of her memories at bay.

Chapter Nineteen Rejection

Aneira sat motionlessly on her narrow bed in her room at the nurses' home at the Infirmary, her head filled with worrying thoughts. The week she'd spent at home had been far from enjoyable. Her parents had cross-examined her endlessly, suspecting her of everything, from pregnancy to going out drinking every night. If only her sister had been there, to diffuse the situation and deflect the awkward questions being fired at her. The drive back to Cardiff had been equally unpleasant, her mother maintaining a stony silence and her father sighing and shaking his head occasionally, while Aneira crouched miserably in the back seat.

She'd so looked forward to going home, thinking she'd be happy there, safe...but the constant interrogation had made her feel like a criminal.

Her mug of coffee lay untouched on the bedside cabinet. She didn't feel like eating much, and the pile of Welshcakes her mother had insisted she take back with her remained uneaten in the old Quality Street tin.

You're far too thin, her mother had kept saying, you're not eating enough. But her appetite was so dreadful, she could hardly manage a piece of toast.

The little room was immaculately tidy, with nothing out of place and smelling sweetly of lavender Pledge. Her yellow uniform dress hung perfectly ironed on the side of the wardrobe, and her plain white nurse's cap was ready for the shift in the morning. Back at work, she thought anxiously, back on Terence Adams ward, back in the company of all the nurses...and Marcus Battencourt. The very thought of him made her stomach churn. How could she have ever thought he was great? The memory of that dreadful night still haunted her dreams. But the huge gaps remained, and although she couldn't remember all that had happened, she knew deep down that Marcus Battencourt had been responsible. But for what?

Only her small bedside lamp provided any light. She looked at her tiny alarm clock. Half past seven. Maybe she should pop over to the canteen in the main hospital, try and get something to eat. Hopefully, Marcus Battencourt wouldn't be about. Or any of his upper-class friends.

A knock at the door made her jump out of her skin.

"You there, Aneira? Can I come in?" The door opened anyway, and Gillian Evans bounced in, as chirpy and cheerful as ever, still wearing her uniform from her early shift. "How's it going then? You better?" Without waiting to be invited, the second-year plonked herself down on the bed.

Aneira blushed."Er, yes, I'm feeling better, thanks." Despite the fact that Gillian was only a few sets ahead of her, Gillian's second year status demanded reverence in her eyes. She'd achieved that much desired single yellow stripe on her cap.

"Bloody hell, Aneira, how on earth do you keep your room so tidy? Mine's like a pig sty!" Gillian surveyed the neat, orderly room incredulously. "Anyway, I haven't come here to compare rooms. Staff Harry, you know, Julia Harry from the ward? Well, she's been asking after you. She's really nice, once you get to know her. Bit of a Tartar when it comes to sticking to the rules, but she's pretty fair. Not like that Staff Lundy on Weston. All sweetness and light, but drops you in it as fast as you can say barium enema!"

"Really? Julia's been asking after me?"

Gillian raised a well-defined eyebrow. "First name terms, eh? Well, she's saying that if you like, to pop and see her, or ring her, whatever."

"Sure." Aneira looked down at her sensible corduroy skirt and fiddled with the pocket. "Thanks, Gillian."

"No problem. Hey, we're going over the Lexington later, d'you fancy coming?"

Aneira was amazed. Invited to join a bunch of second years on a night out? Despite the honour that was being bestowed upon her, she shook her head sadly.

"I'd better not, Gillian, but thanks all the same. I need to get an early night, I'm on at seven thirty tomorrow."

Gillian snorted, derisively. "So am I! And I've got my Phase One as well!"

Aneira gasped. "Your Aseptic Technique? Oh my God! Should you even be going out?" Then she wished she'd said nothing, as Gillian shrivelled her with a look.

"We won't be late, bed by midnight! Anyway, I can do my Aseptic Technique standing on my head! Sister Patel is on an early with us, and you know how sweet she is. Bye for now, then!" Tossing her head defiantly, Gillian left a stunned Aneira, still sitting on her bed, wishing she had even an ounce of Gillian's self-confidence. But the fact remained that the older girl had somehow managed to shake her out of her despondency. Staff Harry had asked after her. That made her feel a lot better. Opening the drawer of her bedside cabinet, she pulled out her Gideon's New Testament, looking for inspiration, for her Thought for the Day...

"And Miss Howells will be along at three o'clock, Nurse Evans, to supervise your Phase One."

Gillian looked at Sister Patel in horrified disappointment. "Won't you be assessing me, Sister?"

Daksha Patel sighed. "'Fraid not. Your clinical tutor has expressed the wish to supervise you, and as we all know, what Miss Howells says, goes. So you'd better be ready for her. I'm on a split shift, anyway." Sister Patel seemed disgruntled. "Sister Winter has had to take emergency leave, her mother has had a stroke, so I've got to cover. Anyway, for your Phase

One I've suggested you do the dressing on the laparotomy in bed one, removal of sutures."

"Oh, Jesus." Gillian had gone as pale as the bedsheets she was carrying. Lowering her voice to a murmur, she continued to Aneira, "Oh my bloody God! Heartless Howells. Oh, shit. She'll fail me, I know she will."

"Oh, you'll be okay." Aneira was desperate to reassure the older girl. "You're really good."

"You think so?" Gillian grimaced. "I hope you're right. Come on, let's get on with the beds..."

Miss Howells' sour-puss face scowled at Gillian, ticking off the boxes on the sheet she was holding. Aneira was praying with every fibre of her being that she wouldn't drop anything or make a huge blunder, as she'd been delegated the role of "dirty"nurse, having to open dressing packs and generally assist the quaking Gillian during her assessment.

Miss Howells was a heavy, lardy woman, with a severe black bob and a moustache on her upper lip. Aneira had never seen such swollen ankles on an otherwise healthy individual, and watched in secret distaste as the tutor's' fleshy neck spilled over her tight mandarin collar. In lurid fascination, she observed how the navy uniform dress stretched tightly over the tutor's vast abdomen and bosom, the metal poppers straining and threatening to release their adipose contents at any moment.

The assessment seemed to go well, Gillian methodically carrying out the procedure with Aneira assisting deftly. Nothing was dropped, the patient seemed happy, but how did Miss Howells feel..?

After the patient was made comfortable and everything had been completed, Miss Howells took the nervous Gillian into the office to complete the paperwork. She frowned, peevishly.

"Well, Nurse Evans. You appear to have carried out the dressing reasonably well." Gillian sighed in relief. "The ward cleaning had been

218

completed before you started, so of course you didn't have to worry about that, did you? You made sure adequate analgesia was given prior to the procedure, you ensured the patient had passed urine before you started. The actual aseptic technique was satisfactory and your instructions to Nurse Thomas were clear. You reassured your patient without speaking unnecessarily over the wound. I was pleased to see that you remembered to remove the sutures alternately." Gillian was beaming now. "However–I have to pull you up on one thing, which could be very important. Attention to detail is vital in nursing, Nurse Evans. Now what do you think you omitted to do?" Crestfallen, Gillian hung her head.

"Um, I'm not sure, Miss Howells."

Smirking in satisfaction at having caught the student out at last, the tutor continued her criticism.

"The window, Nurse Evans, you left the upper window open. Dust could have blown in and landed on the wound area. And there could have been an ensuing infection, yes?"

"But Mr Joseph said he was feeling hot, Miss Howells, he asked me to open it."

"That matters not one jot, Nurse! The prevention of cross infection and the maintenance of a sterile environment is of paramount importance. Don't let it happen again."

"Yes, Miss Howells." Gillian held her breath. The tutor glared at her over her pince-nez spectacles.

"I suppose I'll have to pass you. Congratulations. Here's your paperwork." Ungraciously, she threw the sheet of paper on the desk and marched out of the office, nearly bowling over a lurking Aneira as she went, who immediately rushed in.

"Did you pass?" Aneira was terrified for the older student.

Gillian flashed a wicked grin and lied through her teeth. "Course I did! I knew I'd be okay!"

Mondays in the Infirmary were usually hectic, with the trauma wards mopping up the fractures and head injuries from the weekend's rugby matches, which had naturally also resulted in inevitable excessive partying, plus the theatre lists would be in full swing. The noise levels reached their peak by late morning, with porters transporting patients to theatre, clerical staff rushing between offices, nurses chattering loudly on their way to the canteen and the domestic staff buffing the floors with immense floor cleaners. Then by eleven thirty the clanging of the meal wagons would add to the general din, with doors slamming and lifts clanking their way between floors. So much cacophonous activity, so much high energy, yet come half past eight in the evening, when all the visitors had departed, the hospital sank once more into peaceful efficiency.

Marcus Battencourt drained his mug of tea before checking his appearance in the mirror over the old fire place in the doctors' mess. Irresistible, he thought, smugly, adjusting his new, red satin tie, which had replaced the cravat. He'd gotten fed up with Anscombe always taking the piss. His bleep went off. Terence Adams. Picking up the phone, he rang the ward.

"Marcus here." His smooth voice could have oiled a hundred creaky doors. "There's no post-op analgesia written up for the hernia repair? Sure, no problem, I'll be along shortly. Ciao." Hmm, he thought lasciviously, that was fortunate. Sister Patel was in charge. Now he seriously fancied her. Big brown eyes, long black hair and as slim as a willow. A couple of years his senior, but he'd bet his bottom dollar she was a sweet little virgin - nothing beats a pure, virtuous virgin, he considered. Unadulterated, malleable, clean and unsullied. Ready for him, and him alone. Ready for him to break open that locked box of delights and discharge himself into that tight, snug little cave. His thoughts descended into his nether regions, he was starting to feel colossally randy. But, she was probably destined for an arranged marriage or something, and as likely as not would protect her chastity as though it was the Holy bloody Grail. But he might still get away with a bit of slap and tickle in the linen cupboard...well, you never know. Spraying a quick shot of Gold Spot into his mouth, he did up the bottom few buttons of his white coat, hoping nobody would notice the massive hard on that was rapidly developing.

Mandy was able to complete her handover and escape the ward before nine o'clock. Brilliant, she thought, hurrying along the corridor which lead to the stairs, I'll be able to wash my hair and dry it before I go to bed. Absorbed in her thoughts about hair-washing and the following day's date with Andy, she didn't initially notice the tall figure of Marcus Battencourt striding towards her.

As they approached each other, he watched her walk his way. Now she's no sweet virgin, he thought contemptuously, she's just a little slag. He'd seen all the photos Neil had taken of her – there'd been nearly twenty. Christ, they were seriously erotic. Not an uncorrupted maid, but maybe still worth a crack.

"Mandy!" He put his hands on her shoulders as though delighted to see her. "Where have you been? Haven't seen you for absolutely ages! How are you?" She was quite tasty, he decided, pretty face, small waist, big tits, big arse, and if his memory served him well, delightfully plump thighs. He imagined what it must be like, prising them apart and delving into what ever glories lay between them...

"Er, hello, Dr Battencourt." She wanted to get home. What was this prat doing trying to chat her up?

"Oh, call me Marcus." He grinned down at her, narrowing his eyes in what he considered to be a tigerish way.

"I've got to get home, I'm a bit late. Sorry!" She tried to shake him off but his hands remained firmly on her shoulders.

"Don't run away from me, baby doll, I was just wondering if you were free tomorrow? Fancy a drink or something?" At the 'or something' he crinkled his eyes even more.

"Sorry, I'm spoken for. Now I really need to go! Sorry and all that!" She flashed a triumphant smile at him, before scuttling away towards the stairs. Unable to resist it, she looked back. "You're losing your touch, Battencourt!" She called over her shoulder. "Nobody wants you any more!" And with a laugh she was gone, her head high and with a great feeling of satisfaction.

Bitch, bitch, BITCH! How fucking DARE she. He felt a white hot wave of fury sear through him, sod the post-op meds, he thought angrily, they can wait. Unable to stop himself, he set off in pursuit, his long legs descending the stairs two at a time, until he caught up with her just as she was pushing open the heavy rubber doors at the back of the hospital.

Flinging her around, he grabbed her by her collar and pulled her up so that her face was near his. "What did you say?" There was menace in his voice. "What the fuck did you mean by that?"

"N-nothing!" Alarmed by his venomous tone, she looked around desperately, her eyes massive with fear, hoping and praying that someone else would be passing by in the dark alleyway.

"Who the hell d'you think you are?" He sprayed her face with spittle as he hissed out the words. "You're nothing but a cheap tramp! A tart! A slag! Everyone knows how easy you are, Staff Fucking Jacob! You know what they all say, don't you? 'Have you climbed up Jacob's ladder, yet?' And you have the bloody cheek to insult me! ME? I'm warning, you, Mandy, you'd better watch your Ps and Qs or I'll-"

"Or you'll what?" Richie's grim voice cut through the darkness. "Take yer hands off her, Doctor Battencourt, or you'll have me to deal with."

Marcus released her abruptly. He tried to laugh it off. "We were just having a little chat, weren't we, Mandy? Just a friendly little chat. Messing about! Nothing to be alarmed about! Now don't you have some work to do, Mr Porter? Don't you need to go and push some trolleys somewhere? Or take some shit to the furnace In other words, get lost!"

Mandy gazed imploringly at Richie. Please don't leave me here with Marcus, she wanted to shout.

Richie took a step closer to him, scowling. "I'm warning you, Doctor Battencourt, don't push me any further!"
Marcus took in Richie's six foot four bulk, and decided maybe he better had beat a hasty retreat. He'd deal with Mandy at some later date, he thought.

Attempting to save face, he straightened his tie. "Well, I'll be off then. See you around, Mandy." Flouncing around, trying to recover his authority, he stalked importantly back through the rubber doors, not bothering to look back.

"Staff Jacob, you okay? Did that upper class twat hurt you?" Mandy could have wept at the genuine concern in Richie's gruff voice. Marcus may not have succeeded in hurting her physically, but she was shaking like a leaf. She'd never dreamed he was capable of such verbal brutality.

Struggling to maintain her composure, she smiled. "I'm okay. He's nothing but a bloody plonker. I turned him down when he asked me for a date, that's all. I don't think he liked that very much! Reckon I've wounded his pride."

"Shall I walk you home? It's my break soon, nobody will mind."

"No, I'll be alright. But thanks. Our dear Doctor Battencourt will be back on the ward by now, harassing some other poor woman. Cheers, Richie, you're one in a million!" She gave him a quick hug, before turning and heading for the Gap in the Wall, still with a forced smile on her face,waving goodbye to him as she went.

Slowly returning to the Porters' Lodge, Richie scratched his head in puzzlement. What the hell was going on in this hospital? He suddenly felt overwhelmed and quite depressed. Coming to a stop by the Lodge's door, he pulled out the incriminating photo of Mandy. Glancing at it in distaste, he sighed heavily. And what the hell was he going to do about that? Who could he discuss it with? Did Mandy even know? Shaking his head ruefully, he entered the Lodge and put the kettle on.

"Where's Sister Patel?" Marcus scanned the ward, irritably.

"She's a-gone 'ome." Maria Esposito didn't hold any truck with the likes of Marcus Battencourt. "I'm in charge tonight, Doctor. You come to write up da post-ops?"

"Er, yes." Damn and blast, he fumed. He'd been looking forward to a nice little flirt with Daksha Patel, and here he was, faced with this middle-aged Italian S.E.N.

"The charts are on the desk." She searched for the keys in her pocket, before unlocking and opening the drugs cupboard . "I'll just get out the Pethidine ready. Now where's da student to check before I bleep Night Sister..? Nurse Bevan?" She bustled out of the office in search of the elusive student, leaving behind a grinning Marcus Battencourt. The evening wasn't proving too bad after all, he thought in satisfaction.

Chapter Twenty Fame

Julia and Mitch were curled up on the sofa together, watching the news on the tiny black and white television. They'd just managed to get rid of Charlie, who'd been hanging around making a general nuisance of himself.

"He can't half talk, your friend." Julia snuggled up closer to Mitch. "I really like him, but God, he could bore for Wales!"

"Ah, that's Charlie for you." Mitch's hand started its familiar journey up her leg. "But the bastard said he wouldn't be long. He said he's only going to the Spar to buy some tinnies."

"Meaning..?" Julia's hand also found its way up Mitch's tightly jeaned leg.

"It's er, a bit risky for any hanky panky."

Julia giggled. "I love your euphemisms, Mitch! Hanky panky, rumpy pumpy!Why don't you just come clean and just say you fancy a bit of sexual intercourse?"

"I fancy a bit of sexual intercourse. There! Happy? Now, Julia, how's about it, then?"

She offered no resistance, and allowed his wandering hand the freedom to roam northwards, to the waistband of her black tights, pulling them down swiftly, while she unzipped his jeans, caressing his erect member until he groaned with pleasure.

"You hot little madam," he whispered in her ear, "I'm going to have to take you in a minute if you carry on like that!"

"Take me, then, you fiend!" She gazed up at him so wantonly that the tights were whisked right down in a second, also her pretty red knickers, before he entered her with a great sigh of delight.

"There's something unbelievably erotic about shagging you with your uniform on!" He paused in his rhythmic thrusts. "But I'm going to make you happy first, you naughty nurse, you!" He slid down the sofa, and his tongue found her tender rosebud, flicking it lightly then licking it slowly until she shuddered rapturously.

"Brace yourself, my darling, for here I come again!" And he re-entered her, his thrusts gaining in momentum until he was satisfied.

"Hey! I'm home! Whoo-hoo! Get your knickers back on, Julia! Do your flies up, Mitch!" And the front door banged, giving them just enough time to make themselves decent. Julia wriggled about uncomfortably, trying to ease the knicker elastic from between her buttocks.

Charlie looked at the flushed pair in amusement. "You randy buggers!" He chortled. "I only have to go out for a few minutes and you're at it like a pair of rabbits!"

"Bugger off, Charlie!" Mitch was only too aware of the wet patch next to Julia's thigh. Please don't get up to go to the loo, Julia, he thought desperately, and to make sure it couldn't be seen, he wriggled over as close to her as he could.

"Ooh, making room for me?" Charlie grinned wickedly, and threw himself down next to Mitch. "What's on the box then?" He opened a can of lager, taking a noisy swig and belching happily. As if in answer to his question, the familiar opening bars of Led Zeppelin's "Whole Lotta Love" filled the room.

"Top of the Pops." Mitch's tone was dry. "We just thought we'd watch it for a bit, I wanted to watch other bands and see how it all comes across. Our band's off up there next week, in case you'd forgotten."

Don't remind me, thought Julia miserably.

"Shit, yes! Of course! Mitch the rock star! Whoo hoo! Turn it up then. Can I come up with you?"

"Sorry, Charlie, no hangers-on at all, I'm afraid." Mitch glanced at Julia, who looked seriously down in the dumps. "Not even Julia is allowed." He kissed her forehead apologetically.

"Hey!" Charlie nudged Mitch in the ribs. "All them rock chicks drooling over you! They'll be on a plate for you, man!"

"Aw, piss off, Charlie!" Mitch had had enough of his flatmate's teasing. He stood up. "Anyway, we're buggering off out now. Julia's going home to change and then I'm taking her out for a Chinese." He pulled her to her feet, got their coats and left Charlie alone in the flat, shutting the door behind them.

Charlie settled down to enjoy the all-girl group jigging about on the screen, pretending to sing their hit single. He quite fancied the one with the long, dark hair, the top she was wearing was nice and low as well. Opening a packet of salt and vinegar crisps, he started stuffing them hungrily into his eager mouth. In his haste to scoff them, he dropped a few onto the vinyl sofa. Not taking his eyes off the singers' swaying bottoms for a second, he mindlessly groped for the fallen crisps and popped them into his mouth. A faint yet familiar aroma reached his nostrils, so he sniffed his fingers in casual curiosity. Then he looked at them, glistening and shining in the light of the TV. How come his crisps suddenly smelled of bleach? Then the full horror of the situation immediately dawned on him. His stomach turned over. Jesus!

"You dirty bastards!" He screamed in realisation. "FUCK! SHIT! Jesus CHRIST! I don't believe it!" He leapt to his feet, throwing the crisp packet into the bin, spitting crisp fragments everywhere, retching all the while, until he reached the kitchen sink, where he put his face under the cold tap, allowing the full force of the water to rush into his mouth and around his lips. Snatching up the ancient, smelly Brillo pad, he scrubbed away at his teeth until his gums were bleeding.

Just wait until that bastard gets home, he thought evilly, spluttering and coughing. He wildly plotted his revenge while he searched in the bread bin for a packet of biscuits to demolish instead.

The calm, cloudy Cardiff night allowed the loved-up pair an untroubled walk back to the nurses' home. Along the brightly-lit City Road, with its restaurants and takeaways, the spicy, tantalising smells of Bangladesh, Turkey and Italy mingled enticingly with the aromas of Szechuan and the odd burger bar.

Julia and Mitch had no real desire for food, despite their plan for a Chinese meal. They wandered along the road together, hand in hand, simply happy to be in each other's company.

"About the Top of the Pops thing..." Mitch knew Julia was fretting about it. "I honestly wish you could come."

She said nothing, but continued to stare ahead, smiling slightly, watching the headlights of the cars race along the road, fixing her mind on remaining serene and non-confrontational.

"Say something." He realised she was finding it hard to be honest. "You look like the bloody Mona Lisa! All sweet and untroubled, hair in a middle parting, trying to smile! Say something, for Christ's sake!"

"Alright." She swung around to face him, her grey eyes bright with unshed tears. "I love you to bits, Mitch Walker, I have never loved a boy before. You have my heart in your hands, and now–now... Now I think it's all going to be snatched away from me in a week or so."

"Why d'you think that?" He held her delicate face in both his hands. "Why on earth should you think that? Just because I'm going to London for a few days?"

She resumed her brisk pace along the pavement. "Because of what that Steph said. I'm a hindrance to you, Mitch, an anchor around your neck, a bloody albatross!"

"You've been reading too much Coleridge and got it all mixed up! Stop walking so fast!" He stopped her, and pulled her close. "Look. I've met hundreds of girls during my music career—as you have met boys in your nursing—and yes, I've gone out with a few, and yes, I've slept with a couple, but no-one has ever meant as much to me as you have, Julia. Not one of them has ever inspired me to write a bloody song! Not one of them has ever caused me sleepless nights. You are beautiful, funny, kind, clever...and I worship you. I love you." He lifted her sad, troubled face to his and kissed her gently. "Never doubt me. Please trust me. I will never ever betray you."

Raising her eyes to his, she sighed. "I believe you, Mitch. With all my heart. We are here in Cardiff, happy and together. But when you reach the bright lights of London, it'll be different for you. And don't forget, we must remain a secret. Miss Snazzy Saunders insisted on that!"

They put their arms around each other, walking more slowly, until they reached the junction with Porthnewydd Avenue and were almost back at the nurses' home, Mitch wishing he could convince her that all would be well, and Julia trying her hardest not to mind the inevitable separation and all it would entail.

Cali the Jamaican domestic was always thorough in her work. She enjoyed her job, took pride in it, was diligent beyond belief. The pay wasn't fantastic, but it helped cover the costs of her Open University sociology degree. She was determined to be a social worker one day. She didn't care that she was regarded, along with the porters, as way down the pecking order in the Infirmary. Her work was dirty, heavy and thankless, but she weathered it all with her unique brand of single-mindedness. If she could get this degree, and achieve her dream, she would be able to provide so much better for her young children as they grew up. Her husband had deserted her a few years ago, but she didn't miss him, not Cali. She was her own woman, a woman who had planned her destiny and was hell bent on making it happen.

She'd emptied all the bins in the doctors' mess, hoovered and washed the floor and was now on her knees in the tiny stock room attached, quietly checking the supplies of disinfectant and disposable dusters. Hearing the door of the mess opening, she kept perfectly still, as silent as a mouse. This was the part of her job she loved the most–the gleaning of interesting gossip and useful information. The hospital grapevine would collapse if it wasn't for Cali. She searched in the pocket of her maroon uniform for her paper handkerchief. Now was not a good time to sneeze, and she was sure she could feel a biggy coming on. Thankfully, she was able to stem it in its tracks, and crouched down once more, concentrating intently. It's those two toffee-nosed doctors, she thought, irritably, the ones who looked down their upper-class noses at her, regarding her as though she was something nasty on the soles of their shoes. When she was absolutely certain they had settled down in the lounge area, she peered discreetly around the door. They had their backs to her.

"Oh, well done, Battencourt!" Neil Hancock slapped his colleague on the back, pocketing the small object quickly. "Looks like being an entertaining weekend after all. You on call?"

Marcus Battencourt settled back on the shabby, dented sofa and picked at his immaculately groomed fingernails. "Only tomorrow night, thank God, then just the routine stuff on Saturday before yours truly can put his feet up for a well-earned rest." The doctors' mess was empty except for the two of them, they thought.

"Got anything lined up?" Neil drew deeply on his More cigarette.

Marcus wrinkled his nose in distaste. "D'you have to smoke those disgusting things in here? You just smoke them for show, don't you? I bet you wouldn't be seen dead with a packet of Embassy."

Neil chuckled, and blew a cloud of smoke up into the air, watching it spiral up languidly to the ceiling. "Bollocks! I enjoy it! Anyway, you haven't answered my question! Any sweet little nymphs on the agenda? Bit of a disaster with that first year, wasn't it? That Aneira? I bet you were bloody shitting yourself there!"

A scowl furrowed Marcus's otherwise bland expression. "I prefer not to discuss that. Not at the moment. Anyway, sweet nymphs are in rather short supply at present."

Cali's blood pressure began to rise. Bastards, she thought.

"Plenty of nymphos, though!" Neil grinned, lasciviously, putting his feet up on the battered coffee table. "Pity about that little student, mind you. I reckon it would have been akin to bedding a Sindy doll! Nevertheless – back to the subject! What about considering some of my left overs? What about Mandy?"

Marcus resentfully remembered his brush off. "Who wants to go out with a slag like her? Nah, I think I'll give that Lundy girl a bash, you know, the one on Weston."

"Bit tubby for you? Even so, I think she's been around the block a bit too, so she must be well-versed in the art of lust."

"How do you know?"

"Ah..." Neil tapped his nose mysteriously.

"Yes, I agree, she 's pretty overweight, but also very pretty."

"But no sweet virgin!" They both laughed. Marcus got up to make some more coffee.

Inside the stock room, Cali clenched her teeth in anger.

Neil continued his analysis. "So what d'you reckon is preferable? An innocent maid with a nice tight pussy, or a woman of experience, one who knows what she's doing?"

Marcus pondered on that one. "I think the perfect answer is to have an experienced woman, then get the obs and gynae chaps to sew her up nice and snug!" Amused at his own lewd attempt at humour, Marcus chuckled nastily, adding two sugars to the mug.

Neil smirked. "Well, if you're gonna try Lundy this weekend, I doubt you'll need any, er, assistance, will you?" He reached into his pocket and pulled out the small specimen bottle, waving it happily. "She's as easy to get your leg over as a five inch fence. You enjoy those chubby rolls of flesh, my friend, you enjoy!"

"I intend to!" Marcus stirred his coffee so vigorously it slopped over the rim. Hastily mopping it up with a grubby dishcloth, he resumed his position on the sofa. "You never know, she may be up for a threesome. I'll put it to her. She's so fucking desperate, she could well agree to anything. Maybe you can watch..?"

Neil threw his friend a lecherous look. "Is that a promise? I'll hold you to that. Mind you, you'd better get your snorkel ready for Staff Lundy, all that voluptuous blubber! You'll need it to catch your breath if you go down on her, she may not let you up for air! And a torch when you have to wade through the rolls of flesh to find her pussy!" Cackling away in mirth at his own joke, Neil lit another cigarette.

"I have no intention of going down on that one. Christ, what do you take me for? I wouldn't be seen ever again. No, she'll just get her knickers off like a good little nurse and I'll have my wicked way. Anyway, she's not obese, you twat, just pleasingly plump." But his expression had gone cold. He was getting pissed off with this conversation.

However, Neil was enjoying himself. "When you consider things, between the two of us, I reckon we've had at least ten per cent of the female employees in this hospital. I mean, only last month, I screwed Kerry from Medical Records - now she was a real goer-then good old Carolina Morris from Flanders – up for anything, she was, bloody crazy spinster – but the best one was Mandy Jacob, I reckon. That was a fun evening. With the benefit of hindsight, I don't think we'd have even needed the er, assistance anyway!" He sighed, reminiscing happily.

By now, Cali was seething. Bloody nobs, she thought, furiously. Unable to hold back any longer, she marched into the room, her eyes blazing in temper.

"For shame on you!" She could bellow when she felt like it, and she certainly felt like it right now. "I heard you! Slagging off Staff Lundy and Staff Jacob, talking filthy stuff! Talking about the women as though they're pieces of meat! Tearing apart their reputations like a couple of evil vultures! How dare you! Who the hell do you think you are? Some kind of sex gods? You've no respect for women, you deserve to be reported! And then making fun of Staff Lundy because she's not an anorexic stick insect!" Standing in front of them with her hands on her hips, Cali was a formidable sight. At five foot ten and fourteen stone, she was like a vengeful Amazon. "I won't forget this, mark my words. She's not fat! And for that matter, neither am I! But I could make mincemeat of you two if I so desired!" She jabbed her finger at them. "And you two would be there on the floor where you belong! You're disgusting, the pair of you!" She slammed the door as she left, leaving the two doctors dumbfounded.

"Jesus! Did she hear anything dodgy?" Neil couldn't disguise the alarm in his voice.

"Who cares?" Marcus sighed, picking up the Telegraph. "She's only a bloody domestic. Thick as shit, probably."

His bleep went. Picking up the nearby phone, he put on his best smooth voice.

"Marcus here, how may I be of assistance?" Then he cleared his throat. "Mr Anscombe?" He stood up straight. "Yes, of course, I'll be down to clerk him immediately. On my way, sir." Putting the phone down, he rolled his eyes at Neil. "Fucking Anscombe. Bloody intestinal obstruction in Cas."

Cali strode down the main corridor, her big hands in tight fists, intent on seeking out her partner in crime in the hospital's underground network. Together they formed the unofficial but universally recognised management of the porters, domestics, cooks, electricians and the rest of the ancillary staff. In her head, she replayed the scene she'd just witnessed. Those two doctors were unlike any others she'd ever come

233

across, with their arrogance and posh voices. They were up to no good, she was sure, but what?

Arriving at the Porters' Lodge, she pushed open the door. Steve hastily removed his feet from the table and stood to attention.

"Where's Richie?" Cali demanded, her mere presence making Steve squirm.

"Um, gone home, Cali, you've just missed him. Sorry."

"Humph." Without an explanation she turned around and stormed back into the main part of the hospital, as if she was a matron of old.

The following Sunday, Julia was at lunch break with the other nurses from the ward. It had been an incredibly busy morning, with two emergency admissions, four arranged admissions scheduled for theatre the following morning and a seriously ill post-op patient from the night before who had developed a massive haematoma under his wound. To cap it all they'd also had to deal with an unheard of impromptu ward round by Mr Robinson the consultant.

The staff canteen was crowded, the smell of Sunday dinner enticing even the off-duty nurses and doctors to queue patiently for this comfort food.

"Your song is number seven in the charts, Julia! You must be so chuffed!" Daksha Patel tucked into her roast chicken dinner.

"You bet I am." She'd finally got used to the fact that Mitch would be far away from her for a few days, but he'd said he'd ring her on the communal payphone at the nurses' home as soon as he could. "Also, the band's going to be on Top of the Pops this week! I can't believe it!" Examining her roast lamb critically and removing all the fat, she shovelled the last juicy piece of meat into her mouth.

Gillian Evans' eyes nearly popped out of her head. "Top of the Pops? Wow! That's amazing! Are you going up to be there with him? What will you wear?"

Julia's face fell. "Not allowed. That bloody woman, the record producer woman, you know, well she's completely vetoed it. He's not even allowed to say he's got a girlfriend. C'est la vie, I guess..."

"Oh, that's a shame!" Daksha was all sympathy. "Are you off Thursday evening? We could all watch it together?"

"That's a cracking idea, Sister!" Gillian was getting really enthusiastic now. "We could all bring a bottle of wine, and some crisps, and have ourselves a regular little party!"

"Why not?" Julia was laughing. "D'you all want to come over to Porthnewydd Avenue? The common room is huge and there's a colour TV there as well."

"Better and better! I'm a day off and I can be over by about half six?" The junior sister clapped her hands together, excitedly.

"Excellent, Daksha. Can you come, Gillian?"

The second year blushed, ecstatic to be included in this plan. "I'm an early, so yeah, I'll be there! Shall I ask Aneira as well? She's on an early too, I think."

"Of course, yes, you ask her!" Julia's mood was lifting rapidly. "We'll be quite a crowd at this rate! I'm sure Mandy is a day off, and she may want to bring Andy..."

"You having a party, Staff Harry?" Richie sat on a table opposite them, his tray crowded with a plate of Sunday dinner, apple pie and custard, a cup of tea and a Mars bar.

"Yes, I suppose you could say we are! Do you want to pop over? And your missus as well if she wants?"

Richie's broad face beamed with pleasure. "Well, that's very kind of you staff. Not sure my missus can make it, the baby's teething bad, see. What's the occasion?"

Gillian couldn't help herself, blurting out at top volume, "Julia's boyfriend is a rock star and his band's on Top of the Pops this Thursday! And he wrote the song about her! You know, the song called 'Julia!' It's number seven!" Her voice carried out over the canteen, reaching the pricked up ears of Neil Hancock. His flat expression gave nothing away, however, and he continued to pick at his beef curry.

"Well, fancy that! That's good news!" Richie grinned around at the nurses. "Seeing as it's a sort of celebration, I'll try and pop in for the show, I only live around the corner from here as you know. I'll ask the missus, and if she can get the mother-in-law to babysit, she'll come too, but I doubt she will, mind."

"Well this is turning into quite an eventful lunch break, ladies!" Daksha Patel pushed her knife and fork together. "But it's time to go back to work, I'm afraid!"

"Hey! Richie, my boy!"

The deep, Caribbean voice stopped him in his tracks. Turning around outside the canteen door, he saw Cali waiting at the foot of the stairs, her arms folded, always a sign of trouble.

"Cali! You okay?" He lumbered his way down the narrow steps. "What's the matter? What's up?"

"We can't talk here." She lowered her voice mysteriously. "Let's go somewhere quiet, private."

Richie grinned. "Hey, Cali! People will start talking about us!"

She scowled, pursing her lips. "I ain't kidding, Richie. I'm upset, I am. Real upset." They walked together along the first floor corridor. She was

236

only a few inches shorter than him, she realised. What a formidable pair they must look, marching along. She proudly put her chin in the air to emphasise that fact. They stopped outside Pharmacy, which was closed as it was a Sunday, and stepped into the small, dark porch.

"It's them two toffs. Them doctors, you know, the la-di-da ones."

Richie was on full alert. "You mean Hancock and Battencourt?"

"Them's the ones." She was so close to him he could see she actually had freckles on her dark skin. "Up to no good, those two."

"What they done?" Richie took a step back. Cali always had this habit of getting really close when she wanted to talk to him.

"Well, it's like this." And she told him everything she'd witnessed in the doctors' mess a few days ago.

"So what d'you reckon they're up to, Cali?"

She shrugged. "Dunno. But it's something bad, I can tell you. The way they was talking about women, about nurses..."

Richie turned away, deep in thought. What he may have lacked in any formal education was more than made up for by sheer animal instinct, gut feelings, and they were usually right.

"Hey, you paying attention, Rich?" Cali stepped in front of him, staring him right in the face.

"Course I am, Cali. I just need time to think about this, that's all. But believe you me, I feel the same as you. I just need time, that's all, a bit more time..." And he left her standing there in the Pharmacy lobby, her hands on her hips, frustrated at Richie's apparent lack of reaction. Well, she thought angrily, I'll be keeping my eyes and ears peeled even if you don't, Richie.

He wandered back down to the Porters' Lodge, his heart heavy. What if those two doctors had something to do with that photo? Steve had said that Hancock had dropped it. I'll have to do something about it, sooner than later, he thought. But what?

The journey up to London in the van had been fraught with problems. Just outside Swindon they'd had a flat tyre, which took Jeff over an hour to sort out. Then, as they'd reached the services outside Reading, there'd been a diversion, which took them down through Hungerford and Newbury before they could rejoin the motorway at Slough. The four hour trip had taken over six hours. Despite Jeff's unflappable driving and Dai's accurate map reading, when the band arrived at the Robin Hood Hotel, they were exhausted and irritable. Night had fallen; the menacing, heavy clouds had decided to discharge their wet contents onto the whole of west London and the four young musicians were heartily fed up. What a bloody launch from the platform of stardom...

"Where the hell do we park the van?" Mitch was in despair now. It was dark, cold, so much colder than Cardiff, and he was hungry. Plus he wanted to find a phone box so he could try and ring Julia.

"Do not worry, oh ye of little faith." Jeff's calm demeanour managed to pacify him. "I've had a word with the porter. Seeing as we're about to become extremely famous, he's given me the key for the staff car park around the back. I'll be back in a Jeff!" Mitch smiled at their old, familiar joke, and started lugging their equipment into the reception area.

Try as he might, the ten pence piece refused to go any further into the coin box, and there was a five pence piece stuck half way in the other slot as well. Mitch seethed in frustration. For Christ's sake, he thought, you'd think that in London of all places things would work properly. Stepping outside the booth, he wondered what he could do. Julia'd said she would hover near the pay-phone in the nurses' home between seven and half past. It was ten past already. Nothing for it, he decided, I'll just have to be 'fit,' as Julia was fond of saying, one of her comical Llanelli-isms. Taking a deep breath, he wandered over to the receptionist at the other side of the foyer.

"Er, excuse me?"

The fair haired young man in the beige suit and lilac shirt looked up from his paperwork and smiled, going slightly pink. "Good evening, sir, I'm James, your receptionist until midnight. How may I help you?" He was clearly as camp as hell, and completely bowled over by the sight of this tall, young Welshman.

"Um, I know it's terribly cheeky, but the public phone isn't working, and I need to ring home as soon as possible..."

"So you want to know if you can ring from here, yes?" What a lovely boy, thought James, fancy him ringing home to his parents. He must be very caring.

Mitch nodded, hopefully. "I'll pay for the call, of course."

James giggled conspiratorially. "Ooh, there's no need for that! It'll be our little secret!" He put the phone on the desk. "Dial away! But press 9 for an outside line." James moved away discreetly, pretending to shuffle some papers about, all the while ogling Mitch.

Neither of them were aware of the other three band members chuckling away behind the large potted plants outside the entrance to the restaurant.

"I won't let him forget this," whispered Dai, rubbing his hands in glee, "his first proper groupie!"

Back at the desk, Mitch managed to get the line out and rang the nurses' home. Within seconds it was picked up.

"Mitch? Is that you?" Her breathless voice sounded so relieved.

"Yes, it's me, Julia!" He was grinning like a Cheshire cat now. James pricked up his ears. Julia? Probably his sister, he thought, organising the pens on the desk.

239

"It's so lovely to hear your voice, Mitch!"

Feeling slightly inhibited, Mitch lowered his voice to a whisper. "It's lovely to hear you, too, Julia. I wish you could be here with me, sharing my room, you know what I mean?"

At the other end of the line, she laughed in delight.

James looked as though he wanted to cry.

"Oh wouldn't it be great if we could have a night in a hotel together! What's the hotel like, Mitch? Oh, I miss you so much!"

"It's fine, I'm sharing with Jeff. He snores." He lowered his voice again. "I miss you too, so, so much. I can't wait to hold you in my arms again."

James was looking positively sick by now.

"Will you be able to ring me again? I'm hosting a little party of sorts tomorrow, so all us nurses can watch you together!"

"You can depend on it. And don't forget, Julia, the song is yours."

Realising he was out of luck, James sighed sadly and started to polish the counter. Never mind, he thought to himself, better luck next time.

Mitch always thought that hotel restaurants at breakfast time were interesting places, not that he'd been to many. He often wondered where all these people were going during their visit to London, where they were from, were they on holiday, on business..? I bet none of them would guess where us lot are going today, he thought, helping himself to some cornflakes, before sitting down next to the others.

"Hey, lover boy! Who's got a new admirer, then?" Eddie chortled, all the while chomping away at his bacon and eggs with gusto.

"What are you on about?" Mitch was so nervous he couldn't have faced a cooked breakfast, but nothing was going to put Eddie off his grub, it seemed.

Dai grabbed the brown sauce. "That cute young man at reception, he's got the hots for you, boyo!" The three laughed, enjoying Mitch's acute embarrassment, especially when his rejected suitor minced his way into the restaurant with a pile of menus in his arms. James waved discreetly in their general direction and winked at Mitch.

"Go on, Mitch, wave back!" Jeff was killing himself laughing now.

"Piss off, you lot!" Mitch buried his face in the Daily Express, thoughtfully provided by the hotel. "Anyway, Jeff, if you stuff any more baked beans into your fat gob, you'll explode. And you know what beans do to you! The audience will be asphyxiated if they're anywhere near you, later on!"

"Oh, shurrup." Jeff took a swig of tea. "Ooh, there's toast there as well. I think I'll have some. Could be a long day! I need feeding up!"

"Jesus!" Mitch shook his head in disbelief.

"Fine." Jeff got up to raid the buffet once more. "But don't call me Jesus."

Just as they were finishing off their breakfasts, or in Jeff's case a five course, slap-up feast, the restaurant door was flung open and a blast of Chanel number 5 heralded the arrival of Steph, clad in the tightest of leopard-print dresses.

"Good morning, boys!" She beamed at them from behind her enormous sunglasses. "Sorry I didn't get to see you last night, but I didn't check in until almost midnight. Such a lovely chap on the desk, James, I think his name was. I told him I was in your party-he was so interested! He had no idea you guys were going to be on Top of the Pops! He's asked me to get your autograph, Mitch. I told him to ask you himself, but he said he's too shy!"

Eddie, Dai and Jeff roared with laughter. Mitch felt like curling up with embarrassment, especially as the guests at the neighbouring tables were now staring at them with surprised interest.

Steph looked pleased with herself, and the effect they were all having on the other guests. "Anyway," she clapped her hands together, "we'll need to get cracking shortly."

"Fine," said Jeff, "but don't call me Shorty."

Steph gave him a filthy look. "Okay, we meet at the studios at eleven. I'll see you at the Centre. Just going to order a cab." No way was she going to slum it in that van.

The boys looked at each other in excitement They were almost there.

Bob, the tall, energetic assistant floor manager was nearly having an apoplectic fit as he tried to organise the solo acts and bands into some kind of running order. Nobody was doing as they were told, artists were disappearing all the time; he'd caught one of the drummers snogging with a member of the audience and he had a sneaking suspicion that the lead singer of the band whose record was at number two had locked himself into the hospitality suite with the comely production assistant. The Television Centre was thrumming with lust, it seemed.

Mitch and the boys looked around in awe at all the frenetic activity. Then they looked at each other in despair. Steph had had her way, to a degree. Gone were the scruffy, baggy jeans and random T-shirts. They all sported black drainpipes and tight black shirts, the sort that made Jeff want to keep holding his gut in. He wished he could leave his hanging outside, but Steph was having none of it. She had disappeared ages ago, saying she had a meeting with one of the programme's directors, leaving the band languishing for hours in one of the dressing rooms, with only their fraught nerves, a few curly ham sandwiches and tins of Coke for refreshment.

242

"Thank God you guys are behaving yourselves!" Bob breathlessly rushed into the room, clutching a clipboard as if his life depended on it. "Now are you certain you'll be performing live? Does your record company know and have they agreed? It's not too late to change your minds, but I need to know right now."

Mitch's head was buzzing in reaction to the manic atmosphere, but he decided to brazen it out. Casting a warning glance at the others, he smiled confidently, crossing his fingers behind his back. "Sure, we're playing live. There's no question of us miming. It's all been agreed. Just using a backing track for the female harmonising vocals." Tough luck, Steph, he thought.

Bob ticked a box on his sheaf of papers. "Okay. Well, you're on in about fifteen minutes. Stay where you are, you'll be called over to take your places any second." He rushed off, searching desperately for the dancers, who were on next.

"I've gonna have the two bob bits!" Jeff had turned green. "It's nerves! I'll be back in a minute!" He dashed off to the Gents, holding his stomach in high anxiety.

"Nerves, my arse," Dai sneered, "it's all those bloody baked beans this morning!"

"He'd better bloody hurry up," grumbled Eddie, whose stomach was also performing cartwheels.

Mitch glanced around at the milling audience, who were looking pretty fed up and tired by now, having clapped, cheered and danced for what seemed like hours. The frenzied environment of the Top of the Pops studio was overwhelming, he could hardly think, or even breathe. Would it always be like this?

Just as a couple of sound technicians were rudely pushing past them, yakking away loudly in their London twang, Jeff was back, looking a lot better, tucking his shirt in his jeans.

"I just saw Bowie in the bog!" Hastily, he made sure his flies were done up. "Seriously cool guy! Said hello to me! Can you imagine?"

But there was no time to answer or imagine, as they were being called to take their places on the rostrum at the other end of the studio. Shit.

As glitter balls went, this one was massive, spinning around overhead. Mitch wished he could stare at it forever, it was remarkably hypnotic. The rest of the band stood poised on their individual rostrum, apart from Dai, who was sitting behind his drums, biting his nails, even though there was hardly any nail left to bite. Eddie examined his shiny new shoes; he could see his reflection in them, he realised. Only Jeff appeared composed, having recovered completely from his visit to the Gents earlier. Inside he was quaking. No chance on God's earth of him cracking a smile right now.

The handsome, smiling presenter put his arm around Mitch, holding the mic so they could both be heard. It was stiflingly hot. Mitch was starting to sweat profusely. He hoped the stage make-up so carefully applied by the cosmetic artist would hold up and stop the tell-tale beads of perspiration which were threatening to emerge. The studio lights seemed to be burning a hole into his skull, he could feel his hands shaking. Controlling his anxiety, and putting on a wide grin as previously instructed by the stage manager, Mitch looked straight at camera number five, and prepared himself.

The presenter's smile widened even further. "Well, boys and girls, we now come to our highest climber in the charts! It came in at number twenty-five last week, and now it's hovering at number seven! All the way from Wales, a brand new band, a brand new sound! Say hello to The Mitch Walker Band, and its singer, songwriter, and keyboard player, Mitch Walker!"

A big round of applause, cheers and whoops filled the studio. The presenter's teeth seemed to glitter and sparkle as the lights hit them. Mitch stared at them in fascination. Were those teeth for real?

244

"So tell us, Mitch, what is your song called, and what's it about?" The presenter looked back at the camera and grinned some more.

Right, here goes, thought Mitch.

Chapter Twenty One Revelations

The common room, rather grandly named the TV lounge by the warden, Miss Marshall, was packed full of excited nurses. Daksha, Julia and Aneira sat huddled together on one of the three sofas, the one directly facing the big television. Gillian Evans lay sprawled on the floor, munching her way through a bag of Scampi Fries and Richie sat awkwardly at the communal dining table sipping a bottle of stout. Several other student nurses had got wind of the prestigious event and had bagged the remaining two sofas. Mandy and Andy sat squeezed together in a prehistoric armchair and even Miss Marshall had put in an appearance.

Finally, at two minutes to seven, Daksha got up. "Everyone got a full glass?" She brandished the half empty bottle of Pomagne. "Get ready, now girls, we're about to see Julia's boyfriend become a rock star!" She went over to the TV to turn up the volume. Julia sat on the edge of her seat, gripping the edge so tightly her knuckles were white. She had no idea when the band would be on air, but she supposed it would be around half way through the programme. There were so many butterflies in her stomach it felt as though they were dancing Le Papillon. She paid scant attention to the Motown number, or the New Wave band who had seemed so bloody slick and professional. Please, God, make it go well for him, she prayed, silently.

Legs and Co were elegantly completing their routine, when the camera panned around the audience, coming to rest on the presenter. And Mitch.

"It's HIM!" Her scream reverberated around the room. "He's there! He's on!" Everyone stopped chattering, drinking and munching, and stared intently at the screen.

Mitch was smiling broadly. "Well, the song is called Julia. It's about a lost love, a beautiful girl called Julia."

247

Julia held her breath. The world seemed to stop turning on its axis. All eyes were fixed on the television.

He continued. "But the lost love was found. I found my Julia. She's the light of my life." Looking straight at the camera, he stopped smiling and became serious. "This song is for you, Julia, just for you. You are my world."

There was a collective 'ah' from all the nurses, and even Richie wiped away a tear. That's the little bugger who was hanging around the ward, he realised. Just goes to show how wrong you can be about people. That reminded him, he had that photo in his pocket. He needed to get Julia on her own before he left.

Mitch returned to the band and the song started. Singing it live, Mitch's voice revealed the raw emotion behind the words, and his sad expression was caught beautifully on screen. As camera 5 panned out around the audience once more, Julia could see the rapt expression on the female faces, adoring and worshipful. But the song's mine, she thought, blissfully, he loves me.

There was an almighty cheer in the common room as the song came to an end, everyone standing up and yelling at once.

"You must be so proud, Julia!"

"I'm so chuffed for you!"

"Fancy him writing a song about you!"

Mandy ran over to her and hugged her hard. "Bloody fantastic, chick!"

Miss Marshall, also wiping away tears, walked calmly over to Julia, putting both hands on her shoulders. "A beautiful song, my dear, and dedicated to you as well. Don't let love go, grab it with both hands -" Julia saw Mandy struggling not to laugh behind Miss Marshall's back "- for true love only happens once in a lifetime." Replacing her glasses, she turned around and sedately left the room, like a ship in full sail. Maggie Thatcher, eat you heart out, thought Mandy in amusement.

248

Easing himself to his feet, his back a bit stiff after sitting down in that uncomfortable chair for nearly an hour, Richie edged his way closer to Julia, who was now surrounded by the fawning students

"Er, Staff Harry?"

Breaking away from the adulation for a moment, Julia hurried over to him. "You okay, Richie? Did you enjoy it? What did you think?"

Beaming down at her from his lofty height, he replied,"Oh, it was cracking, Staff. Bloody well pleased for you, I am. And I recognised him too!"

"You did? From when he was a patient?"

"Nah! I gave him a bollocking coz he was hanging around the ward looking for you. Caught him a couple of times. Only at the time I didn't know he..." He looked away, embarrassed.

"He came to the ward looking for me more than just the once? He never told me that!" Julia felt a warm glow rush through her. How hard he had tried to get hold of her. How could she ever doubt someone who was as determined as that?

"Before I go, Staff, is there any place I can have a quiet word with you?" His hands were sweating now, knowing what lay ahead.

"Sure, you can come over to my room, if you like? Mandy and Andy will be there as well, so don't worry, I'll have chaperones!"

"Um, I needs to see you alone, Staff. It's a bit awkward, like."

"Okay." Puzzled, Julia racked her brains for somewhere to have this quiet chat with Richie. "I tell you what. Let's go to the other common room around the front of the house. The one with a piano in it. Nobody ever sits in there, it's too cold and there's no TV."

"Perfect, Staff."

Julia led the way, wondering what on earth it could be about. What could this gentle giant want to tell her that required such secrecy?

Steph's shriek of outrage was obliterated by the screams and cheers of the audience. Her scarlet lips formed a perfect 'O' as she reacted in furious frustration to Mitch's revelation. The stupid, stupid boy! She'd warned him to keep his bloody girlfriend quiet. Jesus. PR would go nuts when they found out. She had to think of some damage limitation, and come up with a solution, fast. Her neck was on the block, now. You idiot, Mitch Walker, she seethed.

As the band left the rostrum and made its way over to where she was standing, she did her best to compose herself. No point in making a scene now, that would be unprofessional, to say the least.

"Well done, boys!" She hugged and kissed them all individually; Dai was so short, he only reached her shoulders. Steph was wearing five inch heels, so she managed to smear her bright red lipstick all over his forehead. He was relieved his feisty little fiancee wasn't around to witness this. Steph hadn't been told about her, he realised, uncomfortably.

"You all did really well. Good idea to do it live, Mitch." Steph led the way through the maze of corridors to the changing rooms, the band following meekly in her wake. "It sounded amazing, and you all looked amazing too." She opened the door of their dressing room. "However, we need to have a little chat, okay?" After they'd all trooped in, she closed the door firmly.

"Right then." She gestured to them to sit down, remaining standing herself. "We need to discuss your private lives, boys, pronto."

Mitch looked at the others. Here we go, he thought.

Back in Cardiff, Julia quietly closed the door behind them. The room was dark, only illuminated by the street light outside. The loneliest room in the whole building, it was shunned by the nurses on account of its stiff formality. Time had stood still for about forty years and the shadowy memories of young student nurses from long ago seemed to linger in its dark recesses.

"I'll keep the light off,"she whispered, "it'll stop the others realising we're in here. What's happened?"

Dreading what he had to do, Richie fumbled around in the pocket of his parka. "You may need to put the light on to look at this. It's your friend Mandy. I don't think she knows about this."

Julia hurried over to the enormous table lamp which had graced the sideboard for over twenty years and switched it on.

"Show me." She held out her hand.

Reluctantly, Richie gave her the incriminating photo. As Julia looked at it, a series of emotions raced through her mind.

"Oh my God!" She felt quite ill, looking at her best friend, apparently unconscious, practically naked, with some fat guy touching her up. She sat down on the faux leather couch, unable to process what she was seeing. "Where did you get this?"

Richie shuffled awkwardly from one foot to the other. "Steve found it in the doctors' mess a couple of weeks ago. He says it was Hancock what dropped it, like."

"Neil Hancock? Dr Hancock?"

Richie nodded miserably. "I didn't know what to do for the best, and seeing as I was coming here tonight, I thought you'd better know. I thought you'd know what to do."

"I feel like tearing it up!" She was livid. "I feel like ripping it to pieces! Oh, Richie!" She burst into angry tears.

Clumsily, he patted her on the back and offered her a crumpled paper tissue to dry her eyes.

"What do we do about it, Staff? I mean, look at it – d'you reckon she's asleep or unconscious or what?"

Julia turned away, fretfully. "Oh, Richie, I think this has something to do with an event that happened a few weeks ago. She went out on a date – well, it wasn't a proper date – with Neil Hancock, but Miss Marshall found her on the steps outside at the end of the evening. She thought Mandy was drunk. But Mandy swears blind she wasn't, and the most worrying thing is that she can't remember anything." She paced up and down on the cold, parquet floor. "I'll have to tell Mandy. We can't have other people knowing about this photo when she doesn't."

"Do we have to?" Richie was feeling worse and worse about the whole situation.

"We must. I'll do it, obviously. Can I have the photo?" She held out her hand, and Richie reluctantly relinquished the offending picture. Then a dreadful thought occurred to Julia."You haven't told anyone else about this, have you?"

"Bleedin' 'ell, Staff! I would never do such a thing. The only other person who's seen it, apart from them bleeding doctors, is Steve, and he never recognised Mandy anyway, thank God."

"You talking about me?" The light was switched on and Mandy and Andy burst in upon the pair. Julia hastily shoved the photo into her pocket.

"What the hell you doing in this dim light, Julia? Hey, have you two suddenly realised you're soul mates? I thought you were happily married, Richie!" Mandy punched him playfully on the arm.

Julia thought quickly. "Oh, don't be daft, Mands! Richie was just asking me about how to go about getting a vasectomy. He was a bit shy." She shot a meaningful glance at Richie, whose face was a comical mask of horror, and had gone a delicate shade of puce.

252

"I'll, er, be off then, Staff. And thanks for the advice. I reckon I've changed my mind about the old, er, vajectomy thingy." And he was gone, glad to be hurrying away from this uncomfortable scenario, and mortified that those young nurses were discussing men's private affairs so blithely.

"You off out?" Julia hastily pocketed the photo before Mandy could spot it.

"Yeah, just down to the Clarence. Andy's starting a new post tomorrow, so I'll be back before ten."

"Oh, that's great!" Julia was relieved to divert the attention away from her and Richie. "What's the new job?"

Andy looked as proud as punch. "Well, you won't be seeing me in uniform for a while. PC Greenleigh-Peters will now be known as DC Greenleigh-Peters!"

"DC? What's that?" Julia looked puzzled.

"Oh, for goodness' sake, Jules, don't you ever watch The Sweeney? He'll be Detective Constable now!" Mandy squeezed his arm in delight.

"Wow! How cool is that? Congratulations!"

"Cheers, Julia. I'm really looking forward to it."

"So if you're still up when I get back Jules, you can put the cocoa on!"

Oh, I'll be up thought Julia, anxiously, I'll most definitely be up.

Steph Saunders prowled around the dressing room like an aggravated wild cat in her leopard-print dress, a murderous expression on her heavily made-up face, sighing dramatically and fiddling with her sunglasses.

"I cannot believe you were so stupid as to announce to the whole world you had a girlfriend."

"Have." Mitch couldn't resist correcting her.

"Shut up, Mitch. I haven't finished yet." She scowled at him before continuing. "You have no idea of the damage you have probably caused by your childish action. Rock stars do NOT have girlfriends. They are available. That's part of the attraction, part of the deal. It's what sets those little girls' hearts racing, and then their little legs go racing off to the shops to buy the merchandise, the records, the posters, the T-shirts. You get my drift?" They nodded, mutely. "They are buying a dream, they live in hope. Now in five seconds flat you have shattered that dream. God knows what the boss is going to say about this." She stopped in her pacing to light a cigarette. Drawing heavily on it she resumed her tirade. "You guys need to think very carefully about your contracts. Your rock music career is in its infancy. You are on the brink of smashing it to smithereens, jeopardising your futures. You -"

"Hang on." Jeff got to his feet, holding up his hand in protest. His impressive height and calm demeanour managed to stop her in her tracks."Sorry to interrupt you, Steph, but maybe we would like to say something now. It's all very well treating us like naughty schoolboys, but I don't recall anything in the contract which mentioned personal relationships. I've read that contract, we've gone through it with Max. So far we have honoured every stipulation. You have nothing to complain about, really."

"How dare you!" She furiously stubbed out her cigarette on a used china plate. "You've only been in the industry for two bloody minutes and here you are laying the law down to me! ME!"

Jeff stood his ground. "I'm not laying any law down, Steph, I'm merely stating facts. And we've been musicians for many years, despite our apparent youth. You can't dictate to us how we live our personal lives. You may prefer it if we were hell-raisers, took drugs, got drunk all the time, smashed our guitars and stuff, maybe that would be better for our so-called image. But we are who we are." The others looked at him in respectful admiration. Steph remained silent, wondering how she could react to this.

"There's something I'd like to say, too." Mitch spoke quietly, remaining seated. "Steph, you're trying to swim against the tide, you want us to pretend to be something we're patently not. I'd like you to reconsider the situation."

"How?" Her response was ungracious. She folded her arms and threw herself sulkily into a leather swivel chair.

"Why don't you go with the flow? We are – more or less – clean living chaps. Jeff here is doing his P.H.D. and Eddie had been considering a move to Stevenage, although I think that's on hold now, as the band is taking off. I'm in a relationship, and Dai's engaged."

"WHAT?!" Steph nearly fell off her chair. "You never mentioned that!"

"Um, you never asked," replied Dai, timidly, cringing under the blast of Steph's blazing eyes, wishing Meinir was there to defend him.

Mitch carried on."What I'm trying, and failing, it seems, to say, is why don't you market us as the boys we really are? Honest, down to earth, the sort of lads girls would be happy to take home to meet their parents. Ordinary. Nothing sleazy or dodgy about us. Promote us as having clean appeal."

She looked at him suspiciously. "Go on."

"We've had a little taste of the high life, of the razzmatazz, the bright lights. And to be honest, it's fun, but not on a long term basis."

"So what are you trying to say? You wanna quit? You'd be in breach of contract." She smiled triumphantly

"Not at all. But our contracts state we have to produce songs for the company, which of course we will do. And do live concerts as well. As long as we fulfil all the terms and conditions of the contract, everybody should be happy." Mitch was determined, a steely look in his eyes.

"But don't you want the fame? The exposure to the media? Your band's name in lights? Most aspiring bands would give their right arms for the chance you guys have been given!" Steph could not believe these boys.

"Not really." Eddie finally chipped in. "We've had a long chat about this, while we were driving up to London. How many bands have been one-hit wonders, Steph? Bursting onto the scene in a blaze of glory, then disappearing just as quickly. We prefer to take things steadily, with Mitch composing and singing, us playing and performing, plus recording. We're realists."

Steph was silent, taking in all that had been said. She huffed, sulkily.

"Very well. I can't force you. Have it your own way. But don't come crying to me if you change your minds. In my opinion, you're throwing away a golden opportunity."

Mitch grinned, confidently. "We can handle that, Steph."

Chapter Twenty Two Teamwork

Mandy happily ran up the stairs of the old wing of the nurses' home, feeling elated. She was going out with a detective! Mr Detective was madly keen on her and Staff Nurse Jacob fancied him something rotten – maybe she was even falling in love with him? A thin strip of light under the door of Julia's room indicated she was still up.

She knocked."Can I come in?" Julia opened the door almost immediately, a bright, forced smile on her face. A smile which soon disappeared as soon as they both sat down on the bed.

"What's the matter?" Mandy could see Julia was upset about something. "Have you had bad news? Is it Mitch?"

Julia searched for the words. "Well, bad news of a sort – but not Mitch, no he's fine, he rang me about an hour ago."

"Well, tell me, for goodness' sake!"

Julia took a deep breath, and looked Mandy straight in the eye. There was going to be no easy way around this. "You remember that night you went out with Neil Hancock? To have your photos taken?"

Mandy nodded, a sinking feeling in the pit of her stomach. "Go on."

"I don't know quite how to put this, Mands, but you were most definitely taken advantage of that night."

Mandy paled visibly. "What the hell do you mean?" She felt as though the room was closing in on her. She suddenly became aware of small details, the regimented line of Body Shop cosmetics on the dressing table, the gap in the curtains where Julia hadn't closed them properly.

"Richie gave me this. It was found in the doctors' mess." Quaking inside, Julia held out the photo. Mandy snatched it from her and gazed at it in disbelief. "Oh, Jesus Christ. Oh my God. What did he do to me? And who is that man? That's not Neil! And he's doing things to me!" She raised her head, her eyes huge with fear. "I don't remember any of this, Jules, nothing at all!" She burst into tears, feeling both scared and utterly ashamed

"Only Richie and I know about it, Mands." Julia put her arm around her. "Richie didn't know what to do with it. He's furious on your behalf. He's devastated for you as well. It's pretty obvious you were out of it, knew nothing about what was going on."

"The bastard!" Mandy wrenched herself away from Julia. "He must have doped me. He bloody well must have! Oh, Julia, Christ only knows what they did to me! D'you think they both screwed me? I was really sore afterwards! Oh, my God! I feel so dirty! And there's probably other photos as well! Oh my God, what the hell am I going to do?" Her normally merry eyes had taken on a crazed, hysterical look.

Julia tried to keep calm and rational. "We'll do nothing tonight, Mandy. We need to think about it carefully. In fact I've done nothing but think about it for the past couple of hours. But this is serious stuff, and I don't mean just the actual photo of you. It's criminal, surely, to slip someone a Mickey Finn, then, you know, take advantage of them?"

"You mean *rape* them, take porno pictures of them, you mean!" Mandy was almost screaming by now.

"Hush! We don't want the Marshall coming up here!" Julia tried her utmost to quieten her friend, holding both her wrists firmly. "Mandy, we can't handle this on our own. I wouldn't know where to start? Why don't we try and sleep on it and have a chat in the morning?"

"Sleep? You have got to be kidding!" Mandy stood up and paced up and down the room. "I've just thought of something horrible, Jules!" An agonised look of despair was etched across her face.

"Tell me." Julia was endeavouring to stay composed.

"Andy! What if he finds out? Those vile pictures could be anywhere, there could be loads of them! Goodness knows where they could end up! He'll dump me! I know he will. He thinks I'm a virgin, or at least pretty unsullied. He's so old-fashioned. Oh, God what a mess!" She threw herself back down on the bed, her head in her hands, weeping afresh.

Julia thought carefully. "Andy could be your best chance of sorting this out, Mands."

"How?" She didn't look up.

"He's a copper. He's in this new post as a detective, well, at least a junior one, but he'll know what to do, won't he?"

"But he'll dump me if he finds out I'm no innocent." Mandy raised her tear-stained face to her friend. "What man would want a girlfriend who allows this sort of thing to happen to her?"

Julia remained silent for a while, all the while imagining various scenarios, before asking quietly,"Mandy, do you love him?"

"Yes. Yes, I think I do."

"And do you think he loves you too?"

"We haven't said as much to each other. But yes, I'd say we've got a fantastic relationship going, and he respects me, he wants to see me all the time – and, dear Lord, he was talking about taking me home to meet his parents!"

"Well, this is the one time you're going to have to put your trust in him. If he dumps you, so be it. But you can't go on like this, worrying all the time and scared. If you are open and honest with him, and you both love each other, surely you can work something out?"

A glimmer of hope lit up in Mandy's eyes. "Do you honestly think so?" She blew her nose noisily on one of Julia's peach Kleenex, kept within handy reach on the bedside cabinet. Julia sighed. "Well, I can't guarantee anything, but if you look at things logically-"

"Oh, it's easy to be logical when it isn't happening to you, isn't it!"

Julia was taken aback at the bitterness in Mandy's voice, she didn't quite know how to react.

Mandy looked regretful."Look, I'm sorry, I didn't mean to be so nasty. I know you're doing your very best to help me, it's just that I feel angry, no-furious-and so horribly scared."

"It's okay, I don't mind." Julia handed her a fresh tissue. "When are you seeing Andy again?"

"Not until next Monday. He's on a course over the weekend, somewhere up in Birmingham, ready for his new job."

"Well, that gives us a bit more time, doesn't it? Look, go to bed, try and get some sleep. I'll give you a knock in the morning. You on a late as well?"

Mandy nodded, glumly.

"Right. Well discuss this tomorrow, when your head is a bit clearer, and form some sort of plan, yes?"

Again a silent nod.

"Remember, Mands, I'm your best mate, and I'm on your side, you're not alone in this, okay?" Impulsively, she reached over and hugged her. "This is not your fault, remember. And I won't breathe a word of this to anyone."

"Not even Mitch?"

"Not even Mitch, Mands. This is confidential, and I won't discuss it with anyone without your permission."

"Thank you, Jules. Where the hell would I be without you?" Mandy picked up the offending picture and left the room, a sad, dejected young girl, wondering what on earth was going to happen.

Sleep was an absent bed-mate that night. Mandy tossed and turned, her sheet twisted and crumpled on top of her. Shame, anger and fear flew in quick succession through her shattered mind. Was I responsible for this, she wondered, helplessly, should I have known better? I shouldn't have led him on, I shouldn't have let him photograph me in my underwear. Giving up any thought of falling asleep, she got up and wandered over to the window.

Gazing out at the darkened garden below, she re-played the events of that fateful evening. She'd trusted Neil Hancock; she'd thought he was a bit of a rake, yes, but not someone who would deliberately dope a girl and then have sex with her. A shooting star flew across the night sky. I wish that night had never happened, she agonised. But it was no good wishing to undo the past, she could only wish for the future to be better.

Feeling powerless and soiled, with a banging headache developing, she took a couple of paracetamol tablets and knocked them back with a swig of flat Coke that she found in the cupboard. She'd hardly swallowed them before her stomach started turning over. Her whole body seemed to be rejecting everything. Mandy rushed over to the sink, where she threw up and up.

Sister Hunter checked the staff rota once more, before removing her glasses and rubbing her tired eyes. So many red 'S's across so many nurses' names. This gastric virus was spreading through the hospital staff like wildfire. It would be a disaster if they had to shut a couple of the surgical wards should this continue. Looking out of her office window for inspiration, seeing the bright lights of Splott twinkling in the night sky, she watched in detached amusement as a large fox ran nimbly across the hospital wall, before jumping down in front of all the massive bins, regarding them in glee, as if undecided which one he was going to tip up first.

Ignoring the tight feeling in her chest, a sure sign of stress, she thought, she reached for her telephone and a Kit-Kat simultaneously.

"Sister Winter? Night Sister here. I was hoping to catch you before you went home. So sorry to delay you. I'm afraid I'm going to have to ask a favour of you." As she waited for Sister Winter's disgruntled reply, she watched the wily fox skilfully flip the lid off one of the bins and help himself to the remains of a chicken curry. Clever little chap, she thought fondly. Then, steeling herself, she listened to her colleague's aggrieved response, nibbling off the chocolate from the biscuit before munching delicately on the wafer.

For some reason Terence Adams ward had remained largely unaffected by the sickness bug, and was full compliment. Sister Hunter regretted having to take such action, but there was nothing for it. In the morning, Sister Winter would have to request that Staff Harry return to night duty, and a couple of the students as well.

Sister Hunter returned to the lists of names on the sheet. She could take one second year off day duty, but not two. That left just little Aneira Thomas. Despite the fact that it was unheard of to put a student on nights so early on in the training, there really was no other option. She sat back in her comfortable chair and sipped her tea, thoughtfully, wondering whether she should unwrap another Kit-Kat. At least it would give her another opportunity to keep an eye on the child, she mused. The events of a few weeks ago had preyed heavily on her mind. Maybe this would reward her with the chance to get to the bottom of things, once and for all. So much had changed in the world since she had trained to be a nurse, all those years ago, in the post-war era. So much had changed in C.C.I. On the whole the students were as diligent as ever, as keen and as willing to learn. But only too often there were the flies in the ointment of hospital life, the student nurses who were only interested in going out partying, staff who acted frivolously, obsessed with fraternising, and the doctors who...ah, yes, the doctors...

She shoved the duty rota back in the drawer, straightening her navy uniform. Almost time to start the ward rounds, she decided, time to assess the nocturnal situation of the hospital, keep an eye on the routine activities and keep under surveillance anything remotely unusual. I missed my calling, she thought, folding up her Kit-Kat wrapper neatly before throwing it into the waste-paper bin, I should have joined the police force...

The first floor main corridor was quiet. An ancient auxiliary nurse, obviously an old retainer from Sister Hunter's time, hurried towards the stairs, homeward bound.

"Evening, Sister," she muttered as she scuttled past, holding her mackintosh closely about her waist, desperately praying that the stern Night Sister wouldn't spot the dark green uniform beneath it. Sister Hunter didn't even register the lowly nurse. She pressed on, her mind focussed on her ward rounds, the night reports...and the prospect of supervising Aneira Thomas once more. Reaching the end of the corridor, she stopped in annoyance at the light switches. Huffing irritably, she turned a couple of them off. "Wasteful," she muttered under her breath, turning right into female surgical.

"I'll be with you when you tell him , if you want." Julia was ready to do anything within her power to help Mandy.

Mandy pulled up her black tights , then smoothed her blue uniform dress down over them. "Thanks, Jules, but I have to do this myself. It's too personal, and I've got to time it right." She stood up to arrange her thick, dark hair into its customary bun.

"Sure, of course, but if you change your mind, you only have to ask, okay?" Julia pinned her fob watch onto her dress, before securing it with her name badge. "I think we should consider discussing the whole event with a senior nurse as well."

"Oh, no! Not yet, Jules! I couldn't stand it. I prefer to have the discussion with Andy first, if you don't mind." She searched beneath her unmade bed for her flat, black shoes, still laced up from her last shift.

"I understand. I'll go and get my things, then we can toddle off, yeah?" But she got no further than the bedroom door, which opened slowly and discreetly.

"Good afternoon, Staff Harry, Staff Jacob." Miss Marshall's immaculately made up face peeped around the door, regarding in distaste the chaos which met her eyes, the dirty plates in the sink, the tights drying on the radiator, the magazines strewn randomly across the floor and the demi-john which was now bubbling away manically as it fermented vigorously. "I tried your room, Staff Harry, then I heard you both talking in here." Mandy looked at Julia warily. Had the warden heard anything?

"You're looking for me, Miss Marshall?" Julia was keen to deflect any attention away from Mandy.

The warden smiled benevolently at Julia. Such a nice girl, she thought, always neat and tidy, a fine example of young womanhood. Unlike that harum scarum Staff Jacob.

"Yes, my dear. I'm afraid the hospital has phoned me. You're not to go in for your shift this afternoon. You're to report for night duty this evening. Staff sickness, you know."

Julia sighed irritably, then started pulling the pins from her hair. "Again? I went on nights only a few weeks ago!"

"I know, it's inconvenient, but they are desperate, especially the surgical wards." Phew, thought Mandy in relief, thank goodness the medical unit is pretty well covered.

"Isn't there anyone else they can ask?" Julia felt bitterly disappointed. She was supposed to be seeing Mitch tomorrow, after her original early shift. She hadn't seen him since Tuesday, before he'd left for London.

"I don't think there is, Staff." Miss Marshall looked regretful. "You see, many of the other surgical staff have either got young children or they're off sick themselves. Are you able to do it? I need to ring the hospital immediately."

"Yes of course I'll do it." I suppose I'll manage to see Mitch before I go in, Julia thought, resignedly, but bang goes the romantic meal for two.

"Thank you, Staff, I'm sure they'll be very grateful." Miss Marshall closed the door quietly, leaving behind a disgruntled Julia.

"Off to byes for you, then." Mandy made a sympathetic face at her friend. "I suppose I'll see you sometime tomorrow. We'll be like ships that pass in the night." Some of her natural buoyancy had returned, Julia thought, relieved.

"Yeah, guess I'll grab myself a Horlicks and turn in for the afternoon. Have a good shift, Mands. And try not to fret too much. Remember, you're in the right, you've done nothing wrong. Some bastard is going to swing for what happened to you."

Smiling weakly, Mandy got her cloak and bag. "I certainly hope so, Julia. I really do."

Aneira Thomas was terrified. But she was also excited. Night duty. And only on her second ward. As soon as she'd been told, she'd rushed to the payphone at the bottom of her corridor to ring her parents. Some of the other first years were in awe of her. But not all of them. Fancy little Aneira being picked to go on nights, they thought, disgruntled. What was so special about her? Their noses distinctly out of joint, they teased her mercilessly.

265

"You watch out for the grey lady, Aneira!" Spotty Lynwen Lloyd taunted, spitefully.

"Yeah! She haunts little first years, glides up behind them and goes BOO!" Delyth Davies chortled, maliciously, scoffing a chocolate eclair, the cream spraying in all directions as she laughed.

"Get lost, you lot." Gillian Evans came to the rescue, elbowing the junior students out of the way as she filled the kettle. "Shall we have a cuppa, Aneira?" The other two scowled and retreated. No way could they challenge the might and authority of a second year. "They're just jealous, those two! Tea or coffee?"

"Coffee, please." Aneira was perched on a high stool in the tiny kitchen. "Is it really as scary as they say? Nights, I mean? What if I can't stay awake?"

"I love nights." Gillian handed Aneira the hot coffee. "It's not scary at all. Nice atmosphere at night. Most of the night staff are smashing, as well. I think we're on with Julia Harry tonight, by the way."

Aneira's anxious little face brightened. "Oh, that's wonderful! It won't seem so scary with her around."

"You learn a lot more on nights, too." Gillian was on a roll now. "I've even been left in charge, once, when the S.E.N. went to break!" She conveniently omitted that she had been on her own for precisely five minutes until the Night Sister had arrived to relieve the S.E.N.

Aneira's eyes were huge. "Goodness," she said, admiringly, "that's amazing! You must have been terrified!"

"It was okay." Gillian assumed the attitude of a worldly-wise and experienced nurse. "But the worst time is around three o'clock. You get absolutely worn out by then, and your eyes keep on closing, it's quite hard to stay awake – unless of course there's an emergency or something. But three o'clock is when a lot of patients tend to pop their clogs!"

"Really?" Aniera's eyes were practically popping out of her head by now.

266

"Yep. And that's a scientific fact. All to do with hormones and stuff. Anyway, drink up, it's almost a quarter past eight and we're not even changed yet. Come on!"

Suitably impressed by the older student, Aneira hurried off to her room to get ready for this exciting yet formidable part of her nursing training.

There was something unique about nights, thought Julia, as she pulled on her thick, black tights for the second time that day. I'm all fresh from the bath, yet my legs feel like jelly and my head is in the shed. Her body was tired, her mind was fuzzy , yet she was restlessly geared for action. Nights certainly muddled up the routine, she thought, gloomily. Trying to sleep during the day prior to the shift usually presented little problem. But when should she eat? A cooked dinner at one o'clock in the morning was okay for some, but not for her. She'd made do with a plate of tinned tomatoes with lots of pepper and a couple of slices of toast at around half past seven. Mitch wasn't due to see her until tomorrow evening, so she needn't worry about over-sleeping and missing him. Actually, when he wasn't around, and it was impossible to see him. it was quite nice to be on nights; a little bit more money for the enhanced hours and she could curl up in her cosy bed after the shift and dream her wonderful dreams...

As she made her way down Porthnewydd Avenue, she gazed up appreciatively at the late winter night sky and the brilliant constellations. Ursa Major courted Leo, such a pretty dalliance, and the moon was making a coy appearance over the eastern skyline of Rumney. March is only just around the corner, she thought, spring is on the way, she could almost feel it in the air. Nana Harry always used to say that the seasons ran in Julia's blood, that she was like the Old People, that she was fey...

But fey or whatever, I'm the girlfriend of a rock musician, she thought, blissfully, wrapping her cape more tightly around her slim shoulders. All is well in my little world, I love my job, my lover is coming home to me tomorrow and …

Then her thoughts became clouded. Mandy. Dear God, what a terrible situation. Mandy was meeting Andy next Monday. How would her friend cope until then? They would see little of each other before the beans were spilled.

Mandy. The best friend a girl could have. Cheerful, kind, exuberant. But also, despite her apparent experience in the ways of Cupid's world, she was naïve and easily exploited. Christ, Julia hated Neil Hancock and all he stood for. As she slipped through the Gap in the Wall, like a little spirit of the night, she suddenly thought that maybe he wasn't alone in his vile schemes. However, her troublesome thoughts were interrupted when she went slap bang into Aneira and Gillian at the rear entrance of the hospital.

"Ready for nights, girls?" She smiled kindly down at Aneira, whose big blue eyes were even bigger with apprehension.

"Oh, don't worry, Staff, I've briefed her thoroughly, haven't I, Nye?" Gillian grinned confidently at the younger girl, just remembering to remove her chewing gum before entering the main corridor. Julia frowned in disapproval as Gillian crumpled it up in a rather dirty paper tissue before disposing of it in a nearby bin. They turned the corner and climbed the stairs to the first floor, two teenagers and a twenty-one year old, ready to care for a ward full of sick men for the next eleven hours. Gillian bounced along with all the cheeky confidence of youth, while Aneira brought up the rear, almost trembling in her size three shoes, feeing inadequate and scared.

"And that's the merry gang, apart from Mr Price, you know, the inoperable bowel cancer?" Sister Winter closed the Kardex and unpinned the keys from her pocket, handing them to Julia. "We've moved him to the cubicle, he's deteriorating rapidly. He's been haemorrhaging per rectum all evening, and you know what that's like for the other patients. He pulled out his I.V.I around six o'clock, but Mr Anscombe didn't want it re-sited. We're just to keep him comfortable. He's more or less unconscious now."

"He hasn't got any family, has he, Sister?" Julia pinned the keys into her own pocket.

"None that anybody knows of. The police brought him to Cas in a right state. He'd been sleeping rough for a very long time. Poor man, a real down and out." Sister Winter looked sad. "But when he was still conscious, even though he was confused, he spoke so nicely, he came across as well-educated. I wonder what makes a man like that become a tramp? But now all we can offer him is plenty of T.L.C. Night Sister has been informed of his condition on the Night Report. Have a good shift, ladies." And then she was gone, leaving the three younger women in the office, ready to start their work.

Julia immediately took charge. "Right, Nurse Evans, can you start the obs, please? Remember to use a trolley and take the pulses for a full minute." Seeing Gillian's face fall, she added, "well, for at least thirty seconds, anyway!" Gillian hurried to the treatment room, smiling broadly.

Julia turned to Aneira, speaking softly. "I want you to be in charge of Mr Price tonight, Aneira." The student blushed at the use of her first name. "We'll check him together now, then we'll do the medicine round . But after that, I want you to spend as much time as you can with him, okay?"

Aneira nodded. "What do I do, Staff? When I'm in there?"

Julia sighed inwardly. She'd forgotten just how junior Aneira was. "I want you to keep him comfortable, as Sister Winter mentioned, oral toilet every couple of hours, I'll send Nurse Evans in to help you turn him and wash him if the haemorrhaging continues, and talk quietly to him."

"But he's unconscious, Staff?"

"Yes, but never forget that when a person is dying, the ability to hear is often there until the very end."

"He's dying?" Aneira's words were just a whisper.

Not wishing to alarm the young girl, Julia replied gently, "Yes, he's dying. Maybe tonight, maybe tomorrow. Sometimes patients can linger for ages despite the fact they're not receiving fluids or food. He's been given plenty of strong analgesics and shouldn't be in a lot of pain. If he starts becoming distressed, you must let me know immediately, we can administer more morphine then."

Again, Aneira nodded. "You know I made a mistake last time I thought someone was dead, Staff?"

"I know. But you learned from that, yes? If you think he's passed away, there's no need to panic, just come and find me, right?"

Aneira took a deep breath. "I will. Thanks, Staff. I'll be okay." I really hope I will, she thought, anxiously.

The journey back to Cardiff was almost as bad as the trip up to London. The weather was good, a clear night, no wind, no rain. But the M4 was practically gridlocked once they reached Bristol.

"Bloody typical." Jeff turned the engine off. "Stuck in the middle lane. To misquote a song, I can see for miles and miles and sodding miles, miles of cars, lorries and more cars. Jesus. To be so close to home and yet so far from my warm bed." He yawned.

"Christ, I want a pee!" Eddie grumbled. "I shouldn't have drunk that Pepsi."

Mitch searched in the glove compartment for something to eat. "I'm bloody starving. I'm sure there was a Mars bar in here."
Jeff had the grace to look ashamed. "Er, that was me, I ate it. Sorry. But I'm bigger than you and my needs were greater."

"Bastard." Mitch slammed the glove compartment shut in irritation.

"I've got some chewing gum!" As optimistic as always, Dai rummaged in his pocket and offered a single, bent stick of Juicy Fruit. Nobody responded, but the disgusted looks on their faces said it all.

Finally, the traffic started moving again. Slowly but surely, the red lights of the vehicles in front began trickling forward, like alien beetles on a dark planet.

"At last." Jeff started the van up again. "Bet it's a flamin' jack-knifed lorry or something."

"Or an R.T.A." Mitch looked superior.

"Whassat?" Jeff was mildly irked, he liked to be the fount of all knowledge in the band.

"Road traffic accident." Mitch was more than happy to share his familiarity with hospital terminology.

"Smart arse." Eddie put his feet up on the back of Mitch's chair. "Anyway, weren't we supposed to be discussing our futures?"

"We were, until Mitch decided he was hungry and you wanted a pee." Jeff was as dry as ever.

"Get your smelly feet off my seat, Eddie." Mitch gave the offending appendages a shove. "Back to our dreams and futures, boys. We've got this meeting with Cosmo on Monday evening, yes?"

Grunts of assent from the others spurred him on. "I don't know exactly what you think about where we go from here. Top of the Pops was okay, but to be honest I found the whole thing totally overwhelming. I'm not into that set-up."

"I agree." Jeff changed up into third gear and accelerated slightly. "I enjoy the playing and the production side of it, and proper live performances too. But I can take or leave the limelight. I've read too many articles about the horrendous things that have happened to other rock bands."

"Um, I'm actually getting married next year, boys. I didn't dare tell Steph that. Meinir will go ape shit if I start touring the globe and stuff." In the darkness of the van, Dai's face was troubled.

"What about you, Eddie?" Mitch turned around to check his reaction.

"Oh, I'm with you guys all the way." Eddie was grinning, happily. "I was sort of hoping you lot weren't gagging for the bright lights, the rock chicks and the groupies. I know that makes us sort of weird, but I really prefer making albums and the creative side of it."

"That's settled then." Mitch sighed in relief. "We need to present a unified approach on Monday. Good lads!"

"Thank Christ for that!" Dai exclaimed, excitedly, pointing at the lights in the distance.

"What?" Mitch didn't think he'd said anything that brilliant.

"The Severn Bridge! We're almost back in God's country, chaps! Won't be long now! Get the toll money ready!"

The old van continued its laborious way along the motorway, carrying the four tired musicians back to their homes, and their real lives.

Chapter Twenty Three The Grim Reaper

Only the overhead lamp shone in the cubicle, casting strange shadows on the plain walls. Reginald Price's breathing was shallow, and his face already seemed to be wearing the waxy sheen of approaching death. Aneira crept closer to the bed, and reached out for his wrist, meaning to check his pulse. As her small fingers touched the thin, gnarled hand, his fingers slowly opened, as if welcoming her youthful touch, and lightly closed around her child-like hand. Aneira didn't think she should remove her hand. Maybe he knew she was there, she thought.

"Hello, Mr Price,"she whispered, "It's Nurse Thomas here again, just to let you know." Gradually she realised that taking his pulse was not so important any more, far better that she just remained where she was, letting the patient hold her hand. He had a nice face, she observed, a kind look about him. His eyelids flickered, as though he understood she was with him.

The cubicle door opened silently, and Julia slipped inside.

"You're doing so well, Aneira," she murmured, "just stay as you are with Mr Price, don't do anything than just stay there, but press the buzzer if you need anything."

The young student smiled up at her, gratefully. Julia slipped away again, to join the other student in giving some analgesics to the post-operative patients who'd had surgery earlier that day.

Reginald Price had been found in Cathays Park, Aneira remembered, by a couple of policemen on patrol. Nobody knew anything about him, other than his name, which he'd managed to mumble when he'd been brought in to Casualty. Even the name he gave didn't match up with any missing persons. Probably a false name, the police had said. Nothing else he'd said had made any sense. Exactly how long he'd been sleeping rough was anybody's guess, and how long he'd been in severe pain and been bleeding remained another mystery. Even his age was a puzzle, but Sister Winter and Mr Anscombe reckoned he was about fifty or so. And now it was too late to help him, too late to save this man, this drifter with an unknown past.

The room was bare, devoid of any of the personal objects that most patients would have cluttered around their beds. Reginald Price wore a hospital gown; his towels were of hospital issue as well, and there was nothing on his locker apart from the oral care tray. Nothing to give him an identity, no clue as to his life history, hardly any pieces of the jigsaw to complete, or even start the picture. It seemed as though Reginald Price had wanted to leave his original life behind him without leaving a single clue as to who he was.

His hand felt cold. She wondered if she should fetch another blanket for him. But that would mean summoning the others, and she didn't want to do that. Taking care not to disturb his hand, she sat down on the chair next to the bed. Even though she was doing very little, it seemed to Aneira that simply sitting there holding Mr Price's hand was important. She felt strangely privileged to be present as a life slowly ebbed away.

Half an hour later, Gillian Evans popped her head around the door.

"Staff says you're to go to break, and I'm to relieve you."

Aneira looked up. "Oh, can you go to break now instead, Gillian? I really don't want to leave Mr Price."

"Sure. I'll let Staff know." And off she went in search of Julia.

Gillian Evans' attitude to life was pretty straightforward. There was no point in worrying (unless she was likely to get the sack or something absolutely devastating like that) and there was every point in living life to the full. She walked happily along the corridor, swiftly compartmentalising the stresses of the ward into the recesses of her mind, and anticipating the fried egg on toast with a plastic covered rectangle of cheese on the side, which she was planning on having for her supper.

There was nobody else around, maybe she was the only nurse going to break now, she thought. That meant nobody to gossip with in the canteen. She could be in for a very boring half hour. Checking her fob watch, she realised it was almost half past twelve, quite late to be off to break. Aneira had better watch out, she could end up not going at all at this rate, and there'd be nothing decent left to eat.

Out of the corner of her eye she caught a swift glimpse of a nurse around the corner of Weston Ward. Maybe it's someone else heading for supper, she thought in pleasure. As she approached the entrance to the ward, she peered into the gloom. Strange, she thought, there's no-one there, must have been my imagination.

Continuing her way towards the narrow staircase which led to the second floor, she was sure she could hear light, rapid footsteps following her. Who the hell was it? Swinging swiftly around, a sense of panic overcame her. There was no-one to be seen – or was that a nurse running silently down the main steps to the ground floor? But wearing grey? A grey cape? No grey uniforms were worn in Cardiff...

Starting to sweat and swallowing hard, she broke into a brisk trot towards the canteen staircase, then raced as fast as she could up the steps until she reached the restaurant door and another real, live person.

"I'm telling you, I definitely saw the Grey Lady!" Gillian drank the rest of her tea and put her knife and fork together defiantly.

Janys Norman had been the only other nurse in the canteen. A self-important S.E.N. of at least six months qualified experience, Janys only just about tolerated perky students like Gillian. She rolled her eyes. "You've been watching too many late-night films,"she said, disdainfully, "you students should concentrate more on your studies."

"Who's been watching too many late-night films, Nurse Norman?" The steely voice of Sister Hunter interrupted the conversation. She sat down at the opposite table, placing her personal, linen-covered tray in front of her.

"The student, Sister. Thinks she saw the Grey Lady down in the corridor. A load of nonsense of course!"

Sister Hunter sighed, taking her time to stir her tea. "The mind is a powerful tool, especially at night. What you imagine you see can seem totally real." She started to cut up her apple into perfectly equal slices. "Ghosts and spirits are frequently the product of a tired mind." She bit daintily into a piece of bread and butter. "You make sure you get enough sleep, Nurse Evans, and no gallivanting about at the expense of sleep when you have to be on duty every night." She smiled knowingly over her spectacles at Gillian, who squirmed in her seat.

"Yes, Sister. I'll be getting back to the ward, then." Gillian grabbed her purse and fled thankfully from the scrutiny of the formidable Night Sister.

Reginald Price was only breathing occasionally now, and although his respirations were shallow, they were noisy and laboured. Aneira was starting to feel stiff from sitting still for so long, but she resolutely refused to leave her post. Julia had checked on her once again, before going to break herself.

"Listen, Staff Sexton from Weston is relieving me for supper, and Gillian Evans is back from hers, so do you want to come with me?"

Aneira shook her head. "Thank you, Staff, but I think I'll stay here. I think Mr Price knows I'm here and I don't want him to think I've just abandoned him."

Julia smiled sadly. Whatever had caused him to retreat from normal life, it seemed quite poignant that during his final moments he had someone waiting with him, someone who cared enough to remain with him until the end and not forsake him.

"Shall I bring you back some sandwiches?"

"Oh, yes please, Staff, plain cheese would be nice, I'll pay you for them later, after...after..."

Julia put a finger to her lips. "Remember what I said about the sense of hearing, Aneira. Anyway, I won't be long."

The minutes ticked by and still Reginald Price clung to his tragic life, reluctant to depart. Aneira's eyes pricked with tiredness and she longed to change her position, but her patient still held her little hand in his.

It was blustery outside, and starting to rain. Heavy drops hit the window and gusts of wind shrieked like banshees around the old walls of the hospital. What a night to be dying, she thought, how bleak and dismal. Closing her eyes briefly, she considered how different it would be to breathe your last breath while gazing out at a beautiful sunset, happy and at peace with yourself and your time on earth. With the image of a glorious sunset uppermost in her mind, she started to drift off to sleep, relaxing into the chair, her hand still held by Mr Price.

In her light, dreamy sleep, she held the hand of a man she seemed to be fond of, the setting sun was reflected in his spectacles, and they were walking together along a sandy beach. The man suddenly released his grip on her hand – she awoke with a start.

Reginald Price's hand hung limply at the side of the bed. Aneira looked in trepidation at his face. His mouth hung open slackly, and he was no longer breathing. His eyes were half open, but dull and lifeless. Cautiously, she tried to find his pulse, and failed. Instinctively, she looked at the clock on the wall. Almost two o'clock. She picked up his hand, and replaced it on his chest.

"Goodbye, Mr Price," she whispered, sorrowfully, "you can rest properly now." She felt a slight rush of air flutter past her, and the sweet smell of violets briefly filled the room, before fading away almost as quickly.

Rising awkwardly to her feet, she opened the cubicle door. Julia had just returned from break and was coming out of the office. She took one look at Aneira's face and realised that Reginald Price had passed away.

"He's gone?"

Aneira nodded, unable to speak.

"I'll just check, let's go in together?" Julia put her hand on the young girl's shoulder. "You should be very proud of yourself. You're a kind, dedicated nurse. Well done."

Aneira swallowed, keeping in check the tears which were threatening to cascade down her face, and followed Julia into the room.

There was nothing really to be afraid of, Aneira thought, gazing at the motionless body on the bed, Reginald Price just seemed to be sleeping. There had been no struggle at the end, no desperate fight to continue living, he had quietly slipped away. She wondered where his soul was, if he could see her and Julia in his room, next to his bed. Was he looking down at his old self..?

Julia checked his vital signs, then closed his eyes, gently. "Rest in peace, Reginald," she whispered, "may God welcome you into his arms." Looking back at Aneira, she continued, "Can you remember what time it was, Aneira? When he passed away?" She reached up to open the small window slightly.

"Three minutes to two."

"Good girl. We'll get the doctor to confirm the death, and we'll bleep Night Sister as well. Once that's done, we'll do the last offices. Do you feel up to that?" Julia wished she could make this easier for her.

"Yes, Staff, of course."

"But I want you to go to break first. If you don't want to go up to the canteen, just make yourself a cuppa and go in the kitchen. Sister Hunter won't mind, I'm sure."

"How much were the sandwiches, Staff?"

Julia smiled. "Don't worry about it. My treat. Now off you go." Time to bleep the doc, she thought.

Just as she was picking up the phone to bleep the S.H.O., the office door swung open and Anscombe stood there, scowling.

"Bloody Cas," he grumbled, "sent up a bloody abdo pain to female surgical, and she's ninety years old with bloody faecal impaction! Jesus!" He threw a pile of notes onto the desk, irritably.

"Cup of tea, Mr Anscombe?" He was obviously at the end of his tether, thought Julia, deciding to forgive him for his harsh words a few weeks ago.

"It's okay, Staff." He sighed, wearily. "I'll make it myself. You've got enough to do." He attempted a smile.

Julia thought quickly. "Well...I was about to bleep Dr Battencourt to confirm a death, but seeing as you're here..?" Anything to avoid having to have contact with that upper class lout, she thought.

"Sure. The old guy, yes? The tramp?" He headed for the cubicle, Julia following in his wake.

Anscombe completed his brief assessment of the body. "Time of death, Staff?"

"One fifty-seven. Can we lay him out?"

"Sure. I'll be hogging your office, if you don't mind, so much bloody paperwork to complete."

"Yes, of course. I'll make sure you're not disturbed."

Giving her a brief nod of gratitude he marched from the cubicle. What a strange man, Julia thought, hot-tempered, sarcastic beyond belief, geeky-looking, but such a brilliantly proficient surgeon.

She glanced at Reginald Price. I wonder who he was, what he was running from, she pondered. But surely to God he's at peace now.

Aneira tied the plastic apron behind her back, before helping Julia wash Mr Price's body and put the shroud on him. Julia gave her a sharp glance. The young nurse looked extremely pale.

"Are you okay, Aneira? Do you want me to call Nurse Evans instead?"

Aneira shook her head. "No, I'll be fine, Staff."

They carried on, performing this final nursing care with sensitivity and sorrow. There was no wedding ring to remove and give to a grieving widow, no items of value whatsoever.

"We'll just wrap Mr Price up in a sheet, then I'll call the porters." Julia started folding the bottom sheet over the lower part of the body. Aneira passed her the other side of the sheet and it was tucked neatly under the shoulders.

Everything was going well, Julia reflected, as she held up the corner of the sheet in readiness to complete the final stage of the last offices. Just as she started to cover Reginald Price's face, Aneira started to feel as though her head was spinning, that all this was a nightmare. She gave a stifled sob. What she really wanted to do was shout out "Leave him alone!"

Stopping the process abruptly, Julia went round to the other side of the bed.

"What's the matter? Is it all too much?"

Aneira nodded vigorously, the tears pouring down her cheeks. "It's just, like, you know, he reminds me of my father, Staff. He's the same age, and when you went to cover his face, it all seemed so final, and- and- oh, God! It made me think that how awful it would be if it happened to my father! He could be someone's father, couldn't he?"

Julia felt so sorry for the girl. She remembered her own first experience of laying out a deceased patient, an elderly woman who had died of pneumonia, and how it had reminded her of her own grandmother.

"Look, I'll go and call Nurse Evans. You take a break. It's been a hard first night shift for you, go and get yourself a cup of tea or something."

Aneira hurried from the cubicle, weeping quietly, her small shoulders heaving in her distress.

Julia followed her as far as the door, looking for Gillian Evans. Then she spotted her, at the desk in the middle of the ward, sorting out the various forms for the next day.

"Nurse Evans? Can you leave the fluid charts for now and give me a hand here, please?"

She sat on a tall stool in the ward kitchen, in the dark, weeping quietly, her head in her hands. That poor, poor man. What a way to end up, dying in a hospital cubicle, with no family around you, and two strange young women laying out your body. She'd never known such intense sadness, it was bordering on engulfing her completely.

Suddenly the room was flooded with light.

"What on earth's the matter?" The stern figure of Anscombe stood in the doorway, the kitchen light reflecting brightly in his thick-lensed glasses.

Aneira blew her nose noisily. "Sorry, Mr Anscombe. I'm just a bit upset, that's all. Staff Harry told me to come in here and have a cup of tea."

Anscombe went to the cupboard to look for a mug. "And you haven't made the tea yet, have you?"

"No." Her voice was a mere whimper.

"Right. I suppose I'll have to do it for you, then, won't I?"

She couldn't see his face, he had his back to her. "Er- thank you, sir."

Putting two tea bags into a couple of mugs, he turned to look at her properly. Her face was blotchy with crying, her white hat was askew and her fluffy blond hair was falling down from its orderly bun. She looked absolutely terrible.

"Is it that tramp? The one who just died?"

"Yes, Mr Anscombe. I'm sorry."

"No need to be sorry." He filled the mugs with hot water. "Milk and sugar?"

"Just milk, please."

"You know, it's perfectly normal to be upset when a patient dies. We are allowed to feel sad. We'd be robots of we didn't feel a modicum of emotion when we lose someone who's been in our care."

Aneira wasn't sure what the word 'modicum' meant but gave him her undivided attention. "Even you, Mr Anscombe?"

He handed her a mug before continuing. "Even me. That poor chap didn't have any family." Aneira started weeping again. "But if he did, and they'd all been there around the bed when he died, don't you think they'd have thought how much you cared if they could see you were sad?" Aneira looked up at him in surprise. He continued, softly. "It seems to me you are a very kind person, Aneir – Nurse Thomas." He put his arm around her shoulder. "Try not to be sad for too long. You've got other patients to look after, remember that. And yourself."

They failed to notice the austere figure of Sister Hunter as she passed by the entrance to the kitchen. She raised her eyebrows in surprise at the unexpected sight of the formidable Mr Anscombe comforting the distressed first-year. Well, I never, she thought, before going in search of Julia, wonders will never cease.

"And there he was, our esteemed senior registrar, consoling Nurse Thomas! I would never have thought he was capable of such empathetic kindness." Sister handed the report back to Julia. "But there you go, the world holds more wonders than we will ever know."

"Yes, Sister." Julia wondered which cliché would fall next from the Night Sister's straight-laced lips. "I've rung the porters, they won't be long."

"You've all done well this evening, Staff. I know Nurse Thomas is distraught, but I'm afraid it's in her make up. She'll make an excellent nurse, however she'll suffer along the way, sensitive little creature that she is. But I may be proved wrong, she could be made of sterner stuff than I give her credit for. After all, you can't judge a book by its cover."

Julia smiled to herself. "No, Sister."

The ward doors opened, and the porters arrived with the trolley reserved purely for the deceased. It resembled a normal, empty trolley, but with a concealed undercarriage, where the body would be placed, hidden from public view, on its final journey, down to the mortuary.

A buzzer sounded at the bottom of the ward.

"I'll get that, Staff. It's been a long time since I had any proper patient contact. You sort the porters out." Rolling up her sleeves, the enigmatic Night Sister tore off a plastic apron from the dispenser on the wall, before marching smartly but quietly down the ward.

Chapter Twenty Four Disclosures

Still groggy from her daytime sleep, Julia tottered downstairs at five o'clock, still wearing her pyjamas. With her burnished hair loose, and not a scrap of make up, she looked about fourteen, yet to Mitch's eyes as she opened the front door, more appealing than ever.

"God, I've missed you!" He enveloped her in a bear hug after she'd ushered him inside, kissing her slowly and thoroughly, letting his tongue roam desirously over her small, white teeth.

Breaking free to catch her breath, she laughed softly. "Shall we go up to my room? The Marshall has gone to the cinema, so we should be okay."

Following her up the stairs like a hound on a scent, he snaked his hand around her waist until he could feel her bare breasts bobbing about in unrestrained freedom. "Your nipple is like the rubber tip of a pencil, you naughty girl! You're obviously very pleased to see me!"

"Stop it!" She giggled, happily. "Someone may hear you!"

"I thought it was perfectly acceptable for you to entertain gentlemen callers until midnight, anyway! So why play the coy innocent with me, you shameless hussy!"

Julia replied, archly,"Miss Marshall expects all her young ladies to act with decorum, and allowing one's lover to follow one to one's room in one's pyjamas,well that's tantamount to announcing to all and sundry that you're about to jump into bed with him!"

Mitch pretended to be disappointed. "Well aren't you?"

"That depends." She opened the door to her room.

"On what?"

"On how quickly you can make me happy!"

Chuckling wickedly, he picked her up, slammed the door behind them and threw her on the bed.

They lay in the darkness, appreciating the closeness, relaxing into their post-orgasmic glow.

"Stop trying to claim more territory!" He shoved her gently.

"I'm fed up of lying in the wet patch," she complained, wriggling against his hips.

"Quit complaining. Come here."

She snuggled up to him, content and replete. "Well, fair play, you met the challenge most admirably, young man. Five minutes flat isn't bad going!"

"Hey! It went on for longer than that!"

"Ha ha ha! No need to be so indignant! I meant it took you precisely five minutes to make me happy!"

Mitch smiled into the shadows of the unlit room. "You're such a randy bugger, Julia, and I love you for it." He planted a kiss on her head.

"I told you, that's what us redheads are like!" She kissed him back, just reaching his lips above the stubble of his chin.

There were so many things to discuss, so much to talk about, yet neither felt much like speaking. They were content just to lie there, close and warm, happy and secure.

However, after ten minutes, curiosity got the better of her.

"What was it like, then? Top of the Pops and all that?"

Mitch rolled onto his back, examining the cream British Home Stores lampshade hanging above the bed.

"It was everything and nothing. Does that make sense?" Without waiting for a reply, he carried on. "It was overwhelming, I suppose. Yes, it was incredibly exciting – Jeff saw David Bowie in the bog – but for me it lacked substance. We didn't feel as though anyone was really interested in us as a band, we just felt we were a novelty, a commodity, a new act to be applauded and cheered, then on to the next singer or whatever. We were treated well, everyone was helpful and respectful and we were made to feel really special, you know? It was a fantastic experience, but it wouldn't bother me if it never happened again."

"Not even to see Legs and Co in the flesh again?" Julia interjected, slyly, poking him in the ribs.

"Not even them. None of them had legs like yours." He smiled in the darkness. "They look so tall on TV, but in real life they're not."
"Most dancers are like that." She curled her arm around him. "I hated the thought of you being there with all those groupies and adoring girls in the audience."

"Didn't you see them? The audience? Christ, what a miserable bunch they were! Mind you, they'd been there all day, being ordered about by the stage manager. Lots of hanging around for them!"

Julia sighed, contentedly. "We all watched you, there were about twenty of us in the common room, even Richie and Miss Marshall were there! Oh, Mitch, you were so bloody brilliant! I was so proud of you! And when you looked straight in to the camera and said the song was about me – well, I could have wept in delight! I think I did weep, actually! Thank you for doing that. But didn't that get you in to hot water with Steph?"

Mitch grinned at the memory. "A bit. But we handled it okay. Now, enough talk about Top of the Pops, I want to fornicate with my little night nurse again." He nuzzled her neck, sending shivers of pleasure down her spine. "Do you reckon there's time?" His hand crept around to her inner thigh, starting to stroke her soft netherhair.

287

She arched like a sensuous cat. "Plenty."

The Clarence was quiet, not many drinkers had ventured out on such a cold, frosty February night. Mandy and Andy were tucked up in a corner of the pub, enjoying their own company, oblivious to the rest of the world. Andy glanced at Mandy when she wasn't looking. Christ, he was bloody fortunate. She was so happy-go-lucky, vivacious, kind...and she seemed delighted to go out with him. Enthusiastic, even. He considered himself a bore, he knew damn well that the other coppers on his shift thought so. They were always teasing him about his stand offish ways, his old-fashioned values. What would his parents think of her, he wondered. He'd never taken a girl home before. The thought of it terrified him. He sneaked another glimpse at her. Mandy was a natural, unaware of her attractiveness, with her lustrous dark curls, her pretty little nose, her dancing, merry eyes...he thought the world of her.

"How was your course?" Mandy took a sip of her red wine. She quite liked the dinky little individual bottles of House Red and House White that had suddenly become all the rage. She'd abandoned her usual halves of lager after reading in a magazine that it was considered much more beguiling to be seen holding a dainty wine glass than a laddish glass of lager.

"Oh, it was fine." Andy checked the frothy head on his pint of Guiness. "It was just a sort of introduction to detective work. There'll be more courses soon, I expect. I'm now a T.D.C." He looked as proud as punch. Mandy looked blank. "I'm a Temporary Detective Constable, an Aide de Camp! Do you fancy some crisps?"

Mandy shook her head, fiddling with the fringe on her scarf. How could she possibly eat anything with this sick, churning feeling in her stomach? Where was this conversation going, how on earth could she get onto the subject of the photo? That sickeningly hateful photo, which was burning a hole in her head and her handbag. Andy was so straightforward, so uncomplicated...so gorgeous. If he dumped her she would be devastated.

But there was no way she could continue living in fear of the repercussions, feeling sick with worry.

The stone-built Victorian pub was not really conducive to the earth-shattering information she would soon have to deliver. Nowhere was, she supposed. She longed to be outside, in constant motion. In desperation she took a hefty swig of her wine, then coughed and spluttered as some of it went down the wrong way.

"You're keen to finish your drink!" Andy chuckled. "Is it that good – or bad?"

"Oh, it's okay." She swallowed the rest of it in one gulp. "But I think I'd rather go for a walk. I know it's cold, but it's dry. Would that be alright?" Her normally merry eyes seemed clouded with anxiety.

"Hey, what's the matter?" The concern in his voice touched her. "You're not about to dump me, are you?"

She forced a smile. "Not at all." Although you may be about to dump me, she thought, worriedly. "Can we go?"

"Sure." He downed the remainder of his Guiness. "Let's go."

Albany Road was similarly deserted. The wide pavements were devoid of the usual pedestrians, all the shops were shut, except the Spar on the corner; Monday evening was certainly not a night to go out expecting a great shebang, it seemed. The desolate street seemed to make the situation worse. It would have been easier in the middle of a crowd, she thought. Safety in numbers.

Mandy slipped her hand into his, and he squeezed it slightly.

"What's the matter, Mands?" His voice was warm, kind, but how the familiar shortening of her name cut through her. She didn't deserve such intimacy. How the hell was she going to do this?

Taking a deep breath, she stopped walking and turned to face him. Her face was a sad blend of anxiety and dread. He'd never seen her look so scared.

"For God's sake, Mands! Tell me! It can't be that bad, surely?"

"Oh, it is, Andy, it's the worse thing that can ever have happened." Trying hard not to cry, she bit her lower lip until a speck of blood appeared on it.

"Tell me. Whatever it is, I promise you, I will understand."

She shook her head slowly. "You will think so badly of me, Andy. You will think I'm a tart, a slag, or worse."

"Jesus *Christ*, Mandy!" He put his hands on her shoulders. "Just bloody say it! Whatever it is, say it!" He was almost in tears himself, by now, his words coming out awkwardly.

"Right. I'll tell you. But you mustn't interrupt, or say anything, okay?" He nodded, mutely. She carried on. "Before I even knew you, about a couple of weeks before we met, actually, I agreed to do a photo shoot for one of the doctors, he's an amateur photographer. He bought me dinner, then we went to his place to do the photo thing, you know, boudoir shots, that sort of thing. He said he was trying to build up a portfolio. He gave me some wine, but only two or three small glasses. After that last glass I don't remember a thing."

Andy frowned, opening his mouth to speak, but she silenced him, taking both his hands in hers.

"Miss Marshall the warden found me later that evening on the steps of the nurses' home, in a terrible state. I had to call in sick the next day, I felt so dreadful. After that, this doctor avoided me constantly. If I passed him in the hospital he'd run away like a scalded cat. I was very upset for a while, but then I just put it down to a bad experience. Then I met you." She raised her eyes to his, fearfully. "But last Thursday, after you'd dropped me off, Julia showed me a photo." Here goes, she thought. "I was most definitely drugged that night, and was taken advantage of in the most horrible way. The photo shows me undressed, unconscious and it's pornographic." She swallowed hard. "I also think I was raped."

Andy stood as if turned to stone; his face, normally a shade paler than alabaster, had turned deathly white.

On the other side of the city, the icy stars glittered down on a modest, rented terraced house in the middle of Grangetown, a tiny, two bedroomed house, sparsely furnished but full of maternal love. Despite being bone-achingly tired after a long shift at the Infirmary, Cali was determined to finish her assignment on time. But her thoughts kept meandering all over the place and it was hard to concentrate. The pile of books lay largely untouched on the table, accusing her of laziness, she imagined.

She'd arrived in Wales in the late sixties, filled with hope and excitement, a young Jamaican woman determined to make a better life for herself. Only trouble was, she reckoned wryly, as she attempted for the second time to read a paragraph about inequalities in health, she'd brought her husband with her. Bastard, she thought, remembering the drunken fights, the women, the poverty. Within a couple of weeks, she was pregnant, putting pay to any ambitions of training to be a nurse. Baby number two followed in hot pursuit of the first, and Cali was tethered to the shackles of motherhood and an errant, alcoholic husband. But not for long. Thanks to her incredible resilience, tough attitude to life, and an Amazonian physique, she swiftly booted him out the night he finally returned home on the arm of a peroxide-haired prostitute from the pub down the road. She hadn't heard from him since.

Cali slammed her text book shut with an irritable sigh. Pete Townsend's book on poverty and socialism was just not managing to cut the mustard for her this evening. She looked through the lounge window, watching a train hurtle past through the darkness, along the railway line just yards from the square of concrete she called a garden.

Absent mindedly, she took a chocolate digestive from the half-empty packet on the small dining table and dunked it into her rapidly cooling mug of tea, before demolishing it in two bites. I'm eating too many of these, she thought, miserably. But there was never enough time to eat properly herself, not after making nutritious food for the children, and more often than not, insufficient money as well.

Her two daughters were curled up in front of the electric fire, engrossed in their favourite television programme, Charlie's Angels. Cali allowed them this one enormous privilege, providing they had done their homework, and done it well. She had great ambitions for her children, she wanted them to be doctors, or solicitors, not a lowly domestic like her. But first she had to climb the social ladder herself, and get her degree. However, for some reason she couldn't settle down to her studies this evening. I'm tired, she thought, so tired of juggling everything, sorting out babysitters, making sure the house was clean, the washing done, that she arrived promptly in the Infirmary for her shifts and got to her part-time job in the filling station down the road as well. But she knew there was another reason for her lack of application to her studies on this cold, February evening.

Ever since she'd overheard the conversation between Battencourt and Hancock, she'd mulled it over incessantly. Why hadn't Richie seemed that interested? His apparent indifference had nettled her, festering away in her mind and eating away at her like an annoying worm that had got into her head.

Richie was one of the few men she liked and trusted, she thought, remembering with affection how kind he'd been to her when she'd started her job at the Infirmary five years ago. His wife had even minded the girls for her a few times, although that would stop, now that they had a baby of their own. Her older daughter, Petunia, giggled at some idiotic stunt that so often occurred at the end of the TV show, while the younger one, Tamara, continued to gaze goggle eyed at Jaclyn Smith. Cali smiled, indulgently, then frowned as her thoughts turned once more to the doctors.

292

She'd have to speak to Richie again, she decided, when he wasn't in a rush, when there was plenty of time to talk properly.

Feeling pleased with her decision, she tidied her books away for the evening.

"Right, my sweet little dumplings, it's time for your bath."

The silence was so highly charged Mandy could feel it, could sense it physically, every fibre in her body tingling, on high alert, making her insides turn to jelly. She felt like a specimen under a microscope, as though the whole world was examining her, judging her.

Andy was breathing heavily, unable to meet her eyes. Hopelessly aware of his revulsion, she suddenly found herself taking note of random things; the mannequin sporting a purple raincoat in the shop window across the road, the special offers advertised outside the Spar on the corner - three packets of Happy Shopper Rich Tea biscuits for fifty pence, the stray dog trotting quickly across the road, dodging the cars with a skill gained from years of practice.

Finally, he raised his eyes, looking at her with infinite sadness. "I don't know what to say."

Something inside Mandy snapped. "I just knew it!" She burst into noisy weeping. "I knew you'd say that! I knew you'd hate me! I knew you'd think I was a tart, a slag!" She turned around and started to run in the direction of Rochester Funeral Home, tears blinding her, despair filling her heart. Unable to run for long in her high heeled boots, she slowed to a walk, sobbing all the while, as though her heart would break. The orange street lights seemed to glow down at her accusingly, illuminating her, putting her into the spotlight, a guilty, fallen woman.

Aghast, as if turned to stone, he watched her run away from him. A small figure racing away from him, away from all the repercussions, out of his life. He couldn't bear it. He couldn't let her go, he needed her, he loved her. Shaking off the mental paralysis that had taken hold of him, he sprinted after her, desperate to catch her.

So absorbed was she in her personal hell, she didn't hear him as he came to a halt behind her, breathless with agitation.

"Stop!" His anguished voice pierced the night. He grabbed her arm and whirled her around. Fixing his kind, hazel eyes on her ravaged face, he brushed away the tears and streaks of mascara."Come here, Mands." She fell into his arms, like a fugitive seeking sanctuary, hugging him tightly, never wanting to let him go. She wept louder than ever, hardly stopping for breath.

"Hush." He stroked her hair. "I love you, Mands. I absolutely bloody love you. Never doubt me. Never leave me."

She looked up at him through the haze of tears in amazement. "You're not angry? Or disgusted?"

"Why should I be angry with you? I know you think I'm a bit old-fashioned, but I'm not that bad. You have been assaulted, abused, you're a victim. I am totally horrified about what has happened to you. But it wasn't your fault, was it?"

"But I'm no innocent virgin, Andy. That's what you'd hoped I was, isn't it?" Her voice was pitiful. "And I wasn't a virgin before that horrible night, either. I may as well be completely honest with you. Do you still want to tell me you love me? Shop-soiled goods and all that?"

"You're being ridiculous, now, Mandy. Anything you did before we met is of no consequence. It's how you are now, now that we're together, that's what matters to me. Yes, I still want to tell you that I love you."

Smiling in relief, she hugged him again. "And I love you too, Andy. I'm so besotted with you. You make me so happy."

Arm in arm, they started to amble slowly along the street, unsure of where they were going, both reeling from the impact of Mandy's disclosure.

"I need to see this photo. We'll need to escalate this. I need to get those bastards who did this to you." He stared grimly ahead. "Christ, I could fucking murder them." Then he looked embarrassed. "Sorry, I didn't mean to swear in front of you."

"No need to say sorry. But about the photo - I don't want to show you here, Andy. Shall we go back to my place? I can make us a cup of tea?" She smiled up at him, hopefully.

"Sounds like a plan. Let's go."

Andy held the photo at its edge, as though it was contaminated, hating even to touch it, gazing down at it in disbelief. How it wounded him to see the girl he loved displayed like a piece of meat, being manhandled by some shitty, evil bastard. Outrage and anguish waged a battle inside his head. But he had to stay in control, if only for her sake.

Mandy huddled next to him, eyes downcast, mortified beyond belief.

"I'm so sorry," she whispered.

He squeezed her arm. "This was not your fault, understand? You are a victim of crime, Mands. The men that did this are criminals, animals." Turning to look at her sad, little face, he continued. "What do you want to do about it?"

Not expecting this, Mandy was taken aback. "Do about it? I hadn't thought about that. What do you think I should do? My only concern was telling you. I've been sick with worry."

"Look, I'm going to put my coppers hat on now – although C.I.D. don't wear hats -" he managed a wry smile "- and I'll try and put it in perspective. We know that you were drugged, you were forced to do things you were unaware of, against your will, with no consent. Things were done to you, without your permission or knowledge. In all probability you were raped, maybe there was more than one man involved. It's a good few weeks since it happened, so you can't be checked for forensic evidence or anything." Mandy shuddered at the thought of having had to endure that. "Unfortunately, there's every chance there are more photographs in existence. If this is escalated, it could be really hard for you, Mands. But, ethically, I can't really ignore it."

"Oh, Jesus." She put her head in her hands and sighed heavily. "I don't know what to do." She glanced up at him, pleadingly. "Can I have time to think this over, Andy? I need to get my head around it all."

"Sure." He hugged her.

"And what did you mean when you said it would be hard for me?"

"Lack of evidence. We only have your word and one photograph. The perpetrators would only have to deny it, your word against theirs. If it actually went to court, the defence would tear you apart."

"I need time, Andy, I definitely need more time. Is that okay?"

He nodded. "Take as much time as you want, Mandy, I'm ready whenever you are. But I'd give that bastard Hancock a very wide berth from now on. Don't have anything to do with him, don't even speak to him, understand?"

"Of course. That won't be difficult." She kissed him softly on the cheek, before asking, uncertainly, "But what do you want to do about next weekend? Meeting your parents?"

"What about it?" He smiled down at her. "We're expected at eight, so you'd better not be late!"

"Who's a poet and doesn't know it!" She giggled. How relieved he felt to see once more that happy face he loved so much.

As they embraced each again, Mandy buried her face in his Aran sweater, breathing in the scent of his Brut after-shave, and reflected on the way things had worked out. The world seemed a good place once again. Her topsy-turvy room was like an old friend, it had witnessed all her sadness and her joy. It felt as though she had been given a second chance at real happiness, and she certainly wasn't going to throw it all away. She no longer felt so frightened. She had Andy well and truly on her side.

Chapter Twenty Five Initiation

"So he was okay about everything?" Concern written all over her face, Julia poured the boiling water into the two mugs, making the tea bags bob up and down in hot, milky ponds. Mandy was stretched out on Julia's bed, wearing her oversized, fleecy red pyjamas, steadily munching her way through a packet of Jaffa Cakes – someone had told her they had less calories than other biscuits, so down the hatch they went. She hardly tasted them, but was comforted by the mechanical eating.

"He was more than okay, Jules, he was amazing. He was understanding, kind – but at the same time he was bloody tamping, furious, do you know what I mean? He wanted to throttle him, them, whoever was there." She took the tea from Julia. "But I've been thinking. Would you do me a favour?"

"Anything, as long as it's legal." Julia tucked into a piece of hot toast, the melted butter dripping down her chin.

"I need to do something, something unpleasant, but it has to be done. For Andy's sake as well as mine."

Julia glanced over at her, curiously. "Spill the beans."

"Will you come with me to the Special Clinic? I need to get myself checked."

"You mean -"

"Yeah! The bloody GUM clinic, you know, through the Blue Door down by East Wing! That secret passage where you sit without a name, where you're just a number. Will you come and be just a number with me, Jules? I want to make sure I'm one hundred per cent okay. Before – before I'm in a situation with Andy – oh, you know what I mean?"

"Yes, of course. Of course I'll come with you. But I refuse to be a number! I'll just be your chaperone! Anyway, you haven't got any symptoms or anything, have you?"

"None at all. I just had that episode of thrush a few days later, but I get that occasionally anyway. No, I very much doubt there's anything amiss, but there's no way on God's earth I'm going to take any chances."

"Well, you make the appointment and let me know. I'll write my shifts down for you, so you can work around them, Is that okay?"

"Oh, that's great, Jules. I'm not looking forward to it, but if you're there it won't seem so awful. It's the one thing I can do for him, after he's been so supportive and kind."

"What do you intend to do about taking it further?" Julia licked her fingers clean.

"I'm not sure." Mandy frowned, considering things carefully. "It's all a bit soon to make a decision, really. And there's no rush, is there?" She crumpled up the Jaffa Cakes wrapper and threw it in the bin, missing her target as usual.

Julia hoisted herself from the rug on the floor and put her empty plate in the sink. "Maybe. Maybe there is, though. I mean, do you think Hancock could strike again? With someone else?"

"I hadn't thought of that. I see what you mean. I'll give it some thought, Jules. I'll be able to think more clearly in the morning, after a good night's sleep."

"Okay, Fanny Ann. You toddle off to bed, and we'll sort it out tomorrow."

"Nite, Jules." Yawning her head off, Mandy retreated across the landing to her own room and the promise of peaceful slumbers.

Julia checked her clock. Eleven o'clock. Peering out between the curtains, she watched the rain beating down on the dark street. How bleak and dismal it all seemed, winter had loitered too long, spring was overdue. Grateful for her warm, cosy room, she closed the curtains together more tightly, and started to brush her teeth. A whole day off tomorrow, she thought, concentrating diligently on her molars, and I get to see Mitch as well. Happy days.

The intense atmosphere of William Meckett ward never managed to faze Mandy. She thrived on the high level of pressure. How on earth could Julia prefer surgical, she pondered, as she changed an IV fluid bag. All those patients coming and going, you hardly got to know any of them properly. Sister Blake was giving handover to the late shift and all the patients had more or less been fed and watered. Only a couple more tasks to complete before she went to lunch.

She looked around for the first-year. Where was that useless student, she thought. Catching sight of Sheila, the reliable auxiliary walking down the ward with a pepper pot, she stopped her. "Have you seen Nurse Rees, the student?"

"Oh, I think she went off to the sluice, Staff. Sister asked her to collect an F.O.B."

"But that was about a quarter of an hour ago. What on earth can she be up to?"

Sheila's pleasant face creased into a smile. "Goodness only knows, Staff, she's not the brightest card in the pack, is she? I'd better get along, Mr Beehnuck in the bay is refusing to eat his lunch unless I get the pepper for him!"

Mandy laughed. The poor renal patients, denied the luxury of adding salt to their food because it could be toxic to their systems, would yearn, beg and clamour for pepper as a substitute. It was a wonder they didn't spend their mealtimes sneezing their heads off. Some of them even demanded pepper on their boiled eggs each morning...

The student was still in the sluice. What the hell could she be up to, Mandy thought, puzzled. Nurse Rees was bent over a bedpan, concentrating hard, her tongue sticking out over her teeth as she struggled to do something – but what was she doing?

"Nurse Rees?"

The girl swung around, startled, her untidy brown hair dangling down over her forehead. Jesus, what a little scruffbag, thought Mandy in despair.

"What are you doing?"

"Um, I'm collecting the F.O.B., Staff."

Thank God she's remembered to put plastic gloves on, Mandy observed. "Let's have a look."

Peering over the student's shoulder, Mandy wanted to burst out laughing. The girl had not just collected a tiny sample, she was intent on packing as much faeces into the pot as she possibly could. It was practically spilling over the top.

"Right. Well done, Nurse Rees. I think that's quite enough, don't you? Put the lid on – if it will go on - and wash your hands, and make sure the form for Path Lab is correctly completed, okay?"

"Yes, Staff."

"And next time you have to collect a sample for F.O.B. remember you only need a titchy, tiny amount! You don't need to pack it all in until it's overflowing. I'm sure Path Lab will be delighted with your efforts!"

Stifling a chortle, imagining the horrified faces of the lab technicians as they pulled out the specimen, she left the sluice.

Regaling Sister Blake with the student's latest escapade, she grabbed her bag. "I'm off to lunch then, Sister, if that's okay?"

302

"Yes, my dear, you go, but could you take this x-ray form down to Radiology on your way? The new house officer filled it in wrong."

"Yes, of course, Sister. I'd quite forgotten it's February!" A standing joke amongst the permanent staff on the wards, February and August were the changeover months for the newly-qualified doctors, with many hiccups, disasters and mess-ups as guaranteed consequences.

Having delivered the corrected radiology form, Mandy belted back up the stairs as fast as she could. There'd be nothing left, she felt certain, and she was absolutely starving. She could already smell the roast beef as she ran up the steps, but her heart was set on some cheese and potato pie with chips. I'll never look like Julia, she thought glumly, I'm too greedy. Just as well Andy liked her exactly as she was, pleasantly curvy and womanly – his words. Her mind preoccupied with loving thoughts of Andy, she was unprepared when she almost collided with Neil Hancock on the second floor corridor.

Shit, she thought, damn him. Mumbling a hasty apology, she tried to sidestep him, but he grabbed her arm.

"What's the rush, pretty lady?" His suave remark made her skin crawl. "No time for a chat? How are you? Haven't seen much of you around these days." He was practically purring, like a great, predatory panther.

"Get stuffed, Hancock." She wanted to spit in his face. "Let me go."

Neil Hancock feigned disappointment. "I thought we had a thing going. I just wanted to know if you fancied coming over to my place again, you know, another photo shoot or something? You looked amazing in those photos, I thought you and I could pick which ones were best." His teeth were dazzlingly white, but there was a piece of cabbage stuck between his lower incisors.

"If you don't let my arm go right now, I'll scream." She wrenched her arm out of his grip. "I have nothing to say to you. Piss off." He released his grip, allowing her to storm off, neither of them recognising an off-duty Sister Hunter who'd been loitering idly near the staff notice board, wearing a pink sweater and a pair of sensible black slacks, her grey hair hanging loosely in a plait. She'd been listening to the conversation with increasing interest.

Thoroughly nettled, Neil Hancock cleared his throat and called after her. "Well, if you change your mind, I'm on Flanders. Ciao!" Common little bitch, he thought angrily.

As he made his way downstairs to the trauma ward, he wondered uneasily what had made her have such an obvious change of heart. He'd thought he'd managed to manipulate her totally, by the silences, the avoidance. She should be a sitting duck by now, ready and willing for the next time he fancied a leg-over, gagging for him. The silly cow should be grateful he'd resumed communication, he considered. Anger swiftly replaced any brief anxiety he may have felt, and he walked resolutely back to his ward.

Marjorie Hunter turned her attentions back to the notice board, reading but not absorbing notices about kittens needing homes and bicycles for sale. I wonder what is going on in this hospital, she pondered. Ignoring the recurring tightness in her chest, she decided to make it her business to a keep a very close eye on events, in any way she could.

It was clear to Andy that a huge effort had been made in readiness for his visit. Gone were the dirty dishes in the sink, the FloorDrobe had disappeared, all Mandy's clothes had been put away neatly and the radiator could actually be seen, not a pair of black tights or greying knickers in sight. She'd obviously been spraying Airwick around the place as well.

"Someone's been hard at work," he chuckled, making himself at home on the single bed.

Hastily shoving an errant magazine under the bed, Mandy pretended to be offended. "What are you on about? It's always like this!"

"Come here! I haven't spent all afternoon looking forward to seeing you to discuss your housekeeping!" He pulled her to sit down next to him. "I'm so glad everything's okay between us, Mands. I couldn't bear to lose you."

"Me too." She snuggled up to him, putting her arms around him. "There's something I need to tell you, Andy."

"Oh, God, not more revelations!" His face fell.

"Not at all." She smiled reassuringly at him. "I just want you to know that I got myself checked out at the hospital special clinic recently, you know, because of what happened, and all is well."

"You went there? On you own?"

"Julia came with me. It was awful, I hated having to do that, but it was really important to make sure all is okay. Oh, and I saw that tosser Neil Hancock in the corridor the other day. He tried it on again. I told him where to go."

He hugged her. "Well done. You're a brave girl, Mandy, I'll give you that. You nurses are made of sterner stuff than us coppers give you credit for. I know you need time to consider what you want to do about taking things further, but I'm here when you're ready. You are important to me, more than you'll ever know."

She leaned against him, enjoying the closeness. "You've made my world complete, Andy. You're everything I've ever dreamed of. I've never met anyone like you before." She sighed, happily.

"I feel the same, Mands. I'm going to make your head massive now, but you need to know that you're stunningly pretty, you've got an incredible figure – no, don't look like that - and you're one of the kindest, sweetest natured girls I've ever met."

He started kissing her, gently at first, then more insistently. She responded with alacrity. He pulled her down on top of the cavorting kittens which adorned her pink duvet. Breathing heavily, he reached

305

slowly for her breast, tenderly caressing it over her fluffy blue sweater, before reaching under the soft fabric to undo her bra.

"God, I want you so badly," he murmured as he unclipped the peach satin bra, her voluptuous breasts springing forth into his eager hand.

Within a few minutes, he'd dispensed with her outer garments and was able to enjoy the sight of her curvaceous body, clad only in a pair of peach satin panties.

"Christ Almighty, you're gorgeous," he groaned, as she straddled him on the bed, "never, ever go on a diet, you are stunning." He reached up to fondle her luscious breasts, leaning up to kiss each dark nipple.

Suddenly, he flung himself back on the pillow with a heavy sigh.

"What's the matter?" Mandy started imagining all sorts of issues. Was he secretly repulsed by her, by the sordid knowledge of her recent assault?

"Mands. There's something you should know. I don't know quite how to tell you." He couldn't quite meet her eyes.

"Tell me, for goodness' sake! Come on, we have no more secrets, remember?" She lay down next to him, stroking his chest, playing with the buttons on his shirt.

"You're not going to believe me when I tell you. Promise you won't laugh at me?"

"Have you got a tattoo or something? A girl's name from your seedy past?" She grinned cheekily at him. "I won't mind! Show me!"

He sat up. "It's nothing like that. Mands, I know I'm twenty-four, but I haven't had many girlfriends – oh, shit, there's no easy way to put it. Mandy, I'm still a virgin."

In the dimly-lit room, Mandy slowly kissed him. "I don't care," she whispered, "I don't care if you are a bloody Casanova or a celibate saint. I

306

love you. Shall I tell you what feels nice for me?" He nodded, his eyes glazed with yearning.

She unbuttoned his shirt, until she reached the waistband of his jeans, sensually stroking his groin, feeling his response beneath her probing fingers.

The jeans and shirt were soon a thing of the past. As the pair lay on the narrow bed, Mandy slowly inched his boxer shorts down. Andy moaned quietly, aroused beyond belief. Unable to prevent it, his carnal pillar rose to the occasion.

"Wow, you're a big boy!" Mandy giggled, taking it in her small hand. Andy looked down his body to enjoy the highly erotic sight of his proud member being held in her fingers; her nails were painted a pale, shiny pink, he noticed. "Now we're going to slow things right down, or you'll end up erupting like bloody Mount Etna." She wriggled onto her back. "Take my knickers off, Andy." Obediently, he did as he was told. "Now I want you to find a tiny rosebud down there, it's very sensitive, and if you stroke it gently and, most importantly, slowly, you'll get me nice and ready for you when you enter my cavern of delight!" Her playful tone helped to relax him. As he started to kiss her once more, he allowed her to take his hand and place it on her mons veneris, where he started to caress and stroke her until she was quivering with unbridled lust. Her writhing response turned him on even more. I must be doing it right, he thought.

"Take me to heaven, Andy, don't stop! Please don't stop! Oh- oh – oh my God!" She shuddered as she climaxed.

Positioning himself on top of her, he parted her legs, probing her entrance with his fingers, his eager phallus following, seeking its ultimate gratification.

She opened her legs further. "I'm so ready for you, Andy!"

He couldn't wait any longer. So great was his desire to enter her, he aimed his weapon of seduction at his goal, and without any further instruction from Mandy, he plunged into her.

"Ah!" His groan of satisfaction was involuntary, and he gave himself up to a rhythmic thrusting, until he exploded into her, after just ten seconds. Detective Constable Andy Greenleigh-Peters had finally lost his virginity.

The plush office was as tropical as ever and the four boys sweated profusely as they waited for Steph.

"Why can't she ever be on time?" muttered Jeff, glancing at his watch, irritably. He had to finish his assignment and hand it in tomorrow. As if on cue, the door was flung open and Steph marched in bossily, but with a beaming smile on her perfectly made up face. She was followed by a middle-aged man in a creased beige suit.

"Evening, guys!" She grinned around at that them. "I'd like you to meet Bill Hockenhull, our C.E.O. He's come all the way down from London to congratulate you."

The four stood up, wondering what was coming next.

"Nice to meet you at last," he regarded them coolly, his smile not quite reaching his pale grey eyes. He accepted a large whisky from Steph, before continuing in his refined mid-Atlantic accent. "I know the top ten was announced last night, and you chaps were hovering around number five, but I've had it on reliable authority that next Sunday you'll probably be straight up there at number one, providing sales continue as they are."

The boys looked at each other in amazement. They'd done it. Fucking hell, Dai mouthed inaudibly at the others.

Grinning from ear to ear, Mitch finally broke the stunned silence. "Jeez, that's bloody cool!" He laughed in delight. "I can't wait to tell Julia!"

Steph threw him a warning look. "Oh, it's top secret right now. Mum's the word, okay?"

Slightly deflated, they nodded assent. She carried on. "And it's not definite anyway. But Mr Hockenhull thought you may prefer to reconsider your, er, disinclination of embracing the limelight."

Taking a big swig of his drink, the C.E.O. smirked at her. "Oh, please call me Bill, Steph."

She's blushing, realised Mitch, amused. Aloud, he said. "Actually, we've done nothing but discuss the subject of our self-promotion etcetera, and we still feel the same, all of us." He glanced around at the others, who were nodding in agreement. "It's amazing to have achieved everything in such a short time, but we are absolutely adamant that we don't really want to go down the mugs, posters and screaming groupies road. We are serious musicians, we want to compose, produce, and-" he couldn't stop himself from quipping "- deliver the goods as promised and agreed in our contracts."

Steph sighed, and flashed a look at her boss which clearly said, "See what I have to put up with?"

Putting his empty tumbler down on the glass table, Bill Hockenhull strolled over to the window. There was still enough daylight for him to see the cathedral in the distance, but, annoyingly, not enough darkness for him to see his own reflection adequately. Turning back to his audience, he cleared his throat slightly.

"Fair enough. It's your choice. But I would like to offer you another opportunity. It's been proposed by the board, after consultation with Steph here -" he gave a her a cheesy smile "-that we send you stateside, to Boulder in Colorado actually, to do some serious recording. There's a well-known female vocalist and songwriter who's been in touch with us. She must remain anonymous at this stage, but she is extremely keen to collaborate with you. You'll be there about two or three weeks, all expenses paid, of course. Now don't tell me you're gonna turn *that* down!" He held his arms open, expansively.

"When?" The ever practical Jeff was thinking of his job and his thesis.

"In a few months, say the beginning of September? That should give you enough time to sort out passports, visas, time off work and so on."

"That's fantastic!" Mitch could hardly believe their luck. "Colorado! Boulder! That's where The Shining is based!"

"Sounds good to me!" Jeff, happy that his orderly life could continue, started to feel the thrill of this fortuitous prospect.

At last, thought Steph wryly, the little sods are actually enthusiastic.

Eddie rubbed his hands in glee. "Bloody hell, I've only ever been to Spain before! Christ, I've always wanted to go to America!"

Dai felt excited, but how was he going to break this to Meinir?

Mitch felt elated, but how was he going to break this to Julia?

"Why did you belt off to the bathroom?" Andy sipped the disgusting cup of coffee Mandy'd made him. Little chunks of Marvel were floating unappetisingly on the surface, and she'd run out of sugar.

"Aha,"she replied mysteriously, tapping her nose, "us girls have to keep ourselves fresh!" Nice and sweet for what I've got in mind, she thought naughtily.

"Fresh for what?"

"Fresh for round two!" Mischievously, she allowed her hand to creep down under the sheet, and started to fondle him. Instantly, he rose to the occasion, his manhood stiffening rapidly in response to her sensual attentions.

"Shall we do something a bit different?" She removed his coffee. "Do you think we should be a bit more, you know, adventurous?" He loved the way she wrinkled her cute little nose when she was teasing him.

"I'm game if you are!"

Sensing his enthusiasm, she slid under the sheet towards his pelvis, and delicately licked him, making him shudder with delight.

"That's bloody wicked of you, Mands! But bloody lovely!"

She carried on with her ministrations, then stopped, coming up for air, before he got completely carried away. "Your turn now."

Compliantly, he also slid underneath the sheet. His eager hands grabbed hold of her well-proportioned hips, digging his fingers into her plump buttocks. Burying his face in the soft fuzz of hair, breathing in the scent of Pears soap, his probing tongue sought her tiny love button. Finding her obvious pleasure an incredible turn on, he licked her slowly, then quickly, pushing his fingers inside her at the same time.

Closing her eyes in ecstasy, she sighed. "Oh, you're good, Andy, so good! Don't stop, don't stop – ah!" Her whole body convulsed as she climaxed.

"That was unbelievable," she whispered, recovering from her second orgasm in forty-five minutes, "now it's your turn. Come to me, my darling boy, come in to me, I'm oh, so ready for you!"

He acquiesced immediately. There was no stopping him now...

Chapter Twenty Six Acceleration

The ward clock showed ten past one. Another seven hours or so to go before she could stumble back to her little room and go to sleep. Aneira was relieved this was her last night shift. She found nights long, arduous and occasionally alarming. Looking down the dimly-lit nightingale ward, she could see that most of the patients were sleeping, but there were a couple of post-operative patients who were quietly sighing in discomfort. Maria the S.E.N. had popped into the kitchen to eat her dinner, there'd been nobody in the hospital to relieve her to go to the canteen, and Aneira was far too junior to be left alone on the ward, even for a few minutes. Thank goodness, she thought.

Jimmy, the male auxiliary from Mauritius, was being shared between Terence Adams and Llanfair, and he'd been called over to the female surgical ward to help out, much to his displeasure. "Bloody women," he'd grumbled as he'd gathered his belongings, "always complaining and wanting bloody bedpans. Give me male surgical any day of the week."

Aneira loved C.C.I. It was so different to her first placement, which had been on a modern medical ward. The old Victorian building seemed to have a personality of its own; how many dramas must have been played out here, she wondered, how many tragedies, how many lives saved...

Her reverie was interrupted.

"Nurse!"

Aneira hurried over to the patient who'd had his hernia repaired the previous day.

"What's the matter, Mr Boswell? Are you in pain?"

Mervyn Boswell's face was creased up in discomfort. He was perspiring heavily. "You could say that." He made a feeble attempt at a smile.

"I'll just check your chart." Feeling confident and experienced, Aneira reached for the treatment chart at the end of the bed. "You last had an injection just over three hours ago, so it's a bit soon for another."

"I'm in agony, Nurse." He winced in pain.

Her confidence ebbing away, Aniera considered what she should do. "Okay, I'll get Nurse Esposito. She's at break, but I'm sure she won't mind. I'll only be a minute."

"Thank you, Nurse." Mervyn Boswell squeezed her hand. "You're a little darling."

Maria was munching her way through a Tupperware box filled with cold arancini, savouring every garlicky mouthful and dreaming longingly of her home town Taormina, in Sicily. How good it was to put her feet up for a few minutes. The shift had been heavy, she reflected, and the little student was still pretty green, but what she lacked in experience and confidence, she more than made up for in enthusiasm and dedication. However, her hard-earned escapism was rudely disturbed by Aneira arriving breathlessly at the kitchen door.

"Sorry to bother you, Nurse Esposito, but Mr Boswell is complaining of severe pain, and he's not due any more pethidine until at least two o'clock. What shall I do?"

Suppressing a heavy sigh, Maria got to her feet. She could finish her dinner at her next break – if she managed to have one.

"I guess-a we better call da S.H.O. I go bleep him. You go tell da patient we will sort it out, and make sure he has passed urine, if he has-a da full bladder he will have more of da pain."

"Okay, thank you." Aneira gratefully retreated back to the ward, heading first for the sluice to fetch a clean urinal for her patient. She liked working with Maria. She was conscientious, diligent and dry humoured, but extremely fair and kind to the young student.

Switching the sluice light on, she noticed that Jimmy had left a used bedpan on the work unit, there were used plastic gloves and aprons everywhere and the Sluicemaster was full to capacity, with its hatch open, ready to be set to go.

"Bloody men!" She muttered, with uncharacteristic annoyance.

"Yes, bloody men, indeed," came an unexpected voice behind her. Swinging around, she came face to face with Sister Hunter.

Blushing a deep shade of scarlet, Aneira stammered out, "Oops, sorry Sister. It just slipped out!"

Sister Hunter beheld the chaos in the sluice for a second before replying.

"I have already forgotten what you said, Nurse." Was that a hint of a smile playing around the senior nurse's lips? Serenely, she continued. "You get along and see to your patient, Nurse Thomas and I will tidy up in here." And give Jimmy-boy a piece of my mind when I catch hold of him, she thought.

To Aneira's dismay, it was Marcus Battencourt who was on-call that night. But at least she didn't need to have anything to do with him. Busying herself with checking the IVI's and adding up the fluid charts, she kept a wary distance between herself and the office, where she could see him studying the various treatment charts with Maria.

Sister Hunter had also just returned to the office, after doing a magnificent clean-up operation in the sluice, in order to check the control drug with Maria.

"Let the student give the pethidine, Maria." They had worked together for many years. "She's very capable, but needs her confidence boosting." She patted the S.E.N on the shoulder. Marjorie Hunter looked as pristine as ever, despite having been up to her fastidious elbows in faeces only ten minutes earlier.

"Nurse Thomas? You come-a here to check da pethidine with Sister Hunter." Maria's resonant Italian voice carried down the ward, a little too loudly, but none of the sleeping patients seemed to have been disturbed.

Reluctant at having to be in the same room as her malefactor, Aneira bit her lip as she joined the two qualified nurses in the office. Marcus Battencourt took no notice of her at all. He was engrossed in a copy of the British National Formulary and had a pile of treatment charts in front of him. His very presence sent shivers down her spine, he terrified her. Out of the corner of her eye she watched his cold, pale face, his thin, pursed lips as he concentrated on his work. How could she ever have thought him attractive, or kind? All she could see now was a hard expression, devoid of any compassion or tenderness. How could I have been so stupid, she wondered, sadly.

Maria removed the pethidine ampoules from the drugs cupboard, counted and checked them with Sister Hunter, before taking one out and replacing the rest, then locking the cupboard door.

Both nurses signed the control drugs register, which lay open on the desk. Aneira read it dutifully, then accompanied Sister Hunter to Mr Boswell's bed.

Drawing the curtains around the bed, the night sister handed Aneira the small tray which contained the already drawn-up analgesic. "You can give it." She smiled encouragingly at the young student. "I will watch you. Just wash your hands first. Go on, you'll be perfectly fine. You've done it before?"

Aneira nodded, before whispering, "This will be my third injection, Sister."

316

"Good. Off you go."

After washing her hands thoroughly at the nearby sink, shaking slightly with nerves, Aneira approached the patient. "I'm just going to give you an injection to stop the pain, Mr Boswell." She pulled back the sheet, to gain access to his leg. "I'm just going to clean your thigh with this little swab." Aneira wiped the skin clean, using the small Medi-swab in the tray. "You'll feel a tiny prick in a minute."

Marjorie Hunter had to look away for a few seconds, trying to compose herself and not smile. Even Mervyn Boswell managed a slight snigger. But Aneira, unaware of her comical words, was intent on completing her task perfectly. Removing the cover of the needle, she held the syringe in her right hand, using her left hand to hold the skin on the patient's thigh. She looked up at the night sister for encouragement, who nodded, reassuringly. She quickly inserted the needle until it was almost completely in the flesh, then withdrew to check she hadn't hit a blood vessel. Happy that everything was going well, she pressed the plunger down, completing her procedure.

"There, all done!" Aneira rubbed the injection site with the Medi-swab.

"Well, that was great, Nurse! I didn't feel a thing!" Mr Boswell winked at Sister Hunter, who smiled back conspiratorially. Drawing back the curtains, the night sister led the way back to the office.

"Now we'll make sure to sign the drug chart, Nurse Thomas, and then I will be off to Llanfair. Nurse Esposito? Have you had your break?"

"Not properly, Sister. Can I go finish now? I only go to da kitchen."

"Yes, off you go. I'll be around later on. Any problems, just bleep me." And off she went, heading for Llanfair ward and the reprehensible Jimmy, wincing as a stab of pain shot through her upper abdomen.

Maria turned to Aneira. "You be okay? I only in da kitchen again."

"Yes, of course, I'll be fine." Aneira felt on top of the world. She had given her third injection, the patient hadn't screamed in pain (like the first one had) and she hadn't hit the bone with the needle (as she had the second time.) Life was good.

Leaving Aneira to clear away the used syringe and needle, Maria wearily returned to the kitchen, popping her head around the office door as she went.

"I only in da kitchen," she repeated for Marcus Battencourt's benefit. "Da student is on da ward, but you can call me if anything important, yeah?"

Without even lifting his blond head to acknowledge her, he merely lifted his hand and waved her away, impatiently.

Arrogant prat, thought Maria, *lanciatore*, as she retrieved her arancini once more, settling down to enjoy them in the kitchen.

She stinks of bloody garlic, the stupid cow, Marcus Battencourt thought, irritably.

Aneira painstakingly completed the post-operative observations on the three patients who were recovering from surgery, even using a small ruler to make sure her recordings were neat and tidy. The only trouble was, these patients were situated close to the office, where they could easily be seen by the nursing staff. That meant she kept on seeing Marcus Battencourt's head as he continued to write up the medications. He was taking ages.

She rolled up the blood pressure cuff and returned the machine to its place near the central desk in the middle of the ward. Wishing to remove herself from Marcus Battencourt's view, she retreated to the dimness of the very first bed on the right hand side, the opposite side to the glass panelled office. He wouldn't be able to see her from there.

A sudden movement in the office caught her eye. She shrank back into the shadows. Was he coming out into the ward? Her heart started beating uncomfortably fast. She couldn't bear it if he spoke to her. But no. He was standing up, with his back to her. Pressing herself against the wall, masked by the bunched up curtains at the top bed, she peeped out at him.

Marcus Battencourt looked furtively over his shoulder, then returned his attentions to the controlled drugs cupboard. He looked about him once more, scanning the ward - for me, she thought, fearfully - before opening the lock and reaching inside. Aneira held her breath. What on earth was he doing? Doctors didn't go into that cupboard. And Maria had the keys pinned inside her pocket. Her eyes were so widely fixed on the events that were unfolding they were stinging and smarting. Thank goodness Mr Boswell had fallen asleep and couldn't witness what was going on, or call out her name.

Marcus Battencourt pulled out a brown bottle, and was pouring something out into a universal container, onto which he screwed the top, then hastily shoved into his pocket. Checking once more that his actions hadn't been observed, he took the brown bottle over to the sink and seemed to be topping up the bottle with water from the tap, before swiftly replacing the cap and restoring it to the cupboard. He was so quick, his movements so deft, it was incredible. The actions of an accomplished practitioner.

Aneira could hardly believe her eyes. He was taking something from the controlled drugs cupboard. He was stealing. He was stealing a controlled drug. Oh my God, she thought, panicking, please don't let him see me. Her breathing was deep and fast, her heart pounding loudly against her ribcage. Surely he'd be able to hear her?

The office door opened. Aneira pressed herself even harder against the wall, making sure that the bed curtains were concealing her. Tiny pearls of sweat glittered on her frightened face as she realised the enormity of what was taking place. All her beliefs about what was good and right dissolved in those wretched moments. He would come by any second, she would be discovered, he would be furious she'd seen him, he would...

She could have wept with relief when she heard his footsteps walk away from her, and through the double doors which led to the corridor.

The terrified young girl sat down at the central desk, trembling, her thoughts in a turmoil. What had been in that bottle, she wondered. Why had he been taking it? More importantly, what should she do about this? Remembering his threats when she was in hospital as a patient herself, she was reluctant to make any rash decision.

Aneira was never more grateful to see Maria, as she returned from her break.

"All okay, cara?" The S.E.N. pushed open the door of the office. Aneira rose shakily to her feet and followed her in.

"Yes, all up to date. No problems." She smiled bravely.

Maria fussily turned the dripping tap off at the sink. "I wish people would take da trouble to turn taps off properly! Right then. All is hanky dunky." She never got her English slang quite right. "I do a quick spot of knitting, now. Sister Hunter, she no be back for a good hour." She pulled out a multi-coloured jumper and started to knit away furiously.

"Nurse Esposito?"

"Yes?" Maria started a new row, clickety-click went the needles.

"Apart from pethidine, omnopon and morphine, what else is kept in the controlled drugs cupboard?"

"Ooh, quite a few things, diamorphine ampoules for injection – that's heroine - and some things like diazepam tablets. And some whisky for da old boys! But it's only found on some wards. It's a-going outa fashion." She laughed.

"Whisky?" Aneira echoed, thinking that now was her chance. "Anything else? Other liquids?"

"Hmm." Maria considered the question. "Let me think. Well, there's always a bottle of Brompton's on most wards. We don't use it much, these days, though."

"Brompton's?" Her voice was no more than a murmur.

"Yeah, Brompton mixture contains morphine, cocaine, ethyl alcohol, syrup, and chloroform." Maria slipped two purl then knitted three. "Some of the old school pharmacists would blend it up with a drop of da brandy for da dying patient. Made it nice to taste, yeah?"

"So it makes the patient sort - of out of it?" Aneira's felt wave of abject distress wash over her. Oh my God, she realised, I was certainly out of it.

"Sure! Makes their sleep sweet and deep. What could be better, yeah? Drift away on a cloud of pain-free sleep. Now why you ask?"

"Just wondering. I've, er, got to do an essay next week on pain relief. That's been an interesting answer."

The knitting needles clicked on, one-two, three-four, slip one, double purl. "You a-worried, chick? Something bothering you?" Maria hardly took her eyes off her knitting.

Aneira's exhausted eyes fluttered slightly. "Nothing at all. Nothing's bothering me, Nurse. Nothing at all..."

Forgive me Lord, for my blatant lies. She bent her head and longed for the clock to race forward, to hurry towards a time when she could be happy and safe once more.

The night sister hadn't put in a reappearance after all. Maria had mentioned she'd rung the ward around five o'clock saying that she'd had to go off duty, suffering from extreme indigestion. Forlornly, Aneira put on her black cardigan and fetched her handbag from under the desk. The day staff were already bustling about, serving the breakfasts and starting the bed-making. As she wearily made her way down the staircase to the ground floor, she thought hard about what she should do, whom she should tell. Sister Hunter had been the obvious choice, but now she was unwell and probably fast asleep in bed.

As she unlocked the door of her tiny room and removed her cap, she suddenly realised with striking clarity that there was one person she could confide in, one person she could trust. Julia.

Aneira raced along Porthnewydd Avenue as fast as her little legs could carry her, adrenaline coursing through her veins, rendering her completely oblivious to the beautiful morning. The sun was rising over Rumney and there was a definite promise of a glorious day ahead.

Swamped by her red mackintosh, her white blond hair streaming out behind her like a mermaid, she knew she must be quite a sight as she ran down the pavement, but she didn't care. She was utterly focussed on getting to Julia as quickly as possible. Entirely grateful for her sensible nurse's shoes, she would probably have broken many a local record for the four hundred metre sprint. She didn't register an astonished Mr Anscombe doing a double take as he drove past on his way to the Infirmary in his ancient Volkswagen Golf.

Julia would either be on a late shift or a day off, she reckoned, as she hadn't been present at the morning handover. But what if she was having a lie-in? Well, Aneira would simply have to suffer the consequences if she disturbed Julia. And once the staff nurse heard what she had to say...

Breathlessly, she knocked on the door of the big, Victorian house, then rang the bell for good measure.

Minutes ticked by. Surely there was someone at home? Ringing the bell again, keeping her finger pressed on it for a very long time, she prayed that the door would open.

Her prayers were answered.

"Goodness me!" An early morning Miss Marshall opened the door a couple of inches, squinting at Aneira in the bright morning sunshine. Pulling her dressing gown more tightly around her waist, she opened the door properly. "Whatever's the matter, child? Why are you creating such a noise at this hour of the morning?"

"Sorry, so sorry," she panted, "but I need to see Staff Harry. It's urgent, Miss Marshall."

The warden could see that the student was considerably distressed. "You'd better come in, then. But Staff Harry is more than likely still fast asleep, unless she's on an early, in which case -"

"No!" Aneira interrupted frantically. "I've just come off nights, Julia – sorry, Staff Harry – she wasn't with the early shift. Oh, please can I come in and talk to her?"

Miss Marshall sighed heavily in disapproval. "Oh, very well, if you must." She beckoned to Aneira to enter the hall. "Wait here, I'll go and call her."

"Thank you, Miss Marshall." Aneira sank gratefully onto an old stool next to the public telephone. "Thank you so much."

Chapter Twenty Seven Pieces of the jigsaw

"Come in, sit down, do you want a coffee?" Julia rubbed her sleepy eyes, her bedtime plait hanging heavily down her back.

"Er, okay, please, if you're having one." Aneira took a seat on the only easy chair available, looking around in wonderment at the qualified nurse's personal living space. The room was much bigger than hers, quite grand, in fact, with its high ceiling and massive bay window overlooking the main road. A huge poster of Roxy Music dominated the wall opposite the bed, and a couple of spider plants jostled for attention on the small window sill at the other side of the room. A clean blue uniform was ready and waiting for the next shift on a coat hanger on the back of the door. All neat and tidy, thought Aneira, immediately identifying with Julia's need for an orderly existence.

Handing her a mug of steaming coffee, Julia sat down on her unmade bed. "Sorry it's only Coffee-Mate. Ran out of milk last night, I think Mandy used it up." She stifled a yawn.

"That's okay, thanks." Aneira took a sip and winced, it was much too hot. "I'm sorry to have disturbed you so early, Staff."

"Julia."

"Yes, sorry, Julia. I had to see you, There's something awful I need to tell you."

"Go on." Julia smiled gently at the younger girl, who was clearly in a high state of anxiety.

"Right. I'll just tell you everything that happened, then you can tell me what you think, what you think I should do. Maybe I'm being silly, maybe -"

"Just tell me."

Taking a deep breath, Aneira launched into her account of the night's events.

"Dr Battencourt was on the ward last night, he was writing up some post-op meds. I was alone for a short while, on the ward, Maria had gone to the kitchen for her break. Everything was fine, I was quite happy. I'd just given my third injection, and I did it well." She smiled, slightly, remembering. "Well, I was just finishing the obs, when I noticed Dr Battencourt moving about in the office. Staff – Julia - he opened the controlled drugs cupboard, although I don't know how he could have done that, as Maria had the keys, and he measured out something from a brown bottle, and then topped the bottle up with water. I think he took some of the Brompton's mixture. It is a controlled drug, isn't it?"

Julia was stunned, unable to say a word, but nodded.

"And there's more. That night when I was taken to Casualty, I'd actually spent the evening in Dr Battencourt's house, I'd been with him all night. All I remember is having a curry, drinking a lot of lemonade and then I don't remember anything at all. I think I passed out or something. And when I was up on Weston ward, he came to visit me, and, oh Julia, he threatened me! I wasn't to say anything! I wanted to tell you so badly, but I was scared out of my wits by him, he was angry and swearing at me. I didn't know what he would do to me." Aneira looked down at her creased yellow uniform. Should she have said all that?

Julia exhaled loudly. "Of course. It's all starting to come together." She closed her eyes in revulsion, trying to assimilate all this information. Taking both Aneira's hands in hers, she continued. "He doped you, Aneira, he tried to dope me, I'm pretty sure of that, and I think he probably gave some of that Brompton's to Dr Hancock as well, for him to use. I can't tell you any more about that right now, it's confidential. What a bastard, what an absolute bloody bastard. And that Hancock as well. Those two are up to their necks in this, I'm absolutely certain."

"So what do we do about it?" Aneira looked ready to burst into tears.

326

"Don't know. Let me think." Julia got up and paced about her room. "It will have to be reported, of course, but this is serious stuff. He's stolen from the hospital, he's guilty of theft of a controlled drug, he has doped you – and almost bloody *killed* you, he's given the stuff to Neil Hancock and if I'm correct, I think Neil Hancock has used it in order to rape someone."

Aneira almost choked on her coffee, her face a mixture of horror and disbelief. "Oh my God, no! Who has he raped, Julia? The poor girl!"

"Can't tell you, sorry, not right now. But I think the best thing to do is to have a chat with Andy – he's Mandy's boyfriend, he's a copper – because if we do anything rash now it could have implications if this turns out to be a criminal case. I have no intention of giving those sods any prior warning if the police are going to be involved."

"Police?" Aneira whispered, shocked. "It's really that serious?"

"Oh, yes, I reckon it is." Julia 's expression was grim. "Rape, doping, theft. It's extremely serious, Aneira."

"Hang on, hang on! I'm coming!" Mandy hastily pulled her pink dressing gown over her bra and knickers. "You can stop knocking! I've heard you loud and clear! This had better be good! I'm a day off!" Annoyed at being disturbed at the ungodly hour of half-past eight, she flung open the door.

"Julia!" She regarded the two girls in surprise. "Nurse Thomas! What's up?"

"Can we come in?" Without waiting for a reply, Julia pushed Aneira in to Mandy's room, closing the door behind them.

"Makes yourselves at home, why don't you?" Mandy folded her arms in mock irritation.

"Sorry, Mands, this is an emergency." Sitting down on Mandy's bed, she indicated to Aneira to do likewise. Sitting down gingerly on the crumpled

327

duvet, Aneira looked round in amazement. Such a contrast between the two staff nurses' rooms. Any effort Mandy had made when anticipating entertaining Andy had disappeared, and dirty laundry was strewn randomly over the floor, the sink was overflowing with used mugs and several pairs of panties were drying on the radiator. Six unlabelled bottles of wine were lined up under the sink, and two used demi-johns waited forlornly for their turn to be washed.

"When are you seeing Andy next? Is he coming over today?" Julia couldn't get the questions out fast enough.

"What's up?" Mandy frowned. She'd never seen Julia so wound up before. "He's been on another weekend course, he'll be leaving the college, or whatever it's called, early afternoon. He's supposed to be picking me up around half six."

"Bugger."

"Look, are you going to let me in on this? Why are you so desperate to see Andy?"

Julia sighed in frustration. "Okay. Here goes. But no interruptions, right?"

Mandy nodded her agreement.

This is going shake her to the core, thought Julia, taking a deep breath. "Aneira witnessed Marcus Battencourt stealing some Brompton's mixture from the drugs cupboard last night. He topped the bottle up with water. She also disclosed to me the truth about the night she was taken to Cas – by her knight in shining armour, bloody Marcus Battencourt."

"His name does keep on cropping up," Mandy muttered.

"I said no interrupting! Aneira had spent the evening with him, the whole evening. He never found her on the steps outside the Infirmary, he'd been with her the whole time, in his house. So he lied. Basically, Mandy, it would seem he's been stealing the Brompton's and he doped Aneira with it." She looked at Mandy meaningfully, before continuing. "And we don't know who else he's been sharing it with."

Realisation dawned on Mandy's face. "Jesus! Those bloody scumbags are in it together. They must be! So you reckon Neil Hancock slipped me some of the Brompton's mixture that he got from Marcus Battencourt?"

Aneira looked up at her in surprise. "You've been drugged too?"

"I haven't told her anything." Julia was quick to reassure her best friend.

Mandy got up and started pacing up and down the untidy room. "She may as well know, Jules. Aneira, I was drugged by Neil Hancock, he took pornographic photos of me, then he raped me. That upper class tosser, that vile, arrogant inbred, Jesus bloody Christ!" She burst into angry tears. "I could murder the pair of them. Who the hell do they think they are?"

Aneira sat silently, shocked at the revelations of the distraught older girl.

Julia was finding all this so stressful, her thoughts were in a turmoil. "We haven't told anyone else yet. That's why I needed to know when Andy was seeing you. He of all people can tell us the best way about this."

Stopping her pacing abruptly, Mandy turned to face the two on the bed. "I'll ring Directory Enquiries and get the number of the college – I think I can remember the name of it – and I'll ask them to get Andy to ring me as soon as he can. I'll say it's a family emergency about his sister Mandy. He'll get it. He'll know I need to speak to him pronto. But in the meantime, what shall we do?"

Julia's mouth was set in a straight line. "Nothing. We say and do nothing which could give either of those two buggers an inkling that their little game is up. If we report them to the Nursing Officer, she'd probably tell Mr Robinson for starters and they would be forewarned. They would certainly set about destroying any evidence – such as those photos, Mands."

"I agree." Mandy started pacing again. "What about Richie? He found the photo, didn't he?"

Julia looked uncomfortable. "Not exactly, He found Steve with it, but Steve never recognised you, thank God."

Mandy squirmed at the thought of Steve's adolescent, lecherous hands handling that photo, but tried to put it at the back of her mind. There were more important things than her own feelings right now.

"Right. This is what we'll do," she said, "I'll get hold of Andy's number. Julia, try and get in touch with Richie before you go to work, he could be invaluable to us, bleep him if he's not in the Porters' Lodge. Tell him what Aneira has said, but warn him to keep quiet about it. Let him know that I am involving the police through Andy, but we mustn't let the cat out of the bag until Andy tells me what to do." She looked at Aneira, whose face had gone ashen with fear and sheer tiredness. "You're exhausted, chick, you'd better go and get some sleep, you'll need it. I've a feeling your presence will be in demand before too long, crucial witness, probable victim and all that. Don't mention anything of this to anyone, understand?"

Aneira nodded. "Will everything be alright, Staff? Julia?" She looked from one to the other, helplessly.

"I certainly hope so." Mandy's face was murderous. "I'll see those two rot in hell before I give up on this."

While Mandy was downstairs on the payphone trying to contact Andy, Julia used the hospital-linked internal phone to try and contact Richie. Thankfully, Miss Marshall had disappeared into the depths of her apartment and was no longer loitering in the foyer.

She thanked her lucky stars when the phone was answered almost immediately by Richie himself.

"Richie? It's me Julia."

"Hya, Staff! Everything okay? Does T.A. need old Richie?"

"I'm not in work, Richie. I'm in the nurses' home. Something's come up. I can't say too much on the phone, we could both be overheard." She wouldn't put it past switchboard to have a sly eavesdrop. "It's to do with that photo and it's serious. Can I meet you before my shift starts?"

"Sure. You come to the Lodge by twelve, and I'll make sure we're not interrupted. Does that suit you?"

"Perfect, Richie, thank you. I'll see you later."

As he put the phone down, Richie had a sense of foreboding, of imminent trouble. He felt unsettled and worried. But there was one other person he wanted to be at this meeting. Cali.

The two staff nurses ran headlong in to each other on the first floor landing as they finished their respective phone calls.

"Got to get dressed quick!" Mandy rushed in to her room. "He could be ringing me back as early as ten o'clock when he has his break and there's no way I'm letting any pesky student hog the phone! I'll be waiting right by it. How did you get on with Richie?" Flinging off her dressing gown she hastily scrambled into her jeans and sweater.

"Meeting him at twelve." Julia collected her towel and made her way to the bathroom. "I wish I could get hold of Mitch. I can't really ring him in work about this, and there's no bloody phone in his flat."

"You wouldn't be able to tell him anything, anyway, would you? This has to be kept quiet until I've spoken to Andy."

"Yeah, I guess you're right. Oh, Mands, what a mess." She opened the bathroom door. "Keep in touch, yes? Ring me on the ward if anything happens, it's extension 435."

"As if I didn't know that number by now." Mandy attempted a weak smile, while brushing her hair with more energy than was warranted. At least, she thought, snagging the brush on a tangle, it was good to be doing something proactive, it felt good to think that Battencourt and Hancock could finally be about to get their comeuppance.

"Aw, Staff! I want to ring my brother! It's really important!" Jess McVicar's petulant face irritated the hell out of Mandy. "I have to ring him now, he'll be going to work soon!"

Mandy rudely shoved her out of the way. "Brother, my arse! I very much doubt you want the phone to demonstrate your brotherly love, Miss. More likely you want to chat with your darling bloody boyfriend for hours on end. Now, bugger off, I'm expecting an extremely important call." The student sulkily edged away. "And no loitering outside the door. If I catch you hanging about you'll know all about it. Now, scram!" The student scrammed accordingly, leaving Mandy alone in the phone room.

She glanced at her watch. Quarter to ten. She hoped Andy wouldn't be too long. There was only so much rank-pulling that the student would tolerate.

How many love-lorn students had hung around this phone, she wondered, looking at all the posters on the wall, how many homesick young girls had waited patiently for their parents to ring them back after they'd used up all their change on the outgoing call. Sitting down on the hard, uncomfortable chair next to the coin box, she counted all the taxi cards which someone had thoughtfully stuck on the back of the door. Twenty-five. Noticing the small poster advertising the hospital radio, she realised she'd never tuned in to C.C.I. Sandie. The cartoon image of a happy, smiling nurse with a ten inch waist and a short skirt, holding a transistor radio, did nothing to dispel the popular image of a sexy nurse. Sorry, Sandie, she thought, glumly, you do nothing to help our cause...

She jumped out of her skin as the phone rang shrilly, breaking the silence.

"Andy?"

"Who else?" It was so good to hear the warmth in his voice.

"Listen carefully, Andy I know you don't have much time."

His voice became serious. "Fire away."

332

"There's developments. Massive developments. A student nurse called Aneira Thomas witnessed one of the doctors, Marcus Battencourt, stealing a controlled drug from the ward last night. It's a liquid that can be added to a drink without it being noticed. And that same student was drugged a few weeks ago, ended up in Casualty unconscious, and guess who she'd spent the evening with?"

"This doctor?"

"Correct, Watson. And that same doctor visited her on the ward and threatened her to stay quiet. Julia also thinks he tried it on with her as well, but she got away in time. And this Marcus Battencourt is big buddies with Neil Hancock, the one who took that photo of me. The one who bloody raped me that night." Her voice was an angry hiss by now, and tears threatened once more.

There was a heavy sigh at the other end. "Jesus. What a bloody situation. You know this will have to be escalated, now, Mands?"

"I'd have been devastated if you'd have said anything else."

"So, basically we have a doctor who is stealing a class A drug from the hospital, possibly – no, probably supplying his mate with it, administering it to a girl with intent to rape her, but in the process causing her bodily harm, and subsequently threatening to harm her. We also have the other doctor giving you this drug, causing you harm, taking porno photos of you and raping you – we assume."

"Assume?! Of course he did!"

"I've got my copper's hat on now, Mands."

"Yes, of course, sorry."

"No need to say sorry. Now, I want you to do nothing, nothing at all, understand?"

"Yes."

333

"I'll discuss this with the senior officer here, and then I'll ring my seniors in Cardiff. We'll be moving fast on this one, Mands, don't you worry. It'll be an unpleasant time for us all, and I won't be allowed to be involved in the case, on account of my relationship with you. I'll be around tonight as arranged, but if the senior officer wants me, I'll let you know. But never forget something really important."

"What?"

"I love you desperately, I'm with you all the way. You mean the world to me."

She smiled. "I love you too, Watson. With all my heart."

Chapter Twenty Eight Escalation

The glorious February day was lost on Julia as she hurried down the road to the Infirmary at ten to twelve, her mind preoccupied with Aneira's disclosures and what would happen next. Mandy had said the case was being referred to the police and that they mustn't do anything themselves.

She had no desire to do anything, anyway. The less contact she had with Marcus Battencourt the better. How could he ever have become a doctor? How could he act in such a way, and that Neil Hancock as well? Just as well she wasn't seeing Mitch this evening, it would be so incredibly difficult to keep quiet about all this. As she walked briskly down the road, hands deep in her pockets, she watched all the cars rushing past, all with their own agendas, their own personal goals. I bet none of them could possibly imagine my situation, she considered, broodingly. And what on earth would her ward colleagues say when the proverbial hit the fan? She groaned, inwardly. But Richie needed to be kept informed, whatever happened. He needed to be prepared. She and Mandy owed him that...

The Porters' Lodge was straight out of a Dickens' novel, Julia thought. A coal fire burned cheerfully in the grate, the walls were a deep, grubby cream, yellowed from years of cigarette smoke, having borne witness to decades of low-level hospital scandal and intrigue. The gossip of many years was ingrained into those dilapidated walls. Several incongruous items of furniture were scattered around the small room and a disused oil lamp completed the vintage look perfectly. Richie was busy making tea.

"Milk and sugar, Staff?" He held the tea strainer over the mugs. No tea bags for Richie, he believed in old fashioned values, good, honest hard work, and making proper tea.

But she had no chance to reply, because the door was thrown open and in walked Cali, almost bursting out of her maroon overall, a fierce expression on her broad face.

"Cali?" Julia was thrown out of her Victorian reverie into confusion. "Why- um-what are you doing here?".

"I asked her, "Richie intervened, brandishing an enormous brown teapot. Julia looked from one to the other, confused.

"What's she doing here?" Cali glanced at Julia, defensively.

"Let's all sit down, shall we?" Richie locked the door, and pulled up a couple of chairs at the oil cloth covered table. "Right, Staff, you go first."

Wondering where on earth to start, Julia began her account.

Cali's eyes could not have grown any bigger as Julia recounted the events of earlier that day, giving them the full story, but omitting Mandy's identity. Richie was feeling more and more angry by the minute. He had known those toffs were up to no good. But this?

"So we have to wait until the police get involved now." Julia felt worn out, the emotional tension was exhausting, and she hadn't even started her shift yet. "We're not to do anything. Just wait."

"I bloody knew it,"Richie muttered, "bloody bastards – sorry, Staff, Cali – I'd love to get my hands on 'em."

"Well, don't do anything stupid!" Cali's assertive voice boomed out.

"Keep yer voice down, Cali!" Richie hastily shushed her.

Ignoring him, the Jamaican woman continued. "I overheard them, those two rasclaats. They were slagging off the nurses they'd been having it off with!" Richie cringed at her coarse words, but Cali continued, relentlessly. "They were boasting about it! And I saw that Battencourt giving that Hancock a small bottle of something – I saw him! I gave them a piece of my mind, I can tell you!"

Julia could just imagine the formidable Cali tearing a strip off the two doctors, she'd have loved to have seen that.

Richie slapped his forehead in annoyance."I forgot to mention, Staff, last week I caught Battencourt shouting and swearing at Mandy. He looked proper angry, he did. He's a nasty piece of work, he is."

"Poor Mands!" Julia hadn't known about this, it must have been when she was on nights or something, and they hadn't seen much of each other. "But the main thing now is that nobody rushes off and muddies the water, okay?" The other two nodded. "I wanted you to be aware, Richie, because you will possibly be needed as a witness, and now it seems Cali will be as well, maybe even Steve. Mandy and I thought it best to inform the police first and let them do their job. If we'd gone straight to the nursing officer, then she would have contacted the consultants immediately, who would naturally have called the doctors in to explain themselves. That would have given them ample time to get their stories straight and destroy any evidence. Well, that's what Mandy and I thought, anyway. I know it goes against protocol, and we should probably have notified the hospital first, but real crimes have been committed. Once I know that all is well, and the police are acting, then of course I'll report to management."

"That makes sense, Staff." Richie drained his tea.

"But Mandy and I will probably be hauled over the coals for not telling management first." Julia sighed despondently, looking down at the foxes and hounds which decorated the oil cloth. "We didn't know what to do for the best." Raising her face to the others, she carried on. "But how could Marcus Battencourt have had access to the cupboard? I realise any of us qualifieds could have left the cupboard door open if he was in the office – I mean, who would have suspected him of anything? But he would have had to have been really quick."

Richie considered this. "Well, Staff, all he would have needed to do was make an impression of the key once he got hold of it. On a piece of plasticine or a bar of soap or summat. Then off to get a key made. As easy as that, I suppose."

"You two gals are brave ones, you both are." Cali reached forward and took Julia's hand. "You can count on me to back you up. You are sure doing the right thing, to hell with hospital policy, these two ain't just bad doctors, they're lawbreakers, villains! I'll stand up in court and swear on the Holy Bible, I will!" She got to her feet to emphasise her point, jabbing her index finger down hard on a fox's little nose.

"You can count on me, too, Staff." Richie patted her on the shoulder.

Julia got up to go. "Well, it's off to work for me. I'll be on pins all day, waiting to hear if something has happened. What time are you two working until?"

"We're both doing a long day, nine until nine." Richie jangled his bunch of keys in his pocket. "I'll pop up to T.A. later on, Staff, make sure you're alright and stuff, you know?"

"Oh, you're kind, Richie!" Julia stood on tiptoes and pecked him on the cheek. He went crimson with pleasure.

"Hey!" Cali put her hands on her hips. "Ain't I getting no kiss, then?"

Bursting out laughing, Julia hugged the domestic. "You're amazing, Cali! You'd better come check on me as well!"

Feeling happier than she'd felt all day, Julia fastened her cap in place, took off her coat and made for Terence Adams ward. How on earth would this shift end, she wondered.

Locking the door of her tiny apartment behind her, Marjory Hunter checked her immaculate appearance for the last time in the passage mirror. Forty years she'd lived in the Infirmary, forty happy years. She had no need of a big house, she was content with her little flat at the very top of the old hospital. But when she came to think of it, she probably spent more time in her office than she did in her own quarters.

Nobody knew the real Marjory Hunter, the Marjory who zoomed off around the globe during her annual leave, rubbing shoulders with the rich in Monte Carlo, scaling the heights of the Matterhorn and occasionally whooping it up in Ibiza Town, although that had in fact been quite a few years ago...

Nobody knew about the ginger tom who kept her company during her free time; pets were not allowed, but Tweedledum was a good mouser, and kept himself to himself, preferring the solitude of his mistress' accommodation to any fussing and petting from the hospital staff. No, she thought in satisfaction, there's so much about me that nobody will ever know...

Satisfied that her hair was perfectly pinned up and her starched, frilled hat was in its proper place on top of her iron-grey bun, she marched stiffly down the flights of stairs, making for the Night Office. She liked to be early, to be prepared in case there were staff shortages, to be in control. Checking her fob watch she saw it was almost eight o'clock. Excellent.

The sound of familiar upmarket male voices stopped her in her tracks. She peered over the stair well. There they were, two miscreants if ever there were. Neil Hancock and Marcus Battencourt were deep in conversation.

"How was Lundy, then?"

There was a wicked chuckle. "Oh, roly poly, pudding and pie, I had my hands full, I can tell you!"

Another laugh, but from the other doctor. "So did you need any assistance? Did you need to loosen her up a bit? Did you need to use, you know, our secret weapon? Can't be much left now!"

The first one sniggered. "No need to loosen her up at all. She was gagging for it, let me do anything I liked, went down on me like a lamb. Oh, it was all on a plate. But she's gone all moony on me now, keeps running after me in the corridor and stuff. Why can't these bloody nurses get it? They're only fit for one thing, and once they've satisfied my, er, desires, they can jolly well piss off!"

More guffaws of laughter.

"She wasn't like a sweet, snug little virgin, then?"

"Not really, it was a bit like waving a stick – a very big stick, naturally – in the Mersey Tunnel. She could do with a bit of gynae intervention, tighten her up a bit."

"Doctor Hancock, Battencourt?"

The icy voice of Marjory Hunter stunned them into silence. Marcus Battencourt looked up to locate the voice, and saw the Night Sister leaning over the stair rail, a look of absolute fury on her face. She ran lightly down the rest of the stairs to join them.

"I've had my concerns about you both for a while, especially you, Doctor Battencourt." Her voice was deadly quiet. "You make sure you leave my nursing staff alone. Do you understand?" She marched off, as stiff as a ramrod, her clever mind working overtime as she reflected on what she had overheard.

Neil Hancock had gone as pale as his perma-tan would allow. "Do you think she heard us properly?"

"Not sure. Nah, she can't have. Anyway, what we do in our spare time is our own business, innit?" And with a confident swagger, Marcus Battencourt strutted off in the direction of the female surgical ward, but decided that he would first make a detour, he'd grab himself a coffee, then pay a social call to Terence Adams...

Every time the phone rang in the office, Julia nearly jumped out of her skin. Nothing from Mandy or Andy so far, nothing remotely linked to the police. The shift was quiet, just as well, really, she thought, as once again she was on duty with the work-shy Maggie Hubert. At least the student

Susan Bowen was perfectly capable and was getting on with the work industriously. Surveying the ward, she appreciated with gratitude the fact that the supper dishes had been cleared away, and the patients were all tucked up neatly in bed, waiting for their visitors at seven o'clock. That was the great thing about male patients, she surmised, they were undemanding, didn't fuss about how their lockers looked and didn't ask for bedpans just when the visitors were queueing outside the ward, waiting to come in. Julia often wondered how anyone could possibly wee – or worse - in a bedpan with only a thin curtain separating them from the rest of the world. She hoped she'd never have to find out for herself. Richie had popped up to the ward just before the suppers were being given out. Good old Richie, she thought, one of life's solid, dependable characters. His wife was a lucky woman. But she swiftly reminded herself that she was also lucky, fortunate beyond belief to have someone like Mitch in her life.

By twenty past eight she was just completing the night report. No seriously ill patients to include, thank goodness, no new admissions and no deaths. Maggie Hubert was ringing the bell to indicate that visiting was over, and was imperiously ordering stragglers to leave the ward immediately. Clearly, that was the part of her job she enjoyed the most. Susan Bowen was down at the bottom of the ward chatting to a lonely old man who hadn't had any visitors. At least she wasn't sitting on the bed, Julia thought, with a smile. Reaching over the desk for a clipboard, she heard the office door open.

Marcus Battencourt.

Her heart sank. What could he possibly he want ? She hadn't bleeped him, there were no patients needing clerking and no meds needed writing up.

"A word." He looked angry, his pale, aristocratic features contorted into a mean-looking mask.

"I beg your pardon?" She was starting to shake. Her mouth felt dry. Had he found out something? Had someone let the cat out of the bag? She felt as though the four walls of the office were closing in on her.

"Not here. I don't want that shitty little auxiliary barging in, or that poxy student. In the treatment room, now." There was no arguing with the menace in his voice, but she tried to buy herself time.

"I – I was just writing a report, I have to finish it, or -" He grabbed her arm, hurting her, and steered her swiftly out of the office and into the adjacent treatment room.

"Finish it later. You and I are going to have a little chat." He shoved her roughly onto a chair, then closed the door, after putting the sign outside, "Treatment in Progress, Do Not Disturb."

Looming over her, he put one hand on the closed door, effectively blocking her exit. "What have you been saying to that Night Sister, eh? What tall tales have you been telling her? Come on, out with it!"

Confused, she stammered, "I don't know what you're talking about!"

"Don't fucking *lie* to me, you conniving bitch!" He almost spat the words into her face, he was just inches away from her. His breath reeked of garlic and pure hate, he was breathing heavily and it was revolting. "You've been running up to that frigid cow Sister Hunter, haven't you? Spreading lies and rumours about me? Haven't you?"

Julia could hardly get her breath, she was so frightened. "N-no! That's not true!"

His fury erupted and he slapped her hard across the face.

Bursting into tears of pain and fear, she put her face in her hands. "I haven't spoken to Sister Hunter, I haven't seen her for ages!"

"Stop your snivelling, you stupid *bitch*. I know your type," he snarled, "you pretend to be all goody goody, but all you're interested in is ruining my reputation, and that of other doctors. Go on, admit it!"

"I'm leaving." She stood up, but he pushed her back down again.

"Not so fast, my pretty little one. I'm not done with you yet. How would you like it to have your reputation torn to shreds, eh? It can be done, you see, only too easily. And that poncy boyfriend of yours won't like that one little bit, will he."

His reference to Mitch made Julia's terror ignite into an indignant, defiant temper. Rising to her feet once more, forgetting her promise to say or do nothing, she pushed against him in an attempt to get to the door, all common sense deserting her.

"How dare you threaten me!" Her voice was getting louder. "You of all people! The great destroyer of women! The biggest misogynist of all time! Well, we all know what you've been up to, Marcus, you're done for!" Tears of rage were pouring down her cheeks. Shit, she thought, panicking, I shouldn't have said that. Oh Christ...

His sudden silence was more terrifying than his verbal tirades. His eyes narrowed and he edged closer to her, before whispering, "What the fuck did you just say?"

"You heard me!" She was screaming now, hysterical and reckless. "You're nothing but an evil son of a bitch, Marcus, you're a waste of space! We know all about you and your thieving, your doping, your -"

"Shurrup!" He launched himself at her, his hands reaching for her throat.

Oh, Jesus Christ, he's going to kill me, she thought, her legs almost giving way beneath her, oh Holy Mary, I'm going to die!

As his hands closed around her neck, she somehow managed to scream. "Help! Help me!" Her voice sounded a million miles away.

His hands tightened, she couldn't breathe properly, there was no more air, she couldn't utter another word. Frantically, she kicked out at the chair behind her, and it toppled over with a loud crash.

She tried to knee him in the groin, but only succeeded in losing her balance, awarding him more purchase. Her world was turning black, she had no fight left in her. As she felt the strength seeping away from her

343

body, she closed her eyes in desperation, starting to sink to the floor as her knees buckled.

There was a sudden loud bang.

The door had been violently thrown open, and Cali stood there, enraged and fearsome. Rapidly taking in the situation, she roared, furiously,"Take your hands off her you evil scumbag!" Without waiting for him to comply, she launched her massive, five foot ten bulk at him, landing an blisteringly accurate left hook on his cheek "Take that, you swine!" Marcus Battencourt fell over like a skittle, crashing to the floor, knocking over a trolley in the process. He lay on the tiled floor, utterly dazed, his nose bleeding and his jaw throbbing madly.

Julia sank onto her knees, struggling to catch her breath, angry red marks around her neck, momentarily too shocked even to cry.

"Jesus, Cali," she gasped, "who the hell taught you to fight like that?"

"My husband," she replied, as she reached for the treatment room phone.

"Doctor Marcus Battencourt? Neil Hancock?" Richie didn't think the three officers looked much like policemen. He peered at them closely through the perspex of the Front Desk window. Two of them were scruffily dressed in jeans and bomber jackets, and the other one was wearing a smart suit – he supposed he was the main man – and looked more like a bloody film star than a copper. But they had I.D on them. And of course, he'd been expecting them.

The senior guy smiled politely. "Yes, we'd very much like to speak with them, it's urgent. Can you tell us where to find them?"

"Dr Battencourt is on duty this evening, Dr Hancock has just gone home, I saw him leave only five minutes ago."

The senior detective turned to his junior colleagues and murmured, "Get Johnson on to it, quick. Tell him to get to Hancock's place ASAP." The more junior officer moved away to the other side of the foyer and started to use his radio.

Richie observed all this with mounting anxiety. "I'll just have to ring their boss. He'll know where Dr Battencourt is. Can I ask what it's about?"

"We can't divulge too much, but it's a police matter." A slick smile from the detective.

Thanking his lucky stars that he'd still been on Front Desk duty when the police had arrived, Richie retreated into the little office and immediately bleeped Mr Anscombe.

"Sorry to disturb you, sir, but some policemen have arrived here at Main Entrance, and they're looking for Dr Marcus Battencourt."

All that could be heard at the other end of the phone was an explosion of blaspheming. Richie waited for Anscombe's outburst to stop. He could see the three detectives waiting patiently in the foyer, talking amongst themselves.

Lowering his voice, he spoke quietly but urgently into the phone. "Sir, there's something you need to know!"

"What?!" Anscombe was fast losing patience. He'd just finished an emergency laparotomy in theatre, he was tired, and now the bloody police were asking for Marcus Battencourt. What the hell was going on?

Richie continued in a low voice. "Some dangerous drug has been pilfered from T.A, sir, and Dr Battencourt was seen stealing it. Also that same drug could have been used on that little student from the Valleys, you know, the one who ended up in Cas. I just wanted you to have the heads up, like."

There was a brief silence before Anscombe kicked off again. "Jesus *Christ!* Of all the - Jesus!" And he slammed the phone down.

Returning to the perspex window, Richie smiled nervously. "Um, I did tell him, sir, but he put the phone down on me..."

Without betraying any annoyance, the senior detective remarked coldly, "I suggest we cut the crap and get on with locating Dr Battencourt, don't you?"

"And find this little shit, pronto," the more senior of the other two muttered to his colleague.

"Please show us where he is, as quickly as you can." The senior detective frowned at Richie, who was busy fumbling for the key to lock the door. But before he got much further, the internal phone rang. It was Cali. Listening to her agitated voice on the other end, he turned to the detectives, turning pale with anxiety.

"We'd better hurry, things is happening up on the ward."

Chaos ruled on Terence Adams. Having heard shouts, screams and crashes from the treatment room twenty yards away at the other end of the ward, Susan Bowen rushed to the door find out what was going on, only to be rudely pushed away by a frenzied Cali.

"Go and look after the patients," she hissed. "Go find that lazy cow Maggie. Just act normal!" Frightened by Cali's stern manner, Susan meekly did as she was told. Just as she was opening the sluice door in search of the auxiliary, Mr Anscombe was belting down towards the office, his mind full of vengeance and vulnerable, innocent young women.

"Where's Staff in charge? Where is everybody?" he bellowed.

"Treatment room, sir." Susan pointed in the direction of the room where she'd heard all that hell breaking loose. What on earth was going on? Anxiously, she tried to do as advised by the domestic, and carried on acting as though nothing was wrong.

"What's the matter, nurse?" Old Mr McDermott in the bed next to the sluice was agog with curiosity. "What's all that shouting? Is everything alright?"

"Er, yes, of course it is. Just a slight disagreement between the porters, that's all!" And with a forced smile, she continued looking for Maggie, eventually locating her in the store-room, having followed the smell of illicit cigarettes.

Anscombe shoved open the door, unable to believe what he was seeing. Marcus Battencourt was slowly getting to his feet, holding his chin in agony. Julia Harry was kneeling on the floor, her hair in disarray, tears pouring down her face and vivid red fingermarks around her neck. Cali stood protectively in front of Julia, her arms spread wide, ready to have another crack at Marcus Battencourt, should it be required.

A wave of absolute, white hot fury washed over the registrar. "You complete and utter bastard!" He lunged at Marcus Battencourt, grabbing him by the lapels of his white coat. "You little snake. And you call yourself a doctor?" He started to shake him violently. "How dare you treat my staff like this! And that poor, fucking innocent student as well? You were responsible for that as well, go on, admit it! I'd like to ring your bloody neck!" He looked around the room, his eyes wild. "Who punched him?"

"I did, sir." There was a note of pride in Cali's voice.

"Well done." Anscombe didn't take his enraged eyes off Marcus Battencourt for a second. "I'd like to punch you too, into the back of beyond, into the cesspit where you belong, you stinking piece of shit!"

"I think we'll take over from here, leave him go, Mr Anscombe." The cool voice of the senior detective suddenly cut through the pandemonium. The three policemen entered the room, followed by a breathless Richie.

"Detective Inspector Samuel Enoch." He showed his I.D. "Marcus Battencourt, I am arresting you on suspicion of the theft of a class A drug, administering a substance with intent to rape, actual bodily harm and an offence against the person. You are not obliged to say anything, but

347

anything you do say will be taken down in writing and may be used in evidence against you. Do you understand?"

Everything stopped. It was as though the world had ceased turning on its axis. The pungent smell of antiseptic, the bright, cruel lights, the clean, white treatment areas now lightly splattered with blood from Marcus Battencourt's nose, they all provided a harsh backdrop for the traumatic scene. In the days to come, Julia was to remember this moment as if it was played in slow motion. Anscombe gradually releasing his grip on Marcus Battencourt. Cali shrinking back towards the wall. Richie's mouth dropping into a perfectly round O. And Marcus Battencourt. Oh yes, Marcus Battencourt reducing into himself, his arrogance a thing of the past, his veneer of confidence shattered and his massive ego in smithereens. All that was left was a malevolent streak housed in a vaguely attractive body. He was like a vampire seeing the sun rise, thought Julia, he was confounded, helpless, yet still full of hate.

As Marcus Battencourt was led away from the ward by the junior detectives, D.I. Enoch and the others remained in the treatment room.

Cali was the first to speak. "Hey, Mr Anscombe, sir. Look at Staff Harry's neck – she'll be okay, won't she?"

"Let me see." Anscombe crouched down next to her, gently examining her neck and throat.

"Who witnessed the assault?" Enoch took out his notebook.

Cali was eager to help."Me, sir. That bastard Battencourt was trying to strangle her. I decked him, I did. He went down like a ninepin." Richie glanced at her in awe.

Enoch cleared his throat. "Ahem, I didn't hear that, but well done." He turned to Anscombe, who was busy checking Julia's pulse. "She's going to be okay?"

Anscombe stood up. "I think so. But she should be seen in Cas, just to make sure. You'll be wanting photos as well, yes?"

"Of course. Plus statements from you all." He flipped over a page in his notebook, starting to jot down the information as it was unfolding.

"Detective Inspector Enoch?" Sister Hunter hurried into the room, then, taking in the scene in horror, went pale. "What on earth has happened? Is this the work of Doctor Battencourt? I take it he's been arrested?" She rushed over to Julia. "Are you alright, my dear?"

"I'm sending her to Cas." Anscombe ran this fingers through his untidy mop of dark hair. "Can you call a porter and a wheelchair, Richie?"

"Yes sir." Richie picked up the phone.

"I'll accompany her, Mr Anscombe." Sister Hunter helped Julia to her feet and into a chair. "And I'll inform her parents."

"Please, Sister, I need someone to let Mandy know what's happened. I want her to get in touch with my boyfriend." Julia's voice was just a croak.

"All in good time, my dear. We need to make sure you're alright, first."

Having made several recordings, Enoch snapped his notebook shut. "I must say, Sister Hunter, it's a pleasure to meet you at last. You've been absolutely invaluable." Everyone looked at her in surprise.

"Oh, it was nothing, Inspector. I've been keeping tabs on Battencourt and Hancock for a little while. I know there was nothing substantial to go on, but I felt it my duty to observe and of course report my more recent concerns this evening. Their attitude, their lewd references to my female staff members, it was all very worrying."

"Well, I have to commend you on your prompt phone call this evening. Of course, we'd already been informed about events from a different source, but your swift action facilitated our response. Thanks to you, it meant we already had the doctors' home addresses so we were able to apprehend accordingly. Well done."

Sister Hunter smiled wearily. "It was my nursing duty, Inspector, to protect my staff. By the way, I neglected to advise you of further information."

Enoch looked at her, quizzically. "What's that?"

She smiled. She was enjoying this.

Chapter Twenty Nine **Resolution**

Marjory Hunter examined D.I. Enoch's finely chiselled profile with interest. If only she could turn back the clock, she thought, wistfully. Here was a man who would at one time have been worthy of her attention. Tall, clean-shaven and handsome, fifty or sixty-something, his sharp blue eyes missing nothing. But now it was too late, far too late. Dragging her thoughts back to the current crisis, she frowned before answering Enoch's question.

"If Staff Harry is comfortable about going to Casualty without me?" She looked meaningfully at Julia.

"Yes, of course, Sister. Maybe Cali and Richie can come with me? I don't need a wheelchair, I can walk." She got up, slightly shakily. Richie immediately rushed over to support her. "No, Richie, honestly, I'm fine. Let's go."

"Er, Miss Harry." The Inspector referred to his notebook. "I'll be in contact tomorrow. In the meantime, please don't discuss this case with anyone else." Julia nodded, crossing her fingers behind her back.

Richie led the way, followed by Cali, who, despite Julia's protests, had her strong arm around her waist.

Once out of earshot, Julia whispered to Richie. "You will ring the nurses' home, won't you? Get in touch with Mandy, tell her what's happened? Ask her to try and get in touch with Mitch for me? She knows where he lives. I don't know how long I'll be in Cas, but I expect Sister Hunter will show up before too long."

"Sure, Staff, don't you worry, I'll ring from the Lodge as soon as you're safe in Cas."

351

The incongruous trio walked slowly down the corridor, doing their best to avoid the curious stares of the night staff hurrying to start their shifts.

"Okay, Sister Hunter." The Inspector opened his notebook once again, pen at the ready, perching precariously on a stool.

"Oh, please call me Marjory." She smiled, politely. Anscombe looked amazed. Marjory Hunter *flirting?* She continued. "It's not very comfortable here, shall we retire to my office? I'll have a word with the night staff first, they'll have to make do with a handover from the student. I won't be a second." She marched stiffly from the treatment room, leaving the two men alone.

"Will you be available to make a full statement tomorrow, Doctor?" Enoch smiled genially at Anscombe.

"It's Mister." Anscombe was in no mood to be dictated to by a policeman, especially one as smooth and smarmy as this one.

"Sorry?"

"I am Mr Anscombe. I'm a surgeon, a senior registrar."

"Very well, *Mister* Anscombe. May we contact you here tomorrow?"

Anscombe scowled. "You may. But after my theatre list, if you don't mind."

Cantankerous bastard, thought Enoch in amusement, getting to his feet as Sister Hunter opened the door. Aloud, he took great pleasure in saying, "Well, that'll be all from you, Mr Anscombe, I need to speak with Miss Hunter in private." It was satisfying to be able to dismiss the perverse doctor so effectively, and watch him glowering as he stomped away, his hands in the pockets of his white coat...

352

Anscombe felt wave after wave of alternating emotions rush through him as he made his way to the car park, pulling off his white coat on his way. How could he have been Battencourt's mentor and not had an inkling as to what was going on? How could that bastard have been stealing a controlled drug from the ward? Dear Lord, what the hell was Mr Robinson going to say when he rang him? But most of all, the image of a pale, unconscious Aneira Thomas kept floating into his head. A naïve, vulnerable young woman, a slip of a girl, that's all she was; he remembered her wavy, blond hair, her sweet, innocent smile, her total lack of guile. She'd nearly been raped... nearly died. His hands clenched into tight fists, as he imagined a variety of suitable, extremely painful, punishments for Marcus Battencourt...

"Help yourself to milk and sugar." Sister Hunter poured the tea into two beautiful Royal Worcester teacups.

"I won't delay too long, Marjory. I need to get back to the station to assist my colleagues with Battencourt and Hancock."

"Very well." She sat authoritatively behind her desk, regarding the suave, good-looking Inspector with slightly more than professional interest. "I became concerned about the behaviours of Doctors Battencourt and Hancock a few weeks ago. I had overheard a few conversations between the two which were unsettling and unsavoury. I'd also overheard quite a few nurses discussing the pair; they were, without exception, upset and perplexed, usually having been dumped or ignored – post-coitally, of course."

"Of course." He looked concerned.

She continued. "Then the admission of a young, vulnerable student nurse to Casualty only served to deepen my concerns. I am not an eavesdropper, but I also happened to catch a conversation between that domestic, Cali, and the senior porter, implicating the two doctors." Enoch nodded, sympathetically. Sister Hunter carried on. "I made it my business to contact the personnel department – they were very helpful indeed – and as well as ascertaining the home addresses of the doctors, I was able to find out which schools they'd attended as boys. They both did their medical training here in Cardiff, of course, and there's no record of any misconduct. But interestingly, they both went to the same public school – St Valentine's in Oakminster. Co-incidentally, I have an old friend who worked there as Matron, until she retired last year. I rang her. She remembers those two well, very well indeed. There was a bit of a scandal, something about the pair of them attacking and sexually assaulting the daughter of the school's caretaker. They were aged fifteen at the time, and she was just fourteen."

Enoch's eyes opened wide and he leaned forward. "Were the police involved?"

Sipping her tea, daintily, Sister Hunter continued. "No. Both boys came from affluent families, and money can shut mouths very effectively. The young girl had a termination of pregnancy at a Harley Street clinic. She claimed that she had not given consent, and that both the boys had abused her, then threatened her. Nothing was ever proven. They were all under age. The boys were suspended for a month in order to let the dust settle."

"But the girl's parents – surely -" Enoch spluttered on his tea.

Sister Hunter held up her hand to silence him. "As I said, money shuts mouths. Despicable, I know, but that's what happened."

Samuel Enoch wished he was at home, watching a rerun of Z Cars. This was all getting too sticky for words. "Despicable, as you say. You do realise, Marjory – you're sure it's okay to call you that?"

She nodded, smiling enigmatically, inclining her head, allowing him to proceed.

"You do realise that this information will now be transferred to the investigating team in that area? This case is mushrooming, and will require absolute discretion. And of course, co-operation."

"I understand fully, Sam."

He raised his eyebrows at her familiarity. Her face creased into a broad grin. "Or should I call you – Sexy Sam?" She laughed, mischievously.

Enoch stared at her as though for the first time. She removed her glasses and he saw an attractive woman of uncertain age, a bright, sparkling mind behind those inquisitive eyes and a manner that was both assertive and assured.

She laughed, quietly. "Oh, I do my homework as well as you policemen. I had to work terribly hard to identify the person – you - in whom I should confide and share my concerns. In the course of my delving I discovered to my great amusement that your junior officers call you Sexy Sam. And I can see why, naturally!"

Enoch gaped, astounded. "Er, ahem. Right. Well, that settles it, then. Thank you Sister – Marjory - for your invaluable information." He stood up. "I will be in touch tomorrow. I assume you will be available..?"

"Until ten o'clock, Sam. After that I will be tucked up in bed – alone, of course!" She crinkled her eyes in amusement at his discomfiture. "And it has been a great pleasure making your acquaintance."

He took her outstretched hand. For a split second she thought he was actually going to kiss it. "The pleasure was all mine, Marjory. Until tomorrow." Executing a semi-formal bow, he hastily left the small office, but murmuring as he went, without meeting her eyes, "You've been in the wrong job all these years, Marjory. Where the hell were you when the force needed you..?"

As he hurried down the deserted corridor, she watched him go, his well-cut suit hanging beautifully on him, his gait powerful and confident. What a fine fellow, she thought, what a pity time has passed me by...

The indigestion was severe now. Reaching into the top drawer of her desk, she pulled out a bottle of antacid. Unscrewing the top, she held it to her lips, taking a most unladylike swig before sighing in relief.

Samuel Enoch swung his black Aston Martin V8 out of the car park and turned right to join Porthnewydd Avenue. He had ignored his fleet car that evening, preferring to take his own. As the car purred smoothly down the road he tried to make sense of the events of the evening. The February night heralded no sign whatsoever of spring, the earlier fine weather had gone; there was no rain, but the heavy clouds deliberately concealed any stellar intervention. He passed a couple of uniformed officers who were strolling slowly along the pavement, chatting to each other. The optimism of youth. Samuel smiled, glad those days were long behind him. So many ideas were festering in his mind. Why weren't new recruits to public service screened before they were accepted? Those two warped, evil doctors had slipped through the net, they had no business being part of a great, honourable organisation like the NHS. Something surely needed to be done at government level to address this. Battencourt was possibly a sociopath, maybe that Hancock as well. Neither seemed to feel any remorse for their actions, they knew exactly what they'd been doing, but had been able to rationalise it in their depraved, corrupt minds. It made him feel sick to the core. And there was a strong possibility there was another individual involved as well, according to that Greenleigh-Peters, the novice detective. Battencourt and Hancock would probably spill their guts once the pressure was on...

The plastic evidence bag on the passenger seat would require immediate action, that was for certain. The brown bottle of Brompton's would be sent without delay to the Public Analyst for testing. Samuel's mind was a hive of activity, sleep would evade him for hours, so many threads to consider...

He had to slow right down when a mad-looking woman started ambling across the road, wearing nothing but a shiny red leotard, a feather boa and black fishnets. Oh, Christ, he thought as he recognised her. Bloody hell! Caitlyn McDuff! He hadn't seen her for years. The last time he'd bumped into her was when she'd chained herself to the main doors of the Welsh Office, claiming the place was full of aliens – she may have had a point there, he thought wryly. Bringing his thoughts back to the present, he felt worn out. Jesus, there was so much going on, so many charges that needed to be made against those two doctors, so many witnesses, where the hell was he going to start? Pausing at the traffic lights by the funeral parlour, he reflected on his conversation with Marjory Hunter. What a formidable woman, he thought, with a smile. But what a pity she behaved just like all the other women who crossed his path. She was damned attractive in a severe, almost Spartan sort of way. He could just imagine her in tight black leather with a whip in her hand. He chuckled to himself, changing down into second gear as he pulled away. But not as attractive in a million years as that crosspatch registrar. Samuel exhaled slowly as he approached the headquarters. Anscombe's irritable, surly face, caustic remarks and masterful attitude would certainly haunt his most private, secret dreams tonight...

It felt strange lying on a trolley in Casualty. Julia had objected, but Sister Peters had insisted.

"I'm not having you fainting or anything like that, my girl, you've had a dreadful ordeal and you are in a state of shock. Now lie back, be a good lass and let me take your blood pressure."

Julia winced as the cuff tightened uncomfortably around her arm.

"Not bad, a hundred over sixty. A bit low, so you stay put, young lady. The medical photographer is coming over as soon as he has finished his supper, and he lives in Llanedeyrn so he could be another half hour."

"But it's gone half past nine. Surely they don't work evenings?"

"You're staff. We pull out all the stops for our own. I don't know the ins and outs about what happened, and I know you can't tell us anything, but word is getting around that you were attacked, and everyone is bloody shocked beyond belief."

Sister Peters tidied away her equipment, and tenderly checked the marks on Julia's neck. "What a bastard to do that to you," she murmured, "let's hope he goes down for a long, long time. I've been told that you won't be

357

interviewed until the morning, you've got Sister Hunter to thank for that, she always puts us nurses first! Now I'm just going to the office to start a Cas record sheet, so try and rest. I'll be back in a few minutes." She briskly drew the curtains around the trolley.

Julia closed her eyes, half-heartedly attempting sleep, but the Casualty lights were so bright, and her thoughts so vivid that it was impossible. She kept re-living the moment when Marcus Battencourt's hands closed around her neck. The old man in the trolley opposite was moaning in confusion, calling out for his mother, wanting Mammy to take him home. Apart from him she was the only patient. She picked absent mindedly at the addressograph which Sister Peters had fastened around her wrist.

Suddenly, someone was drawing the curtains back, someone so dear to her, whose face she'd been desperately longing to see for hours.

"Mitch!" She attempted a shout but it came out like a squawk. She held out her arms to him, tears springing to her eyes, and he leapt forward, embracing her tightly.

"God, Julia! I've been so worried!" Pulling away slightly he saw the ugly marks on her neck. "Who the hell has done that to you? What's happened?"

"I'm not sure where to start." Her voice was still husky, but not as bad as it had been earlier. "It's impossible to tell you everything here, I could be overheard and I've been told not to discuss the attack with anyone."

His face fell. "Not even me?"

She tried to smile, whispering, "I want to get out of here, Mitch, so I can tell you everything, absolutely everything. I have to wait to have these – these marks – are photographed, then can we go? There's no reason for me to stay, is there? I mean, I'm fine. Oh, Mitch, I just want to be with you."

He hugged her again, lightly touching the livid fingermarks on her neck. "We'll do whatever you want, Julia. But if – when – I discover who has done this to you, I'll kill him. I'll bloody murder him."

"You'd better join the queue." Julia smiled, cynically. "There's a lot of people who want to do exactly the same thing. How did you find out I was here?"

He sat down on the chair next to the trolley, running his long, sensitive fingers through his untidy mop of hair. "Mandy and Andy came round in a taxi, Richie the porter rang Mandy in the nurses' home. They picked me up and then dropped me off here. They've gone back to Mandy's room. They don't know much more than me about what happened. I expect they're waiting to see you when you get home."

"Oh, it's so good to see you." She closed her eyes in relief. He leaned over and kissed her gently on her lips.

The curtains were once again pulled open, and a plump third year student nurse stood there, some documents in her hand. "Sister Peters wants me take some basic details, Staff. Is that okay?"

Julia nodded. "Sure. Mitch will stay here, though." She squeezed his hand.

"You bet." Mitch was deadly serious. "I'm not letting her out of my sight." The student did a double take.

"Oh, my God! It's Mitch Walker!" She went crimson. Hastily lowering her voice, she added shyly, "Could I possibly have your autograph?"

Mandy's room looked almost overcrowded with the four of them all squashed in together. She'd made an effort to tidy up, so at least there was sitting space on the bed and the easy chair. She and Julia were perched up at the pillow end, Andy was at the bottom, and Mitch was pacing up and down like a caged lion, unable to sit still, his face deathly pale. It was now eleven o'clock, they'd been talking for over an hour, dissecting the evening's events and analysing them. Several mugs of Mandy's disgusting coffee had been drunk and the four of them were high on both caffeine and adrenaline.

"Jesus, I still can't believe it." Mitch finally sat down on the chair. "I mean, aren't doctors supposed to take an oath or something?"

"They must refrain from causing harm or hurt -" Julia managed a few hoarse words.

Mandy finished off for her. "And live an exemplary personal and professional life."

Andy looked up. "Hippocratic oath?"

Mandy nodded. "Some of it."

Mitch linked his fingers in agitation, flexing them, making a loud click. "Well those two sodding bastards have hardly kept their promise, have they? How long d'you reckon they'll get, Andy?"

Andy exhaled thoughtfully. "Bloody hell, I dunno. I'm only a rookie detective. But if you think about the whole situation logically, from beginning to end, there's a multitude of things to consider." He turned to Mandy. "Is it okay to speak openly, you know, about everything?"

Mandy agreed with a single, determined nod. "Go ahead, Andy, it'll all come out soon enough anyway."

Andy got to his feet, and replaced Mitch in his pacing up and down the room.

"I call him Watson for fun." Mandy whispered in Julia's ear.

"If we start at the very beginning - "

"It's a very good place to start -" Mandy couldn't resist it. "Sorry, Andy, carry on."

Flashing her a look of mild annoyance, he continued. "Essentially, we have two junior doctors whose regard for women, particularly nurses, is diabolical. One of them has been seen stealing a class A drug from the ward. We think both of them have used the drug to dope women, rape them, take pornographic photos of them. One of them gave a girl too much of said drug, rendering her unconscious and endangering her life. And of course, the recent assault on Julia. Plenty of witnesses as well; we've got Julia, Mandy, Richie, Cali and of course, Aneira the student."

"So what d'you reckon? Twenty years?" Mandy looked hopeful.

Andy shrugged. "CPS will have to get a conviction first. This could take months."

Julia shivered. "They won't be allowed bail, will they?"

"I very much doubt it. These are serious allegations."

Mandy got up. "More coffee anyone?" They other three looked at each other, appalled at the thought of yet more revolting coffee.

Mitch was the first to speak. "Er, no thanks, Mandy. Any more of your lovely coffee and I won't get any sleep tonight. Mind you, we should really be opening a bottle of Champagne right now!"

Julia, Mandy and Andy looked at him incredulously.

Julia grinned. "Don't tell us -"

Mitch laughed at their surprised faces. "Yep! We've done it! We're number one! My bloody song, the song I wrote for a nurse -" he smiled at Julia - "it's number bloody one!"

"Why didn't you say?!" Julia ran over and sat on his lap, hugging him in delight. "Congratulations!" She smothered his face with kisses, until he broke away, laughing.

"I didn't say anything because I had more important things on my mind."

"Aw..." Mandy and Andy sighed in unison.

"Oh, I'm so happy for you." Julia snuggled in to his arms. "What a lovely ending to such a terrible day."

"Talking of Champagne..." Mandy leapt off the bed and burrowed into the depths of her wardrobe, pulling out a dark green bottle with no label. "Home-made elderberry wine, anyone?"

Marjory Hunter left the female medical ward with a satisfied smile on her face, having completed a ward round with Staff Lundy and extracted a little bit more useful information from her. It had been harrowing in the extreme when Battencourt had attacked Staff Harry, but now he'd been apprehended, they could all sleep safely. Why did these young women allow themselves to get into such situations, she wondered, why couldn't they see some men for what they really were? In her day, when she had been a student in the great London teaching hospitals, the risks had been there alright, for a student nurse to be taken advantage of, but the strict rules and regulations had served as a protective barrier. Thank God for that, she thought, thank God I got away lightly...

She turned left out of Weston Ward and decided on a whim to do a ward round downstairs on paediatrics. Glancing with approval at the spotless floors and recently emptied rubbish bins, she felt a surge of pride as she advanced down the corridor towards the stairs. Her stately, dignified walk was imitated by many young students behind her back, but secretly they all admired her.

The hospital at night was Marjory's domain and she loved it, feeling as always that she was part of the structure itself. The Victorian building was both awesome and comforting; the yellowing walls with green tiles, the Nightingale wards, the many fire escapes with staircases leading up to the heavenly heights of the ancient Infirmary, so many nooks and crannies... She wondered how long it would all last, before the great god of Change reared its ugly head.

Reflecting on this evening's overwhelming events, she wondered how it would all develop. Poor Staff Harry, what an ordeal she'd been through.

362

She'd told her to take a couple of weeks off sick. That nurse was an exemplary member of staff, a dedicated practitioner with an excellent work ethic. She should go far. Unless, of course, she committed the stupidest of crimes and fell in love, which, unfortunately seemed highly likely to Sister Hunter, having seen her in the arms of that pop star boyfriend of hers earlier on. She sighed. Love. What a gamble, what a sorry pseudonym for a quick tumble between the sheets...

The corridor stretched ahead of her, empty of any living being apart from a solitary radiographer walking towards her with a bundle of X-rays in her arms.

I must be getting old, Marjory thought suddenly, my legs feel like lead, I've no energy. Without warning, she began to feel light-headed, dizzy. Grabbing hold of a nearby wheelchair, sending it spinning off into the centre of the corridor, she doubled over in agony as a spear of excruciating pain seared across her chest and down her left arm. An unimaginably tight band crushed her rib cage, radiating up into her neck. As she sank to her knees, the ringing in her ears became deafening, a singing choir of angry angels. This is it, she realised in panic, this is it, as the darkness descended upon her. Unaware of the racing steps of the radiographer hurrying to help her, but hopelessly aware of the racing steps of her impending doom, Marjory Hunter closed her eyes for the last time, relinquishing her spirit to the final mystery, and she knew nothing more of this earth.

Chapter Thirty Two weeks later

Her royal blue lurex dress scratched her thighs and her nurse's feet already felt sore in the silver high heeled sandals. The price we women pay to look good, thought Julia wryly, but she knew she had to make a good impression this evening, for Mitch's sake.

"Where you to?" The taxi driver held the car door open for her to get in.

"The Angel, please." Julia settled down in the back seat, struggling to pull her short dress down to a more modest length. She hadn't dressed up like this for ages, it felt strange. What will all the other women be wearing, she wondered, would there even be any other women there, apart from that man-eater Steph Saunders. Mitch's record was still at number one and Cosmo Records was hosting a reception for the band in the Angel Hotel, during which members of the press would be interviewing and mingling with the musicians.

Julia stroked her throat, a habit she'd developed since the attack. The marks had almost disappeared now, but she still preferred to cover up any remaining traces of them with a few dots of ivory Pan-Stik, which she'd rubbed in gently. The nightmares had gradually stopped and she had started to sleep a bit better.

As the taxi drove past the Infirmary, Julia gazed upwards at the gothic rooftops of the hospital. She thought sadly of Sister Hunter. Such a sudden, unexpected death, she'd seemed perfectly healthy only hours earlier. The entire hospital had been stunned, shocked beyond belief at the news. Marjory Hunter had been loved, feared and revered by every single member of staff, nursing and otherwise, she'd been part of the establishment.

Sister Winter had rung Julia to ask how she was, and had told her that the night sister's death had been caused by a massive myocardial infarction.

Fast, furious and deadly. Julia tried to halt the tears which threatened to course down her made-up cheeks. Sister Hunter had been an enigma, sometimes stern and strict, then suddenly humorous and kind-hearted. But always efficient, hard-working and fair. At least, she considered with a sorrowful smile, she had departed this life in the place she'd loved the most. Julia wondered if she'd been lonely, living in splendid isolation in that little apartment of hers, tucked away at the very top of the hospital. She'd never mentioned any family, but then, she'd been a very private person. Had anyone ever actually known her? The hospital chapel would be packed for tomorrow's memorial service, that was certain. Just as well it was going to be at half past two, because tonight was going to be a late one.

The taxi pulled up outside the Angel. Now all I have to do is find Mitch, she thought, nervously.

The tall, willowy redhead in the shimmering blue mini dress stood immobile at the entrance to the Delavere room. Unaware of the stir she was causing, and the admiring glances of the journalists, Julia fumbled in her bag for the invitation.

"That's Mimi Magda, the new face of Fabergé." One reporter felt sure he recognised her.

His colleague put his glasses on to get a better look. "Nah, that's Mirranda, you know, that new singer, Mirranda with two 'r's."

Completely oblivious to their interest, Julia handed her invitation to the snooty waitress at the door and searched anxiously for Mitch.

And there he was. Striding over towards her, grinning from ear to ear, his arms open. Crushing her in a massive bear hug, he whispered softly, "You look bloody stunning, Julia, Christ, I just want to whisk you away and go to bed with you."

Pulling him even closer so she could reach his ear, she murmured, "Is that what this dress is doing for you, you randy bugger!" She tweaked his nose playfully.

Releasing her embrace slightly, she wanted to giggle. He was wearing a dinner jacket and a tie. Mitch! Wearing a shirt and tie! "Well, who's done up like a dog's dinner, then?" She punched him, teasingly.

"Don't ask," he groaned, "the Saunders has had her way, she insisted." Julia scanned the room for the other band members, and spotted them at the far side of the room, all looking equally uncomfortable in their get up, Dai in particular, as his suit was at least two sizes too big. His plump little fiance, Meinir, was clinging to his arm, out of her depth in this social setting, dressed quite inadequately in a pair of black trousers and a purple, sparkly top.

Steph Saunders lost no time in marching over to Mitch and Julia, a proprietorial look on her face. Her hair was now jet black, jelled back severely, and she wore a red cat suit, unzipped to the navel, with a huge gold medallion dangling between her Duo-Tanned breasts.

"Hello, Julia." Her tone was icy, no smile lit up her vermilion lips. "How nice to see you again. I must say, you certainly scrub up well. No-one would ever think you were a nurse!" With a brittle, tinkling laugh, she accepted a glass of Champagne from a passing waiter.

Bitch, thought Julia, angrily. Putting a fake, beaming smile on her face, she laughed back."What did you expect, Miss Saunders? Did you think I'd turn up in my blue uniform and hat, with shit still on my hands?" Another false laugh. Her retort was not lost on Steph, who bristled with annoyance.

Somebody banged a gong. "Ladies and gentlemen, the buffet is served."

Thank Christ for that, thought Mitch in relief, ushering Julia towards the small side room, where attentive staff were standing at the ready.

367

The Angel had certainly provided the company with a magnificent buffet. Several tables were groaning with expensive food; smoked salmon slices, cold roast beef, cheeses of every description, salads and exotic fruits were beautifully presented on silver chargers, and elaborate flower arrangements were placed at regular intervals along the snowy white tablecloths. The members of the media, keen to capitalise on this free dinner, stuffed themselves silly, overloading their plates, talking with their mouths full of French bread, garlic mushrooms and devilled eggs, spraying each other with crumbs in their excitement.

Julia sipped her Champagne, watching Mitch work his way through the throng of journalists and executive members of Cosmo records. She'd lost count of the number of times he'd been photographed, with the band, without the band, with Steph Saunders and even once with her, much to Steph's chagrin.

"This cheese is cowin' lush." Meinir took another big bite of the French bread which she'd liberally spread with Brie. "Never 'ad it before. Bloody gorgeous, it is." She chomped away happily, greedily eyeing the puddings which were being borne aloft by the waiting staff.

"Where are you from, Meinir?" Julia tried to balance her glass in one hand and take a bite of quiche at the same time.

"Bridgend." Chomp, chomp went her brightly lipsticked mouth.

"Ooh! My best friend is from Bridgend!" At last, thought Julia, we've something in common. "She's a nurse with me in the Infirmary."

Meinir stopped troughing for a few seconds. "You're a nurse? Of course! Song for a Nurse! I keep forgetting that! Oh, I'd have loved to have been a nurse, I'd have been good at it as well, I think, you know, handing the surgeon instruments and saving lives and all that. But I thought, nah, I'll be a hairdresser instead, better hours and more pay. Mind you, we're both on our feet all day, innit?"

Julia looked away, unable to think of a suitable reply.

Out of the blue, the band's number one record began to play, and everybody cheered and clapped. As it finished, Steph Saunders got up onto a small rostrum to make a speech.

"Evening, everyone!" She adjusted the microphone then rubbed her hands together. "I think the band needs no introduction." Everyone laughed politely. "Song for a Nurse is in its third week at number one, which is absolutely fantastic for Cosmo!" Polite cheers and more applause. "The Mitch Walker Band has proved itself as the most financially viable product Cosmo has ever signed. Plus they're all incredibly well-behaved! Maybe they should be called the Little Saints!" She flashed a brilliant smile at the gathering. "The plan for the future is that they carry on writing and recording, plus a few carefully selected live concerts, and - here's the big news – they're off to the States in the autumn to compose and record with none other than Kirsty MacBride." Gasps all round. "She's seriously interested in the band and has requested their input, a collaboration on a new album. So they'll be jetting off to Colorado in October, making their mark for Cosmo Records!" Amidst the acclamation and congratulations, Julia felt her heart sink. Mitch hadn't mentioned this. Would she lose him? And Kirsty MacBride was a seriously brilliant musician, ten years older than Mitch, but stunning in an ethereal sort of way, all long blond hair and a dreamy expression. Trying hard to be brave, she struggled to smile and clapped her hands with as much energy as she could muster.

Meinir clearly hadn't been kept in the loop either. The look on her face said it all, she was livid, and for once, speechless.

The flip side of 'Song for a Nurse' started playing, but Mitch leaped onto the rostrum, grabbing the mic from a surprised Steph.

"Hey you guys! I want you to meet someone! The inspiration for the song! May I present – Julia!" He beckoned to her. "Come here, come on, I want them all to see you."

Reluctantly, Julia pushed her way through the crowd, which parted like the Red Sea, joining Mitch.

He put his arm around her proudly. "This is my Julia, my muse, the beautiful girl who inspired me to write the song – and many more in the future, I hope. Now, there's something important I need clarification on, Julia."

She frowned, puzzled. What on earth could he be talking about? Out of the corner of her eye she could see Steph Saunders turning away, seething.

"Julia, is your passport up to date?" He was loving this. The crowd held its collective breath.

"Er, I'm not sure." Julia bit her lip.

"Well it had better be! Because you are coming with us to Colorado!" The place erupted with cheers, apart from Steph Saunders, who slunk away, defeated.

Unable to believe her ears, Julia threw her arms about him, kissing his cheeks, his lips, then finally engaging him in a minute long necking session. The crowd went wild.

Meinir poked Dai in the ribs, fuming.

"Don't worry, mun," he cuddled her ample waist, "you're coming too."

The service had been beautiful. The hospital chaplain had delivered a poignant, pertinent eulogy, bringing tears to the eyes of the staff present in the little chapel, including the men. All the nurses who attended wore full uniform, plus their cloaks, and each carried a single red rose. Trevor Bodenham from Medical Records played Marjory Hunter's favourite song on the small organ as they all filed back out into the hospital.

"I never knew she liked the Moody Blues!" Mandy whispered to Julia.

Julia smiled sadly. "Pretty appropriate, I guess, 'Nights in White Satin'. Well, her nights have finally reached their end, haven't they?"

"When's the funeral?" Mandy found herself stuck behind Mr Robinson as they queued to leave the chapel.

"Not sure about that. Daksha mentioned something about Sister Hunter wishing to donate her body to medical science, but then I heard Sister Winter talking to Mr Anscombe, saying something about having her ashes scattered on the Matterhorn of all places."

"Talking of Mr Anscombe, look over there, Jules. I cannot believe what I am seeing!"

Swivelling around to get a better look, Julia's eyes nearly popped out of her head, for there stood Anscombe with Aneira Thomas, who was wearing civvies. He had his arm around her shoulders, and was gently dabbing her tear-stained face with a handkerchief.

"Well," decided Mandy, grinning, "let's go and check this one out!"

The two staff nurses hung back for a while, allowing the crowd to disperse, then edged their way closer to the registrar and the student, who were deep in conversation near the altar.

Aneira, despite her tears, was looking radiant in a pale lilac mohair dress, her hair flowing over her shoulders and down her back. She looked like a cherub.

"Hi there." Mandy suddenly felt lost for words, and Julia was similarly affected. They instinctively sensed they were intruding on a very private moment.

"Hello, Julia, Staff Jacob." Aneira sniffed quietly, then looked up questioningly at the registrar. He nodded, gravely. She returned her attention to the other two girls. "I have some news for you."

Julia and Mandy looked at each other incredulously, but remained silent, allowing the young girl to continue.

"You see, Mr Anscombe – Alan – and I have been seeing each other recently, and I will be giving up my nurse training, because he has just, this very morning, asked me to marry him." She shyly stretched out her left hand, upon which was the most exquisite ring, a huge diamond solitaire, sparkling in the candlelight of the chapel. There was an astonished silence.

"Well, knock me down with a feather boa!" Mandy gasped, wanting to laugh and cry at the same time.

"Oh, congratulations, sweetheart!"Julia embraced the younger girl. "I'm so happy for you!"

Anscombe looked as proud as Punch. "Aneira and I will be making the arrangements as soon as I have spoken with her parents, we see no point in delaying."

"But- what about your training? Don't you want to become a qualified nurse?" Mandy couldn't believe all this.

Aneira smiled adoringly up at her fiance. "It was my decision. I like nursing, but a lot of it terrifies me. I feel so much happier now." Her small, pale face was ablaze with sheer joy.

Anscombe awkwardly squeezed her narrow shoulders, clearing his throat. "She will be safe with me, I will look after her."

"Well, we wish you all the very best, sir." Julia could see that behind the gruff exterior, the registrar was besotted with his young fiancee, he was bursting with pride. The love and affection in his voice when he spoke to Aneira was evident. But what an incongruous pair, she thought, amused, the stern, sarcastic surgeon and the shy, shrinking young girl. But then, she considered, opposites do attract.

"Julia?" Aneira's voice brought her back to the present. The young girl was blushing deeply.

"Yes?" I hope to God she's not pregnant, was Julia's immediate thought.

"I was wondering, I was hoping if you would agree to be my bridesmaid?"

372

Julia laughed, delightedly. "Of course I will! I'd be more than happy!"

Suddenly, the sombre occasion had brightened, so much cause for celebration. The red roses which lay discarded on the chairs seemed to be a sign of happiness, of better things to come. As she gathered them up, Julia felt sure that somewhere, somehow, Marjory Hunter was looking down on this, and was giving them all her blessing.

"Oh, c'mon Staff." Cali was unhappy about the assignment which had been delegated to her by Miss Graham, the nursing officer. "I can't go in there on my own. She was like the Queen, she was. Poor Sister Hunter, God rest her soul. How can I go rummaging through her stuff? It ain't right, it ain't right at all." She stuffed the disinfectant-soaked mop roughly into the bucket.

Mandy buttoned up her black cardigan, hurriedly, desperate to go off duty. "Oh, Cali! I'm about to go home! I'm seeing Andy later on and I need to wash my hair and stuff!"

Cali harrumphed sulkily, splashing water all over the cloakroom floor. "Well, I ain't happy. Not at all."

Sighing in frustration, Mandy removed her hat. "Oh, alright, then. But it's almost quarter past four. I really need to leave by half past five."

Cali brightened. "Oh, thank you, Staff. I have to be away by then myself, I have to pick up the girls from the childminder." She wrung the mop thoroughly, then removed her plastic apron, immensely pleased at having got her own way.

The compact apartment was just like Sister Hunter herself. Neat, tidy, immaculate, and everything in its place.

"She had a cat, you know that?" Cali closed the door behind them, dumping a pile of carrier bags on the floor. "A great big ginger tom called Tweedledum. Only a few of us knew that." She smiled, proudly.

"Really?" Mandy led the way reverently into the small bedroom. "Who's got the moggy now?"

"Me, Staff." Cali grinned broadly. "My girls have always wanted a cat, and nobody else put in any offers, so I took him home with me on the bus a few days ago, in a cardboard box. He didn't like that much, I can tell you."

Mandy smiled at the thought of the poor cat being transported through Cardiff on Cali's substantial lap, mewing in distress, then turned her attention to the enormity of the depressing task ahead of them. It would obviously take more than just an hour or so. Maybe they'd have to make several visits.

The bed was perfectly made, and had been turned down in readiness for Marjory Hunter's return after her night shift that fateful day. A crisp, white broderie anglaise nightdress was laid out on the pale blue counterpane – no modern duvets for the traditional night sister. A pair of sensible navy slippers had been placed with almost military-like precision at the side of the bed. It was all so personal, so poignant, all those preparations that were never needed after all. Mandy felt a lump in her throat, and tears sprang to her eyes.

"It's all so sad," she whispered.

"Oh, c'mon, Staff," Cali hugged her, "don't take on so. She's at rest now, a hard-earned rest, too. I bet she's looking down at us, wishing she was here to boss us about."

Mandy reigned her emotions in. "You're right, Cali. Let's get started."

"God, she certainly got about a bit." Mandy glanced briefly through the hundreds of photos which had been filed neatly in albums and stored on

374

top of the wardrobe. "She went to South Africa, Singapore – and here's a picture of her in a mini-skirt, in St Tropez, it looks like! What a pair of legs! What a bloody figure! And all hidden beneath that uniform. I wonder why she never married?"

Cali gave her a cynical look. "Like as not she was cleverer than most, Staff." She folded a few petticoats and added them to the pile of underwear on the bed. "I'm going to make a start on the ornaments in the sitting room, okay?"

"Sure. I'll carry on here. You know, going through her things like this makes me realise that we didn't know her at all. And none of us actually tried to get to know her, either. I feel quite guilty about that." Mandy looked glumly at the albums, wondering what on earth they were going to do with them.

"She lived her life the way she wanted, Staff, so don't go fretting. Now, I know I'm only a domestic, and you're a staff nurse, but I'm telling you to get a move on, time is not on our side." She bustled efficiently out of the bedroom, leaving Mandy with her melancholic thoughts. With a heavy sigh, she opened the bottom drawer at the base of the wardrobe, starting to pull out the various perfectly folded garments, putting them in one of the carrier bags.

We'll need bigger bags than these, she thought gloomily, reaching for another bag. Fancy, she mused, all your life being packed away into Tesco carrier bags.

She pulled out the final item, and looked at it in puzzlement, then incredulity, as realisation dawned on her. She held up the long, grey hooded cloak, a big grin spreading across her face. Oh, Sister Hunter, you wicked, naughty woman, she laughed to herself. Hastily, she shoved it into a spare bag, before Cali came back. I'll be keeping that, she decided, oh yes, indeed, that's one part of her life that will definitely be perpetuated. Nice one, Sister Hunter!

THE END!

Acknowledgements

Song For A Nurse was written hot on the heels of Rhiannon, my first book, only taking about nine months to complete. I was spurred on by the success of Rhiannon, knowing that self-publishing was the way forward.

I trained as a nurse in Cardiff, so was able to draw on my own memories in order to weave this tapestry of hospital life at the end of the 1970's. City Central Infirmary is totally fictitious, but no doubt there will be many nurses who read the book who will find some descriptions nostalgically familiar! Remember, dear colleague – this is one hundred per cent fiction and all the characters are formed in my vivid imagination!

I would like to thank Tudor (a hugely respected retired pharmacist) for his opinion on controlled drugs and their effects, also his lovely wife Pat, a wickedly humorous retired nurse. Diolch!

Rob Lewis, a retired policeman, proved invaluable when I needed to establish certain "police things" and his beautiful wife Helen (another retired nurse) was always on hand to explain my requirements to him when necessary.

Once again, Ken McDermott (lead guitarist and a fellow musician in the band) was patience personified when I arrived at the dreaded formatting stage. His skills were first-class and I would not have got through this stage without his help. Ken's attention to detail was unbelievable and his methods meticulous. He implemented his considerable talents in designing the book cover. His charming wife Beth provided lots of cups of tea and I am indebted to her. She also outclassed her husband (an ex-photographer) when she took my photo for this book.

My family is gradually getting used to my strange writing habits now, and my husband actually bought me a writing desk for Christmas – YES! Thank you all, Phil, Sally and Patrick, and a woofy thanks to Rosie, Bob and Red, my gorgeous dogs.

A brief acknowledgement to Richie, my friendly local butcher, who has maintained a faithful interest in my writing: Richie longed to be in this book, so I awarded him the honour of starring as Richie, the super-hero porter. Richie is the kindest, most warm-hearted butcher in Wales!

Lastly, thank you Christine Price! Once more you have come up trumps with a beautiful drawing for the cover of the book. What a team we are!

I would like to dedicate this book to all the nurses I have ever worked with, the ones who taught me everything I know and the ones who were great friends and colleagues. You are all wonderful.

About The Author

Sonja Collavoce was born and brought up in Llanelli, South Wales. Despite studying languages at A-level, she left home at eighteen to train as a nurse in Cardiff, qualifying as a Registered General Nurse, then as a midwife and finally as a health visitor. She is married with two grown-up children and has three dogs. Sonja has also had poetry published and has performed her work at the Chapter Theatre, Cardiff, during the Dylan Thomas centenary festival. She continues to play keyboards in a rock band, and also sings two songs herself, Wuthering Heights and Babooshka. This is her second novel.

Printed in Great Britain
by Amazon

22293300R00215